PRAISE FOR

Next Year in Havana

"[A] flat-out stunner of a book, at once a dual-timeline mystery, a passionate romance, and paean to the tragedy and beauty of war-torn Cuba. The story of sugar heiress Elisa watching Cuba fall into revolution as Castro rises is intertwined with the modern-day tale of Elisa's granddaughter Marisol as she returns to Cuba after Castro's death. Both women fall for firebrand revolutionaries, but Cuba itself emerges as their true love interest, threatening to break both women's hearts as Elisa and Marisol each grapple with what it is to be Cuban, what it is to be an exile, and how to love and live in a homeland riven by revolution. Simply wonderful!"

—Kate Quinn, *USA Today* bestselling author of *The Alice Network*

"An evocative, passionate story of family loyalty and forbidden love that moves seamlessly between the past and present of Cuba's turbulent history . . . Kept me enthralled and savoring every word."

—Shelley Noble, *New York Times* bestselling author of *Whisper Beach*

"Chanel Cleeton's prose is as beautiful as Cuba itself, and the story she weaves—of exile and loss, memory and myth, forbidden love and enduring friendship—is at once sweeping and beautifully intimate."

—Jennifer Robson, *USA Today* bestselling author of
Somewhere in France

"An undeniably personal and intimate look at Cuba then and now, wrapped around the gripping story of two women torn between love and country." — Renée Rosen, author of *Windy City Blues*

continued . . .

BERKLEY TITLES BY CHANEL CLEETON

Fly With Me

Into the Blue

On Broken Wings

NEXT YEAR
in Havana

CHANEL CLEETON

BERKLEY
NEW YORK

BERKLEY
An imprint of Penguin Random House LLC
375 Hudson Street, New York, New York 10014

Copyright © 2018 by Chanel Cleeton
Excerpt from *When We Left Cuba* copyright © 2018 by Chanel Cleeton
Penguin Random House supports copyright. Copyright fuels creativity, encourages diverse
voices, promotes free speech, and creates a vibrant culture. Thank you for buying an
authorized edition of this book and for complying with copyright laws by not reproducing,
scanning, or distributing any part of it in any form without permission. You are supporting
writers and allowing Penguin Random House to continue to publish books for every reader.

BERKLEY is a registered trademark and the B colophon is a trademark of
Penguin Random House LLC.

Library of Congress Cataloging-in-Publication Data

Names: Cleeton, Chanel, author.
Title: Next year in Havana / Chanel Cleeton.
Description: First edition. | New York : Berkley, 2018.
Identifiers: LCCN 2017027806 (print) | LCCN 2017032141 (ebook) | ISBN
9780399586699 (ebook) | ISBN 9780399586682 (softcover)
Subjects: LCSH: Cuban American women—Fiction. | Family secrets—Fiction. |
BISAC: FICTION / Contemporary Women. | FICTION / Cultural
Heritage. | GSAFD: Love stories.
Classification: LCC PS3603.L455445 (ebook) | LCC PS3603.L455445 N49 2018
(print) | DDC 813/.6—dc23
LC record available at https://lccn.loc.gov/2017027806

First Edition: February 2018

Printed in the United States of America
9 10 8

Cover art: *Havana* © by Christopher Morre; *Background pattern* © by YanaDesign
Cover design by Sarah Oberrender
Title page art: *Floral Border* © by IndiPixi / Shutterstock Images
Book design by Kristin del Rosario

Para mis abuelos
For my grandparents

Acknowledgments

This book has truly been the book of my heart and I owe an enormous debt of gratitude to the many people who played a role in bringing it to fruition. Thank you to my amazing agent Kevan Lyon and editor extraordinaire Kate Seaver, whose constant encouragement, support, and guidance made this book possible. I am so grateful to work with both of you and cannot thank you enough for all you have done for me.

Thank you to everyone at Berkley for giving me this opportunity. I couldn't have asked for a better publishing home. Special thanks to Ivan Held, Christine Ball, Claire Zion, Jeanne-Marie Hudson, Craig Burke, Erin Galloway, Ryanne Probst, Roxanne Jones, Fareeda Bullert, Kim Burns, and Katherine Pelz for making my books a reality; to the amazing subrights department for all of their hard work; and to the Berkley art department for the stunning cover and for capturing the essence of *Next Year in Havana*.

Thank you to my wonderful friends, especially A. J. Pine, Jennifer Blackwood, and Lia Riley. I can't imagine what I would do without you. Thanks to the lovely Jennifer Robson for reading *Next Year in Havana* and for the kind words.

I am so grateful to my readers and to all of the bloggers who have supported my books throughout the years and who joined me on this new adventure. Thanks for reading!

This book never would have been possible without my wonderful family and the strength and courage of those who came before me.

Thank you for sharing your stories with me and for preserving a piece of Cuba I can always hold on to. I am so grateful for your insights on this novel and for your love and support.

To my family—my heart—*thank you.*

NEXT YEAR IN HAVANA

chapter one

Elisa

HAVANA, 1959

"How long will we be gone?" my sister Maria asks.

"Awhile," I answer.

"Two months? Six months? A year? Two?"

"Quiet." I nudge her forward, my gaze darting around the departure area of Rancho-Boyeros Airport to see if anyone has overheard her question.

We stand in a row, the famous—or infamous, depending on who you ask—Perez sisters. Isabel leads the way, the eldest of the group. She doesn't speak, her gaze trained on her fiancé, Alberto. His face is pale as he watches us, as we march out of the city we once brought to its knees.

Beatriz is next. When she walks, the hem of her finest dress swinging against her calves, the pale blue fabric adorned with lace, it's as though the entire airport holds its collective breath. She's the beauty in the family and she knows it.

I trail behind her, the knees beneath my skirts quivering, each step a weighty effort.

And then there's Maria, the last of the sugar queens.

At thirteen, Maria's too young to understand the need to keep her voice low, is able to disregard the soldiers standing in green uniforms, guns slung over their shoulders and perched in their eager hands. She knows the danger those uniforms bring, but not as well as the rest of us do. We haven't been able to remove the grief that has swept our family in its unrelenting curl, but we've done our best to shield her from the barbarity we've endured. She hasn't heard the cries of the prisoners held in cages like animals in La Cabaña, the prison now run by that Argentine monster. She hasn't watched Cuban blood spill on the ground.

But our father has.

He turns and silences her with a look, one he rarely employs yet is supremely effective. For most of our lives, he's left the care of his daughters to our mother and our nanny, Magda, too busy running his sugar company and playing politics. But these are extraordinary times, the stakes higher than any we've ever faced. There is nothing Fidel would love more than to make an example of Emilio Perez and his family—the quintessential image of everything his revolution seeks to destroy. We're not the wealthiest family in Cuba, or the most powerful one, but the close relationship between my father and the former president is impossible to ignore. Even the careless words of a thirteen-year-old girl can prove deadly in this climate.

Maria falls silent.

Our mother walks beside our father, her head held high. She insisted we wear our finest dresses today, hats and gloves, brushed our hair until it gleamed. It wouldn't do for her daughters to look anything but their best, even in exile.

Defiant in defeat.

We might not have fought in the mountains, haven't held weapons in our glove-covered hands, but there is a battle in all of us. One Fidel has ignited like a flame that will never be extinguished. And so we walk toward the gate in our favorite dresses, Cuban pride and pragmatism on full display. It's our way of taking the gowns with us, even if they're missing the jewels that normally adorn them. What remains of our jewelry is buried in the backyard of our home.

For when we return.

To be Cuban is to be proud—it is both our greatest gift and our biggest curse. We serve no kings, bow no heads, bear our troubles on our backs as though they are nothing at all. There is an art to this, you see. An art to appearing as though everything is effortless, that your world is a gilded one, when the reality is that your knees beneath your silk gown buckle from the weight of it all. We are silk and lace, and beneath them we are steel.

We try to preserve the fiction that this is merely a vacation, a short trip abroad, but the gazes following us around the airport know better—

Beatriz's fingers wrap around mine for one blissful moment. Those olive green–clad sentries watch our every move. There's something reassuring in her fear, in that crack in the facade. I don't let go.

The world as we know it has died, and I do not recognize the one that has taken its place.

A sense of hopelessness overpowers the departure area. You see it in the eyes of the men and women waiting to board the plane, in the tired set of their shoulders, the shock etched across their faces, their possessions clutched in their hands. It's present in the somber children, their laughter extinguished by the miasma that has overtaken all of us.

This used to be a happy place. We would welcome our father when he returned from a business trip, sat in these same seats three years earlier, full of excitement to travel to New York on vacation.

We take our seats, huddling together, Beatriz on one side of me, Maria on the other. Isabel sits apart from us, her pain a mantle around her shoulders. There are different degrees of loss here, the weight of what we leave behind inescapable.

My parents sit with their fingers intertwined, one of the rare displays of physical affection I've ever seen them partake in, worry in their eyes, grief in their hearts.

How long will we be gone? When will we return? Which version of Cuba will greet us when we do?

We've been here for hours now, the seconds creeping by with interminable slowness. My dress itches, a thin line of sweat running down my neck. Nausea rolls around in my stomach, an acrid taste in my mouth.

"I'm going to be sick," I murmur to Beatriz.

She squeezes my fingers. "No, you're not. We're almost there."

I beat the nausea back, staring down at the ground in front of me. The weight of the stares is pointed and sharp, and at the same time, it's as if we exist in a vacuum. The sound has been sucked from the room save for the occasional rustle of clothing, the stray sob. We exist in a state of purgatory, waiting, waiting—

"Now boarding . . ."

My father rises from his seat on creaky limbs; he's aged years in the nearly two months since President Batista fled the country, since the winds of revolution drifted from the Sierra Maestra to our corner of the island. Emilio Perez was once revered as one of the wealthiest and most powerful men in Cuba; now there's little to distinguish my father from the man sitting across the aisle, from the gentleman lining up at the gate. We're all citizens of no country now, all orphans of circumstance.

I reach out and take Maria's hand with my spare one.

She's silent, as though reality has finally sunk in. We all are.

We walk in a line, somber and reticent, making our way onto the tarmac. There's no breeze in the air today, the heat overpowering as we shuffle forward, the sun beating down on our backs, the plane looming in front of us.

I can't do this. I can't leave. I can't stay.

Beatriz pulls me forward, a line of Perez girls, and I continue on.

We board the plane in an awkward shuffle, the silence cracking and splintering as hushed voices give way to louder ones, a cacophony of tears filling the cabin. Wails. Now that we've escaped the departure area, the veneer of civility is stripped away to something unvarnished and raw—

Mourning.

I take a seat next to the window, peering out the tiny glass, hoping for a better view than that of the airport terminal, hoping . . .

We roll back from the gate with a jolt and lurch, silence descending in the cabin. In a flash, it's New Year's Eve again and I'm standing in the ballroom of my parents' friends' house, a glass of champagne in one hand. I'm laughing, my heart so full. There's fear lingering in the background, both fear and uncertainty, but there's also a sense of hope.

In minutes, my entire world changed.

President Batista has fled the country! Long live a free Cuba!

Is this freedom?

We're gaining speed now, hurtling down the runway. My body heaves with the movement, and I lose the battle, grabbing the bag in the seat pocket in front of me, emptying the contents of my stomach.

Beatriz strokes my back as I hunch over, as the wheels leave the ground, as we soar into the sky. The nausea hits me again and again, an ignominious parting gift, and when I finally look up, a startling shock of blue and green greets me, an artist's palette beneath me.

When Christopher Columbus arrived in Cuba, he described it as the most beautiful land human eyes had ever seen. And it is. But there's more beyond the sea, the mountains, the clear sky. There's so much more that we leave behind us.

How long will we be gone?

A year? Two?

Ojalá.

Marisol

JANUARY 2017

When I was younger, I begged my grandmother to tell me about Cuba. It was a mythical island, contained in my heart, entirely drawn from the version of Cuba she created in exile in Miami and the stories she shared with me. I was caught between two lands—two iterations of myself—the one I inhabited in my body and the one I lived in my dreams.

We'd sit in the living room of my grandparents' sprawling house in Coral Gables, and she'd show me old photos that had been smuggled out of the country by intrepid family members, weaving tales about her life in Havana, the adventures of her siblings, painting a portrait of a land that existed in my imagination. Her stories smelled of gardenias and jasmine, tasted of plantains and mamey, and always, the sound of her old record player. Each time she'd finish her tale she'd smile and promise I would see it myself one day, that we'd return in grand style, reopening her family's seaside estate in Varadero and the elegant home that took up nearly the entire block of a tree-lined street in Havana.

When Fidel dies, we'll return. You'll see.

And finally, after nearly sixty years of keeping Cubans in suspense, of false alarms and hoaxes, he did die, outlasting my grandmother by mere months. The night he died, my family opened a bottle of champagne my great-grandfather had bought nearly sixty years ago for such an occasion, toasting Castro's demise in our inimitable fashion. The champagne, sadly, like Fidel himself, was past its prime, but we partied on Calle Ocho in Miami until the sun rose, and still—

Still we remain.

His death did not erase nearly sixty years of exile, or ensure a future of freedom. Instead I'm smuggling my grandmother's ashes inside my suitcase, concealed as jars in my makeup case, honoring her last request to me while we pray, hope, wait for things to change.

When I die, take me back to Cuba. Spread my ashes over the land I love. You'll know where.

And now sitting on the plane somewhere between Mexico City and Havana, armed with a notebook filled with scribbled street names and places to visit, a guidebook I purchased off the Internet, I have no clue where to lay her to rest.

They read my grandmother's will six months ago, thirty family members seated in a conference room in our attorney's office on Brickell. Her sisters were there—Beatriz and Maria. Isabel passed away the year before. Their children came with their spouses and their children, the next generations paying their respects. Then there was my father—her only child—my two sisters, and me.

The main parts of her will were fairly straightforward, no major surprises to be expected. My grandfather had died over two decades earlier and turned the family sugar business over to my father to run. There was the house in Palm Beach, which went to my sister Daniela. The farm in Wellington and the horses were left to my sister Lucia, the middle child. And I ended up with the house in Coral Gables, the site of so many imaginary trips to Cuba.

There were monetary bequests, and artwork, lists upon lists of items read by the attorney in a matter-of-fact tone, his announcements met with the occasional tear or exclamation of gratitude. And then there was her final wish—

Grandparents aren't supposed to play favorites, but my grandmother never played by anyone else's rules. Maybe it was the fact that I came into the world two months before my mother caught my father in bed with a rubber heiress. Lucia and Daniela had years of family unity before the Great Divorce, and after that, they had a bond with my mother I never quite achieved. My early years were logged between strategy sessions at the lawyers' offices, shuttled back and forth between homes, until finally my mother washed her hands of it all and went back to Spain, leaving me under the care of my grandmother. So perhaps because I was the daughter she never had, yet raised as her own, it made sense that she charged me with this—

No one in the family questioned it.

From her sisters, I received a list of addresses—including the Perez estate in Havana and the beach house no one had seen in over fifty years. They put me in contact with Ana Rodriguez, my grandmother's childhood best friend. Despite the passage of time, she'd been gracious enough to offer to host me for the week I'd be in Cuba. Perhaps she could shed some light on my grandmother's final resting place.

You always wanted to see Cuba, and it's my greatest regret that we were unable to do so in my lifetime. I am consoled, at least, by the image of you strolling along the Malecón, the spray of salt water on your face. I imagine you kneeling in the pews of the Cathedral of Havana, sitting at a table at the Tropicana. Did I ever tell you about the night we snuck out and went to the club?

I always dreamed Fidel would die before me, that I would return home. But now my dream is a different one. I am an old woman, and I have come to accept that I will never see Cuba again. But you will.

To be in exile is to have the things you love most in the world—the air you breathe, the earth you walk upon—taken from you. They exist on the other side of a wall—there and not—unaltered by time and circumstance, preserved in a perfect memory in a land of dreams.

My Cuba is gone, the Cuba I gave to you over the years swept away by the winds of revolution. It's time for you to discover your own Cuba.

I slip the letter back into my purse, the words blurring together. It's been six months, and yet the ache is still there, intensified by the moments when I feel her loss most acutely, when she should be beside me and is not.

The sight of the *merenguitos* she would make me on special occasions, their sugary taste dissolving on my tongue in a cloud of white powder, the sound of my childhood—our musical icons: Celia Cruz, Benny Moré, and the Buena Vista Social Club—and now this, the wheels of the airplane touching down on Cuban soil.

I miss my grandmother.

Tears spill onto my cheeks. It's not merely the absence of her; it's this feeling of connection as the airplane taxis down the same runway that carried her away from Cuba nearly sixty years ago.

I stare out the window, treated to my first glimpse of José Martí International Airport. At first glance, it looks like the countless Caribbean airports I've flown through on vacations in my life. But underneath it all there's a sense of recognition and a thrill that runs through me. A sigh that escapes my body as though I've been holding my breath and can finally exhale.

It's that sensation of being away for a long time and returning to your house, the sight of it greeting you—both familiar and changed—stepping through the doorway, dropping your bags on the ground next to you with a sense of completion, your journey over, and taking in your surroundings, surveying all you left behind, and thinking—

I am home.

chapter two

I step off the plane, heading through the airport, my bags clutched in hand. All my life Cuba has been this mythical entity, at times tangible, at others an ephemeral presence removed from my grasp. But now it's real, and while there's nothing romantic or glamorous about the arrival hall, excitement fills me.

Unfortunately, the romance of the moment is dimmed by the tedium of time. Minutes pass, nearly an hour going by before I near the front of the immigration line. I take note of the number of immigration officers sitting behind counters, the ease with which the tourists in front of me are processed. Officially, I'm here on a journalist's visa, writing an article for the online travel magazine I freelance for in Miami—an article on tourism in Cuba now that restrictions have eased. I pitched it to my editor as a multi-part series focusing on introducing Americans to Cuba and sealed the deal with my offer to finance my own travel. Unofficially, of course, my grandmother's ashes are in my suitcase.

There's a process for returning an exile to Cuba for burial, but after speaking to family friends who faced the same challenges— denials, red tape, and government intervention—this seemed like the easiest route, one undertaken by many Cubans each year. As I smuggle my grandmother back into the country, I swear I can feel her looking down on me and smiling, thoroughly delighted to slip something past the regime she loathed.

All my paperwork is together, visa in hand, as I shuffle forward in the immigration queue, praying my makeshift urn makes it through without any issues.

I present my documents to the official, my heart pounding as I answer his questions in Spanish, in the language I've spoken my entire life. There's a strange divide here, the sense that we are connected—countrymen—and yet, not. Despite the Spanish American mother, I've always considered myself more Cuban than anything else, and in Miami it's never been an issue. My grandparents are Cuban, my father Cuban, therefore I am Cuban. But will it matter here that my skin is lighter than many of the country's citizens, that my blood is not fully Cuban? Am I an outsider here or is the ancestry I claim enough?

He waves me on, and I head through with my bags, nerves filling me as I slide my carry-on and my grandmother's ashes through the X-ray machine while the Cuban officials ensure I'm not smuggling contraband into the country. The belt heaves and sighs as my bag sails through. I hold my breath—

I make my way through the X-ray machine and wait, sure this will be the moment when they flag my bag, images of being led to a windowless interrogation room tucked away in the airport flashing before me. The sheer fact that tourist travel to Cuba is still prohibited for Americans hammers home the unpredictability of this situation, the reality that I am venturing into murky waters and uncharted territory.

While no one questioned my grandmother's wishes to have her ashes spread in Cuba or her decision to entrust me with the task, my trip has been met with caution within the family, especially those who had firsthand experience with the regime.

Never forget where you are, Beatriz warned me. *The rights you enjoy here will vanish once you land in Havana. Never take that for granted.*

My great-aunt Maria sent me daily emails filled with news articles and travel information from the State Department in the weeks leading up to my departure, the State Department's words emboldened in my mind . . . *may detain anyone at any time . . . if you violate local laws even unknowingly . . . arrested . . . imprisoned . . .*

Nothing like the potential of capricious imprisonment to instill fear inside you. I don't doubt Cuba is different from any place I've traveled before, but at the same time, I can't quite reconcile the images I've seen on TV and in the news over the years—brightly colored antique cars, crashing waves, and romantic architecture—with the stark portrayal my great-aunts warn of.

My great-aunts are protective of me and my cousins, but when they speak of Cuba there's another level of fear present, one that hints at unspoken horrors whose impact has not lessened with time. I've tried to explain to them that things are different now, that it's not 1959, that the revolution is over, the U.S. Embassy reopened in Havana, and we've entered a new dawn in Cuban-American relations.

Nothing I said lessened the worry in their eyes, and when Maria insisted I carry her rosary tucked away in my bag, given the risk I'm taking with the ashes, I didn't protest. I can likely use the extra luck.

I shuffle forward in the line of travelers.

Just let me get my grandmother through, and I promise I'll stay out of trouble for the remainder of my trip.

My gaze is riveted to the X-ray machine.

Another officer gives me a cursory nod, and I grab my bag from the belt once it has sailed through, a chorus of hallelujahs filling me as I make my way through the airport.

I pick up the rest of my luggage from the baggage area and

make my way through customs, the nerves subsiding with each step I take, my unease making way for excitement akin to the night before Christmas. I've waited my whole life for this moment.

I exit the airport and get my first true glimpse of Havana, take my first breath of Cuban air. There's a slight breeze in the air, but beneath it the humidity hits me full force, my hair beginning to stick to the back of my neck. January in Havana feels a lot like January in Miami. I reach into my bag and pull my sunglasses out, sliding them onto my face.

The sidewalk outside the airport is cheerfully chaotic, friends and families hugging one another, loud voices yelling in exuberant Spanish, people placing luggage into the enormous trunks of brightly colored cars. Most of the cars are nearly sixty years old, some even older, but their age is reflected more in the style than in their condition, as paint shines, chrome gleams, pride of ownership evident in many of the vehicles.

I scan the sea of people, some holding small signs with names scrawled upon them, looking for Ana Rodriguez. I'm eager to meet the woman my grandmother told me about, her words filled with nostalgia and affection.

We were inseparable from the time we were little girls. Her family lived next door to ours, and we used to play together in the garden. Did I tell you about the time I tried to climb the wall separating our houses, Marisol?

I always envisioned the friendship between my grandmother and Ana as a Cuban version of Lucy and Ethel—with my grandmother in the role of Lucy given the stories she told me.

"Marisol Ferrera?"

I turn at the sound of my name and come face-to-face with a man leaning against a bright blue convertible with a massive chrome grill and white accents running down the sides.

"Yes?"

He pushes off the car, the hem of his white guayabera fluttering in the breeze as he walks toward me, all long-limbed grace.

He greets me in smooth English, holding his hand out to me. "I'm Luis Rodriguez. My grandmother asked me to pick you up. She's sorry she couldn't meet you, but she wasn't feeling well."

I take his hand, his calloused fingers rubbing against mine, his handshake firm, his skin warm. His thumb grazes the inside of my wrist as his hand releases mine, and a tremor slides through me.

I blink, my gaze narrowing slightly as I study him, wishing I'd paid more attention to what Beatriz told me about Ana's family.

He looks to be about my age or a couple years older—mid-thirties, perhaps. His hair is full, a few shades lighter than mine—more brown than black—his skin a deep tan, his eyes a dark brown. Crinkly lines surround his eyes, adding character to his face. A close-trimmed beard covers his jaw.

He's handsome in that way some men are—as though the sum of their parts while individually nondescript creates a charisma about them that makes you stand up and pay attention.

"Is she okay?" I ask, responding in Spanish, ignoring the flutter of nerves taking residence in my stomach.

His full lips curve into a smile, the punch of which I'm not altogether prepared for, and I get the impression I've amused him.

"She's fine," he replies back in Spanish. "She tires as the day wears on."

My grandmother was seventy-seven when she died. Ana is nearly a year older.

"She's excited to meet you, though. She's spoken of little else these past few weeks."

He leans forward, lifting my large suitcase in one hand, grabbing my carry-on with his other.

"Are you ready? Is this everything?"

I nod. He ignores my protests that I can carry my own bags, and

I follow him to the car, unable to resist the urge to slide my hand over one of the sleek curves.

"First time in Cuba?" he asks as he sets the smaller bag down and opens the passenger door for me.

"Yes."

I sit on the giant bench seat, my gaze running over the car's interior. The seats are covered in leather that looks like once, long ago, it was white and has now turned to cream. I imagine my grandmother sitting in a car like this, wearing one of the dresses I've seen in the few photographs that remain from her life in Cuba. For a moment, I time-travel.

I wait while Luis loads the bags into the trunk and makes his way to the front seat, firing up the old engine. I reach instinctively for the seat belt, freezing mid-motion when I come up empty.

Right.

I truly have time-traveled.

"This is amazing. Did you restore the car on your own?"

"I have a cousin. He's good with his hands." He gives the dashboard an affectionate pat. "She's temperamental, but if I treat her right, she doesn't let me down."

I grin. "Your car is female?"

"Of course."

He navigates back onto the road with a honk and a wave out the window for the car behind us.

A mix of classic cars and boxy, more modern-looking vehicles pass by us on the road. Some are in near-pristine condition like Luis's; others appear to be held together by ingenuity and prayer. The car accelerates, and I grip the doorframe as palm trees pass us by, the vehicle surprisingly fast for its age. The wind blows my hair around my face, the breeze somewhat alleviating the heat.

We hit a few bumps in the road, the terrain rough, my body tossed around without the security of a seat belt. The landscape changes to giant signs proclaiming the greatness of the Cuban Revolution, the supremacy of communism. Fidel Castro's face stares back at me, followed by images of Che Guevara, his hair billowing in the imaginary wind. These are the monsters of my childhood, and it's strange to see them in this context, venerated rather than vilified.

"So you're a writer?" Luis shouts over the sounds of the wind and the cars rushing past us.

"I am," I shout back. "Freelance, mostly."

It's taken approximately a decade of writing magazine articles and blog posts for me to consider myself a writer, and part of me still waits for someone to call me out when I use the moniker. Writing is not a profession anyone in my family respects or understands—my salary has too few zeros, my schedule is too erratic, the prestige of my career choices not nearly enough. They view it as an eccentric hobby, an anecdote trotted out at parties, a source of bemusement rather than something that—mostly—pays the bills. They would have been much happier to see me working at Perez Sugar—well, besides my grandmother.

Life is too short to be unhappy, Marisol. To play it safe. To do what is expected of you rather than follow your heart. Look at us. One day we had everything, the next it was knocked over like a castle in the sand. You never know what life will throw at you.

She bought forty copies of my first magazine article, handing the periodical out with a smile to anyone and everyone that crossed her path, proclaiming that her granddaughter had written an excellent piece about organizing your closet that had inspired her to transform her own spacious dressing room.

"What do you write?"

I'm surprised by the genuine interest in the question rather than the disinterested politeness I'm used to or the quips about when I'm going to get a "real" job.

"Lifestyle pieces," I answer. "Travel, fashion, food, that sort of thing. I'm working on an article on Cuban tourism now that relations are opening up."

"Do you enjoy it?"

It's funny, because I think he's the first person to lead with that question. Typically people want to know where I've been published, if I've written for a "big" entity, if I'm successful by whatever metric they've decided matters—money, fame, notoriety. I like him better for getting to the heart of it—the reason behind why I write.

"Most of the time. It's fun. I like traveling and seeing new places, enjoy meeting new people. It's usually a puzzle—I know where I'll end up, the words I'll use to get there, but the magic comes when I sit at my computer and string sentences together to reach the heart of what I'm trying to say. There's always a new challenge, a new surprise waiting for me when I begin researching."

And I like the freedom it brings, but I don't say that. I grow restless if I'm in one place too long, and while I always return to Miami, the familiar itch springs up after a month or so. An itch that has infected other areas of my life since my grandmother died, her loss and the memories she left behind making me examine my own legacy—thirty-one, unmarried, childless, driven by a career I like, but don't love.

"So it's the quest you enjoy?"

I never really thought about it that way, but—

"Yeah, I guess it is."

We pass by a wall decorated in a mural of Cuban flags, and I sneak a sidelong glance at Luis. His arm rests on the seat next to mine, inches between us.

Has he ever left Cuba? Do the Cubans who remained resent those who left? Are they worried we will attempt to retake the things we lost when the revolution came? Would he leave if he could? Does he wonder about the world beyond Cuba's shores? It's strange to be in a place that is so cut off from the rest of the world, to realize we likely view life through such different lenses.

"You can just ask me." A smile plays on his lips as his gaze flicks to the rearview mirror. "I can practically feel all the questions in your mind pushing to get out."

I open my mouth to object, but he shakes his head, his gaze back on the road.

"Journalists."

There's a sort of indulgent affection in that word.

"What do you do?" I ask instead of responding to his statement.

"I'm a history professor at the University of Havana. I teach courses on Cuban history. If you have questions about the city for your article, I'm happy to answer them."

"That would be great, thanks. I have a list of places I want to see—the Malecón, the Hotel Nacional, the Tropicana—but I'd love to visit sites locals frequent as well."

"I'm happy to show you around, then."

I didn't expect a built-in tour guide when I accepted Ana's invitation to stay with her, but I'm grateful for his help. Besides, it's not exactly a hardship to be shown around Cuba by a handsome, intelligent man.

"How much do you know about Cuba?" he asks.

"I was raised on it," I answer proudly. "My grandmother's favorite pastime was to tell me stories about Cuba, the house where she grew up, trips to Varadero, attending dances in the squares. Cuba was part of my everyday life. In the food we ate, the music we listened to. It still is, but now that my grandmother is gone it feels more removed."

"Was your father born here?"

"No. He was born after my grandmother left in '59."

"And he didn't want to visit with you?"

I shrug. "He works a lot. He runs the family company, and that keeps him busy."

My father is a man of business and action, not prone to sentimentality or self-discovery. When relations between the United States and Cuba normalize—*if* they normalize—I fully expect him to pave a way in the new market. But this? Chasing down his family's legacy? No.

"Sugar, isn't it?"

I nod, wondering what else his grandmother told him about us.

"My grandmother wanted her ashes spread here. She told me I'd know where to scatter them, but after talking to her sisters, I haven't decided where would be ideal. They gave me some ideas, but I'd like to visit the places and get a feel for them myself. She trusted me with this; I don't want to let her down."

My grandfather was buried in a cemetery in Miami, but my grandmother's letter made it clear that she didn't want to be buried on American soil.

I always said I would go back, and now it's up to you to fulfill that wish for me, to reunite me with those I left behind.

"I'm sorry for your loss. You were close?"

"She was like a mother to me."

He nods as though he understands that my words are not said lightly. "My grandmother spoke of her often and fondly. She hoped they would see each other again."

"My grandmother thought she would return," I reply, the grief creeping up on me the more I speak of her. Talking about her is always a double-edged sword—it keeps her close to me, but it also makes me feel her absence more acutely.

Luis turns onto another road, and I experience my first glimpse of Havana.

I've seen pictures, of course, but there's nothing like viewing it in person, the buildings towering before us. Many of the exteriors are adorned in vibrant colors—coral, canary yellow, and turquoise—the sun bathing them in an amber glow. The walls match the flashy cars surrounding us, the paint on the structures peeling in places. Clotheslines hang from intricate wrought iron and stone balconies, clothes flapping in the breeze; power lines zigzag across buildings. People are stacked upon one another here, crammed into any available space, spilling from the buildings.

The architecture is breathtaking, though. Ornate black iron lamps are posted as sentries along sidewalks. The detail on the buildings is truly remarkable, intricate carvings and scrollwork adorning apartments. But pieces of plaster have crumbled off, leaving gaps on the walls, and there's a faint sheen of gray that adorns the landscape as though the entire city needs a good scrubbing.

Havana is like a woman who was grand once and has fallen on hard times, and yet hints of her former brilliance remain, traces of an era since passed, a photograph faded by time and circumstance, its edges crumbling to dust.

If I close my eyes I can see Havana as she was, enshrined in my grandmother's memory. But when they open again, the reality of nearly sixty years of isolation stares back at me, and I'm grateful my grandmother isn't here to witness the decay of the city she loved so faithfully.

"It was beautiful once," Luis says, surprising me. Our gazes catch.

"Yes. You can see that it was."

"Each year it ages a bit more." He sighs, turning his attention back to the road. "We paint, plaster, attempt to keep it together, but a project of this magnitude?"

The rest lingers between us. Without money, there's very little they can do.

"Old Havana is better than most of the neighborhoods. They preserve it for the tourists, so if you want a glimpse of what the city was like before, you'll see it there."

The Spanish founded the old part of the city in the sixteenth century. From what I've read and the stories I've heard, Havana is divided into different neighborhoods, each distinct for its own reasons. Part of the attraction of staying with Ana rather than in a hotel is that her family still lives in the house next to my grandmother's—the house where generations of Perezes were born and raised.

"What can you tell me about Miramar?" I ask, referring to my grandmother's old neighborhood.

"Which do you prefer—the history professor's perspective or that of the man who's lived there his entire life?"

"Both, I guess."

"The story of the Cuban people—the modern history, at least—is a story of adapting. Making the most of the limited resources the grand revolution affords us—" There's a hint of disapproval in the way he says "grand revolution," as though he's committed blasphemy.

"Miramar has survived better than most parts of the city because the embassies are there. Some of the houses are run-down, but it could be worse. Many of the regime's generals and high-ranking officials now live in the homes that were once occupied by Batista's cohorts, by Cuba's wealthiest families." This time the disapproval rings clear. "That's progress, you see. We rid ourselves of the worms and look who moved in to replace them."

The candor in his words and the manner in which his voice fairly drips with scorn surprises me.

"We opened a *paladar* in our home," Luis continues. "It's filled with European tourists, because most Cubans could never afford to eat at our restaurant if it wasn't subsidized by the high prices tourists pay—well, high for us anyway."

I've heard about the informal restaurants Cubans have begun running out of their homes with permission from the government. I have a list of the top-rated ones in Havana to add to my article, and the *paladar* run by the Rodriguez family is on it.

"Does your grandmother do the cooking?"

"For the most part. Everyone who comes into the restaurant is welcomed like family. It's harder each year as she gets older, but she enjoys hosting our guests. I help out when I can."

"And your parents? Do they live in Miramar, too?"

He doesn't answer me for a moment, his fingers tapping against the leather steering wheel. He turns down a side street, the ocean making a sudden appearance. It's a perfect Tiffany blue; the waves crash in foamy white caps.

"My father died when I was a boy. Fighting in Angola."

"I'm sorry." I hesitate. "He was in the military?"

"He was. An officer in the army. He fought in Angola in '88. The battle of Cuito Cuanavale. Died a hero. My mother works in the *paladar* with my grandmother."

He offers this last piece of information with deceptive candor; I recognize it for what it is—offering more information than I asked for so I won't ask for more.

Silence falls between us, and I'm content to spend the rest of the drive staring at the scenery, imagining my grandmother walking down these streets, standing under the lamppost, dipping her feet in the water lapping along the shore. I see her sisters here, too—Beatriz causing mischief wherever she goes; Isabel, who passed away almost two years ago and who spent her life with a perpetual shroud of sadness for the love she lost; and Maria, the youngest of my great-aunts who was little more than a child when she left.

The neighborhood reminds me of the Spanish streets in Coral Gables, and I see why my grandmother gravitated toward that part of Miami when she first came to the United States, how she found her own enclave where she attempted to recreate the country she loved and lost.

Enormous palm trees dominate the landscape, their intricate, spindly trunks a testament to the island's resilience against Mother Nature and the hurricane-force winds that often batter its shores. The homes themselves exist in varying states of decay, ghosts of a society carried away by revolution. And yet beside the rubble are tall, modern hotels designed to attract European tourists, a smattering of shops and bars that clearly cater to similar clientele. An empty fountain sits off to the side, broken, its mermaids forlorn and aimless, as though it's been frozen in time by a sorcerer's spell.

We continue on, and the city stirs, people walking down the street, waiting at a bus stop.

We drive down the Quinta Avenida, past embassies lined up in a row. And then there are more houses—overgrown lawns, empty swimming pools in the backyard visible from the road. There's more space here, the estates a bit larger, and from the condition of the houses, it appears Miramar has fared better than most of Havana, even as my surroundings are still so different from what I'm used to and a far cry from the opulent splendor my grandmother described to me.

The houses were fashioned after grand European estates, materials brought in from France and Spain on great big ships. Their gardens were impeccably manicured, flowers blooming, the smell of oranges in the air, the immense palm trees casting shade upon us all.

Luis points out the Russian embassy as we pass by. It's impossible to miss—the building is austere and towering, shooting into the sky like a missile.

Luis makes another turn in the big car, as though he's navigating a boat into a slip, and we're on the street where my family lived.

Luis stops in front of a house, and despite the rambling appearance, the faded paint, I recognize the structure behind the iron gates immediately.

It was painted pink, the palest color, like the inside of a seashell. Beatriz used to stand on the upstairs balcony like a queen holding court.

And where were you, Abuela?

Swimming in the pool in the back with Maria, probably. Or reading in the library. We would make our way into the kitchen, and the cook would sneak us food before dinner. My mother hated it, of course, which was largely the appeal.

I remove my sunglasses, wiping at my face as I open the door and get out of the car, walking toward the house, staring at the palm trees, the steps leading up to the front door. From Beatriz, I learned the house was built in the Baroque style by Perezes generations past. The image in front of me doesn't compare to the photographs I've seen, smuggled out by family friends and former employees over the years, but the shadow of its former glory remains.

"Who lives there now?" I ask as Luis comes to stand next to me, silent, his hands shoved into the pockets of his khakis. The sleeve of his guayabera brushes my bare shoulder, a hint of the weight of his body beside mine.

"A Russian diplomat moved in decades ago." His breath catches as our arms graze. "When I was a teenager."

My grandmother's bedroom was in the back of the house, a view of the ocean from her window, and I yearn to sneak back there and explore.

"Are they in residence?"

Perhaps I can convince them to let me look around? Of all the places I've considered spreading my grandmother's ashes, her childhood home seems like the best option.

"Not at the moment, no."

The sun shines down on the building, encasing it in the same glow that bathes everything here. The sky is an explosion of color, every shade of blue you can imagine; white cotton clouds spread throughout.

I've never seen a more beautiful place in all my life.

"It's gorgeous," I whisper more to myself than him, taking a step forward, my hands curving around the wrought iron gate in front of the property.

Everything fades into the background, and it's just the house and me.

A minute passes by. Two.

I pull back reluctantly, loath to leave. When I turn to face Luis, he isn't looking at the house, but at me.

"Are you ready to drop your bags off and settle into your room?" he asks, his gaze speculative.

I nod, words momentarily eluding me.

Luis holds out his hand, indicating for me to proceed. I offer to carry the bags again, but he refuses, following me as I walk along the sidewalk to the house next door to my grandmother's.

The Rodriguez house is three stories tall and painted a pale yellow. Compared to the other residences, the mansion is relatively well-kept, wearing its age with dignity and grace. A restaurant awning hangs over one side of the building, indicating the house's changed stature in life, people milling outside on one of the patios where tables have been set out for diners. Large, nearly floor-to-ceiling glass-paneled doors open to the outside, exposing an indoor dining area.

We walk up a gravel driveway, Luis leading me toward the front doors. He opens them with a creak, and we step over the threshold. The entryway is cavernous, the marble floor cracked and scuffed, but still impressive. Judging by the empty spaces on the walls and in the room, much of the furniture is long gone, the remaining pieces in surprisingly good condition despite their age.

My grandmother told me Ana's family was in the rum business before Castro nationalized it, and even fifty years of communism haven't fully erased the vestiges of their wealth.

The walls are a pastel green color. A heavy gold mirror with a delicate fleur-de-lis covers one wall, the gilt tarnished in places. Another wall is covered in a hodgepodge of artwork and aged photographs. A chandelier hangs from the ceiling, a double staircase leading up to the house's second floor.

"Your home is beautiful."

Luis removes his sunglasses and smiles. "Thank you."

"Marisol?"

I turn.

She walks toward me from a doorway off the entryway. Even with the addition of over fifty years, I recognize her instantly from my grandmother's old photos.

Ana Rodriguez is a petite woman—an inch or two shorter than me—with a compact build. Her dark hair curls beneath her ears, her cheeks are pink, a broad smile on her face.

In three steps she crosses the entryway, holding out her hands and clasping mine.

"Marisol."

My name is said with a rush of affection, and any lingering nerves I possessed about staying with a stranger disappear completely. She treats me as one would a granddaughter she hasn't seen in weeks rather than a guest, engulfing me in a hug. Tears prick my eyes. There's something in her manner, in the way she carries herself that reminds me of my grandmother. She smells as though she's come from the kitchen, an apron tied around her waist, mouth-watering scents I recognize instantly—*mojo* and black beans—greeting me.

I'm not normally a crier, but between my grief and the nostalgia of the moment, it's difficult to keep my emotions in check. These are the stories of my childhood come to life, the spirit of my grand-mother, my family, our legacy, everywhere I turn.

Ana smiles, tears swimming in her brown eyes.

"You look like Elisa."

I do. I inherited my grandmother's nearly black hair and I wear it long like she did when she was younger. Our faces are similar—heart shaped—and I have her mouth. I inherited her petite stat-ure, too.

A twinkle enters Ana's eyes. "Perhaps a bit of Beatriz as well."

In terms of compliments, there is no higher praise. Aunt Beatriz is the beauty of the family, and the broken hearts that have trailed behind her are legendary.

"Thank you."

"How is she? Beatriz?"

"She's good. She sent gifts for you."

"Is she still—"

She doesn't need to finish the question.

I grin. "Of course."

My great-aunt has caused scandals that span countries and con-tinents.

"And Maria?"

"She's doing well. She stays busy with her grandchildren, my cousins."

"I was sorry to hear about Isabel. And your grandmother."

I nod, the emotions still too raw for words. It's being in this place, feeling as though I'm inhabiting a corner of my grandmother's life while she's gone that tugs at my heart. That's the thing with grief—you never know when it will sneak up on you.

Ana squeezes my hand, gesturing toward her grandson.

"Come. Let us take you to your room. You must be tired after the trip. Rest and then we'll talk."

I allow her to shepherd me up the immense staircase, leading me toward the guest room she has prepared for me. Ana explains in a matter-of-fact tone that the house has been divided up into apartments where other families live.

Luis trails behind us, bags in hand.

We stop in front of a heavy wooden door that looks as though it belongs in a Spanish monastery.

"I hope this room will be comfortable," Ana says as she pushes it open.

The bedroom is small and clean, the windows open, white linen curtains fluttering in the breeze. There's a bed pushed up against the wall, an aged wood table beside it. A chipped glass vase filled with colorful flowers sits atop it. A matching wardrobe is stuffed in the corner, a gilded mirror on the wall, the edges cracked and tarnished, adorned with fat carnelian stones.

"It's perfect."

And it is.

Luis sets my bags down near the wardrobe and excuses himself, leaving me alone with Ana.

She hugs me again, her scent engulfing me.

"Rest. We'll talk later."

She leaves me, the door shutting behind her, and I browse around the little room, unpacking my things and changing into a pair of pajama pants and a tank top. I set aside the gifts I brought Ana as a thank-you for hosting me—after hours spent scouring the Internet for travel tips, I hope I've found items she will use and enjoy.

I climb under the covers, a faint breeze coming in from the open windows. I stare up at the ceiling, the plaster cracking, chunks of white paint missing, my eyelids growing heavier with each moment that passes. The events of the day hit me in waves, the adrenaline crash coming on strong.

I roll over to my side, pulling the worn sheets up to my face, my eyes drifting shut. I smell the gardenias my grandmother described to me, and the jasmine, the scent of roast pork wafting up from the *paladar* below. The faint sound of a saxophone drifts up to my room, and I recognize the familiar strands of "La Bayamesa."

This is family, home, the most fundamental part of me. I could be sitting in my grandparents' elegant residence in Coral Gables, or off in Europe, and all it takes is the scent of *mojo*, the sound of my people, to ground me.

The breeze blows my hair across the pillow, and the smell of jasmine calls to mind a memory of me as a little girl—my grandmother's perfume and the feel of her hand stroking my hair when she put me to sleep at night.

Tell me a story.

When I was a girl in Cuba . . .

I fall asleep.

chapter three

Elisa

It's the perfect dress for a night like tonight—elegant without the obvious sophistication of the gowns our mother orders us from abroad, a neckline a touch more daring than I usually wear, a hem exposing the calves I've sunned by the pool at the Havana Biltmore Yacht and Country Club.

I pull the white dress designed by Manet from my closet, my fingers skimming the lace. The bodice is fitted with pale pink flowers, the waist tucked in, the skirt full. I bought it on a shopping trip with Beatriz last month after we saw it in El Encanto, and I've been waiting for the perfect occasion to wear it. This seems better than any. I snuck a pair of my mother's shoes from her closet—the palest pink to match the flowers—after she and our father left for their trip to Varadero.

I dress quickly, struggling a bit with the tiny buttons in the back. Once the dress is on, I choose a pair of earrings from the wooden vanity in the corner of my bedroom, staring at my reflection in the three-way mirror perched on top of it. I select one of the glass bottles sitting atop the surface, spritzing the perfume on my wrists, rubbing it behind my ears, the scent one I save for special occasions.

"Are you ready?" my sister Isabel hisses from the doorway, her gaze drifting toward the hallway. None of the servants are likely to tell on us, but Magda's the unknown; our nanny is more family than anything else, nearly as concerned with the reputation of the Perez family as our mother is. This isn't the type of party we normally attend, like all the ones where we stand in full-skirted ball gowns and long white gloves wearing heavy diamond necklaces around our necks.

My brow rises as I take stock of Isabel's outfit; clearly I'm not the only one who raided our mother's closet. The dress is one our mother has worn to parties before—black, fitted, and far more daring than anything she's ever allowed any of us to wear. If this is Isabel's choice for the evening, I can only imagine what Beatriz has come up with.

"I'm ready." I pick up my clutch from the dresser, my fingers stroking the beads.

"Where's Beatriz?" I ask, careful to keep my voice low. Magda has the uncanny ability to sneak up on us at the most inopportune moments, a lesson Maria has learned more than anyone else; being the youngest has its drawbacks.

"Waiting in the car."

The car was another battle with our mother, one Beatriz ultimately won.

Isabel's gaze darts toward the hallway and back again.

"And Maria?" I ask.

"Sleeping."

Keeping our outing a secret from our little sister is as crucial as hiding it from Magda. Maria has bribery down to an art form President Batista would envy, and the price for ensuring her silence for not telling our parents we're attending a party would likely be steeper than we would want to pay. The last time Maria caught Isabel sneaking back into the house after a date, she made out with Isabel's favorite pearl earrings and a dress from Paris.

I follow Isabel down the hallway, our heels drumming against the marble floors. Our house was built in the mid-eighteenth century by the first Perez ancestor of note, a French corsair who amassed a fortune through ill-gotten gains and won himself a wife of impeccable lineage. He built her one of the largest and most ostentatious mansions in Havana, one that's been renovated and updated throughout the years by various Perez heirs. The end result is a cavernous mansion brimming with gold leaf and marble. I've always thought the corsair had more money than taste, but considering he won himself a title from a Bourbon king along with his bride, he possessed enough cachet for our mother to proudly claim him as an ancestor.

In the beginning, our legacy came from smuggling and the corsair's more nefarious activities. Soon his children and grandchildren began diversifying the family's fortune, and through an advantageous marriage in the late nineteenth century, the Perezes became sugar barons.

For better, worse, and the truly horrific, sugar has molded Cuba's fortunes.

The corsair stares us down as we tiptoe through the hall, and while the rest of our ancestors seem to disapprove of this act of rebellion from atop their oil-and-canvas perches, I fancy that our pirate ancestor with his dark hair and even darker eyes twinkling with mischief would have wholeheartedly approved.

We slip our shoes off at the top of the staircase in an act of choreographed sisterly precision. The marble is cool against my toes despite the warm air tonight, the moon casting a sliver of light across the steps. We freeze as noises coming from the general direction of the kitchen filter throughout the house.

Is the risk we're taking really worth the reward of a night of freedom?

The punishment? Temporary removal to the country. Forced attendance at teas and luncheons, parties where we're jettisoned from one eligible son of one of our father's business associates to another. Life as usual.

They're fighting in Cuba's eastern provinces, in the Oriente, boys not much older than me, boys who should be at university— who would be at university if Batista hadn't closed the University of Havana out of fear years ago. The revolutionaries are fighting throughout the country, storming the Presidential Palace, seeking to overthrow the government, to end Batista's corruption, and yet, behind the high walls of our Miramar home, the ancien régime reigns supreme. My mother has no time for revolutions; they wreak havoc with her balls and teas.

It is a strange time to be Cuban, to feel the stirrings beneath your feet, hear the rumblings in the sky, and to continue on as though nothing is happening at all. Stranger still to be a woman in Cuba—we vote, but what does a vote mean when election outcomes are a foregone conclusion? The women in our family attended the best schools, grew up with a slew of tutors, each one more harried and harassed by all of us—Beatriz, in particular—but Perez women do not work no matter how much we might wish to do so. We are useless birds in a gilded cage while our countrywomen serve in the government, while some plot revolution. Times have changed in our little island, a tinder lit, spreading like wildfire throughout Cuba, meanwhile our estates are a bulwark against modernization, change, freedom.

And so occasionally, we do exceedingly foolish things like sneaking out of the house in the dead of night, because it's impossible to stand near the flame consuming everything around you and not have some of that fire catch the hem of your skirt, too.

We make it to the front door, pausing once for a maid completing her duties for the night, a song under her breath. Once the maid has finished dusting the entryway table, Isabel exits first, leaving me to close the heavy front door behind me with a wince. I slip my mother's sandals back onto my feet, freezing at the sight of Beatriz lounging against her convertible.

Her dress looks as though it was painted onto her voluptuous body, and I don't know where she bought it or where she's been hiding it, but you wear a dress like that when you want to create a scandal. She flaunts it beautifully.

Of all of Emilio Perez's daughters, Beatriz is the most apt to court scandal, to push at the edges of the cage, occasionally breaking free. She fights with our parents about attending university, wants to study law, quotes philosophers and radicals. And she insisted we sneak out tonight.

"Are you ready?" Beatriz asks. Her gaze runs over me, and when she doesn't say anything, I relax slightly. Beatriz's sartorial elegance is undisputed in Havana.

"I thought we talked about discretion," Isabel grouses beside me. "Parking your car in front of the house where anyone can see is not discreet."

"No one will say anything," Beatriz scoffs. "They're too terrified of our mother to broach the subject."

Our father runs his businesses, but our mother rules our home with a jewel-covered fist.

"You're too careless," Isabel retorts.

I tune them out, their bickering a common refrain in our household. My gaze drifts across the high stone walls to my best friend Ana's house. I count the windows as I've done for years until I reach the second floor, settling on the third one down. The light is on in her bedroom—

"Elisa!"

Isabel gets into the car's back seat, waving me on while Beatriz somehow slides into the driver seat despite her constricting dress.

I follow my sisters out into the night.

The party is at a house in Vedado, a few blocks away from the University of Havana. The host is a friend of a friend of a friend of Isabel's boyfriend, Alberto. Beatriz navigates a parking spot, and once she's parked we exit the car, and I trail behind her and Isabel. Guests spill out of the entrance, the house brimming with noise and music, vibrating with laughter.

It's a pretty enough structure—two stories tall and painted in a clean white color. A balcony juts off the second floor, more guests filling the space. At first glance, it's obvious we're overdressed. Significantly so. We might as well announce to the entire room that we aren't from here, that we belong to a different part of the city. Our aim tonight is anonymity; our names and faces are relatively well-known, but I doubt this crowd spends much time poring over the society pages of *Diario de la Marina*.

Beatriz charges through the crowd, her hips swaying, a woman on a mission. She was so intent on coming here tonight that I can't help but wonder if Isabel isn't the only one dating a man our parents don't wholly approve of. At the same time, if Beatriz were dating someone inappropriate, she would be the last to hide it. No, she'd proudly parade him in front of all, seating him at the grand dining room table our mother had shipped from Paris to compete with her rival and best friend whose own dining room table sailed from England.

Benny Moré is on the record player, couples dancing anywhere and everywhere, their bodies a little closer than you typically see at my mother's formal parties, hands drifting a little lower, fingers clutching fabric, their cheeks pressed against each other. The women dance with a freedom I covet, their hips sinuous, their movements leaving no doubt that they embrace every ounce of femininity God gave them. There's passion of varying degrees and inspirations throbbing in the air, occupying the cracks and crevices of the party, tucked away behind clasped hands, soaring above bent heads. A sort of frenzy that seeps into your bones.

The crowd swallows Isabel and Beatriz up until I'm left alone, standing on the fringes of the party in my too-formal dress, searching for a familiar face, someone else who's somewhere they shouldn't be, torn between discomfort at the raw emotions lingering under the surface and a faint prick of envy.

I accept one of the drinks they're generously passing around, the rum sweeter than any I'm used to—stronger, too—finding a comfortable place against the wall where I can observe everyone. In a family like mine, you grow accustomed to watching from the shadows. I've never been like Beatriz, happiest taking risks. Nor am I Isabel—truculently in love, or Maria, prone to outbursts. This—watching couples dance, listening to music, taking the occasional sip of rum—is more than enough for me. At least, it was.

And then I see him.

Strangely, I notice the suit before I notice the man. Cuban society is not quiet society; we flaunt our wealth and status like peacocks. He is no peacock. His suit isn't impeccably tailored to fit his frame, and it isn't designed to impress. It's functional—a no-nonsense black that drapes a tall, lean body. I like him better for the simplicity; I'm more than a little tired of peacocks.

He's speaking with two other men, his hands shoved in his pockets, his gaze cast downward. He has a strong jaw, sharp cheekbones, and a surprisingly full, lush mouth on a hard face. His skin is a shade or two darker than mine, his dark hair an unruly mess curling at the ends.

He doesn't smile.

I sip the rum, watching him, attempting to guess his age. Most of the party appears to be a little older than me—in their early twenties, perhaps—and while there's a severity about him, he doesn't look *that* much older.

His lips move rapidly when he talks, his hands in constant motion.

My foot taps in time with the music, mimicking the beat of my heart as I watch him, willing him to look at me, to notice me.

And miraculously, he does. Maybe the dress is a little magic.

He turns, mid-conversation, his hands lingering in the air like a conductor instructing a symphony, surveying the crowd, the same hardness in his eyes that's stamped all over his face. There's a hunger there, though, beneath that hardness—a hunger I've seen before—the kind that looks at the world and isn't afraid to say it isn't good enough, that there must be more, to demand change. He looks like a man who believes in things, which is truly terrifying these days.

My breath hitches.

His eyes widen slightly, as though he can hear my breath over the sound of Benny Moré, the laughter and sin spilling all over the party.

He doesn't appear callous, merely as though life has tested him and roughed his edges. His gaze rests on me, and those lips pause for a moment. He doesn't do the polite thing and glance away, or pretend he was looking at something else and just happened to catch me in his path. No, he settles in and looks me over, and slowly, so slowly, a smile spreads across his face, and suddenly, surprisingly, he's handsome.

I freeze, my mother's voice in my ear—*don't fidget, smile—not too much—put your shoulders back*—until her voice disappears, floating above this party she would never approve of, and in the space of a heartbeat he's standing in front of me, a little taller, a little more broad shouldered than he appeared to be across the room.

I swallow, tilting my head up, staring into solemn brown eyes.

"Hello," he says, offering a perfectly ordinary greeting in a voice that is anything but.

"Hello," I echo, traversing one thousand guesses surrounding who he is, what he does, why he crossed the room to speak to me, in the time between those hellos.

His lips curve, those eyes softening a bit. "I'm Pablo."

I turn his name over and over in my head, testing out the sound of it to my ears alone before giving him my own.

"Elisa."

An elbow brushes past me, jostling me. I lurch forward, the rum in my glass tipping precariously, entirely too close to Pablo's black suit. He reaches out, steadying me, his hand connecting with my arm.

I blink again in an attempt to right myself. My drink isn't the only thing that's tilted on its axis.

"I've never seen you at one of Guillermo's parties before," he says.

Guillermo must be our host, the friend of a friend of a friend, or something or other, of Isabel's boyfriend.

"I've never been to one before."

He nods, that same solemn expression on his face, and I revise my guess about his age. He is older, late twenties or early thirties perhaps.

Another person nudges my back, and Pablo shifts, putting his body between me and the rest of the crowd, his hand exerting the faintest pressure on my elbow to steady me.

The song changes, the tempo increasing, guests dancing to the spirited beat as we remain pressed up against the wall, his hand on my elbow. His fingers are long and lean; they tell the story of a man who works with his hands, slightly incongruous with the dark, well-worn suit and the party's solidly Havana crowd.

Pablo's hand falls to his side. I look up.

His mouth is parted slightly, his gaze narrowed as though he doesn't know what to make of what he sees.

Another body bumps into us. The rum lists in my glass.

Pablo leans into me, his voice rising to be heard over the loud music, the laughter. My heartbeat thrums, equal parts nerves and anticipation running through my veins.

"Do you want to step outside?" he asks. "It's quieter out there."

It seems the most natural thing in the world to give him my hand and follow him out of the party.

chapter four

Pablo leads me through the house, his steps guided by purpose and familiarity. We weave through the crowd, and I search for Beatriz and Isabel as we walk, but I can't find them in the throng. Every so often Pablo turns around and glances at me, his fingers laced with mine. We step out into the night, the backyard nearly empty as we walk toward a palm tree to the side of the house. The backyard abuts another, the lots small and crammed together.

He's right—it is quieter outside, the roar of music and partygoers now a low hum.

I look up at the sky, the stars shining down on us, taking the opportunity to compose myself. When I glance back at him, he's not looking at me, but up at the stars as well, his gaze hooded.

I jump at the sound of a boom off in the distance, then another, and another. The explosion is far away, relegated to another part of the city, but these days it could signal anything—gunfire, fireworks, bombs.

I glance at Pablo, his attention no longer on the sky, but focused on me; his expression is unreadable, as though he has grown immune to the sounds of violence and armed revolt.

"Those probably aren't fireworks," I comment, my heart pounding.

"Probably not," he agrees.

I wait for him to say more, for him to remark on the recent violence, but he's surprisingly quiet. I'm used to men who fill conversations, offering me little opportunity to speak.

"How long have you known Guillermo?" I ask, searching for someplace to start. It's more private out here, but it was easier back in the party, the music and people filling the spaces and silences in our conversation. Now it's up to us, and I'm at a loss for words. I know how to speak to people from my own world, people who have mastered the art of speaking without saying anything at all, but I can't imagine having such a conversation with the boy—man—standing before me. He seems like the sort who parses and weighs his words with economy and care.

Pablo doesn't answer me right away, those brown eyes piercing, his gaze lingering on my feet, and I immediately regret my decision to wear my mother's fine Parisian shoes.

His are black, the leather creased in places from wear.

"Years," he replies absentmindedly, his gaze still on my ridiculous shoes. "We've known each other for years."

I shuffle back and forth, my mother's voice in my ear again— *Don't fidget, Elisa.*

Surely, this time a little fidgeting is warranted.

"How do you know Guillermo?" I press on, motivated not only by his answer but a desire to remove his attention from my footwear. His manner makes me a bit bolder, the inclination that he's also off-balance, a tension threading through his silence.

This time he looks into my eyes, a ghost of a smile on his mouth.

"We went to law school together years ago."

The University of Havana has been closed for two years now, so he must have graduated a while ago.

"How do *you* know Guillermo?" he counters.

"I don't. He's a friend of a friend of a friend of my sister's boyfriend.

Or something like that. I came with my sisters." The words escape in a whoosh. I take a deep breath. Then another. "Are you from the city?" I ask, attempting to place him in the insular circle of Havana society.

"Just down the street, actually."

It isn't the nicest neighborhood, but far from the worst.

There's a twinkle in his eye when he asks his next question, and before the words leave his mouth, I know these stupid shoes have given me away.

"Miramar?"

I nod, slightly embarrassed by the knowing tone of voice, the images my neighborhood's name conjures up. Havana's wealthiest citizens live in our own private enclave, and the rest of the city knows it.

I was raised from birth to be proud of being a Perez; we all were. My sisters and I cannot work, but that doesn't mean we don't do our part to carry our family's mantle, that it hasn't been instilled in us that we must never tarnish our family's reputation, our every word, every action reflecting on the Perez name, the legacy of our ancestors resting on our shoulders.

Still—this is the point in the conversation when I wish I had more to contribute, that I could share career ambitions or something similar. It has not escaped my notice that so many of my countrywomen are far more accomplished than me.

Thanks to our father's insistence we had the finest education, are well acquainted with the classics. Thanks to our mother's influence we have been trained in the art of entertaining—hosting dinners, organizing charity functions; living, breathing decorations that form part of the trappings of our family's empire. Times are changing in Cuba—how long will we be little more than ornaments?

Pablo walks forward a bit before turning back to face me, his shoulders listing with the effort, and I'm surprised by how lean he is, the suit hanging from the slope of his shoulders.

"What's life like in Miramar?" he asks.

"Probably what you'd imagine."

I feel as though I've become a point of curiosity, an exhibit like the island of crocodiles at the Havana Zoo, those mighty animals sunning their backs with contempt for the gawking tourists and locals who point and exclaim over their size. Being a Perez in Havana—one of the sugar queens—is akin to wondering if you should charge admission for the window into your life—the stories they print in *Diario de la Marina* and the like. Beatriz welcomes the attention, Isabel attempts to cast off the veneer of notoriety, and I'm somewhere in the middle. Maria is too young to care either way; her chief amusements are still playing in the pool and the backyard.

"Fobbing off marriage proposals and attending parties all day?" Pablo teases.

I fight back an utterly unladylike snort. "Yes to the parties. No to the marriage proposals."

"Then the men in Miramar are fools."

His tone is light, bantering, but the solemnity in his gaze makes my heart pound.

Suddenly the nerves are too much, and I turn, looking out to the direction of the sea. I can't see it, but I can hear the sound of the waves crashing along the Malecón.

Pablo's voice comes from somewhere behind me in the dark night. "You missed a button. On your dress."

I swallow.

"May I?" he asks.

I nod, my mouth dry. My mother would be thoroughly appalled to see her daughter standing outside a party such as this one, a strange man buttoning her dress. My mother would be thoroughly appalled, and yet I turn, lifting my hair, bringing it to the side, baring my nape to him.

A tremor slides through my body.

Pablo steps behind me, close enough that his fingers brush against the line of tiny buttons running down my spine. It feels like an eternity before his fingers slip the button through the slim hole, setting it to rights. It could be my imagination, but I swear his fingers twitch against me, or perhaps it's my own body that shudders. There's a novelty to this that catches me off guard. He is both old and new at once, and I can't ignore the voice inside me that's pushed out my mother's now—

Pay attention. This is important. He is important.

Pablo releases a deep breath, stepping back. I turn to face him.

There's surprise on his face, the kind that sneaks up on you and isn't entirely welcome.

"You're very young, aren't you?"

The words themselves are tinged with the faintest hint of disapproval, but I can't shake the feeling that the sentiment is directed more to himself than me.

I swallow, tilting my head, refusing to be cowed. "Nineteen."

Nineteen and a pampered bird in a gilded cage.

He gives a soft little laugh, his hand running through his hair. It's a bit long around the edges, unkempt, as though it's been some time since he visited a barber. It's a stark contrast to his clean-shaven face, his tanned skin at odds with an attorney's days spent indoors behind a desk. My father knows a host of attorneys, men who bow and scrape before him. Does he know this one?

"Nineteen is very young."

He says the words more for himself than me, an aside in an internal conversation he seems to be having.

I have older siblings; my interactions with men I'm interested in may be limited, but I'm well versed in the art of standing up for myself when I need to.

"And you?"

I toss the question out like a challenge.

"Thirty."

The number isn't shocking, nor is the age difference. My mother stopped celebrating birthdays ages ago, but the chasm between my own parents is impossible to miss.

"Not that old," I say, even though I doubt he's merely speaking of physical age. I feel new and shiny next to him; in contrast, he's *interesting*—a sanded-down veneer covered in telltale signs of experience.

"Perhaps." He's silent for a moment, that word a door shutting on me, the conversation, whatever this is.

"I should go," I say, taking a step forward, away from him.

Pablo's head bows slightly. "I'm sorry."

I don't move.

"I shouldn't—" His voice breaks off and he shakes his head. "I'm in a foul mood tonight. I didn't come here looking for a party, only to speak to Guillermo, and I certainly didn't come here expecting to meet you. That's no excuse for being rude." He takes a deep breath. "A friend died recently. I came to talk to Guillermo about it. I'm—" He pauses again, as though he's searching for the right words. "I'm at a loss," he finally says.

"I'm sorry about your friend." My feet, those shoes that seem filled with ideas and ambition, take a step toward him, then another.

I rest my hand on his arm, the hem of my dress brushing against his trousers, a hint of tobacco and spice filling my nostrils. The body beneath my palm is all tightly coiled strength. His eyes are wide.

This—touching a man I barely know—is wholly inappropriate.

Everything about this evening has firmly teetered away from respectability, and he's right, he was a bit rude earlier. I should go inside, find my sisters, and return home. This man isn't one of the tame boys my parents have trotted out in front of me as suitable escorts. He possesses an edge even I can't miss.

There's that flame, licking at my skirts again.

"Was he a good friend?"

"He was a good man," Pablo answers after a beat. He takes a step back, putting distance between us, doing the appropriate thing when logic and reason seem to have picked their skirts up in one hand and fled.

It's funny how that little step can change everything, but it does. It's as though he cedes territory, and in his retreat, a burst of courage fills me. Whatever this is, he's equally unsettled, and some entirely feminine urge I didn't realize I possessed has me straightening my shoulders, tilting my head, meeting his gaze, my lashes fluttering closed, happy to play the coquette if only for the span of this evening.

A rueful grin covers his mouth, a glint of admiration in his eyes. His hand drifts to his heart, a hint of mockery in his demeanor. "You must forgive me. I fear I'm at a loss for words. No one ever warned me about the dangers of debutantes."

"And how many debutantes have you known?" I ask, measuring my tone against his in an effort to keep things light between us, even though there's sincerity in the question.

You learn fairly early on that there are men who will attempt to court you because of your last name, because your father is power and they want to grasp it in their greedy hands, because they dream of wealth, and slipping a ring on your finger is the easiest way to obtain it. I don't sense that he's such a man, but the impulse to be wary is there just the same.

"None."

A flutter kicks up in my stomach.

I really should go inside.

"Am I dangerous?" I test the word out and decide I like the taste and sound of it.

His expression turns somber. "I have a feeling you just might be."

The flutter takes flight.

"I should go inside," he says, echoing my earlier words.

He doesn't move.

We both stare at each other, unblinking, the ocean roaring in the background, my heart thundering in my chest. Now I understand a bit better what drives Beatriz and Isabel, how they can throw caution to the wind for one night of freedom. I'm curious in a way I haven't been before, curious and perhaps just a little bit reckless.

Pablo looks pained as the question falls from his lips. "Will you meet me tomorrow? By the Malecón?"

"Yes."

chapter five

Marisol

I sleep longer than intended, the sheets worn and soft, the mattress surprisingly comfortable. The afternoon sunlight has dimmed by the time I wake. I reach for my cell phone, the limited Cuban telecommunications connectivity rendering it virtually useless but for the clock display—it's almost eight o'clock in the evening. I napped for three hours.

It's strange to be so separated from the rest of the world, from my sisters, my friends, my editor, but that's part of the Cuban experience, I suppose, adding to the sensation that I truly have journeyed to the land of my grandmother's memories, firmly walled off from my life back home in Miami. There are a limited number of places where you can get Internet here, and even then it's unreliable at best; there is no service in private homes, and everyone told me to expect to be cut off for the week I was staying with the Rodriguez family. My cell service doesn't work, either, so it's just Cuba and me.

I climb out of bed, padding to the window and pulling back the curtain, staring at the view in front of me. The sky is gold; a palette edged in pinks and blues, the sun a radiant ball of fire as it drifts into the horizon. The ocean is equally stunning. Back home, it would be a multimillion-dollar view, one many would clamor to possess. I've seen some beautiful sights in my life, but my grandmother was right; this really is paradise.

My gaze drifts to the patio beneath my room. A few tables are empty, but the dinner crowd has begun gathering. Glasses clink, silverware scrapes across dishes, and the aroma of black beans and rice fills the air. I grew up eating Cuban food; between my grandmother's love of cooking and the plethora of Cuban restaurants on Calle Ocho and beyond, black beans and rice have always been a staple in my diet.

I pause as Luis comes into view. He walks toward one of the tables, plates in hand, setting them down in front of a family of tourists before exchanging a few words with them in the same flawless English he used when he greeted me at the airport. He bobs and weaves through the tables crammed into the tiny outdoor space, moving past one of the waitresses in a coordinated dance. There's an economy and efficiency to their movements as they pass by each other without speaking.

Luis says something else to one of the diners, offering a friendly smile, and then he looks up at my window and our gazes connect. I don't get a smile, just a faint inclination of his head before he disappears from view, trading places with the same waitress from earlier, a pretty brunette.

In his absence, my attention turns back to the view ahead of me—the ocean and beyond.

The sound of the saxophone returns—low, haunting, each note aching and melancholy. The music fills me with a soaring emotion, and it doesn't surprise me in the least when the saxophone player steps into the little courtyard, his eyes finding mine as his lips press against the instrument, his fingers flying over the keys, playing for the guests. That explains the calluses.

History professor. Musician. Waiter.

The legacy of the Cuban revolution—donning many hats to stay afloat.

Luis doesn't look away from me as he plays, his stare unblinking, sending another tremor through me, his fingers caressing the keys with practiced ease. The first strands of "Guantanamera" drift over the courtyard, goose bumps rising over my skin as the tourists gasp and clap somewhere in the background. It's a beautiful song, one every Cuban knows, the ballad taken from one of our greatest national treasures—José Martí's poem "Versos Sencillos"—and performed by a queen, Celia Cruz. He plays it beautifully.

I force myself to step away, slipping back into the room, running water over my face from a sink in the corner, fixing my makeup. My hair's prone to frizzing in humidity, and it's risen to the occasion provided by the Cuban climate, the black strands cascading down my back in a wild mix of curls. I grab a scarf from my bag, using it to tie my hair back. Minutes later I shut the door behind me, venturing out into the hallway.

The sounds of the kitchen reverberate throughout the house, the footfalls of the residents in the apartment upstairs thudding through the worn ceiling. I follow the smell of food, making my way down the chipped marble staircase to the lower level of the house where the *paladar* is located. The kitchen is tucked in the back, a surprisingly small space for the amount of activity taking place inside it.

The appliances are old and clearly well used, knobs broken off, piecemeal parts strung together. The walls are covered in hanging pots and utensils, the economy of space solved by ingenuity. There are no fancy copper pots and pans here, no double ovens or commercial stoves, no massive center islands, nothing like my grandmother's kitchen in the house on Alhambra Circle in Coral Gables.

The food, though, obviously doesn't know the difference. Black beans, rice, *maduros*—sweet fried plantains—and roast pork await the tourists seated outside, and judging by the mouthwatering smell emanating from the kitchen, they're in for a treat.

Three women bustle around the kitchen—Ana Rodriguez, another woman who looks a lot like Luis, and a third, the waitress from earlier. The waitress has dark hair contained in a tight bun, strands escaping at intervals, a clipped expression on her face as she moves at a frenetic pace.

I duck my head as her gaze runs over my appearance, taking in the sandals that cost more than most Cubans make in a year. When I packed for this trip, I intentionally chose the least flashy pieces in my closet, opting for comfort and simplicity over high fashion. Not that it matters. We both know the difference, and shame fills me at the condemnation in her eyes.

She brushes past me, a plate of *tostones* in hand for the tourists, the scent of the salty fried plantains filling the tiny space. The older woman—she has to be Luis's mother—eyes me as though I'm an alien dropped in her midst before grabbing more food and exiting the cramped kitchen.

Ana turns, a smile on her face, spoon in hand.

"Did you sleep well?" she asks me.

"I did, thank you."

"Good. Are you hungry?"

"A bit, but I can wait. Can I help you with anything?"

I know a thing about Cuban pride, and yet, I feel like an interloper here, an unnecessary burden to a family who has likely faced more than their share.

Ana waves me off and points to a tiny table shoved in the corner. "Sit, sit. You'll eat and we'll chat while I finish up the meal. We have one table left, and then we'll be done for the night."

"How many guests do you serve each meal?"

"It varies by day. About a hundred between lunch and dinner."

The expression on my face must say it all.

She laughs. "You get used to it after a while."

"How long have you had the restaurant?"

A twinkle enters her eyes. "Officially? Twenty years or so. Unofficially, perhaps a bit longer than that. Luis cooked here when he was in university and still does occasionally."

She scoops a heaping portion of beans and rice, and spoons them into a white bowl with a floral pattern along the rim, setting it on the table in front of me where a napkin and silverware lay. A glass of *guarapo* follows, the sweet drink coating my throat in sugar.

Ana gestures toward the plate. "Eat. Then you can have some pork and some plantains."

"Thank you."

The beans have thickened, the taste familiar comfort food. There are subtle differences between Ana's beans and those I've grown up eating in Miami, but their essence is inescapably similar.

"This is amazing."

She beams. "Thank you."

Ana returns to the dinner service for a few minutes while I eat before turning to face me. "I received pieces of the story from my letters with Beatriz, but I gather there's more to your visit than merely wanting to see Cuba or writing an article."

"There is. My grandmother left a letter spelling out her last wishes to me. Her attorney gave it to me when her will was read. Her desire was to be cremated and to have her ashes spread in Cuba."

Ana doesn't seem surprised by this news, which leads me to think this isn't the first time she's heard of my grandmother's request. When Isabel died, she asked to be buried in the United States beside her American husband who'd died a year before. I'd assumed my grandmother would want the same thing—to be buried beside my grandfather at the cemetery in Miami. We'd never discussed it, though.

I'd always thought we'd have more time together. The stroke came on unexpectedly and swiftly, stealing her from us in the night. If we were to be comforted by anything, it was the knowledge that her doctor said it likely had been a painless way to pass.

"And she chose you to do it," Ana says. "You were always her favorite."

"Did she ever tell you why?"

I'm curious for this side of my grandmother I otherwise wouldn't have known.

Ana smiles. "She did."

I wait while she peels and chops a plantain with shaky fingers.

"Lucia is your father's daughter—confident, determined, driven. She pushes herself constantly; for her, the accomplishment is in the attempt."

It isn't an unfair assessment of my sister. I love Lucia, but she's always blazed her own path, determined to make her way despite our family's last name. Her world is her horses, her friends, distinct from the one the rest of us inhabit. She shows up for major family events, is never more than a phone call away, but we've never been that close despite the mere two years between us.

"Daniela is—"

"Trouble," I finish with a smile, no condemnation in the word. Daniela is my favorite sister, the eldest, the adventurous one. She's the closest to our mother, perhaps by virtue of her age, and as far as I know, has never backed down from a challenge.

Ana laughs. "I might have heard something to that effect."

And then there's me.

"Your grandmother saw herself in you. Always. You're the romantic, the dreamer, the one who's searching for something. She always prayed you would find it. You were the most affected by your parents' divorce." Her mouth tightens in a firm line. "By your mother leaving. You needed Elisa and she you."

"And now she's gone."

I've become unmoored with my grandmother's passing; Ana is right—my grandmother was my anchor, and now that she's gone, I'm adrift.

"She was so proud of you, Marisol. Always."

She slides a plate of *maduros* and *lechon asado* in front of me.

"Will you eat, too?" I ask.

"Perhaps a bit."

I wait while she serves a smaller plate for herself, taking the seat opposite mine. Behind her the two women reenter the kitchen, dumping plates into the sink with loud clunks before exiting again.

Ana begins eating, and I follow suit. The pork is the perfect mix of succulent meat and fat, the plantains a sweet, sharp bite washed down with the saccharine drink.

"Where will you spread her ashes?" Ana asks.

"I don't know. I hoped you could help me with that. I asked Aunt Beatriz and Aunt Maria, and they offered a few ideas."

I asked my father, as well, but he'd had little to propose beyond the Perez home. He loved my grandmother, but he was much closer to my grandfather in childhood and adulthood.

"What did they say?" she asks.

"They suggested the house where she grew up." The very house that is now inhabited by a Russian diplomat and his family. I can't help but think that my grandmother, my proud grandmother, would view the Russians as interlopers.

Ana smiles. "She would be close by, then. It's a good choice. It was in the Perez family for generations. In its day it was one of the finest homes in Havana, a distinction your great-grandparents were proud of."

"Do you think she would be happy there?"

"Perhaps. Where else have you considered spreading her ashes?"

"I'm not sure. Somewhere in the city, I guess. It seems like she belongs here."

"Yes, she does. She loved Havana, even after it broke her heart."

Ana gets up from the table, clearing our empty plates.

"What was your grandfather like?" she asks from her position at the sink, her back to me.

I rise, ignoring her protests as I help her wash the dishes. The need to stand on ceremony with Ana Rodriguez feels superfluous; despite the fact that we just met, there is an ease to her manner, conveying the impression that a part of my grandmother—a chapter of her life—is here in her childhood best friend.

"I didn't know him as well since he died when I was ten," I answer. "They were happy, though. In love. She didn't date or anything after he died. Wasn't interested in it. She had us—her granddaughters—my father, and her causes. Besides, they were married for almost forty years. I think it was hard for her to move on after spending so much of her life with him."

I remember my grandmother's grief even now, standing beside her in the pew of the Church of the Little Flower as we laid my grandfather to rest, my hand clutched in hers as we mourned. Twenty-one years later I stood in the same pew, staring at the gleaming coffin where my grandmother lay, consoling myself in the fact that they were together again.

Given my own parents' disastrous marriage, my grandparents were the ones I looked up to. Their story was filled with so much love and respect, giving me hope that one day I would find a good man, one I could trust, who would be both friend and partner, who would love me with as much devotion as I loved him.

"Everything Elisa told me about him made it sound like he was a lovely man." Ana smiles at me. "Your grandmother wrote to me when she could throughout the years. She asked me to hold something for you. Let me get it from my room."

She shuffles out of the kitchen, leaving me alone. I sit back down at the table, anticipation filling me. This is what I came for—to let a piece of my grandmother go and to perhaps find new pieces of her that I could clutch to my breast once I did.

The two women from earlier reenter the kitchen, neither one glancing in my direction, as though I've become part of the table and chairs.

I stand and introduce myself.

They both stare back at me; the elder woman speaks first.

"I'm Caridad. You met my son, Luis, earlier."

So I was right; this is Ana's daughter-in-law. She possesses her son's height and his angular face, his graceful manner of moving.

"Yes. He was kind enough to meet me at the airport."

"We needed him here at the restaurant. It was busy today."

She delivers the words with dart-like precision, the remainder unspoken—*and we needed Ana's help today while you were busy chatting with her during the dinner service.*

My cheeks heat at the subtle rebuke as she passes by me without another glance.

The younger woman meets my gaze with a flinty stare.

"I'm Cristina. Luis's wife."

Disappointment shoots through me with a particularly lethal and effective stab. Silence fills the kitchen as we stare at each other. Here I feel the resentment I feared when I first planned my trip to Cuba, the unspoken censure that I'm not a real Cuban, that I'm a traitor to my people because my family left this country behind.

The exiles in Miami and around the world hate Castro because he took their country from them, because he took everything, really. But I see a different kind of anger here, simmering below the surface, contained in Luis's mother and his *wife*. For the most part, Cubans who left prospered whereas those who stayed behind still appear to be struggling despite the promises they received from the government.

Cristina walks past me, leaving me alone in the kitchen that's stuck in a time warp, a product of the fifties modernized by make-shift repairs and a make-do attitude.

How would my grandmother have fared in this version of Cuba? Somehow I can't imagine her making black beans and rice on an old stove. My grandmother was a study in contradictions depending on her relationship with you—the affectionate constant of my childhood juxtaposed against the woman who ran Miami's exiled society with a jewel-covered hand.

Her family had struggled after the revolution, of course. She told me stories about adjusting to an entirely new way of life in the United States, mourning the one she'd left behind in Cuba. Still—

It took my great-grandfather years to build back all he lost from the revolution, the tangible things at least, but once he did he bought one of the grandest estates in Palm Beach to show the world that not even communism could take down the Perez family.

"Did my grandmother go to bed?" Luis asks as he walks over the threshold to the kitchen carrying a pile of dirty dishes.

"No, she went to her room for a moment."

He sets the plates down on the tiny counter, his mouth in a firm line, his eyes tired. "She needs to rest. Try telling her that, though. She lets us help to a point, but she still works harder than she should at her age."

Luis washes the dishes, his back to me, and I walk over to the sink, picking up one of the rags and drying the ones he's already cleaned. He shoots me a curious look but doesn't say anything. My hands tremble as I wipe the cloth over a plate.

The dishes are a hodgepodge. Some are clearly the remnants of expensive sets with elegant stamps on the back. Others are plain and cheap. Luis treats them all the same, his soapy fingers methodically scrubbing them with a worn cloth. His nails are neatly trimmed, his fingers lean, devoid of a ring.

How long have they been married?

The need to fill the silence tugs at me.

"You play beautifully."

He doesn't respond.

"I heard you earlier on the saxophone," I add.

Nothing.

"Have you been playing long?"

The side of his mouth quirks up. While the women in the house—Ana excluded, of course—appear to view me through a filter of mistrust and disdain, he seems indulgently amused, as though I am some bizarre creature taken out of her habitat and dropped in the middle of an environment where I clearly don't belong.

"Since I was a child. My father taught me."

The father who died in Angola. I feel a pang of sadness for his mother who was left to raise a child in Cuba as a widow—surely no easy feat.

"How old were you?"

"When he died?"

"Yes."

"Seven."

I swallow. "I'm sorry."

Luis rinses one of the plates, handing it to me, his fingers ghosting over mine for a moment before he turns to the next one, repeating the motions as though he's producing parts on an assembly line.

I search for something else to contribute to the conversation only to come up short, silence filling the kitchen save for the rush of water and the clunk of plates being set on the tiny countertop.

Ana returns a moment later, a box in her hands.

I finish drying the last dish and join her at the table while Luis excuses himself.

The box is a dark wood with a small gold clasp, a little bigger than a shoe box. It's the sort of thing you'd expect to reside in a gentleman's study holding cigars or cash or jewels with mysterious provenances.

"It was your great-grandfather's." She smiles, handing it to me. "Elisa borrowed it."

My great-grandfather Emilio Perez. Sugar baron. Batista supporter.

He died before I was born, but I've seen old family photos of him. He was handsome, tall, and distinguished. The stories I've heard from my grandmother and great-aunts give the impression of a man more concerned with business than family, but a man they loved just the same.

"When families left Cuba, they didn't know how long they would be gone," Ana explains. "Most thought Fidel's regime would be temporary. They weren't able to take items out of the country, but they also weren't comfortable leaving them in their homes for fear the government would seize them or others would steal them. So they buried them in their backyards and hid them in the walls of their homes for when they returned."

My heart pounds.

"Your great-grandfather buried a large box of items in the backyard." She hesitates. "Beatriz has it now."

This is the first I've heard of Beatriz having some secret box of family possessions.

"How did Beatriz end up with it?"

"That's Beatriz's story to tell. Let's just say your great-aunt has led an interesting life. More so than you probably realized."

Considering the myth-like quality surrounding Beatriz, I'm not entirely shocked.

"The contents of this box, though, were your grandmother's. We buried the box together under a banana tree the night before she left Cuba. When the Russians moved into your family's home, I snuck back over there and dug it up before they could find it."

I gape at her.

She chuckles. "Beatriz isn't the only one willing to take risks." Her hands stroke the wood. "It was the right thing to do. Elisa wouldn't have wanted it to fall into someone else's hands. Especially the people who took her home. I told her years later that I had the box, and she asked me to keep it for her. To keep it for you."

She slides the box toward me.

"I don't know what's in it. She never told me and I never looked. Go through it. If you have questions, find me."

Ana reaches out, her hand covering mine.

"She loved you very much. Adored your father. Your family was her entire world. Her letters were filled with stories of all of you, so much so that I feel as though you're a part of my family, too.

"She was trying to make the best of a difficult situation. You can't understand what those times were like, how our world was shattered in the span of a few months. Whatever you find, don't judge her too harshly."

Later, I sit on the edge of the bed in the guest room, staring at the wooden box, running my fingers over the edges. My grandmother was nineteen when she left Cuba, and I try to imagine her as a young girl, caught in the midst of such political turmoil. If I had a box—not much larger than a shoe box—in which to place my most important possessions for safekeeping, what would I choose to guard? What did she save?

The hinges creak as I open the box.

Yellowed pages stare back at me, covered in ink, tied together with a red silk ribbon. Letters by the look of them. I set them aside. Next is a ring.

My heart pounds.

The center stone is a diamond, set in an art deco style, smaller diamonds cut in emerald and round shapes surrounding it. The ring itself isn't large, but it's elegant and clearly antique, the craftsmanship superb.

We never grew up with family jewelry whose origins extended past my grandmother's time. Everything remained in Cuba after they left and eventually our valuables disappeared. In some ways, it's as though the Perez family was invented in 1959. So this piece of family history is everything.

I slide the ring over my finger, delighted it fits.

There are other items in the box—concert programs, a white silk rose, the petals still soft, a faded map, a matchbook from a Chinese restaurant in Havana—treasures that clearly possess more sentimental value than monetary.

I go for the letters first, starting with the top one, expecting to be greeted by my grandmother's familiar, loopy handwriting. Instead it's slanted, all hard lines and black ink. Masculine.

I begin to read.

chapter six

Elisa

I barely recognize myself anymore—last night I snuck out to a party with my sisters, today I am walking along the Malecón, on my way to meet a man whose last name I do not know, whose family I do not know, who my family would likely never accept.

We are the source of my mother's greatest pride and also the instrument of all her ambitions. That Isabel at twenty-three is not yet married is a travesty my mother is unable to reconcile, compounded by the sheer volume of marriage proposals received and summarily rejected by Beatriz—who at twenty-one should already be presiding over a home of her own, a child tucked away in a nanny's safekeeping. My unmarried state is hardly a priority with two older sisters, but it is no small thing, either. Love is for the poor. In our world, you marry for status, for wealth, for family.

And yet here I am.

The Malecón is one of my favorite parts of the city—five miles of seawall that showcase Havana at her most beautiful, especially during the moments when the sun sets, the sky exploding into a series of golds, pinks, and blues like the colors that adorn the heavy paintings that hang on our walls.

I pass a fruit vendor selling pineapples, mangos, and bananas. He offers me a toothy grin before returning to his customers.

I've chosen another white dress to wear to see Pablo—one of my favorites, another purchase from El Encanto. It was harder than I anticipated to sneak out of the house today. Maria wanted to come with me, and Magda kept glancing at me suspiciously as though she could tell something had changed.

This is to be a onetime indulgence.

I will see him, and I will let myself have this hour or so to enjoy, and then I will return to Miramar and the dinner party my mother has planned for a judge—one of my father's cronies—whose son she hopes to foist onto Isabel. I will see Pablo, and then I will forget him, save for the very late hours of the night when I am alone and cannot sleep, or when I walk along the promenade, the waves licking at my skin.

When I arrive at the point where we agreed to meet, Pablo is standing at the edge of the seawall, looking out over the water. It's surprising that I can already recognize him merely by the slope of his back, the dark hair, the manner in which he carries himself—but I can.

My pulse quickens.

I duck my head from prying eyes as my strides lengthen. It's risky being seen in public with him, in the daylight, but in this, too, I can't refuse.

Pablo turns as I walk toward him, almost as though the same string that yanks me toward him binds him, too.

A white rose dangles from his fingers.

My mouth goes dry.

We meet in the middle of the sidewalk, and by the look in his eyes, I'm immeasurably glad I wore the white dress.

"I wondered if you would come," he says, his voice low.

"I questioned it myself a time or two," I admit.

Pablo holds the flower out to me, and I take it from his hands, the silk soft against my palm, the simple beauty of it tugging at my heart. I'm grateful for its resilience, that I won't have to watch it age and turn to dust, that I may tuck the rose into a drawer somewhere and pull it out, stroking its petals when I feel the need to remember.

"Thank you." My words are both far too little and all I can afford to give.

"Would you like to walk?" he asks.

I nod, not quite trusting my emotions enough to speak.

Pablo positions himself between the street and me, although really, both sides possess equal treachery. On the one side there are the lanes of traffic, cars whizzing by, the opportunity for recognition high. On the other there is the water, the ocean crashing over the seawall, splashing pedestrians, the sea invading the street with Poseidon's angry wrath. Today, though, the waters are relatively calm, and there is little chance of the salt water marring my dress, merely the walk sullying my reputation.

We walk in silence, Pablo measuring his stride against mine, seemingly content to follow my lead and opt for silence rather than meaningless conversation. I clutch the rose in my hand, every so often stroking the soft silk; each time I do there's a hitch in his stride, as though he is aware of every twitch of my fingers, the rise and fall of my chest, the sound of my heart thudding in my chest. The wind blows a strand of my hair, and I tuck it behind my ear, only to be rewarded by his sharp intake of breath.

The air around us crackles with energy.

I avert my gaze from him, needing the moment to collect myself. As I survey the landscape around us, the others walking along the promenade, it's impossible to miss that there's a tension emanating all around us.

There are fewer tourists than you typically encounter on the Malecón. The attacks at the Montmartre cabaret and the Tropicana have rattled nerves and people are on edge. Then there are the bombs exploding around the city at random intervals, interspersed between parties, elegant dinners and lunches, and trips to the beach.

And Nero fiddled while Rome burned.

Some of these explosions make the newspaper the next day; other times they don't and we're left wondering if the loud booms, the screaming, were figments of our imagination, the product of a city poised for the next burst of violence. It's hard when a country descends into such turmoil, harder still when there are so many groups vying for power, attempting to feast on the carcass of a dying island.

There are—were—the Organización Auténtica, an ill-fated group of guerrilla fighters; the Directorio Revolucionario Estudiantil, a group of students from the University of Havana; the mostly defunct Federación Estudiantil Universitaria, another group of students from the University of Havana who together with the DRE fought their way into the Presidential Palace and attempted to assassinate Batista last year; members of the Communist Party whose uneasy alliance with Batista wanes; the 26th of July Movement fighting Batista's army in the Sierra Maestra mountains; and any number of other enemies Batista has garnered over the years.

The waves crash over the seawall ahead, spilling onto the road, their white foamy caps full of such energy that they appear alive. We pause and wait for the sea to cease its angry assault, and I take the opportunity to do what I've wanted to do since we began walking. I stop and look at Pablo, my gaze hungry, lingering over his features, the faint lines around his eyes, the hint of darkness beneath them, as though he did not sleep well last night.

"I saw you in the paper this morning," he says, standing just a bit closer to me than is necessary to be heard over the sound of the waves, the noise from the street.

I flush. "I didn't take you for someone who reads the society pages."

I'd counted on that, actually.

This time it's his cheeks that look a bit ruddy. "I'm not. At least, I wasn't until today." He swallows, his Adam's apple bobbing. The words hover in the air between us, unspoken—

Until I met you.

"You know who I am, then."

"Yes."

I look out to the sea, my heart pounding. "Then you know this afternoon is all I have to give."

There is a difference between small rebellions like sneaking out at night with my sisters and big ones like falling in love with a man and going against my family's wishes. I stand on the precipice of one, and I need the reminder, perhaps more so than he does, that I must not under any circumstances allow myself to give in to the temptation. It's not just my reputation, or my mother's and father's, but it's Beatriz's reputation, and Isabel's, and Maria's. I've seen firsthand what can come of going against our parents' wishes. More-over, it's not lost on me that at nineteen, I have limited skills, that if I was cast out of the family I would have a very hard time supporting myself, especially with the employment challenges facing Cuba.

"Yes," Pablo responds.

My gaze sweeps across the seawall, at the people around us. There are so many different versions of Cuba before me—tourists, locals—all of us inhabiting different realities within Havana. Which one is his?

"Tell me about yourself."

So I will have something to hold on to when I must forget you.

"What would you like to know?" he asks.

Anything. Everything.

I start with the little I do know about him. "You mentioned you grew up in Vedado. Does your family still live there?"

"They do. My parents and two sisters." His voice cracks. "I haven't seen them in a while, though. I've been away."

There's a hint there, a thread of family discord I'm uncomfortably familiar with lingering behind his words. There are natural pauses in conversations when one speaks of family estrangement—the inadequacy of words to convey the unnatural state of breaking from those to whom you are bound in blood, the pauses physically manifesting themselves in an empty chair at an ostentatious dining room table that hailed from Paris. I know all about those pauses—a relationship severed at the knees, a sibling lost to ideology, a family forever fractured.

I fight to keep the tremor from my voice.

"Are you back for good now?"

I'm not quite sure which answer I wish to hear. This will be easier if he is to go—a clean break.

"No. Only for a short time. I have business in the city."

I wait for him to elaborate, and when he doesn't, I press on.

"Do you like your job? Practicing law?"

I know enough about topics I've studied in heavy books given to me by tutors, but I know little of the practical applications of things. Lawyers dine at our table occasionally; however, the conversation rarely turns to their work or anything of substance.

"I like it well enough, I suppose," he answers. "I enjoy helping people—trying to, at least. Justice in Cuba—" His voice trails off, but I'm not so oblivious to the reality around me to not fill in the blanks.

Most of my education on Cuba's political condition was given to me through the walls of my father's study in the form of the angry shouts and recriminations I've overheard.

How can you justify the way we live? People are starving, suffering. You built your fortune on the backs of others. We all have.

Up ahead, a group of boys dive for coins left by American tourists, the children's bodies bobbing against the waves before disappearing beneath the surface in waters likely overrun by sharks. All for a few coins.

"These are difficult times," Pablo says, his gaze—like mine—on the boys. "So many of my friends graduated from university years ago and can't find jobs. They're frustrated, and they're angry, and they're scared for their future." He turns from the boys, back to face me. "I took some time off from practicing law to focus on other things."

The phrase "other things" dangles ominously between us. The winds of change coming from the former students of the University of Havana—who are now left without a place to study since Batista closed the university out of fear for their subversive activities—have already torn through my life once. This is one afternoon, one indulgence. I don't need to know all his secrets; can pretend he is merely an attorney, nothing more.

"What about you?" Pablo asks.

"What about me?"

"You never really answered me before. What is life like on the other side of the gates?"

I laugh softly, relieved to be back on firmer ground. "Not as exciting as people seem to imagine."

Pablo is silent for a moment, his gaze far more intense than an afternoon walk on the Malecón merits. Everything about him is intense—when he discusses politics, when he looks at me. It's that intensity that has me gravitating toward him; it's refreshing to be around someone who cares more about substance than frivolity. He reminds me so much of my brother—Alejandro has that same determined glint in his eyes, the same conviction underscoring each word.

Pablo grins. "So if you aren't marching all over Havana, capturing hearts, what do you do in your free time?"

"I spend time with my sisters—I have three." And a brother no one speaks of anymore. "I read; I go shopping. We like to ride horses, go to the beach."

I don't mention the social obligations. It all sounds so frivolous and tedious. And it is, this waiting around for a man to walk into our lives and marry us. A part of me envies Alejandro for his ability to cast off the weight and responsibility of being a Perez, the ease with which he is willing to risk everything for his beliefs. And at the same time, there's an anger there I cannot erase. Loyalty is a complicated thing—where does family fit on the hierarchy? Above or below country? Above or below the natural order of things? Or are we above all else loyal to ourselves, to our hearts, our convictions, the internal voice that guides us?

I wish I knew.

"I'm surprised you're not in school overseas somewhere."

"My mother didn't support us going to university. Beatriz lobbied the hardest for it—she would have made an excellent attorney—but in the end, it wasn't worth the fight. My parents have a very traditional view of what it is to be a woman in Cuba, and no matter how much society might disagree with them, they weren't going to change their opinions. A working Perez woman is a blight on the Perez name."

He looks faintly outraged. "So you're just what—supposed to wait around until one day you move from your parents' home to your husband's?"

"Yes."

"What if you never marry?"

"Then I'll stay in our house taking care of my mother until I grow old."

I don't find the idea any more appealing than he does, but I don't know how to explain to him how few options are afforded to us. I suppose I could break from family tradition, go against my parents' wishes, but the truth is there's never been anything I've been passionate enough about to risk severing all ties with my family. I don't possess secret dreams of being a doctor or lawyer. I'm nineteen, and I don't know what my future looks like, harder still to predict when I'm surrounded by such uncertainty.

"And you're happy with that?" he asks, his expression doubtful.

"No, of course not. But you speak as though there are limitless options available to me."

"What if there could be?"

"I have no interest in politics," I reply.

It is both warning and caution—I have no interest in revolution, in even a hint of it. Bombs aren't the only things that go off in Havana; President Batista's firing squads have been especially prolific lately, and no Cuban, regardless of their wealth, is above his notice. My own brother is proof of that. The best thing to do, the smart thing, the way to survive in Havana is to keep your head down and go about your daily life as though the world around you isn't creeping into madness.

"You speak as though politics is its own separate entity," he says. "As though it isn't in the air around us, as though every single part of us isn't political. How can you dismiss something that is so fundamental to the integrity of who we are as a people, as a country? How can you dismiss something that directly affects the lives of so many?"

"Very few can afford the luxury of being political in Cuba."

"And no one can afford the luxury of not being political in Cuba," he counters.

The fervor lingering in his words, the conviction with which he speaks them, transforms him before my eyes. His overlong hair blows in the breeze, his dark eyes flashing, and there's something about the ferocity in his gaze that reminds me of the corsair on our wall at home. This is not the sort of man who waits for permission, but a man of action, a man of deep abiding passion.

What would it be like to have such a man be mine?

"Aren't you tired of keeping your head down and praying for invisibility?" he asks, his voice soft.

His question tugs at me, the undeniable fact that I am both attracted to and repelled by this zeal within him. How many hours have I spent having these very conversations with my brother, and in the end, where did it leave us? I didn't lie—I have no interest in revolution, in armed revolt, in killing. There are women who fight this battle for Cuba's future, but I have no desire to join their ranks, for my presence to be excised from our family as Alejandro's has been. But the freedom Pablo speaks of? The love for his country that infuses each word that falls from his lips? There is beauty behind that sentiment and a devotion that is admirable.

Batista's policies aren't about Cuba or what's best for the Cuban people. They're designed to serve Batista, to increase his wealth, his power, to keep his stranglehold on the island forever.

Do we all dare to hope for more?

Of course.

But it's hard to hope when all you've known is corruption, when your reality is rigged elections and the possibility of more of the same.

I admire his hope; I envy it. And even more, I fear it.

Pablo shakes his head. "I'm sorry. I shouldn't speak of such things."

A rueful smile settles on my lips. "You don't strike me as the sort of man who worries about 'should.'"

"That's true," he concedes, his mouth quirking.

We walk side by side, the sun shining down on us, close but not touching. His lean, tall frame shields me from the view of onlookers. My hair blows in the breeze with the faintest gust of wind, and he inclines his head, watching the strands in the light, his expression softening. My cheeks heat again.

I'm not normally this serious, not normally this shy, but everything about this feels different, important somehow. There are a finite number of minutes left in this one afternoon I've granted myself, and I'm torn between hoarding them, feasting on every look, every word, and making the most of them, filling the spaces in our conversation with words I've yet to seize.

The rose is almost unbearably soft in my hands.

"Have you read Montesquieu?" Pablo asks, the question catching me off guard.

"I haven't."

"You should. His words never seem more true to me than when I am in Havana." He turns away from me, his gaze sweeping over the buildings on the other side of the Malecón. "Montesquieu said that an empire born in war must maintain itself by war."

"Cuba is hardly an empire," I interject.

"True. The spirit is similar, though. When have we ever not been at war? With others—Spain and the United States? With ourselves?"

"Are we to be forever at war, then?" I counter.

Why do men always think war is the answer? Alejandro was eager to take up arms against Batista, to spill Cuban blood, and for what? Batista remains in power, and all it earned Alejandro was exile from Havana. Officially, my parents have told their friends he is studying in Europe, traveling the world. There are whispers, of course, but no one has the temerity to challenge my father or mother, to ask if the rumors are true—my brother, Beatriz's twin, is a radical.

"Bombs are exploding in movie theaters," I argue. "Dead bodies litter our streets. Are those not Cuban lives being taken? Innocents caught in the middle of a fight that is not their own? You speak as though all Cubans should take up arms, but what if we don't want the same things? Then what?"

"And what of those who stand by and do nothing while a tyrant runs our country into the ground, slaughtering our countrymen because they speak out against his injustices? What is the cost of inaction, of turning away when atrocities are committed in the name of Batista? There is a disconnect between those in the city who yearn for change and those who pretend everything is grand. The industries we rely on as a nation—sugar, tobacco, coffee, tourism—enslave us as a nation, as a people who serve others in the fields, in the casinos and hotels run by American scoundrels."

I flinch as the word "sugar" falls from his lips. What must he think of my family? Of me? He is here, walking beside me, and yet, I can't help but wonder if he doesn't see my father as part of the problem. Alejandro certainly did.

"The Americans control so much of our industry, our economy, and who benefits from that largesse? Batista," he continues. "The rich are extravagantly rich, and the poor are so desperately poor."

Everything disappears, the roar of the Malecón, the noise from the road. I can't tear my gaze away from him, the conviction in his voice mesmerizing. With each word that falls from his lips, he's transformed. The serious man I met at the party last night has been replaced by someone else entirely.

"When I am in the country, I see my fellow Cubans without electricity, running water, unable to read, their children unable to go to school," Pablo says, his gaze once again on those looming buildings. "When I am in Havana the lights are on, people walking down the Paseo del Prado as though they do not have a care in the world. There are other parts of the city—far too many—where people are suffering tremendously, yet it still feels as though Havana exists in its own self-contained bubble. I was a boy in '33 when we overthrew Machado. I understand that people are tired of violence, tired of conflict, tired of Cuban blood spilling. But—"

"I have a brother—" The words tumble out without thought, the secret that isn't really a secret at all. "He shared those thoughts once."

Beside me, Pablo stills as though he is adept at reading the pauses in a conversation, the tense, unfinished sentences and words uttered in a whisper.

"Families can be hard," he says after a moment.

"Yes."

"Is he safe?" he asks, as though he, too, knows a thing or two about the precariousness of going against one's family, defying one's president.

"I hope so."

I wish I possessed more optimism to inject in those words.

"In any event, I have not read Montesquieu, but I will search for his work in our library." I flinch as the word leaves my mouth, but really, what's the point in pretending? He's seen the newspaper, knows my last name now. As much as I envy Alejandro his freedom, I lack the ability to cast off my family, to repudiate them and all they stand for. They—we—are flawed, yes. But the legacy and blood that binds us is inescapable.

"Yes—my father has a library in his home, the walls brimming with books," I continue, my tone dry. "I'm sure you think us decadent. We are decadent. My family's fortunes were cast a long time ago, and those of us born under the Perez name have enjoyed the benefits of that wealth."

"And would you apologize for it?" His tone is idle, but there's real interest behind his words.

"For my family's fortune? For the grand house and the rest of it?

You could strip away the paintings—except for the corsair, I am indeed quite fond of him—and I do not think I would mind." I cast a sidelong glance his way, attempting to take his measure. "Or perhaps I would be better served by exclaiming my disgust with our wealth and the shame that it brings me? Or tell you of our charitable endeavors, the men who served in the military and died for Cuba's independence, my father's efforts to work with Batista drafting the 1940 Constitution, the ancestors who have served in the national legislature?"

I sigh.

"Perhaps our legacy will always be that we have more than we ever need in a country where many do not have enough. And even so, I see the limitations my father faces—the whims of the sugar crop that was once booming and now keeps him up working late in his office. I overhear his strained conversations—the broken promises, the fears over the direction in which the country is headed. Even the wealthy are not immune—we have friends who have been thrown in Batista's prisons; we fear the firing squad as much as the poor. My own brother is evidence of that. Money buys us the proximity to power, but in this current climate that proximity is a target on all our backs."

My little speech leaves me a bit breathless, the ferocity of it catching me off guard. When was the last time anyone asked me what I thought? How I felt about the world swirling around me? When was the last time I was able to utter Alejandro's name? I sneak a peek at Pablo, wondering if I've scared him off—the girl who is too free with her opinions.

Instead, a gleam of admiration enters his gaze.

"You're brave, Elisa Perez."

In a family such as mine, there are varying degrees of bravery, but I'll take the compliment all the same, even as I wonder just how brave I really am.

"Why me?" I ask, pushing the limits of my alleged bravery a bit further, indulging the curiosity turning over in my mind.

A moment passes before he answers me. "Because you're comfortable in your own skin. Because you appear content to show yourself to the world exactly as you are without deception or artifice. That's a novel quality these days, and I suspect, in Miramar, even more so."

It's the sort of compliment whose very nature makes testing the veracity of it exceedingly difficult, and the pleasure of it seems best savored with acceptance rather than dissection. I smile, though, holding his gaze for a moment and lingering there before ducking my head and looking out to the sea.

We both seem content to let the silence swallow us up, for the wind, and the waves, and the car horns to do the talking for us—a trumpet interjecting every so often, our bodies moving in tandem as we stroll along the promenade.

"You're not what I expected," he says finally, breaking the silence between us, his words little more than a whisper, an aside to himself that I'm privy to.

Does he feel it—this thing between us—too?

"What did you expect?" I can't resist asking.

"I don't know. Not this. I didn't expect to meet someone—"

His words disappear with the wind.

They seem safer there.

"Elisa—"

I turn and face him, the sun bright in my eyes, casting a glow around him. I fear he can see every single emotion—the worry, the confusion, the desire—in my gaze, stamped across my face.

Deep down, I know what he is. How can I not? It couldn't be clearer if it was written in the sky before me. Deep down, a part of me gravitates toward what he is, even as I am horrified by it.

"Elisa—" he repeats.

A tremor trails down my spine at the sound of my name falling from his lips, at the husky timbre of his voice.

Enough.

One of us moves. Both of us move. I don't even know anymore. Only that his lips meet mine and it is both everything and nothing that I expected.

For all that I anticipated, imagined, my first kiss, the reality of it comes to me in pieces, fractured moments unfurling themselves.

His hand on my waist. The brush of his fingers against the fabric of my dress. His lips on mine. His breath becoming my breath. His heart thudding against my chest.

He strokes my hair, fisting the strands as the kiss changes, deepening, leading me into treacherous waters until I'm left gasping for air.

Pablo pulls back first, staring down at me with those dark, solemn eyes. I should take a step back. And another. And another, until I'm safely ensconced in the mansion in Miramar.

I step forward, laying my palm on his cheek, my fingers sweeping across the dark shadows just beneath his eyes.

He shudders.

In one step, I know power, the drugging effect of it coursing through my veins. With one step I am removed from the fringes and thrust in the middle of my life. In that space of the step, my world shifts. Everything is different now, and nothing will ever be the same again.

chapter seven

I stay up late into the night reading and rereading the letter Pablo wrote me. He pressed it into my palm after he walked me home, the paper still warm from its place in his pocket, the intimacy of it sending a flutter through my chest. We said good-bye yesterday on the fringes of Miramar so no one would see us together, our parting paltry compared to the kiss on the Malecón. I regret the circumstances between us, the need to keep him a secret, tucked away in the fringes of my life. His words speak of the same frustration within him, the same yearning for more.

I am at a disadvantage. When I went to Guillermo's, I never imagined I'd meet you. And then you were there, so beautiful it hurt. You looked so earnest watching everyone, as though you attempted to commit every moment to memory. As though you feel the same restlessness inside you, the same desire for more than that which life has given you.

I know this is foolish. You have everything in front of you, and I have nothing to offer, no place in your life. It is likely premature to think about these things, to worry about them, when I've only known you a moment. How can time feel both unending and entirely too finite?

Pablo's letter tugs at something inside me like a loose thread, unfurling the tightly wound knot in my chest as I clutch the pages in my hand. Time is a luxury I don't have. Seeing him in person brings its share of risks, and I spend far too much time grasping for words when we're together. Here, in the comfort of my room, reading the words he has written, I learn about him—his family, his passion for the law, his favorite books.

His words linger, long after I've finished reading them, the remnants of our conversation on the Malecón imprinted in my mind. Despite having traveled abroad with my parents, I've seen very little of Cuba outside of Havana, have limited knowledge of the struggles those outside the city face. He's right—we do live in an insular society. But what will change? How can it change?

Hours before dawn I begin crafting my own letter. I'll give it to him when I see him again.

My hand shakes as I put the words on the page, my normally neat penmanship devolving into an unpleasant scrawl. Still, this is easier for me. It's clear Pablo attended university, studied law—he speaks with a confidence and quick-wittedness I both admire and envy. The words I write have only ever existed for me in the pages of the books I read, shoved tightly into the recesses of my mind, uttered in the confines of my home. Women in my circle do not speak of these things in public, and in this house we no longer speak of them in private, either.

In the early morning, I pluck Montesquieu from a shelf in my father's library. I curl up in one of the oversize chairs that has been in our family since before he or I were born, flipping through the pages until the lack of sleep becomes too much for me and my eyes shutter.

When I wake, it's to the sound of the door opening and closing with a gentle thud, followed by light footfalls on the carpet. The smell of perfume announces her presence before I open my eyes— Beatriz's signature scent.

I feel her presence hesitating near me, her body still, waiting to see if I'm still sleeping.

I keep my eyes closed.

A surreptitious Beatriz is a dangerous one, and the feeling that she's up to something has plagued me since the night she insisted we attend the party in Vedado.

The sound of footsteps, muffled by the carpet now, continue and then stop. I open one eye slowly.

Beatriz stands with her back to me, leaning over the wooden desk. Our father prefers to work privately in his study, reserving it as his inner sanctum, but he also keeps a desk here in the opulent library where he entertains guests and business associates as the mood suits him. As far as rooms go, you can't get much more impressive than thousands of antique books collected by centuries of Perez ancestors.

The sound of drawers opening and closing, knobs rattling, fills the room.

My breath hitches. Beatriz turns.

My eyes slam closed.

"There's no use, you know. I've slept in the same bedroom as you before. You snore when you're truly asleep," Beatriz calls out from across the room.

That's the trouble with sisters; they know you far too well.

I open my eyes, rising from the chair, picking up the copy of Montesquieu that tumbled to the floor when I fell asleep.

"Should I be concerned by the fact that you're skulking around Father's desk?" I ask.

Knowing Beatriz as I do, her actions could be the result of a number of things, but it's a not-so-hidden family secret that my father often keeps cash in his desk. Not a lot, of course, but—

Beatriz walks over to me, her gaze drifting to the book perched in my hand.

"Montesquieu? How *egalitarian* of you." A twinkle gleams in her eyes.

I ignore the teasing note in her voice, the curiosity contained there.

"What are you doing going through his desk?" I repeat.

This time it's Beatriz's turn to look abashed.

"Money?"

Beatriz flinches.

"Have you heard from Alejandro?" I ask.

Of all of us, Beatriz and Alejandro are the closest, perhaps by virtue of being twins. She's certainly taken his rift with the family the hardest. Beatriz was born first, and their relationship has always reflected that. She sneaks out of the house at all hours, taking packages bundled up from the kitchen among other items. She claims it's charity, of course, but as I said, sisters always know you far too well.

Beatriz glances at the closed door, fear flickering in her gaze. If our father is willing to disown his heir, then none of us are safe from his ire, even his favorite child.

"Alejandro is in Havana," she admits, keeping her voice low. "He needs money."

"Is that why you wanted to go to the party? To meet up with Alejandro?"

She nods.

"Beatriz."

Her expression turns defiant. "He's my brother. What would you have me do?"

"If Father finds out—"

"He'll what? Disown me, too?"

"Yes."

"Fine. Let him. I can't keep pretending things are normal when they're not, that our family is whole when it is not. What has Alejandro done that was so wrong?"

"He attempted to assassinate the president," I hiss. "Participated in it, at least."

He might not have been one of the men who stormed the Presidential Palace itself, but he planned the failed attack just the same.

"He needs our help," Beatriz argues.

"He needs to leave Cuba," I counter. How long can Alejandro escape Batista's notice? How long before he is killed?

The grandfather clock chimes, cutting off Beatriz's response. I agreed to meet Pablo at a restaurant in the Chinese quarter of the city for lunch. If I leave now, hopefully I won't be late. The unexpected nap took quite the chunk out of my day.

Montesquieu dangles from my hands. "I need to go. We can finish this later."

Beatriz rolls her eyes. "Must we?" Her gaze drifts to Montesquieu and back to my face again. "Meeting Ana?"

We've become masters in the art of reading between the lines of each other's conversations, the art of having our own intimate discussions without saying the words aloud cultivated by the need to circumvent our parents' notice. She doesn't believe for a second that I'm meeting Ana, and in that moment, a truce is born. She'll look the other way while I head off to my assignation, and I won't say anything about her helping our brother—not that I would have anyway. In our younger years, we likely would have sealed our pact with a secret handshake or something similar. Now all it takes is a nod and a few parting words before I'm on my way out of the house—

Only to be stopped by Maria. The curse of having three sisters.

It takes every excuse I can think of to keep Maria from tagging along with me as I walk down the front stairs, the letter I've written Pablo tucked inside my purse. She trails behind me like a shadow.

"Please, Elisa. I just finished my math lessons. We can go shopping. I need a new dress."

I laugh. "I seriously doubt you *need* a new dress."

Even though Maria is the most rambunctious of us all, our mother insists on dressing her as though she's a little doll, each gown itchier and fuller, more and more elaborate than the one before it. The age difference between Maria and me is due in part to the cooling relations in our parents' marriage and punctuated by the loss of the child our mother miscarried. While Isabel, Beatriz, and I have had one another, and occasionally, Alejandro, Maria's age has set her apart, leaving her more firmly in our mother's care.

Maria's lower lip juts out.

I try a different tactic, guilt filling me. "I'm meeting Ana for lunch." *Liar.* "What if we get ice cream when I come back?"

She hesitates. "Coconut?"

Her weakness for sweets is another not-so-well-hidden family secret.

"Whatever you want."

I don't blame her for wishing to accompany me; life in the Perez household has become incrementally more restrictive with each act of violence in Havana. Batista might attempt to convince the rest of the country that the unrest is contained to a few isolated incidents firmly under his control, but our mother isn't fooled, nor is she willing to expose her daughters to anything deadly or unseemly.

More reason why today's outing must be a secret.

I leave Maria playing the piano, our ice cream date secured, and make my way to Central Havana, already a few minutes late. Sneaking out is becoming a habit, one I'm surprisingly good at, and a skill I wished I'd discovered in my younger years. I can only imagine the adventures I would have had.

I walk through the enormous gate heralding the entrance to the Barrio Chino, stepping into an unfamiliar part of the city. Havana and her secrets. When we dine out my parents tend to favor places like La Zaragozana or the many French restaurants that have sprung up in recent years. I can't recall if I've ever been to this part of the city—at least, not since I was a child.

Sugar's heavy influence over our fates and fortunes is evident here, too—it was sugar that brought the Chinese workers to the island long ago. Some of the workers returned to China when their contracts had ended, but many stayed, finding their home in Havana and the countryside.

Looking around me, it's impossible to ignore the fact that my family has played a role in an industry that has supported the economy for so long, and at the same time, taken so much from its people, bringing wealth and prosperity to the island on the backs of so many. Our lifeblood as a nation is also a source of shame. I like to believe my father is a fair man, that he treats his workers well, pays them justly for their efforts, but I am not so sheltered as to believe it has always been thus for those who work the fields. It was sugar that kept us under the yoke of the Spaniards, that brought slaves to our shores, meant workers languished under harsh conditions, gave the Americans a heavy interest and control over our fortunes.

The island gives and the island takes in one fell swoop.

This is the legacy my brother rebels against, the cause that drives him. Is it Pablo's cause, too?

Once I'm through the gate, I'm surrounded by a mixture of Spanish and Chinese spoken around me, the signage in characters I can't read. The scents in the air are familiar, yet not—the smell of roast pig is mixed with seasonings and spices I can't identify, spilling from tiny restaurants and storefronts. Bodies are crammed more tightly together here, and I fight my way through the crowd, looking for—

Pablo leans against a building with a red awning, his gaze scanning the street, settling on me.

He's dressed casually today, his long legs encased in buff-colored pants and a paper-thin linen shirt—a concession to the heat, I imagine. He pushes off from the wall and walks toward me, a smile on his face that has my heart pounding.

"I wondered if you would come," he says once again as though this is becoming our standard greeting, acknowledging the uncertainty between us. He steps forward, pressing a kiss to my cheek.

It's only been a day since we last saw each other, but I can't deny the urgency in my limbs, the eagerness in my heart.

"I'm sorry I'm late. My sisters—" I don't know how much to share with him about my family, this man about whom I know so little. It's one thing to trust him with my heart and another entirely to trust him with my family. "It's complicated," I say, realizing my words offer little explanation.

Pablo nods. "I appreciate you meeting me here. I thought it would be better if we went somewhere you aren't known, where you don't have to worry about being seen."

He's right about that—everyone is busy going about their day; no one bothers to glance our way. There's freedom in the anonymity this part of Havana affords us, which has me standing just a bit closer to him than I normally would. It makes it easier that Pablo understands the risks I'm taking, but at the same time, I can't deny the thread of shame that fills me—surely he deserves better than a girl who fears going against her family's wishes.

"This is perfect. I don't think I've ever been to this part of the city before," I reply.

"We used to come here when we were younger. My father would bring me and my sisters to buy fireworks. You've never seen fireworks such as these." He smiles, and I suspect he's caught in a memory. "We used to fight over who would light them."

I grin. "That sounds like something my siblings and I would do."

"Are you hungry?" he asks after a moment.

I nod.

"There's a good place right around the corner; they have the best Chinese food in the city."

Pablo takes my hand, and I link my fingers with his. I'm grateful I removed my gloves before I came, that I'm able to touch him like this, our bare skin clasped together. His thumb strokes the inside of my palm.

He walks with purpose, navigating the crowds with ease.

We walk past a business Pablo identifies as the famous Pacifico and stop outside a tiny restaurant shoved in between several other businesses on the narrow street. The sounds of the restaurant spill out onto the street, the inauspicious front incongruous with the lively interior.

It's not La Zaragozana, or the Tropicana, but I like it more for the fact that it, too, like Pablo, doesn't stand on ceremony. Other men might have taken me to the finest restaurant in the city in an effort to impress, but I appreciate this more—his desire to show me somewhere special, to share this secret with me.

"I promise the food is some of the best you'll ever eat," he says.

I smile. "It's wonderful."

We walk inside, and an elderly Chinese man leads us to a small table in the back of the space. The restaurant is narrow and long; the tables around us are empty, the front filled with groups of men eating and playing dominoes. I'm happy to have Pablo order for me, content to watch him laugh with the waiter as they converse in Spanish. When he's finished ordering our meal, the man leaves us and we're alone once again.

Neither one of us speaks for a moment that stretches on and on, until I can no longer take the silence. There's too much at stake here for me to be demure, too much that hangs in the balance for me to be my mother's daughter, eyes cast downward and only speaking when spoken to in polite society. Before the kiss on the Malecón, I was content to keep things casual. Now I know that possibility is behind us.

"What do I need to know about you?" I ask, keeping my voice low. We're far away from the rest of the diners, but you never know when the wrong person will overhear a dangerous conversation.

"Elisa—"

I shake my head, cutting off any protest. Perhaps this is fast, maybe it's too much for me to ask these things, but in this climate I'm not sure the rules for polite behavior apply anymore. We are entangling ourselves, and I need to know how risky it is.

"I read your letter. You've given me pieces of it, and I think I know, but I need to hear the rest, need to know what I am getting myself into, what I need to protect."

Our hands rest inches from each other on the table, and even as I attempt to keep my feelings for him at bay, I want him to take my hand again, to feel those calluses against my skin.

Foolish girl.

Pablo sighs. "You have to be careful. You can't trust anyone. The things I tell you, you can't tell anyone. Lives depend on it."

He searches my gaze, and I can feel him assessing, deciding whether he's going to trust me. That's the crux of it, isn't it? Does he merely view me as a silly debutante, pretty to look at but good for little else? Or does he see me as more? As an equal, someone he can confide in, someone he can trust.

"I was in the Sierra Maestra before I came here."

I take a deep breath, steadying myself, even as I'm not completely surprised by his announcement. He is one of the bearded ones—the men who are fighting in the Sierra Maestra mountains, broadcasting revolution on Radio Rebelde, the men my father decries each day.

"How did you become involved with them?" I stare down at my

knuckles, offering a prayer to the heavens that I have not just opened Pandora's box.

"At the University of Havana. I told you I studied law—one of my classmates was involved in the revolutionary movement; I went to a few meetings with him. In the beginning, we marched in protest. There wasn't much organization in place, but we believed we had an opportunity to speak out against the injustices around us."

His voice hardens.

"Batista promised to uphold the 1940 Constitution, to give us the rights we were promised, and then he reneged on that promise. Where is our freedom? Our liberty? How much of this country's wealth goes to the city, to Havana? The capital is littered with American casinos and hotels, populated by movie stars and gangsters treating the country as though it is their own personal playground while Cuban citizens in the provinces can't read, don't have access to basic necessities to meet their needs."

I heard the same sentiments from Alejandro not so long ago.

An oath falls from Pablo's lips, his voice lowering.

"The protests turned violent. It was inevitable, really. Anytime we made progress, anytime we attempted to reach the Cuban people, to spread our message in newspaper articles or on the radio, our words and actions were censored, our supporters hunted. Batista controls everything—the military, the media, the economy. We never stood a chance. And we aren't just fighting Batista; we're fighting the United States, who supports him year after year, who gives him weapons he uses to kill his own people, to maintain his hold on our island. How do a group of students chanting and marching create meaningful change if they aren't willing to embrace violence? How do you gain any power in a world where a few control all of it if you aren't willing to wrest that power from them?"

A chill seeps into my bones as his words hit home. Men like my father. How far is Pablo willing to go in his fight against Batista?

Has he killed? Will he kill? Can we ever find common ground between us—our love of Cuba, perhaps—or are we destined to be on opposite sides?

He cuts off his speech abruptly. "You're upset."

I am, but this hardly seems the time for delicate sensibilities. "Tell me the rest of it."

"I was at the Moncada Barracks with Fidel. The soldiers opened fire on us. We thought we would catch them off guard, that everyone would be distracted by Santiago's carnival festivities, drunk and careless, but we missed something in the planning, and once we lost the element of surprise, it was all over. We shot at them until we had no bullets left—men I'd laughed with, drank with, died beside me—and then we ran. Fidel wasn't so lucky. I escaped, helped him while he was in prison."

That was five years ago. I was a young girl when armed men attacked the Moncada Barracks—the second-largest military garrison in Cuba—in Santiago de Cuba on July 26th in Fidel Castro's failed attempt to seize control of the government away from Batista. The news said that the rebels boarded buses in Havana and followed Fidel to the country, not realizing the details of their mission, failing to understand how suicidal it was—how they were outmanned and outgunned, armed with recklessness, idealism, and weapons that paled in comparison to those of the military. Men were killed that day on both sides, the trials that followed somewhere in the background of my childhood. I played with dolls while he went to war.

"So you have lived a dangerous life."

He shrugs as though he takes no pride in the matter, as though such actions are merely a by-product of doing what he believes to be right.

"I have. It is dangerous to fight for what you believe in. It is also dangerous to speak of the corruption in Batista's government, of our dependence on the United States, to complain about unemployment, the failing economy, how sugar controls all of our fortunes." He breaks off with a curse as I blanch.

I've listened to the same words hurled at my father by my brother, except the difference between Pablo and Alejandro is that I'm familiar with Alejandro's disdain for Fidel and the 26th of July, his belief that they are not willing to go far enough in the change they wish to bring to Cuba, that the "revolution" they call for will not do enough to upend the economic disparities that have plagued our island since the Spaniards came.

"You hate my family," I say, my voice dull.

Another oath falls from Pablo's lips, and in a flash, I see the conflict in his eyes, the truth and the lie contained in his words.

"If only it were that simple. I should hate your family. Men like your father have stolen this country from the rest of us. I should hate your family, but—"

His voice trails off as though he cannot explain the vagaries of the human heart.

"I'm not my family," I protest even as I recognize the falsehood for what it is as the words fall from my lips.

It is a remarkably painful thing to have someone you care about and admire judge your existence, your very identity, the world you inhabit, and deem it rotten to the core. My brother hates everything about being a Perez, and the more he professes his desire to distance himself from our family, the more it seems impossible for him to love those of us who were born into this lifestyle. I am my parents' daughter. How can you love something you denounce with such fervor?

"Of course you are," Pablo says. "It's in your bones, the tilt of your head, the sound of your voice, every step of your stride. You're a Perez, through and through."

And that's the problem. I don't know how to undo a lifetime of behavior, of rules, of manners that have been drilled into me. How to repudiate those I love the most—Beatriz, Isabel, Maria, my parents, Alejandro. We are not Batista, nor do we agree with many of his policies. But where is the difference between sin and survival? Does the benefit we receive from his position of power automatically damn us?

"I wish things were simpler," Pablo adds. "I wish you could live in my world and I could live in yours. I wish there wasn't such a sharp divide between those who have everything and those who simply yearn for a chance at more."

"And you think you can bring that to Cuba?"

"Me and others like me. Fidel Castro for one."

I know little about Castro besides the mentions of him I hear in the news and the derision in my brother's voice. Fidel is calling for those running for the upcoming presidential elections to be shot and jailed; he says he will bomb polling places where people will gather. Perhaps Pablo thinks he is a good man, but the little I've seen of him has yet to convince me, and as much as I might disagree with my brother, I can't ignore his thoughts on the matter, either.

"Were you with Fidel on the *Granma*?" I ask.

"Yes. I've been with him throughout the journey."

"He's your friend."

I don't bother hiding the fact that I'm mildly appalled. My mother has always cautioned us that we are to be judged by the company we keep, and it is difficult to not do the same to Pablo. Just as it appears difficult for him to not do the same to me.

"He is," Pablo answers. "He's also one of Cuba's best chances at stepping out from under Batista's shadow. He's a good man, a lawyer, a reformer, a constitutional scholar, and a student of history."

The bombs going off around Havana—some of them have belonged to Castro's 26th of July Movement. Some of the Cuban blood that has spilled on the streets, the lives lost, have been at their hands, too. Either directly or indirectly, he's been responsible for those deaths.

How can I admire such a man? How can I care for him?

"Isn't Castro in the mountains? Shouldn't you be with him now? What are you doing in Havana?"

He's silent for a long time. "I was with him in the mountains for a while. I was needed here. It's best if you don't know why."

"What happens if you are caught?"

"They question me. Throw me in prison."

"Shoot you?"

He doesn't flinch. "Maybe. Probably."

He takes my hand, lacing our fingers together, his gaze on me. He leans forward, shattering the distance between us, his voice lowering again. "If you don't want to see me again, if you can't understand . . ." His voice trails off. "My family—" Emotion splinters the words. "My family wanted no part of this, either. Wanted no part of me now that this is my life. I understand. They've gone to America. To Florida. We don't speak."

"I'm sorry. That must be hard for you. I can't imagine my life without my family."

"It is."

"When my brother—" I take a deep breath. How much will I trust him with? How much of myself, of my family, should I give? Pablo just shared enough to see himself hanged. Can you have a relationship where you exist in half measures, or does the very nature of love demand you throw yourself into it with gusto?

"It's been hard on everyone." I twist the white linen napkin around in my hands. "He wants nothing to do with our parents, the money, his legacy of running our family's sugar company."

"He's with the Directorio Revolucionario Estudiantil," Pablo says.

The DRE, who a year ago stormed the Presidential Palace and

attempted to assassinate President Batista. With the death of their leader José Antonio Echeverría after he took part in an assault at the National Radio Station of Cuba, the group all but collapsed, many of its members choosing to join the 26th of July fighting in the mountains. My brother has remained in Havana with his friends who refuse to join Fidel and his men.

My stomach clenches. "Yes. How did you—"

"I asked around. Discreetly, of course."

My eyes narrow. "My parents have told everyone he's studying in Europe. Everyone thinks he's studying in Europe."

"The people who know of your brother run in very different circles from the ones you likely see at the yacht club. We're a small, disreputable lot, but word travels quickly." He hesitates, the smile slipping. "Your brother has gained notice lately. His writing is . . ."

"I know."

"You've read his papers?" Pablo asks, his tone fairly incredulous.

"He is my brother."

"But you don't share his views?"

"Of course not. He's still my brother. I don't always like him, don't always agree with him, but I love him." I think about it for a moment. "I'm proud of him for believing in something so passionately, even if it isn't something I believe in. Even as his beliefs drive a wedge between him and the rest of the family. He wouldn't be happy to be a replica of our father; he needs to be—is—his own man. And at the same time, I worry about him. Constantly. With each day he's gone, it feels like he's further and further away from us."

"And where do you fit in all of this?" Pablo asks.

"It's different for me. It's different to be a woman in Cuba."

"Perhaps. But it doesn't have to be."

I shake my head. "You hope for too much."

"And you ask for too little."

"Perhaps," I acknowledge.

We break apart as the waiter sets our plates on the table. Pablo ordered us a dish that looks and smells wonderful, chunks of meat mixed into the rice.

When the waiter leaves, I say calmly, "How long will you be in Havana?"

"A few weeks, maybe. I'm not sure."

Then we'll have a few weeks.

"I want to see you again," he says, his gaze intent. "Can I see you again?"

Perhaps I fell in love with him while walking on the Malecón. Or maybe it was at the party, or a few minutes ago when he spoke of his dreams for Cuba. Or maybe this is merely a precursor to love, an emotion singularly difficult to identify by name when you've yet to experience it; maybe there are stages to it, like the moment when you wade into the ocean, right before the waves crash over your head. And maybe—

"Yes."

Relief shines in his gaze.

Pablo takes my hand, his thumb stroking the inside of my wrist, teasing the soft skin there.

"You're going to be difficult to walk away from, aren't you?" he asks, his voice resigned.

My heart thuds.

"I hope so."

He drives me back to Miramar in a car he says he borrowed from a friend, dropping me off a few streets away from my house to avoid anyone seeing us together.

Pablo turns in his seat to face me. "Would you like to go for a walk with me tomorrow? I have some business in the morning, but we could meet in the afternoon if you'd like. On the Malecón, near the Paseo del Prado."

With each day we spend together, the risk of discovery grows—and yet—

"Yes."

We decide to meet at two o'clock, and then with a brush of his lips against my cheek, he is gone, leaving me walking down the streets of Miramar, my skin warm from his kiss.

My home looms ahead, the pink edifice framed by looming palm trees. I walk toward the gate—

A little scream escapes my lips as a hand closes down on my forearm, tugging me to the side of the fence, away from the view of the house.

"Elisa."

Alejandro is suddenly there in front of me, his hand gripping my arm, pulling me out of view of the street until we're hidden by the massive walls flanking our estate.

My brother's voice is low, urgent, so different from the teasing, mischievous boy I grew up beside. I'm not sure exactly when the change began, when he started looking at the society we inhabited with a different gaze than the rest of us. University, perhaps? He made it through a year at the University of Havana before its doors shuttered, and at some point during that time, he transformed from future sugar baron to revolutionary.

"What are you doing here?" I hiss.

My father made it clear the day he threw Alejandro out of the house—my brother could leave with the clothes on his back and nothing more, never to return again, his name expunged from the family bible, the sugar empire left to whichever one of our future husbands was most deserving in our father's eyes, making us eminently marriageable. While our father's edict hasn't been strictly followed, Alejandro's visits are typically relegated to evenings and days when our parents aren't in residence. That our father is somewhere in the cavernous mansion, our parents returned from Varadero, makes this even more brazen.

"What are you doing with *him*?" Alejandro asks, his eyes dark, ignoring my question completely. His gaze runs over my appearance as though I am a stranger to him.

My heart pounds.

Brothers, too, are both a curse and a blessing.

"Nothing."

"That didn't look like nothing."

What did he see? Me in the car? Walking away from Pablo? That moment when Pablo pressed his lips to my cheek?

"Well it was," I lie. "And it's not like you're in any position to lecture me about being circumspect in my behavior."

"This isn't about being circumspect; it's about your safety. He's dangerous."

"Not to me."

"Especially to you. Do you know what they're doing in the Sierra Maestra? They're animals. Do you know how close he is to Fidel?"

That name drips with scorn falling from my brother's lips. I'm not entirely shocked that my brother knows of Pablo; despite their ideological differences, my brother is every inch my father's heir—he appreciates the value of information: hoarding it, trading it, using it to his advantage.

"He's a good man."

Alejandro snorts. "Aren't we all?"

Something in his tone breaks my heart—what has Batista done to us? What have we done to ourselves?

"You're still a good man."

Alejandro runs a hand through his hair, grimacing. The hand

falls to his side and he stares at it, pained, as though blood drips from his gaunt fingers.

Beatriz and I stood on the other side of the door, our ears pressed to the wood, listening as Alejandro and our father fought that fateful day in his study after the attack on the palace. I know my brother has killed in his private war for Cuba's future—does he dream of the faces of the lives he took? Does he wonder if they had families—wives, children?

Beatriz and I have never spoken about what we overheard that day. Speaking words gives them an unimaginable power, and we're full up on horrible things at the moment.

Alejandro curses beneath his breath.

"What are you doing here?" I ask again, my tone gentler.

"I need to speak to Beatriz."

"Beatriz needs to be more careful. I caught her in Father's study. If it had been someone else who saw her rifling through his desk . . ."

Alejandro lets out another oath. "I'll talk to her. Tell her to be more careful."

He's the only one she listens to, and even that isn't saying much.

"How much longer is this going to continue?" I ask, sagging against the wall.

"What do you mean?"

"Aren't you tired? Don't you want to come home?" I reach out, grabbing his arm, searching his eyes for the brother I've known for nineteen years.

Pain stares back at me.

"How can I? What am I supposed to do?"

"We're your family. We love you."

"Do they love me? Perhaps you do. And Beatriz, and Isabel, and Maria. But our parents? He threw me out."

"You tried to kill the president," I whisper. "What was he supposed to do?"

"Understand."

"He doesn't. They don't. What you're trying to do—this system you want to destroy—is everything to them. It's our heritage."

"That's not something to be proud of."

"Not to you, but it is to them. The things you revile are the things they seek to maintain."

He sighs, his expression haggard. "You think I don't know that? That I don't see that there is little chance for us to be anything other than natural enemies?"

"It's just politics," I argue.

"No, it's not. Not anymore. It's a part of me now. I can't bury it and I can't destroy it. I can't go back to being the pampered prince who was set to inherit a sugar empire forged in other people's blood and sweat. I *can't*." He pushes off the wall, frustration etched all over his face. "Tell Beatriz I'll meet her here tomorrow at noon."

"Alejandro—"

"I can't wait any longer. I meant what I said earlier—that guy is no good for you. Stay away from him." He leans forward, embracing me in a quick hug. His body is much slighter than I remember. What has he been eating? Where has he been living? How is he surviving on his own?

"Alejandro, wait."

He releases me abruptly, turning away, his strides lengthening with each step away from me. It hurts more than I thought it would to watch my own brother nearly run away from me, and minutes pass before I'm able to move again, standing on the pavement between the mansion that feels a bit like a mausoleum and the brother who seeks to tear it down piece by piece.

chapter eight

Weeks pass, my brother absent once more, my life a cycle of ordinary events interspersed with life-changing moments with Pablo. Whatever Pablo does for the revolutionaries, he steals into the city like a thief in the night, providing us with hours together before he's gone again. There's no rhythm to his schedule, at least none I can see, and while I could likely search for a pattern in the news of the day, there are some things I am unwilling to examine too closely. Sometimes he is in Havana for a few days at a time and we are able to see each other once or twice; other times I can get away for a few moments and that is all.

The letters have become a method of keeping him with me when we are forced to part. They exist between dates on the Malecón, two times when he took me to the cinema, the occasional furtive meal.

There's a tension in our interactions together that is stripped away when we write each other, an intimacy to the act of passing our most private thoughts to each other, creating pages and pages of familiarity. I turn his words over in my head when we are apart, inventing imaginary conversations between us, carrying him with me throughout the day, including him in parts of my life the flesh-and-blood man would never be allowed to experience. Our romance plays out as much in our letters as the few times we are able to see each other, so much so that at times the two blend together—the man who clasps my hand and walks beside me along the shore and the version I've conjured in my mind from ink and paper. As greedy as I am for his words, though, there are some worries they can't soothe.

It seems fair that my joy would be tempered by the reality of the situation, as though fate has stepped in and ordered this in a more equitable fashion. My family will never accept him. His friends will likely never accept me. Unless Batista falls, Pablo has no place in Havana. If Batista falls and the rebels succeed, what then? They have declared war on our way of life, on the wealthy, decried the position of families like mine, have urged the Cuban people to rise up against those in power. They have caused a rift in my family I now worry will never heal.

"You're quiet today," my best friend, Ana, says, sipping a soda across from me. We're having lunch outside at a restaurant off the Plaza Vieja. We've been next-door neighbors my entire life; only nine months separate us. Our parents are cordial with one another, social contemporaries, but our friendship has developed organically, two dark-haired girls playing beside each other in the backyard, plotting adventures within the confines of the high walls that contain us. My siblings are my friends because we are joined by birth, the bond strong and unbreakable, but there is freedom in having a friend with whom I can be myself, without the expectations and strings of family dynamics and drama.

"Sorry," I reply. "I hope I'm not poor company." We have the sort of friendship where there's no need to fill the silence; we're content just being in each other's company, but I fear today I am stretching the limits of that. "I have a lot on my mind."

Alejandro came by the kitchen the other day and met with Beatriz. He was always a favorite with the staff; do they suspect his real motives for staying away? Do they support his cause? Their lives would likely be better under Fidel.

"You're not poor company. Is it your brother?" Ana asks, sympathy in her voice.

My brother and Pablo.

With each day, each moment, I find myself falling for Pablo more and more. I'm in awe of him, I think. His convictions, his passion, his intelligence. He's so determined, so driven, his dedication admirable even if we disagree on the best direction for Cuba's future.

I've always told Ana everything, but I can't tell her the whole truth—not about my brother and certainly not about Pablo. I want to protect her, yes, but I'm also afraid she'll condemn me for getting involved with one of them. Her family isn't as close to the president as mine is, but still. Imaginary walls are forming in Cuba, running through families, marriages, friendships.

"My brother came by the house the other day," I answer. "He doesn't look good."

I've told Ana a different version of the story my parents have floated around, a bit closer to the truth—that Alejandro and my father had a falling-out, prompting him to leave the house. Perhaps she suspects the rest of it and is merely too good of a friend to say anything. Who knows? I have far too many secrets these days to unravel them all.

Her eyes widen. "Were your parents home?"

"No, they're in the country. My father's dealing with a strike in one of his factories. My mother's playing lady of the manor, sipping coffee and sitting on the veranda."

"I wish my parents would go to the country," she comments.

"They invited Arturo Acosta over for dinner tonight, and I'm fairly certain they have nefarious intentions."

"Still trying to get you engaged?"

Her lip curls. "With fervor. I envy you the older sisters. It would be nice to have some pressure taken away."

"I don't think Isabel is far from getting engaged," I comment.

"Really?"

"Things seem pretty serious between her and Alberto."

"Your mother is going to have a fit."

My mother has all sorts of problems with her daughters—one is in love with a rebel, the other is dating someone who doesn't have the right last name, and Beatriz is, well, Beatriz. At this rate, Maria's the only one who won't turn out to be a massive disappointment, although she still has a few years in which to change that.

I make a face. "Probably. Although, if one of us—"

The square explodes into a fury of noise.

Rat-tat-tat-rat-tat-tat-rat-tat-tat.

I freeze, my fingers closed tightly around my fork, my hand in midair. It takes a moment for my brain to reconcile those noises—firecrackers, cars backfiring, gunshots . . .

"Get down," Ana shouts, pushing me out of my stupor. Around us people yell and scream, the sound of crying filling the square.

Rat-tat-tat-rat-tat-tat-rat-tat-tat.

I huddle under the table, my arms around Ana, praying one of the stray bullets won't hit us, that they won't come over here and shoot us.

What has happened to our city?

As quickly as it begins, it stops, a deathly silence descending over the block. My body quaking, I look out from under the table. My stomach clenches. People are on the floor, hiding behind cars. Food has spilled from the tables, a stray piece of crusty bread lying on the ground near my face, wine staining the pavement in a deep red. The busy city has stilled; there is no sign of the gunmen. I fight the impulse to run, my gaze still searching.

Will the police come and tell us it's all clear?

Slowly, as if released from a spell, people begin to stand, shouting and gesturing. Ana and I rise from the ground. My legs shake, knees buckling as I grab the table for support. There's a gash on my palm from where I hit the ground, gravel embedded in my skin. The splatter of overturned black beans mars my hand. I wipe it on the linen napkin clutched in my white-knuckle fist. My fingers tremble as a new kind of worry fills me.

It's a strange sensation to feel tethered to violence—to know that somewhere in the city, this explosion of gunfire might have touched someone close to me, either perpetrator or victim—my brother or Pablo.

We drop money on the table for the meal, fleeing the restaurant. Around us people swarm the street, shopkeepers and restaurant owners emerging from their businesses, their voices carrying.

It was the rebels.

No, it was the mob.

Please, anyone could see they were Batista's men. The rebels are making progress in the mountains; what do you expect?

Batista's men? They were common criminals. The crime in this neighborhood gets worse each year. My niece was walking through the neighborhood the other night . . .

"Come on." I link arms with Ana, turning down the street, heading toward the car, panic filling my limbs, my head, my heart.

I stop in my tracks.

Two men lie facedown on the ground in front of us less than one hundred feet away, blood pooling beneath their bodies, their lifeless eyes staring back at me.

How can I not look?

Relief fills me—swift and decisive—

It isn't them.

We're quiet on the drive back to Miramar. Ana's behind the wheel—a good thing considering how rattled I am by this afternoon's events. I sit in the passenger seat, my face tilted toward the open window, the breeze, the hint of salt in the air. Anything to get the scent and sight of blood from my mind. Nausea rolls around in my stomach.

Ana breaks the silence first.

"Do you think it will ever end?"

The hopelessness in her voice breaks my heart. We don't talk about the violence, the madness in the city, but it's clear how much it has affected her, too.

"I don't know," I answer.

Batista has been in power for over half my life. His first term they say he was somewhat progressive—he gave us the 1940 Constitution we aspire to now, which among other things protected women from discrimination based on their gender and gave them the right to demand equal pay. When he returned to the presidency years later, he became a dictator, populist government eschewed for corruption, a hero transformed to a villain. The American mafia runs Cuba now—tourists swarm our beaches, fill hotels Cubans cannot stay in, gamble in casinos built by avarice.

For those of us who have known little else, it's hard to imagine a different version of Cuba, as though we can somehow turn back time and undo the changes his regime has implemented. And at the same time, I can't envision a future when the island isn't as fractured as it currently is.

Ana turns onto our street, the sight of those swaying palm trees calming my nerves a bit. My gaze drifts and settles on a man standing next to a bright blue convertible.

My heartbeat kicks up.

Pablo is dressed casually today, smoking a cigar, far enough away from the house to keep it from appearing as though he's here for me, but close enough that I have no doubt he is.

What is he doing here?

I get out of the car, pleading a headache when Ana asks me if I want to come in for coffee. I keep my gaze peeled for anyone I know as I pass our house, walking toward Pablo. Thankfully, none of our neighbors are out, but one of the gardeners casts a curious glance my way.

I stop a few feet away from Pablo, wanting more than anything to close the distance between us, to relax into his embrace, even when reason dictates I cannot.

"Hello," I say, keeping my voice low.

His smile sends a flash of heat through me, the fire of it instantly banked by the worry tingeing his expression.

"I'm sorry to come. I don't want to cause trouble for you, but I didn't want to leave without seeing you one last time."

My stomach lurches. "You're leaving?"

I've only seen him once since he's been back in the city this trip. He comes and goes so frequently that it is difficult to settle into a routine of seeing each other, the parting and subsequent reunions granting all of our interactions with a sense of urgency.

"My plans have changed," Pablo replies, his voice laced with regret. He reaches out, surreptitiously capturing a strand of my hair and wrapping it around his fingers before releasing me with a sigh. "I have to leave Havana tomorrow. I'm sorry."

I knew this was coming, knew he would have to leave again eventually, but there's still a wave of sadness and a sense of foreboding. When will we see each other again? Will we see each other again? The image of those dead men enters my mind once more, sending a shudder through my body.

"Will you take me somewhere? Anywhere? I need to get out of the city for a moment." I take a deep breath, the pounding in my chest growing more urgent, more insistent with each beat. "I was at lunch with my friend Ana. There was a shooting." My voice shakes as I say the rest of it and breaks over the part I cannot say aloud.

I worried it was you lying dead on the ground.

Pablo's eyes close once I've finished, and he wraps his arms around me, reason be damned, pulling me into his embrace. The top of my head fits perfectly beneath his chin; his lips brush my hair. I lack the energy to worry about who will see us. He's silent for a long time, and then he pulls back and takes my hand without a word. He walks to the passenger side, holding the door open for me while I slide into the seat. In this moment, I'd follow him anywhere.

We drive to the beach, to Celimar, in his borrowed car. He drapes his arm around my shoulders, my body pressed against his. With each moment we spend together the knot inside my chest unravels a bit more, the nerves calming. I never imagined it would be like this; I envisioned pretty words and poetry, not this raw, primal thing that affects me now. Love is a remarkably physical entity—the beat of his pulse at his wrist, the heaving of his chest with each breath, the fluttering of lashes, the line of his jaw. I want to press my lips there, want to know every inch of his body, every movement, want the parts of him no one else sees. There's a greediness to love that I didn't anticipate, either.

When we reach the water, Pablo parks the car and we walk onto the beach. I reach down, removing my sandals and carrying them in my free hand, the other clasped in his. My toes sink in the sand as I walk to the shore, the waves lapping at my feet as I stare out to the sea.

"Was it you today? Your group that shot those men?"

I can't look at him, am not prepared to see the unvarnished truth in his eyes.

"No."

I swallow.

"Has it been your group other times?"

It's a moment before he answers me, his gaze cast out to sea.

"Yes."

I can't decide if I'm grateful for his honesty or if I wish he'd lied instead. I look down at his hands, at the nicks and scrapes that once attracted me, so different from the men of my acquaintance. Now I see blood there, the same shadow of it that lingers on my brother's skin.

How can you love someone who has taken a life?

And yet—

Are they really different from the men who give orders behind desks, who are equally responsible for the bloodshed even if the violence is carried out on their authority and not by their neatly manicured hands? Where do matters of right and wrong fall in times of war? Are my brother and Pablo soldiers even if they aren't in uniform, or are they the criminals my father believes them to be?

I fear I'm not equipped for these judgments, for the moral equivocacy war creates. More than anything, I wish the conflict would end.

"We're to have elections soon. Isn't that what you wanted?" I ask. "A chance for the people's voice to be heard?"

My voice sounds so very young, even to my own ears. What do I know of the emotions running through me, or of the things of which we speak? It's not merely gender or age that separates us; it's life experience. He has seen horrors I cannot fathom, possesses ambitions I cannot imagine.

"The elections only serve Batista," Pablo replies. "He's not a stupid man. Havana is on the brink of revolt; he's fighting a losing battle in the countryside. These elections are Batista's attempt to appease the masses, creating the false appearance of democracy while pulling the strings for his puppet behind the scenes. Agüero's name is on the ballot, but Batista will call the shots if he's elected."

Comprehension dawns, bringing with it a fresh new horror.

"Is that why you're in the city? The election?"

The revolutionaries have been doing everything in their power to disrupt the election for months now.

Pablo dodges my question. "Batista might hold Havana, but his control over the rest of the island is rapidly dwindling. There are places even he can't send his candidate for fear of what will happen," he boasts.

Fidel Castro's infamous threat to attack polling places has left many Cubans afraid to vote. His threats to jail and execute any candidate have left few men willing to run.

"And you support this? You agree with Fidel's actions? You call for democracy, and yet, what is this if not standing in the way of democracy?"

"It's preventing Batista from rigging another election."

"By what, rigging it before he can?"

"No." Frustration fills his voice. "I'm not saying I agree with the threats, with the calls for violence, the attempts to suppress the election, but at the same time, Batista must be stopped. There's no clear answer here. He has all the power at his disposal, and unless we do something to wrest it away from him, this will never end.

"It is not enough to control the countryside; we need to control the entire country, including the government. We must drive him from Havana and show the people they no longer need to fear him and his firing squads, his secret police. We must give them the power to determine their own future, to decide the direction the country will take, but it's impossible to achieve that under the current system."

"It sounds as though you're willing to play the villain in order to defeat one."

"Please don't think that I have become as bad as Batista, that I am driven by the same power and greed that fuels him."

I'm afraid, and that thread of doubt threatens to unravel whatever relationship exists between us. I worry I'm surrounded by madmen who desire to burn the world down without thought for the consequences of their actions, without regard for all the innocent lives that will be charred by the flames.

"Please don't look at me like that." There's a plea in Pablo's voice I haven't heard before and a hopelessness in his gaze.

"Like what?"

"Like I repulse you. As if I'm a monster like Batista and his cohorts. Please, Elisa."

I want to believe he's different, but right now both sides blur before my eyes, each claiming to possess the answer to Cuba's future and willing to do abominable things in order to bring that future about.

"I don't understand. I'm trying, but it's difficult. Doesn't the violence wear on you? The killing?"

"How can I not fight for my country? Nothing changes. If we continue on, if we don't alter our strategy, if we don't give them a war, then Cuba's current state, the government's failure, is our responsibility.

"Look at what Batista has turned us into. Look at what he has brought into the country. Gangsters and drugs—that is Batista's legacy. Not to mention the casinos, the brothels. He has handed our country over to the Americans. They have more power here in a foreign land than we have in our own home. And in turn they give

Batista military aid, weapons he uses against his people to maintain an iron grip on the country. The Americans preach liberty, and freedom, and democracy at home, and practice tyranny throughout the rest of the world. Batista is a despot. You know this."

He's right; but my father was one of the men who donated large sums of money to Batista's presidential campaign years ago, is frequently welcomed at the Presidential Palace. How can I condemn my own family, my parents? That's the difference between me and my brother—for better or worse, I am a Perez before I am a Cuban.

"Batista is bleeding us dry," Pablo continues. "But because he is in bed with the Americans, he is untouchable. He has slaughtered tens of thousands of Cubans, and still he remains in power. We've endured his cruelty for far too long and look where it has left us."

"And yet you think you and your friends can defeat him."

The hubris in his words terrifies me; they are tempting God and the rules of nature to think that such a small group of men can do such a thing.

"Yes."

"And the Americans?"

"If we are loud enough, if our voice is one, if we are successful in defeating him, then what can they do? They will accept us eventually."

I'm not so sure about that. It all sounds so easy when he puts it that way. But if it is so easy, why has Batista held such power over the island for so long?

"And if you aren't successful?"

"Then at least I will have spent my life serving a cause I believe in, a cause greater than myself."

"You think it's worth dying for."

I try to imagine loving something so much that I would die for it. I would die for my family. For my child. For the man I loved. But a country?

"I cannot imagine anything more sacred than the willingness to give one's life for one's country," he answers, his voice solemn.

Those are a martyr's words, and perhaps one day they will honor him in the annals of Cuban history, but I don't want to love a martyr. I don't want this war or bloodshed to touch my corner of the island more than it already has. I don't want to lose him. And suddenly, I feel young and foolish, impossibly coddled. He speaks of revolution, and I worry over my heart.

"Then you are to sacrifice your life for Cuba?"

Pablo attempts a smile. "Hopefully, not. Hopefully, it won't come to that."

"And if it does?"

He wraps his arm around me, his forehead resting against mine, his lips inches from my mouth.

"At the end of the day, the only thing you have left is what you stand for. If I said nothing, if I did nothing, I could not live with myself. I would not be a man. This is the position I choose to take, and for better or worse, I will accept the consequences of my actions."

I take a deep breath.

"Will I see you again?" A tear trickles down my face. "This feels like the end."

Pablo kisses me, his arms wrapped around my waist, his body against mine.

"Have faith, Elisa."

"Will you come back when it's all over?"

"Yes."

chapter nine

Marisol

I place the last letter in the box, momentarily speechless. After all the times I asked my grandmother about her life in Cuba, why didn't she tell me she fell in love? What happened between them? Were they separated by the revolution? Did she forget him when she met my grandfather?

My grandmother loved a revolutionary. I can't quite wrap my mind around it.

My grandmother spent her days decrying Castro's regime, volunteering with groups speaking out against Cuba's government, donating money to causes designed to remove Fidel from power. She went to Mass every Sunday, yet never took Communion because she said her heart was too filled with hatred for Fidel, for the men who stole her country from her. But she loved one.

Did he come back to her?

The letters in my hand fill me with questions, offering little in the way of answers. I have half of their romance—his letters to her—letters my grandmother clearly thought were precious enough to save, but what of her words to him? Did she love him? And if so, why did they part?

I need to know the end of the story, need to know what happened, and Ana's earlier warning returns to me now.

You can't understand what those times were like, how our world was shattered in the span of a few months. Whatever you find, don't judge her too harshly.

She has to know some of it at least. Do my great-aunts know? There's no mention of whether they were my grandmother's confidants in the letters, and there are so many pieces I need filled in for me.

Is her lover alive? Is he still in Cuba?

It's late—just after midnight according to the clock on my phone—but I can't sleep, questions running through my mind. I want to share what I've learned with my father and sisters, and at the same time, I need more information before—if—I tell my family this news. Besides, Cuba's telecommunications challenges don't make it easy. A part of me welcomed the reprieve from real life, but now I feel almost unbearably lonely, cut off from my friends and family.

Why didn't my grandmother tell me these stories? Why didn't she trust me with this?

I need fresh air, the four walls closing in on me. I grab a robe from my suitcase, belting it around my tank top and yoga pants, tiptoeing from the room. The Rodriguezes' part of the house is quiet. Upstairs their neighbors are still awake, domestic noises filtering through the water-stained ceiling. Footsteps thud, joined by the whoosh of water running down the pipes. The faint sound of a baby crying.

The stairs creak, and I wince with each one, praying I don't wake the whole household. I walk past two closed doors and reach the back of the house, opening the glass door that leads to the *paladar*'s outdoor dining area overlooking the water. The wind whips my hair around my face, the lulling sound of the water calming my racing heart.

"Couldn't sleep?"

I whirl around. Luis lounges in one of the chairs previously inhabited by diners. A bottle of rum and a half-filled glass sit on the table in front of him.

The moonlight shifts. I freeze.

A sliver of light illuminates the left side of his face. His eyelid is bruised, a nasty-looking gash on his cheekbone that definitely wasn't there earlier this evening.

I gasp. "What happened? Are you okay?"

Luis reaches for the drink in front of him. He drains the liquid, setting the glass back on the table with an angry clank.

"I was robbed."

"Oh my God. What did they take?"

He unscrews the bottle, filling the glass. He doesn't drink it.

"Mostly, my dignity."

"Did you report it to the police?"

His lips curve in a sardonic twist. "I highly doubt the police would concern themselves with a simple robbery."

"I thought Cuba didn't have a ton of crime. The guidebooks I read mentioned it was fairly safe," I say, feeling a bit foolish with the evidence to the contrary staring me in the face.

He snorts. "Don't believe everything you read. Crime doesn't cast the regime in a favorable light."

"Do you need something for your face? Antibiotic cream, maybe?"

Luis lifts his drink in a silent toast. "I already have it."

He gestures toward an empty chair on the other side of the table with his free hand, and it occurs to me that he just might be a little drunk.

He's married. Go back to your room. Do not sit down.

I sit, and when he slides the full glass across the table to me, the liquid sloshing around the rim, I don't hesitate as I lift the drink to my lips and drain it.

The rum is better than expected. I've seen the brand before in my travels abroad, its distinctive logo jumping out at me as a sign of yet another thing Castro's government has taken, but I've never tried it. Was it once the Rodriguez family's before the rum companies were nationalized?

"Are you sure you don't want to patch up your face?" His eye looks like it must be throbbing; he'll have a hell of a bruise tomorrow.

Luis shakes his head, seemingly unconcerned with the fact that he's sitting across from me beaten and bloody.

Men.

"Rough night?" He gestures to the empty glass in my hand.

It sounds like he's laughing at me again.

"You could say that."

I slide the glass back across the table, and he refills it, taking another sip. His gaze is trained on the sea in front of him rather than on me, but I sense he's waiting for me to respond, and now, an ocean away from my family, I'm so in need of another person to talk to that I do.

"Your grandmother had a box of possessions my grandmother buried in her backyard when she left Cuba. There were letters in there. Love letters. From a man. He was a revolutionary."

Luis is silent, waiting for me to continue. Surprisingly, I do.

"I came to spread my grandmother's ashes because she asked me to, because I knew her better than anyone, or thought I did, but now I don't feel like I knew her at all."

"She never told you about the man?"

"No. I don't think anyone knew. At least if her sisters did, they never said anything. She told me so many stories about her life in

Cuba, and this might be the most important one of all, and she never mentioned it. Not once."

I've never been overly close to my father; he's an affectionate, if distant, parent. And my grandfather died when I was fairly young, so he's little more than a hazy memory. My mother left me in the care of others after the divorce. But my grandmother—

She was the constant in my life, the person I knew would be there for me no matter what, the one person in my family who accepted me without reserve, who didn't attempt to shape me into the Perez mold. That makes this discrepancy between the woman I thought I knew and the woman she was cut the deepest.

"What are you more upset about? The secrecy or that your grandmother loved someone you wouldn't approve of?"

"I don't know," I admit. "My grandparents' relationship was always built up as this great romance in my mind. I didn't have a lot of examples of healthy marriages to look up to—my parents certainly didn't fit the bill."

I'd told myself that one day when I was older, my own relationship would look like theirs, that my children would never grow up in a home as divisive and fractured as the one I was raised in, but rather in a house filled with love and affection like that of my grandparents.

"When I was a little girl, I used to beg my grandmother to tell me about how they met," I explain to Luis. "They married a month later. Can you imagine that—meeting someone and falling in love in the blink of an eye and then marrying them a few weeks later? What is that if not great love?"

I can feel my skin flushing, the warmth prickling me, either from the rum or the topic.

Luis stares at me, his expression inscrutable. "Your definition of romance is a singular one."

I blink. "What's that supposed to mean?"

It sounds like he's faintly mocking me again.

"You speak of passion, but what about companionship, mutual respect, friendship? Why do people always seize on the spark that can peter out as the measure of a relationship?"

Does he have that spark with his wife, or is theirs a steady marriage, bolstered by the qualities he speaks of now?

"Those things are important," I concede. "And my grandparents had them, too. They were married for a long time; I very much doubt marriage can endure without those qualities."

He tips his head in silent acknowledgment.

"But I'd want the spark, too," I say, my voice growing bolder.

Luis laughs, the sound throaty and warm. "I don't doubt it."

He picks up the glass again, bringing it to his lips, his Adam's apple bobbing as he swallows.

I can't look away.

"I imagine a family like yours wouldn't be pleased to have a revolutionary in their midst," he says.

"No, they wouldn't." I hesitate, torn between truth and caution. The rum loosens my tongue. "I grew up hearing the worst about people like Che Guevara and Fidel Castro."

There is somewhat of a divide between the Cubans who left and the Cubans who stayed. There is affection and worry for family members and friends who remained behind, the intrinsic need to help anyone leave Cuba, but there is also a schism. Some believe those who stayed contributed to Cuba becoming what it is now, and in doing so, bolstered Fidel's power and legitimized it. People like my grandmother saw that as another betrayal—one that hurt especially because it came from her fellow Cubans. It is much easier to forgive the stranger than it is one you love.

"It's difficult to imagine my grandmother loving one of them."

"Maybe he wasn't one of them," Luis suggests. "Not everyone involved with Fidel's 26th of July Movement was the same."

I'm embarrassed to admit my knowledge of Cuban political history is fairly limited. I know broad brushstrokes and anecdotes passed on by my grandmother and great-aunts, but I've rarely examined the nuances beyond the simple proposition that Castro and the communism he wrought were bad. It was a truth so strongly accepted in our family, that questioning it, even in the smallest manner, was blasphemy.

"Who were the good ones, then?"

Luis drains his drink, pouring more rum into the glass. He slides it toward me, his fingers grazing mine as I grasp it.

I lift the glass to my lips, the smell of the rum filling my nostrils. The taste of him lingers somewhere on the glass and in the alcohol, or perhaps it's just my imagination.

He looks away, out to the sea again.

I swallow, the rum sending a hot lick of fire down my throat, uncoiling in my belly.

"I didn't necessarily say there were good ones," Luis clarifies. "Merely men who died before they made the full transition from liberating heroes to tyrants. Men with good intentions, at the very least, which is almost but not quite the same thing. I imagine a number of history's most notorious offenders started out with the very best intentions."

I slide the empty glass back to him. He removes the cap from the rum bottle, filling his glass, lifting it to his lips.

"I want to find him," I say, surprising myself even as the words leave my mouth.

The need to learn what happened between them, the puzzle of it, is all-consuming now.

"Of course you do. Journalists." Luis sighs, his expression hovering between resignation and amusement. "What do you know about him?"

"Not much. The letters were unsigned."

"Probably to protect your grandmother if they were ever found. Were there any clues in the letters?"

I think about it for a moment.

"He was an attorney. He met Fidel at the University of Havana while studying law."

Luis flinches, the move *nearly* imperceptible, and yet so slight it speaks volumes. Fidel casts a long shadow even in death.

"That's not much to go on. You don't even know if he remained in Cuba or if he left. If he's still alive."

"I know."

Without the use of Internet searches and genealogy sites, it will be a difficult endeavor. Without a name, it seems insurmountable. And still, I can't help but wonder if my grandmother sent me here because she knew I would need something to seize hold of once she was gone. Ana said that my grandmother asked her to keep the box for me; she had to have wanted me to have this part of her. But if she did, why did she never tell me herself?

"Your grandmother might know something," I add, recalling Ana's earlier words. "Maybe there were other people around who are still in Cuba. I want to try to find him, at least. If he's still alive, if he's in Havana, perhaps I could meet with him."

"Why?"

Luis refills his drink, the alcohol swaying in the bottle, and then he slides the glass back to me. This time I don't pick it up.

"Because she feels like a stranger and she was the only person in the world who really knew me."

Understanding flashes in his eyes as a sense of recognition passes between us. It's obvious in his interactions with Ana that there's a special bond between them, that for a boy who lost his father at a young age, his grandmother has become a rock for the entire family, taking them into her home, running the *paladar* in an effort to give them a better life.

"Tell me you wouldn't do the same," I say.

"If things were different, perhaps I would. But this isn't Miami. You need to be careful. Maybe he was a nice man nearly sixty years ago; that doesn't mean he's the same man your grandmother loved. You don't want to start asking questions, poking into things that will agitate the regime."

"You think finding him—trying to, at least—would be dangerous?"

It seems such a simple thing, to want to know my family's history. The idea that the government would discover my efforts or even care is something I can't quite wrap my head around. It's a love affair, not political insurrection. Were my great-aunts right to worry about me coming to Cuba as much as they did?

"Yes, it could be dangerous. Marisol—"

An oath falls from his lips, and his chair slides against the chipped tile floor with a scrape. His face is flushed, though from the liquor or the conversation, I'm not sure.

"I should go to bed," he murmurs.

The image of him lying next to Cristina assails me.

Married. He's married.

"Thanks for the drink," I offer haltingly.

He doesn't answer me.

I look straight ahead, fighting the urge to turn around, to watch him walk away. I'm too old for a crush. Especially on a married man. I came here to settle my grandmother's ashes, not for this.

"My grandmother asked me to show you around Havana tomorrow," Luis says behind me. "I'll be downstairs at ten."

I open my mouth to protest, but when I turn to tell him I'm fine without a tour guide, he's already gone.

· · ·

The morning comes far earlier than I'm prepared for, my grandmother's love affair spread out on the bedspread, a dull throb in my head from the alcohol. I fell asleep somewhere in the middle of rereading the letters after I returned to my room, my belly full of rum and my mind full of questions.

Was he killed? Were they separated by the revolution? Did he leave Cuba as well? If they were divided by something trivial, why did she never mention him?

I haven't forgotten Luis's warning last night, but I can't ignore the desire to attempt to track down my grandmother's mysterious revolutionary. It feels like this, too, was a charge she gave me—a puzzle surrounding our family's past, and now that the temptation is here, I can't shake the desire to learn who he was and to find him.

I choose my favorite maxi dress from my suitcase, pairing it with comfortable sandals and oversize sunglasses. I pretend I don't spend more time on my hair and makeup than normal, that I'm not preening, but I do and I am.

The ring on my hand weighs heavily, and I stare down at it, envisioning it on my grandmother's finger, as though I'm carrying a piece of her past along with me on my journey through Cuba. I hesitate but slip the container with my grandmother's ashes into my bag as well. Perhaps it's a bit macabre to carry her bones with me, but who knows when inspiration will strike.

I leave the room and walk down the stairs, my steps faltering when I spot Luis at the base waiting for me. He's wearing a white linen shirt and another pair of khaki pants. His eyelid is a spectacularly awful coloration of yellow and green, his cheekbone slightly swollen. He looks tired; maybe I wasn't the only one who passed a sleepless night.

"Are you sure you don't want someone to take a look at that?" I say in lieu of a greeting, gesturing toward his injured face.

His lips quirk. "I'm sure."

"How are you feeling?" I ask, my tone gentling.

"My eye's fine; my head, on the other hand . . ."

His expression is sheepish, so out of character with the glimpses of his personality I've seen so far—intense and serious—that I can't help but grin in spite of my earlier resolve to be oh-so-stoic and proper.

"It was strong rum," I concede. My own head is fuzzy, the daylight shining through the windows in the entryway a little too bright.

"Yes, it was." His gaze drifts over my appearance. "Are you ready?"

"I am." I glance around the room. "Is your grandmother here?"

"No. She usually goes to the market in the mornings to buy food. My mother went with her."

"Do you know when she'll be back?"

"A couple hours, maybe?" A faint smile tugs at the corners of his mouth. "She likes to visit with everyone while she's buying groceries. They all love her." His smile disappears. "Let me guess, you want to ask her about the letters you found."

"I do."

"So despite what I told you, you're still determined to find this man."

"I'm not going to do anything to put your grandmother at risk, but if she knows something, surely answering my questions wouldn't be dangerous."

"Are you always this curious?"

He says it like it's not a compliment.

"I don't know. I guess. Besides, this isn't some stranger we're talking about. This is my grandmother, the woman who raised me.

How can I not take this opportunity to learn more about her? Who knows when I'll have the opportunity to come to Cuba again; *if* I'll have the opportunity to come to Cuba again."

These are uncertain times for both of our governments, and decades of Cuban-American relations are changing on a dime.

Luis shakes his head in resignation. "If you'd like, we can hit up the major sites today and see where we end up. My grandmother will be here when we return. This article you're writing—what kind of tips are you looking for?"

The article has been the last thing on my mind since Ana handed me that box.

"A mix, really. Tourist spots. Things that are off the beaten path."

I can see him turning over the expression in his mind. There's that look again, as though I've amused him. I can't tell if Luis Rodriguez likes me or is vaguely appalled.

"We could start with the Malecón," he says. "It's better at night if you want the full effect, though. That's when everyone comes out. By day, it's not much to see."

The Malecón—five miles of seawall and promenade separating Havana from the Caribbean Sea—has been on the top of my must-see list after hearing about it from my grandmother. It was one of her favorite places in Havana.

I used to stand at the edge of the water and look out at the ocean. You could see all manner of things when you stared into that wide expanse of blue, Marisol. The world felt limitless, as though it was ours for the taking.

After reading the letters and learning what the Malecón meant to her and her lover, about their first date there, I now understand a bit more why the spot was so dear to her.

"Do you have a list of places where you're considering spreading your grandmother's ashes?" Luis asks. "We could tackle those first if you'd like, then do more tourist sites."

"I'm still working on that. I hoped I'd get a feel for the city. I thought something might speak to me."

I expect amusement in his gaze, but he simply nods as though he understands, as if family means as much to him as it does to me.

"Well, why don't you let me play tour guide, and if there's anything you want to see along the way, we can take a detour?" Luis suggests.

He holds his hand out to me, and I know he's only being polite, but my nerves reappear, the tension in my body returning with a vengeance. I give him my hand, our palms connecting, our fingers threading together, and a new kind of energy—excitement and anticipation—enters my body as he leads me down the cracked steps and onto the sidewalk, into the vintage Buick, and out into Havana.

chapter ten

We leave Miramar and drive to Old Havana, the part of the city that's most frequently seen in tourist photographs and iconic images. Here the buildings have retained much of their original state, the architecture harkening back to a time when Spanish influence played a defining role in the island's development, when Cuba was the jewel in Spain's imperial crown. Many of the buildings are in a state of disrepair, but others have been lovingly, painstakingly restored, and it's clear why tourists name this as one of the top sights to see in Havana.

"In the eighties, this neighborhood was designated as a UNESCO World Heritage Site," Luis explains. "There's a movement in place to preserve many of the buildings, but it hasn't been easy. Most Cubans aren't necessarily historians by nature."

It strikes me as surprising, considering exiled Cubans are intrinsic historians. They collect faded photographs, draw maps of Havana neighborhoods from memory, pass down family recipes and traditions as though they're sacrosanct. So much of our history is oral, a by-product of Castro's unwillingness to allow families to take anything but their memories with them when they left Cuba.

"Why?" I pull out my notebook and pen from my bag, and a soft chuckle escapes his lips.

"Practicality, I suppose. There's a luxury in historiography most Cubans lack. They're too occupied with surviving in the present to spend their time living in the past. Plus, there's the added difficulty of how much the narrative of the past has been shaped for them and how difficult it is to get honest information out of the regime.

"It's a real problem because documents that have been around for centuries—marriage records, birth records—are disappearing. We don't have the resources, or enough national interest, to properly preserve historical documents. Our history disappears a bit more each day, and I fear people won't realize how much we've lost until it's too late."

"Are there efforts to restore these documents?"

"There are several programs in place within the academic community, but it's a massive undertaking. Hell, getting bread in Cuba can be a massive undertaking."

We pass by a bright yellow scooter as Luis navigates into a parking spot.

I turn my attention away from Luis to my notebook, jotting down my impression of Old Havana, of the ease with which tourists can get around, for the article I'll eventually write. When all is said and done, my weeklong trip to Havana will be condensed into a two-thousand-word article to be read on flights and in airports by bleary-eyed travelers.

I'm surprised by how busy the streets are, full of tourists and locals alike. The tourists stick out—their shoes new compared to the ones the Cubans wear, cameras in hand, their heads tilted up to take in their surroundings, the beautiful buildings looming around them.

At the moment, most of them are speaking languages other than English, but no doubt that will change as more Americans take advantage of the available visa exceptions and if those exceptions eventually disappear altogether, allowing free American tourist travel.

"Have you noticed more tourists now that travel restrictions with the United States have eased?"

With each question, the tension inside me lessens. I can get through a day with him as long as I focus on the sites before us and not his tanned forearms, the pride in his voice, the sharp intelligence in his words. He's an impressive man, his competence and confidence undeniably seductive.

Luis Rodriguez belongs to my grandmother's time rather than mine, and for someone whose life has been steeped in nostalgia, his manner calls to me. He's a throwback to an era when men were gentlemen, and that alone is a powerful lure.

Married. He's married, Marisol.

"We used to get a steady stream of tourism from the rest of the world, but now there's definitely an increase," he answers. "The demographics are changing, too. There were Americans before, of course, but more of a trickle. And many were Cuban Americans."

"It's going to change things when relations open up even more."

"Yes. It will." He tilts his head, leaning toward me, his voice lowering. The scent of his soap—clean and strong—fills my nostrils. "Once again, Cuba is on the precipice of another change, and we're all holding our breaths to see what, if anything, will come of it."

Luis does a quick, almost reflexive sweep of the street. His voice lowers again, his head bent, close enough to mine that his breath tickles my skin. He doesn't smell like the expensive cologne I'm used to men wearing. There's something intimate about the scent of soap and man, layers stripped away between us.

"We live in curious times here," he says, speaking as though we share a secret. "Throughout history, we've always been dependent on an outside benefactor—Spain, the United States, the Soviet Union, Venezuela. When the Soviet Union fell and we entered the Special Period, a bad situation grew worse. Then Chavez came to 'save' us, sending Fidel tens of thousands of barrels of oil each day in an unholy alliance. They were friends, and in that friendship, we found ourselves beholden to yet another foreign power. Once Chavez died, we faced uncertainty again. And now we're opening up dialogue with the United States after nearly sixty years of hatred on both sides—perceived hatred, at least," he acknowledges. "Castro—Raúl, that is—began loosening restrictions on private enterprise in Cuba because otherwise who knows what would have become of us. And really that was merely a formality, acknowledging black market businesses as legitimate for the first time."

I'm struck by his comments and even more so by the incontrovertible truth behind them. Signs of Cuban pragmatism are everywhere I look, both in their relations on the world stage and in the daily life most Cubans lead here. The legendary cars like the one we're sitting in now are of course eye-catching with their bright colors and history, but perhaps more impressive is the amount of work that must go into making them run for over fifty years.

Luis laughs when I tell him so.

"Yes, we've learned to become inventors, repurposing everything we can. This car is a luxury. My grandfather was a well-known photographer before he died. The regime liked him, and life was easier. The car was his. For many Cubans, though, something as simple as owning a car is an exercise in all the ways the government can screw you over. Getting gas used to be nearly impossible. So yes, I work hard to preserve the one thing I have."

"That must be exhausting."

He shrugs. "It is what it is. In a way, things are better. Having access to the tourists in the *paladar* has made a huge difference. I have friends who are doctors and lawyers, but also work in the big hotels on their free time because they make a fortune in tips. We all live under the shadow of the almighty Cuban convertible peso."

"Why is the Cuban convertible peso so important?" I ask, pen poised for his reply.

"Cubans are paid in Cuban pesos. Everyone makes a set level of pesos every month. But having a private business or working in the tourism industry gives you access to the Cuban convertible peso, which foreigners use here. The convertible peso is pegged to the dollar. The national currency is worth a fraction of it. It's a different world when you're paid in convertible pesos. Cubans make more serving those who come and go, treating the island as a vacation destination, than they do in careers building infrastructure or helping their fellow citizens. And ironically, there is a substantial difference developing in Cuba now between those who have access to the convertible peso and those who do not."

I was prepared for the differences between Cuba and the United States, or at least I thought I was, but I truly feel as though I've stepped into another world. My sisters and I grew up with every opportunity available to us, never had to struggle financially, never knew the kind of pressures I see here. There's a different level of poverty in Cuba that suggests that not only is the deck stacked against you, but someone keeps stealing all the cards.

"And yet you still teach," I say.

"I do. The money is important, yes. And believe me, I have fought hard for us to have the restaurant in our family. At the same time, my students are the future of this country. Eventually, things will change. They have to."

He says the words with a ferocity that catches me off guard, even as they're muttered under his breath.

"And now that Fidel is dead?" I ask.

"I'd like to believe things will change, I *hope* they will, but who knows? Perhaps the infrastructure is too much, his brother too stubborn, the country too entrenched to really change after his death. He hadn't been running the show for a very long time even before his death, but he still casts a long shadow. Older Cubans, the ones who lived through his particular brand of hell, are reluctant to refer to him by name for fear of the ramifications of speaking ill of him, for fear of the perception that they are criticizing the regime. That trend is changing little by little, but words have power here. Deadly consequences."

I'm not sure if he delivers the last lines as a warning to me or a reminder to himself.

"From everything we saw on TV, it looked like people mourned him in Havana," I comment.

"Some probably did. Others put on the show they've been participating in for decades now, because it's expected, because it keeps them and their families safe," he replies.

Luis gets out of the car and comes around to the side, opening the door for me. Does the chivalry come to him naturally or through his grandmother's instruction? It's certainly part of his charm.

Now that we're out of the privacy of the car, the whispered conversations have ceased, and he's all business, history professor and tour guide. We begin walking, Luis pointing out sites as we go, his shoulder occasionally brushing mine.

There's the Capitol building that resembles our own Capitol in the United States. He explains that it's being renovated, scaffolding dominating much of the dome's exterior.

A bright red tour bus passes us, kicking up water lying near the curb. Without breaking stride, Luis puts his arm around my waist, guiding me away, his body between mine and the street. It lingers there for a beat before he lets me go.

The Hotel Nacional de Cuba is ahead, the design and entryway lined in palm trees, reminding me of the Breakers back home. We walk past a row of vintage cars and head inside.

Luis walks behind me, silent, as I explore. He seems uncomfortable here, his hands shoved into his pockets, his head bent, his eyes downcast and hiding whatever emotions linger in his gaze. The contrast between the bisected home he shares with his wife, mother, and grandmother, and the tourists' domain is stark. Thirty minutes pass—we explore the lush gardens, the public rooms, the infamous café bar—and then we leave the hotel behind us, in search of the next landmark.

We walk by the Museum of the Revolution, the old Bacardi building. I'm more interested in my grandmother's Havana, the sites that formed her love of the city, but I mark my impressions of the other places for the article, my grandmother's ashes in my bag weighing heavily on my mind.

Havana is a beautiful city shrouded in sadness, yet the remarkable thing is that it's almost as if the people didn't get the memo. They laugh, and there's a jubilant quality to the air. The frenetic pace I'm used to is replaced by an ebullient atmosphere that gives the impression that life is a big party. The Cubans probably have the least to laugh about compared to everyone around them, but they laugh the loudest.

We continue walking, Luis pointing out more sites and answering my questions with thoughtful precision. It's impossible to walk these streets and not feel a measure of pride as a Cuban for the beauty that is our capital city. The Great Theatre of Havana is stunning architecturally; the Cathedral of Havana is equally so.

I hesitate at the church's entrance, watching the tourists file in.

"Do you want to see inside?" Luis asks.

"Do you mind?"

He smiles indulgently, glancing over his shoulder and gently guiding me out of the path of a group of tourists. "Not at all."

I grab a scarf from my bag, covering my shoulders as we enter the church.

Beautiful chandeliers punctuate the interior, the landscape peppered with elegant statues sculpted and carved to exquisite detail. My grandmother and her siblings were baptized here, my great-grandparents married at this very altar. I imagine my grandmother here as a young girl, sitting in the pews beside her sisters, Beatriz whispering and gossiping to Isabel as the priest says Mass.

The sensation of standing in the spot where she once stood, sitting in the wooden pews where she once sat, brings a tear to my eye. And another. This is a piece of my family's history I didn't expect to have returned to me.

I don't realize I'm crying until Luis silently hands me an ivory square handkerchief, his expression somber. My breath hitches, and I stare down at the fabric in my hands, anything to distract myself from his searching gaze.

His initials are embroidered on one corner of the handkerchief, the fabric slightly yellowed with age. I rub my fingers over the letters there, a smile playing at my lips. It seems somehow fitting that a historian would carry a handkerchief, and I have no doubt his grandmother painstakingly embroidered his initials.

"Thank you," I whisper.

Despite the Catholic Church's difficult relationship with Castro—his attempts to wholly eradicate religion from the country—there are a few Cubans sitting in the pews praying, their heads bent, rosaries in hand. Tourists mill around us—I recognize two men who were at the Hotel Nacional earlier. Clearly these are the popular spots to see in Havana. I make a few notes about the church on my pad.

I turn away from Luis, lingering over the artwork, exploring the side chapels, attempting to soak in every inch of the beautiful building. I've never been particularly religious, but the ambiance adds an air of solemnity to our surroundings.

Luis trails behind me, leaving a few paces between us, and the few times I glance back at him, his gaze is fixed on me and not our surroundings.

"What's it like to be Catholic in Cuba?" I whisper to Luis once he's caught up to me, his earlier warning about curbing my words fresh in my mind.

His gaze sweeps across the church before returning back to me. "Nearly as difficult as it is to be Cuban in Cuba," he replies, his tone dry.

We walk around for a few more minutes, and I pay the extra fee for us to climb the bell tower, the city spread before us. I look out past the terra-cotta-tiled roofs that appear as though they would simply crack off with a strong gust of wind.

"Are hurricanes bad here?" I ask. Growing up in South Florida, I am intimately familiar with the havoc storms can wreak.

"It can be hell," he answers. "Often the buildings are in such a state of disrepair that even relatively mild weather can prove a problem."

He keeps his voice low again, closing the distance between us. Even here, surrounded by tourists, it's clear he's afraid to speak his mind.

Across the water, there's La Cabaña, the infamous prison Che Guevara ran after the revolution. The sight of it sends a chill down my spine when I think about the blood shed there, the lives lost. There's a violence to our history that gets lost somewhere in the telling, buried beneath the beautiful scenery, the deceptively blue sea and sky, the palm trees swaying placidly in the breeze. It's the sound of firing squads that echo in the wind.

"They've built shops there now, a restaurant," Luis murmurs, his body tucked away from the tourists, his mouth hidden in the curve of my neck. "You can gawk at the world's largest cigar in the site where we bled."

There's something so ironically vicious about that.

Luis stands patiently beside me as I take pictures of the land-scape. I've blocked out the other tourists, but he seems faintly amused by the conversations around us; his English is quite good given his ability to understand the British family arguing over whether they're going to return to their hotel or continue sight-seeing.

Once I've finished snapping photos, we leave the church and meander through the streets, drifting from one landmark to the next. I stop occasionally to take more pictures, filling the pad with additional observations. Some journalists use electronics, but there's something about the rhythm of putting pen to paper that I can't resist. It adds to the spirit of my surroundings—I imagine Heming-way scribbling in old notebooks, the ink staining his fingers as he sips a mojito in the late Havana sun.

Havana lends itself to the romantic and idyllic even as the evi-dence to the contrary is everywhere I look. Perhaps that's the double-edged sword to being Cuban—we are both pragmatic real-ists and consummate dreamers.

We walk on, the sun growing brighter, the heat increasing. My dress sticks to my skin, the air pregnant with humidity; it's like being back in Florida again.

There are other landmarks to explore; the father of Cuban inde-pendence, José Martí, is everywhere—on statues and streets. We all claim him as ours, revolutionaries and exiles alike.

"Are you getting hungry for lunch?" Luis asks as we walk down the street.

"Yeah, I am."

We walk a bit farther and leave Old Havana behind, the scenery changing to more run-down buildings, less antique charm. Dogs roam the sidewalk, others lounging in the available shade. The pe-destrians on the sidewalks shift from European tourists to locals. I stand out here, my clothes setting me apart from those on the street, the unmistakable sense that I belong more with the tourists than I do in this Cuban neighborhood, a visitor in the country that should feel like home.

We buy tamales from a stand in Vedado. The cornmeal is warm and moist, perfect paired with the sweet soda I buy from the vendor as well.

I stumble on a crack in the sidewalk, and Luis is there at once, his hold on me steady and reassuring. Out of the corner of my eye, I spot the same two men from earlier at the church and the Hotel Nacional, except now that they're removed from the tourist spaces it's clear that they, like Luis, belong to this part of the city.

"Are you okay?" His hand wraps around my arm, his breath along my skin.

I nod, pulling away, shutting down the urge to lean into him, to relax my body against his. That's the thing about desire—it creeps up on you at the most inconvenient times, too often with the most inconvenient people.

We continue walking, and this time I pay more attention to my surroundings. The vendors in this part of the city aren't selling touristy items, but basic things Cubans can use in their everyday lives—fruits and vegetables, shoes, books. A few doors down, a queue of Cubans line up outside a building that looks similar to a convenience store, dogs hanging around here, too.

"They're getting their food rations," Luis answers when I ask about the line. "On average, your ration book entitles you to rice, sugar, cooking oil, eggs, pasta, and coffee every month. Protein— typically chicken—every ten days. A bread roll every day. Every few months you get salt. Young children and pregnant women receive milk.

"It's never enough," he adds, his voice low once again. "They run out all the time—milk? Forget it. You have to go all over town, standing in lines to get all your rations. It's a job in and of itself. Literally."

I am filled with the deepest amount of shame as I think of all the food I've taken for granted throughout my life, the Michelin-starred restaurants where I've dined.

"Some of the wealthier families hire someone to get their rations for them," Luis explains. "And you used to not be able to buy certain items unless you had the tourists' currency."

"The Cuban convertible peso."

He nods. "See why the *paladares* and businesses like the *casas particulares* where people transform their homes into hotels are so important? Things are slowly changing, and previously banned items are now available to Cubans who pay in regular pesos, but they're so expensive hardly anyone can afford them. While our guests in the *paladar* dine on *ropa vieja*, many Cubans have never even tasted beef. Supply is an issue considering we import the vast majority of our food."

"So where do people go to get the food they need when the government stores aren't enough?"

"The black market."

"What's the penalty if you're caught?"

"It depends on the scale of involvement in the black market, but it's not unheard of for people to be sentenced to more than fifteen years in prison. You can serve a greater sentence for killing a cow than a person in Cuba."

"Jesus."

"—hasn't been to Cuba in a very long time," Luis replies.

Silence falls between us.

I'm at a loss for words. The life he describes is a far cry from mine, and I feel awkward around him, as though the things I could contribute to the conversation are frivolous and shallow in comparison.

I spent so much time listening to my family's stories about the revolution, and yet, I failed to consider how bad things were for those who remained. My family focused on the revolution and its effect on them, but less attention was paid to the current state of things.

Food rations and fear make up Luis's Cuba, and my version of it is something else entirely, one that slips through my grasp more and more with each step I take down the Havana streets. I came here hoping to understand more about where I came from, but now I feel more lost than ever.

We walk toward a section Luis tells me is called La Rampa. Crowds of people stand around with their phones out, their gazes riveted by the mobile devices.

"Wi-Fi zone," Luis explains. "One of a few in the city."

We pass a cinema and what used to be known as the Havana Hilton, Fidel Castro's onetime headquarters and home.

"You get more of a feel for how everyday Cubans live here," Luis says. "Old Havana is great, but it caters to tourists. There's a different ambiance here."

Across the street he points out Coppelia—the ice cream shop Fidel made famous after the revolution.

"It's always busy," he answers when I comment on the size of the line. "Cubans do lines better than anyone. Lines for bread, lines for beans . . ." There's good-natured humor in his voice; I guess if you can't laugh about it then you just might cry.

"You probably don't do much waiting," he adds, and I can't tell if he's speaking generally about life or my family specifically.

Either way, he isn't wrong. Our fortunes haven't changed much since we left Cuba. Castro temporarily derailed them, but it wasn't long before my great-grandfather had rebuilt his empire.

What would our life have been like if we'd stayed? Would I be here on the sidewalk, standing in line for food? Was staying even an option considering Castro's regime targeted my family?

"Do you ever wonder what things would have been like if your family had left?" I ask Luis.

"When I was younger, I thought about it more than I do now. What's the point? I wouldn't be the person I am if I didn't grow up here, in this time, in this place."

Even though we share the same heritage, as hard as I search for commonalities between us, as much as I want to belong here, the differences are glaring.

I am Cuban, and yet, I am not. I don't know where I fit here, in the land of my grandparents, attempting to recreate a Cuba that no longer exists in reality.

Perhaps we're the dreamers in all of this. The hopeful ones. Dreaming of a Cuba we cannot see with our eyes, that we cannot touch, whose taste lingers on our palates, with the tang of memory.

The exiles are the historians, the memory keepers of a lost Cuba, one that's nearly forgotten.

chapter eleven

The day winds down with too much speed, the air turning cooler, the sun sinking lower and lower in the sky. I'm eager to return to the house and ask Ana the questions that have been running through my mind, but I'm also reluctant for the day to end. Luis is good company, and if I'm not mistaken, he's enjoying himself, too. With each hour that passes, he seems more relaxed, his tongue loosening as he teaches me about Cuba.

And then there's the part we don't speak of—the manner in which our bodies shift with each second, the physical distance between us lessening with each breath. Awareness sparks within me, an electric, tingling feeling of anticipation and longing—that infinitesimal pause before lips touch for the first time, the beat when fingers link, the instant when you're unwrapping a present and realize it is exactly what you wanted.

Married, Marisol. He's married.

We drive down a street in Vedado, the old buildings surrounding us capped in the sky's golden rays.

"Why don't we make one more stop?" Luis suggests. "You can't miss the sunset over the Malecón."

That sounds . . . romantic.

"It's getting late," I answer.

And I'm enjoying myself far more than I should. I'm ashamed of my reaction to him, the ease with which I've allowed myself to be distracted from my purpose here—finding my grandmother's final resting place. I want to talk to Ana, to learn more about my grandmother's mysterious love. And at the same time—

I don't want this day to end.

I've avoided the topic of his wife all afternoon, and he hasn't brought her up, either, but she exists between us regardless, her body taking up space on the car's bench seat—the disappearing inches between his hand and my leg, his shoulder and mine, the gap between the whisper of my dress floating in the breeze and the clothes that drape his tanned limbs.

I slide my palms down the fabric of my dress, attempting to release some of the nervous energy that runs from my wrist to fingertip. The water peeks out between buildings, the sky already in transition, and I want to sit on the mighty seawall and get the full effect.

"Are you sure?" he asks. "We could swing by for a minute. It's not something you want to miss."

I hesitate, torn between the need to play it safe and the desire to indulge. Just for a moment. There's a boundary between us I absolutely will not cross, no matter what. So what's the harm?

"Maybe just a minute."

Luis nods as though either answer I could have given him would have been satisfactory, but I don't miss the smile tugging at the corner of his mouth, or the warmth that enters his eyes. My stomach clenches.

He finds a spot to park the car, coming around the side and opening the door for me.

The city vibrates with energy now that the temperature has cooled, people hanging out their windows, lounging on balconies and stoops, calling to one another with good-natured teasing. It's raucous and beautiful, and more than anything, I want to belong here, want this city to become a part of me.

It takes us a while to cross the street. Luis gestures at drivers, tugging me along as we maneuver through the lanes. He stops when a car comes too close, his body between me and the vehicle, shielding me from the oncoming traffic. The vintage cars drive past, the smell of diesel pungent, the roar of their engines in my ears. In this snapshot of Cuba, I see it through my grandmother's eyes, as she remembered it.

At night, the Malecón comes alive.

But there are cracks in the image, and not just the ones on the path beneath our feet, the gaps freckling the surface. It's easy to spot the tourists; the locals approach them selling cigars, scantily clad women offering something more. It's a stark reminder that this isn't the country my grandmother remembered, that underneath the historic beauty there's a sense of desperation.

No one approaches us; perhaps they identify Luis as one of their own. This piece of Havana isn't for the tourists; rather, we're allowed to share their part of the city however briefly.

This is the beating heart of Havana.

Teenagers congregate, laughing and joking around; young couples stroll hand in hand, their walk punctuated by the occasional kiss. Ice cream vendors pepper the landscape. Farther afield, people fish off the seawall. One day will they tear down the beautiful old buildings and replace them with high-rise condos that sell for hundreds of dollars a square foot, touting this unparalleled view of the Caribbean?

We walk down the promenade, our shoulders almost touching. Luis adjusts his stride for the difference in our height. I barely reach his chin.

"Do you think it will change in the future?" I ask him. "If money begins pouring in and the tourists come?"

"Perhaps? We've learned not to look toward the future too much. It's hard to get excited about building things when someone comes behind you and knocks them down again."

"That sounds frustrating," I say, knowing my words aren't enough.

He laughs, the sound devoid of humor. "To say the least."

"How long has the Malecón been part of Havana?" I ask, changing tack.

"They began construction in 1901."

I can easily see Luis standing before a classroom of students as he gives me a rundown on the site's history, can equally imagine his students hanging on his every word. I pull out my notebook and write down a few of the facts he shares with me. Once he's finished speaking, he gestures toward an open space. "Do you want to sit for a moment?"

I nod, following him to the edge. He offers me his hand and I take it, my fingers curling around his as I sit down on the seawall, my legs hanging over the ocean.

He releases me and lowers himself next to me.

"During the day, it's hot," Luis says. "You still see people here, but it changes at night. The temperature cools, the sun recedes. It becomes—"

"Magic," I finish for him, embarrassed by the emotion in my voice. This is the Cuba my grandmother described to me.

"Yes."

A man strums a guitar in the background. Luis's hand is on the stone inches away, his naked fingers long and tapered, his nails neatly trimmed, his skin a few shades darker than mine.

Those inches feel like a mile—or ninety.

His head is bent, his gaze not on the sunset, on those beautiful colors, but on our hands and the distance between them.

My fingers itch to move forward; my palm is rooted to the stone.

"Is there anyone waiting for you back in the United States?" he asks, his voice low.

My heart skips and sputters in my chest.

It takes a moment for me to speak, and when I do, the word is little more than a whisper, drowned out by the crash of sea against rock, a group of musicians playing several yards away, cars whizzing past us.

But I know he hears me.

His hand moves.

An inch. Two.

His pinkie rests against mine, his finger grazing mine. It stays there, his response to my answer—

"No."

We don't speak the rest of the evening, from the time we depart the Malecón to the moment Luis leaves me in the entryway of his family's house with a nod, taking the stairs two at a time before he disappears entirely.

I stare after him—is he going to see his wife?—more than a little ashamed by my behavior this afternoon. Nothing happened, but the desire was there, simmering below the surface. There will be no more tours of Havana with Luis.

I walk up the stairs and into the guest room, setting my bag on the bed and removing the container with my grandmother's ashes. I place the makeshift urn on the desk before heading off in search of Ana. I find her in a tiny room off the kitchen area, seated on a couch in what was once probably a small salon in their grand home and now serves as their only living area. The silk furnishing is faded and worn, the fabric sagging and stretched thin in places, but it's obvious it used to be a beautiful piece.

Ana smiles as I walk into the room, gesturing to the empty chair across from her.

"You've returned. Did Luis show you Havana? Did you have a good time? I'm sorry I wasn't able to go with you, but today is my day for the market, and honestly, the girls never get the good vegetables," she says with a smile.

I assume "the girls" are Luis's mother and his wife.

"Tonight we have *ropa vieja*," she adds.

The mention of the dish reminds me of Luis's discussion earlier about the rationing system in Cuba and the challenges most Cubans face. The meal, which translates to "old clothes," is one of my favorites—shredded beef seasoned with peppers and garlic in a stew-like creation that's served over rice.

"It was wonderful to see the city," I say, rattling off the list of places we went, wondering if my face is as flushed as I feel.

Ana pours me a *cafecito* from a set on the tray in front of us. She takes a sip of the coffee, and I follow her lead.

"I'm so glad you enjoyed yourself. Now, you aren't here to talk about Havana, are you? You opened the box."

I nod.

"You have questions."

"Yes. Did you know my grandmother was involved with a man here in Cuba? His letters to her were in the box she buried in her backyard. I think he was a revolutionary. Did you know about him?"

"I didn't know him. Elisa and I were best friends. We told each other everything. But with him, it was different; she talked about him a bit—not by name, but the occasional allusion." She sighs. "Those were dangerous times. Batista's punishments were merciless. She likely kept her young man a secret to protect both him and the people she loved. I knew she was in trouble, though. And I knew she was in pain." Ana takes another sip of her coffee. "What do you want to know?"

"Everything. What was his name? What happened between them? Was he really involved with Castro? Is he still here in Cuba?"

"I'll tell you what I know, because she wanted you to have the box, the letters. She wanted you to know this part of her life."

"Then why didn't she just tell me? I don't understand why she never mentioned him in all of the stories she told me about Cuba."

"Perhaps it hurt her to talk about him. And there was probably shame, too. Those were polarizing times for the Cuban people; families were torn apart by political disagreements—including Elisa's."

"My great-uncle was disowned for opposing Batista, wasn't he?"

Even now, my great-uncle is a sore spot for my family.

"He was. Your great-grandfather was one of Batista's biggest backers—whether out of expediency or true fervor, I do not know. I was too young to worry about those things. But much of the country did not share those views. There were real problems in Cuba before the revolution. There was no justice, no chance of democracy. Those of us who lived behind the gates of the grand estates in Miramar knew little of suffering. We were surrounded by people who looked like us, who had access to education, who possessed wealth. Our lives were parties and decadence, the violence somewhere in the background. But for many Cubans, those were horrible times.

"A movement began within the country. It started, strangely enough, among children of the elites. Don't forget, Fidel himself was the son of a wealthy farmer. The very people who enjoyed Batista's largesse discovered their children sympathized with the revolutionaries. Their sons fought for democracy and change, and were willing to spill Cuban blood to achieve it. It would be easy to say that the revolution divided us along the lines of poor and wealthy, but it's not that simple.

"It's not shocking to me that Elisa fell in love with such a man, but Emilio Perez would never have accepted his daughter with a revolutionary. And it would have killed your great-grandmother. She was descended from Spanish royalty, and she expected her daughters to conduct themselves accordingly."

"And my grandmother never told you his name?"

"No. He was from Havana, but I'm not sure what part of the city."

"Was he her age?"

He sounded older from the tone of his letters—more worldly, certainly.

"A bit older, I think. Most of the men involved with Fidel's movement were in their twenties or early thirties. Boys, really."

"What else did she tell you about him?"

"One day, we were supposed to have lunch and go shopping at El Encanto. This was a couple months before everything fell apart. Late October or early November. I went to the house to see Elisa . . ."

chapter twelve

Elisa

NOVEMBER 1958

This time he's gone for longer than ever before, and the letters arrive sporadically, delivered through subterfuge and random messengers in his absence, read in the privacy of my room when I can sneak away from everyone and escape into his words.

The fighting is intensifying; the tide is turning, Batista is on the defense, his forces and resolve weakening. Hopefully, this will be over soon and he will be gone; hopefully, I will be back in Havana and we will be together again.

I write him nearly every day, my letters tame compared to the stories he tells me, of sleeping beneath the stars, existing on meager rations. He gives me enough detail that I feel as though I am there with him. There's poetry in his letters, in the manner in which he describes his actions, his fidelity to Cuba, and in his words for me.

I think of you often. I try to imagine you going through your day, laughing with your sisters. I use my imagination to paint a picture of your life. It keeps me company when we're marching, waiting for things to happen. I never realized war would be so much waiting.

I imagine what our future will look like, where we will live, how we will live together. Attempt to envision what my life will look like when we defeat Batista. I think I would like to go back to practicing law, perhaps become a judge one day. I can no longer fathom a future without you.

I write back to him, the act of committing my pen to paper giving me courage to share all that is in my heart.

I want a future with you, too.

I scour my father's library for José Martí's writing, for the men Pablo admires—Locke, Montesquieu, Rousseau; the books are faithful companions as I wait for him. The days between his letters turn into a week, two, and pass by as I spend time with my sisters, shopping with Ana. Alejandro is gone as well, and I can't help but fear that unseen forces are operating within the country, weaving disorder, and two men I care about—deeply—are involved.

The presidential election is held on November 1, and Batista's candidate for president, Agüero, wins under mysterious circumstances. Murmurs ripple through the country—suggesting Batista rigged the vote in his favor. We waited and waited for elections, years, years of promises, years of hope for democracy, years of Batista, and it was all a foregone conclusion. Agüero will be Batista's puppet.

The hope many held in their hearts is now reduced to tatters. After nearly a decade of Batista, we are now to have more of his rule in one form or another. We are fractured between those who are ambivalent to this outcome and those who mourn it. No one seems genuinely happy about Batista—he is not a man who garners great loyalty except perhaps within his most inner circle—but there is a sort of muted relief that envelops my parents.

Our house has become an uncomfortable place, everyone walking on eggshells. The servants smile, but there's an edge to it now, a simmering anger lingering behind the flash of white teeth. Our nanny, Magda, is a buffer between the family and the rest of the staff, both parent by love and employee in our parents' eyes. She's the glue that keeps us together now that the family feels more fractured than ever—Isabel is consumed with Alberto, each day pulling further and further away; Maria is occupied with her games and toys, cocooned in an imaginary world where Cuba isn't cannibalizing itself; and Beatriz and Alejandro—

They always had secrets as twins, but now I fear those secrets run far deeper and more insidious. I've already lost one sibling to this madness; how can I lose another?

Magda walks beside me and Ana as we drift through the store, our gazes lingering on the glittering jewelry ensconced behind glass cases. It seems incredibly indulgent to go shopping in times like these, but without these amusements to pass the time, the days grow stagnant, the waiting and wondering and tension unbearable.

"What do you think about this necklace?" Ana asks, pointing out a pretty set of pearls on display.

"More your style than mine, but pretty. They'd look nice with your new yellow dress."

She smiles. "They would, wouldn't they?" She lingers over them while Magda and I drift to the next set of cases, the next display of exquisite jewelry.

"I wish Beatriz would have come with us," Magda whispers to me.

"Me, too."

"What did she say when you invited her?" Magda asks.

"That she already had plans."

I didn't ask what they were; at the moment, it hardly seems in my best interest to inquire considering how much we've all been sneaking about lately.

"Plans." Magda's expression is grim. "She needs to spend less time up to no good and more time trying to find a husband."

I can't help but grin. "You sound like my mother."

Magda and my mother are strange allies in the house. Their attitude toward me and my sisters might be different, but they work in concert, Magda a gentler, more affectionate version of our mother.

"Your mother knows what she's about. And for as smart as she is, Beatriz can be incredibly foolish."

"Headstrong," I say, feeling the need to defend my sister.

Her expression softens. "Yes. Headstrong. And a bit stubborn, too."

My lips twitch. Beatriz is undeniably stubborn.

I reach out and squeeze Magda's hand, the familiarity of her touch a comfort in these tumultuous times.

Ana joins us, and all talk of Beatriz ceases; Magda, too, shares our mother's devotion to protecting the integrity of the Perez name.

I wander off, half-heartedly looking at jewelry while Ana buys the pearls.

"Elisa."

I turn at the sound of my name, at the faint pressure against my elbow.

My brother is suddenly in front of me, and for a moment, seeing him here in a store we accompanied our mother to when we were younger, it feels as though we have both gone back in time to when things were simpler and we weren't divided by ideology and war.

Alejandro looks better than he did outside our home the day he saw me with Pablo, but he's still unkempt, his appearance so different from the urbane brother I remember.

"What are you doing here? How did you find me?" I whisper, my gaze darting around the store. Magda and Ana are thankfully preoccupied with the pearl purchase.

His expression is grim. "I was waiting for you outside the house. I saw you leave with Magda and followed you. I need to talk to you."

He pulls me into a corner so Magda and Ana can't see us. "I

heard a rumor the other day; they say Batista has arrested some rebels. Fidel's men."

My heart turns over in my chest. "No."

Not Pablo.

"He's alive. They're holding him in Havana. In La Cabaña."

My legs tremble. Batista's prison is notorious.

"They say he's being questioned on Fidel's movements." Alejandro's voice lowers. "Did you know he was Fidel's eyes and ears in the city?"

I suspected. That Pablo is on Batista's radar is a death sentence.

Despite the ideological differences between us, Alejandro's still my big brother, and in this I can't help but search for reassurance.

"What will happen to him?" I ask.

Alejandro's silence is answer enough, even if it's not the one I wanted.

"They'll kill him, won't they?"

He nods.

That's the thing about families. They always tell you the truth, even when you'd almost prefer the lie.

"What can I do?" I ask.

I'm not sure how much more helplessness I can stand.

Alejandro's gaze narrows. "Do you care about him?"

The words are clogged in my throat behind a morass of fear and guilt. "I do."

"Then there's one person who might be able to help."

If helplessness is my Scylla, then the solution is most definitely Charybdis.

I hover on the threshold to my father's study. I've never done this before, never used my family's influence in such a blatant, flagrant attempt to secure what I want. I've been in a daze since my brother came to see me, panic flooding my veins. My father is seated behind his enormous desk, papers spread before him. I wince at the sight of the newspaper shoved into a corner. Has he already read about the arrests? How will I convince him to throw his weight behind freeing Pablo?

He looks up from his desk, and his eyes widen in surprise. This study is my father's domain, and we tiptoe around it, reluctant to bother him when he's working, when it's clear he has little time for our frivolities.

Let him think this is a whim, nothing more. Don't let him see my heart is breaking.

"Elisa, what can I do for you?"

"I have a favor to ask," I answer, nausea rolling around in my stomach.

A brief look of annoyance crosses his face, but he waves me in. "Come in."

I close the door behind me, crossing the Persian rug, and take a seat in one of the antique chairs opposite his desk. The corsair, captured in yet another painting, stares down at me from his place of prominence behind my father. This iteration of him is more dour than the one in the upstairs hallway. They say the corsair was once threatened with the gallows; perhaps this portrait was captured around that time. I now have an uncomfortable familiarity with men who look as though they are on the precipice of hanging by one means or another.

My father leans back in his chair, studying me over his black-rimmed reading glasses. "What do you need?"

My father is an imposing man in both his public and private life. He's never been cruel, but he's not the sort of man who invites confidences. Still, I've always believed him to be fair. He must know Batista's actions are wrong. I've never viewed him as a blind supporter, but rather as a man willing to do anything to survive, a father and husband willing to sacrifice his integrity to protect his family. I take a deep breath. "I have a friend. He's in La Cabaña. Can you secure his release?"

I have the novel experience of seeing true shock on my father's face. He gapes at me, his mouth hanging open like a fish. If I could have avoided this, if there were anyone else I could ask, I would have, but my brother is right, in this I need someone with the kind of power our father wields.

"What did you just say?" he asks, a knifelike edge to his voice.

There is a delicate balance to this, the art of giving away enough to convince him to intervene, but not so much that he will lock me away in a convent somewhere. "My friend is being held in the city. No trial, no charges." It's a struggle, but I fight to keep any emotion from my voice, to stick to a dry recitation of the facts. My father will not be swayed by sentiment, and in this case, I fear any affection I show for Pablo will condemn him rather than save him. "He's innocent," I add hastily.

The lie slips out with far too much ease.

Forgive me, Father, for I have sinned.

"He's a lawyer, a good man. From a good family." I swallow. "Please."

My father blinks, momentarily in a stupor. "You want me to do what?"

"They will kill him. They're probably already torturing him. I thought perhaps—" A tremor racks my body. "I thought you could use some of your connections to see if he could be released."

"How can you ask me this?" my father sputters.

I reach now for some thread of courage I didn't know I possessed, the same courage I admire in those around me—my brother, Pablo, Beatriz.

"Because it's the right thing to do. Because he's a good man who has been put in an untenable position. He hasn't done anything wrong. You know what's happening in Cuba, how paranoid Batista is. You raised us to know right from wrong. What Batista is doing is wrong."

"Not you, too." A wealth of sorrow fills my father's voice.

My breath hitches.

He's silent for far too long. When he does finally speak, I am surprised by the fear flickering in his eyes, stamped all over his face. We never talk of Alejandro, but now I see a glimpse of the weight of my father's loss.

My parents have always loomed larger than life—my mother so glamorous and elegant, my father exuding power and authority. He looks smaller sitting behind his desk, as though recent events have overwhelmed and diminished him. It is a terrifying thing to see fear in your parents' eyes.

"What is your role in this, Elisa? Are you involved with the rebels? Is this your brother's doing?" He whispers the question as though the walls have ears. Perhaps they do these days in Havana.

"No. Not at all." I force a smile, praying he believes me. "He's just a friend. Really more of a friend of a friend. Nothing more. I have nothing to do with the rebels."

"Is this some boyfriend of yours?" His face reddens, his expression turning thunderous.

"No, r-really, just a friend. Someone who was caught up in something." My voice shakes as I tell my father his name, as I shatter the secret I've kept for so long. "He has friends from the university, and their activities have drawn Batista's notice. He hasn't done anything wrong."

My father studies me quietly, and when I think all hope is lost, he sighs. "You need to be careful. I am not oblivious to the goings-on in this house—your sister's relationship with that boy Alberto, or Beatriz—" His voice trails off. "Batista is under a great deal of pressure right now. He had hoped the election would satisfy the people, but it has not."

"Because the people know it was little more than a sham," I mutter.

My father's gaze sharpens, his hand hitting the desk with a loud rap. "Do not think that because we live like this, you are exempt from Batista's gaze. You are correct. He is afraid, and a man who fears his people is a dangerous one indeed."

"How can you—"

"Support him? Please. Spare me the youthful condemnation. How do you think I keep this family safe? Do not come for my help and then cast stones at me for the manner in which I am able to deliver it. The rebels abhor abuses of power, but do not presume that they wouldn't do the exact same thing as Batista if given the chance."

He removes his glasses, rubbing his face, his shoulders hunched over, as though he is tired of this conversation, tired of Batista and Cuban politics.

"I will make a few calls," he says after a pause, "but I cannot offer any promises. If I do this, though, you will make me one—whatever exists between you and this boy, you will stop it. Immediately. I have a duty to protect your mother, your sisters, and I will not shield you if your actions endanger this family. You will not see this boy again. You will not do anything to bring us shame, to attract Batista's ire— am I understood? If you do, you will no longer be my daughter."

I clear my throat, pushing past the unshed tears, the fear, the panic, the shame.

"Yes, sir."

I'm dismissed with a curt nod and a clipped, "You may go now."

My legs shake, a prayer running through my mind as I walk to the door.

Please save him.

chapter thirteen

Marisol

Ana pours us each another cup of coffee once she's finished her story; between the espresso and the secrets, I doubt I'll sleep much tonight. I had hoped Ana would have the answers I sought, but it seems like my grandmother kept her lover a secret even from her closest friend. All I know is that my grandmother loved a revolutionary, that they were separated when Batista threw him in prison. Was he ever released?

"I'm sorry I don't know what happened to him," Ana says. "Elisa told me he was a friend who had gotten into trouble, nothing more. When I asked her about it weeks later, she changed the subject. Your great-aunts may be able to fill in the rest of it."

If they do know more about my grandmother's past, I'm surprised they haven't shared it by now.

"There is someone else who might be able to help," Ana adds.

"Who?"

"Your grandmother's nanny."

"Magda?"

My grandmother and great-aunts spoke of her fondly, but given the age difference between them I never considered the possibility that she would still be alive and in Havana.

"Yes. She's ninety-four now, but her memory is still quite good. She lives in Santa Clara with her niece."

Excitement fills me. "How far is that?"

"By car? A few hours or so depending on the conditions. Luis could take you on one of his days off, if you'd like."

"Are you able to reach her?" I ask, momentarily sidestepping the issue of spending even more time alone with her grandson. Her *married* grandson.

"It's still early—I can call her tonight. We haven't spoken lately, but I make a point of checking in with her every so often. I can see if she'll meet with you before you leave; I'm sure she will. Your grandmother and great-aunts were like daughters to her. Especially Elisa."

The impression Beatriz and Maria gave me when I discussed this trip with them was that they'd lost touch over time, but hopefully Magda can fill in some of the blanks of what my grandmother was like as a child.

"Thank you. I really appreciate all you've done to help me."

"Of course. Elisa would have done the same for me. Any of your great-aunts would have."

The loyalty in her voice is so absolute, so indelible, that I'm taken aback by its intensity, surprised their friendship withstood a separation of nearly sixty years. Does she ever feel as though they left her behind? Does she envy the freedom they found on the other side of the sea?

Ana Rodriguez operates in both spheres—the before and the after—and while I struggle to understand this new iteration of Cuba, there are similarities between it and the one that developed ninety miles away. The same inherent sense of pride, the determination to be successful, the hard work, the entrepreneurial spirit and ingenuity, the pragmatism.

"Has it been hard?" I ask. "Seeing the changes in Cuba?"

I'm eager for this piece of Cuba she gives me. I grew up on the stories of those who left, of exile, of loss, and yet, I never understood it from the other perspective—those who were left behind, who chose to remain, whose lives were shaped by the whims and policies of governments, by ideology.

"Yes." She sighs, taking a sip of her *cafecito*. "The story of Cuba is one of struggles and strife. When we were girls, we were kept from most of it, but the edges seeped through, crawling over the gates. Batista was a harsh president. He loved sugar, loved the money that flowed into the country from overseas, but he didn't love the Cuban people. He wanted to be king over a people who didn't want to be ruled."

"And yet—"

She gives me a sad smile. "Ah yes. But we didn't know then, you see. We had hope. So much hope. Remember, Fidel did not start out as a communist, merely an agent for change, one we desperately needed. He was going to bring freedom to Cuba. Democracy. Elections. He was going to be our future. He promised us a revolution, and he delivered it."

"But at what cost?" I ask.

"Terrible things rarely happen all at once," she answers. "They're incremental, so people don't realize how bad things have gotten until it's too late. He swore up and down that he wasn't a communist. That he wanted democracy. Some believed him. Others didn't."

"Did you—"

"Believe? Support Fidel then?"

I nod.

"No. But what did I know or care about politics? I lived in a world of balls and parties, days at the club, lounging by the pool with friends, shopping for hats and dresses. Batista, Fidel, it was all the same to me. Or so I thought.

"When Batista fled the country, I began to care. Before then, the revolution was contained to whispers between my parents. And then the whispers spread to our dining room table."

"Did your parents consider leaving?"

"They did and dismissed it. They were convinced Cubans would come to their senses and Fidel would fall. 'It's only a matter of time,' my father would say."

Ana's gaze drifts to the room that has clearly fallen on hard times, the lingering trace of its former grandeur a stark reminder of all her family has lost.

"No one realized how far this would go. We thought Batista was the worst we would experience, but when Fidel nationalized our rum business, things began to change." She takes another sip of her coffee, her gaze on some memory I cannot see. "They came to our home one day with a letter saying the company was now the property of the Cuban government. Just like that. A hundred years of labor, of dreams, our legacy erased with one piece of paper."

"I'm so sorry."

I'm not even sure why I'm apologizing or what I'm apologizing for other than the fact that the Perezes have managed to keep their family legacy mostly intact—or at least create a new one—whereas she has lost hers.

"It's been a long time now," Ana replies. "There was nothing we could do. My parents left Cuba six months later. I never saw them again. We kept in touch over the years as best we could, but it wasn't the same."

Even though it was a common occurrence following the revolution, it's difficult to imagine a family being ripped apart in such a manner. There are no Perezes remaining in Cuba; we all made the crossing to the United States, claiming Miami and Palm Beach as our own as we embraced polo and dresses with colorful prints.

"If you don't mind me asking—"

"Why did I stay?"

I nod.

"Life, I suppose. In the beginning, the plan was for us to reunite in the United States. But my husband didn't want to leave. He was a photographer, and he took many pictures of Fidel and others. It was an opportunity for him to see the revolution up close, to glimpse the men who loomed so large above all of us in their natural habitat. As an artist, it was a powerful lure."

She takes another sip of her coffee.

"I was young. I didn't understand the urgency, the consequences of my decision to stay. I didn't want to leave him. I became pregnant with Luis's father, and we had a baby and started building a life here, putting down roots in a fragile earth.

"The thing with loss is that at first, you don't notice. You lose your favorite pair of shoes, but there is still another, and the baby needs to be fed, and your husband had a long day at work, so why worry? And when you lose the next pair of shoes, well, you've already lost one pair so the novelty has worn off. You're upset for a moment because now you've lost two pairs, but dinner needs to be made, and when you took your ration card to get food, they were out of milk and chicken again, and who has time to worry about shoes? And this goes on for a time until you realize you're down to your last pair and they have holes in them, the dirt from the streets covering your skin, the soles falling apart, your toes pinched, and when you're finally able to replace them, there's an overwhelming sense of relief, and you forget you once had twenty pairs, that once you lived like kings, and now you serve on bended knee, fighting for every inch.

"It's poetic justice, of course. We had everything when much of Cuba had nothing. Fidel took everything away so now we all have nothing. We are all equal, you see."

"Except for Fidel, who lived like a king," Luis interjects, sliding into the empty seat next to me without acknowledging my presence. "And so many of his top officials who continue to do so."

How long has he been standing there?

Luis lights a cigar, the flame a bright torch that crackles the paper. A familiar scent fills the air; my father's abhorrence of Castro never extended to the expensive cigars he smuggled into the United States.

"All are equal, but some are more equal than others," I muse.

Luis inclines his head toward me. "Was that an *Animal Farm* reference?"

A hint of what might be admiration lingers in his gaze, coupled with that same indulgent amusement I've come to associate with his reactions to me.

I force a smile, attempting to keep my voice light, to not draw notice to how rattled I am by his presence, how my body shifts once he's around, my attention gravitating toward him. It seems supremely unfair that these pings of energy, these sparks flying around me, have found a target they cannot—and should not—have.

"If the hoof fits, I guess," I joke.

A voice calls out from the kitchen for Ana. She excuses herself, leaving us alone, silence filling the room, its presence fairly screaming with discomfort.

"So you read Orwell?" Luis asks after a pregnant pause.

I shrug. "I have. I'm surprised *you've* read Orwell."

"Why? Because I live in a communist paradise?" A smile plays on his lips.

Playful Luis is perhaps the most lethal version of all. I take a deep breath. "Partly. Everything we hear in the United States is centered on the scarcity of resources in Cuba, the banning of ones the government disagrees with on principle. Things are painted as austere."

"I'm sure that helps with the political rhetoric on both sides," he acknowledges. "The evils of communism and all that. And when it comes to the scarcity of resources, well, it helps the regime sell the idea that we're all equal, that your neighbor has exactly what you have even when your neighbor is a high-ranking government official driving a luxury import."

His voice builds with each word, growing from a murmur to something louder, stronger.

The confidence in his tone, the conviction, is as seductive as it is surprising.

My heart pounds. "You're angry."

There were hints of his discontent earlier, but now something has changed between us, and it feels as though the mask has fallen and he's sharing a part of himself he normally keeps hidden away.

"'Angry' is the easiest emotion," Luis replies. "You'd be surprised what people do when they're desperate, when the dream of a society that provides for its citizens isn't the reality."

"People thrive regardless of their circumstances?"

"Something like that. The irony of the revolution is that it sought to eradicate capitalism, entrepreneurship, but the revolution's greatest legacy has been the rise of a new breed of Cuban entrepreneurs. The black market thrives."

"So where does Orwell in Cuba fit in?" I ask, returning to our original point.

He smiles faintly, his previous rancor erased. "You forget, I *am* a history professor."

"A *Cuban* history professor. I thought Castro discouraged such activity—examining the *why* behind things."

"How can we study history if we only examine the events in a vacuum? Orwell's stocked in the National Library and others. Knowledge is not discouraged in Cuba, only acting upon that knowledge."

"And reading?"

"Reading is encouraged." His lips twist, that tinge of disdain back again. "Few can afford to buy books, however, so we borrow them. My students attend the university for free, which is a great thing, but they still must pay for books, supplies, transportation, food, on limited incomes. How can we afford those things when we're barely surviving as it is? When our ability to support ourselves is limited by the government? The legacy of modern Cuba is that we can enjoy things for a moment, but we cannot truly possess them. The country is not ours; it is merely on loan from Fidel."

If I thought him attractive before, this conversation, the passion that animates him now, is my undoing.

"Do all Cubans think like this, speak like this?" It surprises me to hear the same thoughts fall from his lips echoed by the exiles hanging around Versailles in Miami, sipping espresso and eating *pastelitos* while calling for change in Cuba.

"Some do. Not enough." His voice lowers. "Those of us who want more speak in whispers."

Luis takes a deep breath, leaning forward. His scent fills my nostrils, and once again, we're sharing confidences. A line of goose bumps rises over my skin. I glance away from his dark flashing eyes, his full mouth, simultaneously craving his words and wishing I could build an impenetrable wall between us.

"Existing in a constant state of uncertainty is hell," Luis says. "This restaurant is the difference between putting meals on the table and the days when we went hungry. But how long will it last? The government controls everything."

A curse falls from his beautiful mouth.

"This country. It has so much potential. So much possibility.

But it breaks your heart every single time you dare hope for more. Fidel's great revolution was supposed to bring us equality. Yet so many of the problems that existed before him still do."

"What would you wish it to be?" I ask, meeting his gaze, unable to look away. Have I ever met a man like him?

No.

"Free. Democratic." He lifts the cigar to his mouth, inhaling in one deep breath. He exhales a cloud of smoke. "I would like to shout. The freedom to protest when I do not agree with what my government is doing without fear of retribution. The freedom to listen to music without the fear that the regime will accuse me of being too 'Western' and throw me in jail. I don't want to spend my days looking over my shoulder, wondering if my neighbor is really a member of the secret police, that one of the students in my classroom isn't there solely for the purpose of spying on me for the government, that I won't accidentally say something that could result in me being thrown in jail or worse."

A chill slides down my spine. This is the Cuba my great-aunts warned me about.

"I want to own something of my own," Luis continues. "Something the government can't take from me, something that is mine. If we left, the government would come into our house and inventory every single possession to make sure we didn't take any of it with us. We don't own the furniture, the pieces that have been in our family for generations. The framed photographs on the wall taken by my grandfather. None of it is ours."

The urge to take his hand, to offer comfort, is so strong I reach out before I catch myself. I snatch my hand back, my fingers curling into a fist in my lap. This connection between us—I can't be imagining it—he must feel it, too.

Married. He's married, Marisol.

"I want to be my own person." His words wrap around my heart.

"Not another number in the eyes of the government. Another food ration, another worker, another Cuban who isn't free in his own country."

My heart breaks for him even as I reach for hope in a place where that particular emotion seems perversely futile.

"We survive by not calling attention to ourselves, by being good little soldiers. I am tired of putting on the uniform, pretending I'm someone I'm not, unable to think for myself, burying these thoughts so they don't get me or my family killed. I'm thirty-six years old, and each day the fight filters from my body, the effort to exert myself, to get through a day and meet my basic needs, to care for my grandmother, for my family, to put food on the table, robbing me of much else. They ensure we're so preoccupied with the daily struggle that there's little left over for the most important one, for taking control of our future."

"Do you think things will improve now that diplomatic relations have increased?"

"I hope so. But what change? Will we go from this to serving even more tourists and courting cruise ships? That was the Cuba of Batista's time, when the American mob ran Havana with their hotels and casinos. When Hollywood used this as their playground. Is there no chance for Cuba to be something more? Something greater?"

The light casts a shadow across his face, the bruise there. Luis rubs his jaw, his gaze downcast.

"There are restaurants in Havana my grandmother frequented with her family when she was a little girl. Now only tourists can afford to eat there. We're guests in our own country. Second-rate citizens because we had the misfortune to be born Cuban."

He raises his head to meet my gaze, his eyes defiant. We do not wear humility well.

"Would increased tourism be better, though? Than this?"

"I don't know," he answers, his voice weary. "It's a cruel twist of fate that we've suffered through all we have to merely end up where we started, and in my family's case with far less.

"It's hard to hope," he continues. "We've known worse times, of course. It was hell when we lost the support of the Soviet Union."

The not-so-Special Period.

"Would you ever leave?"

"This is my home; it's all I've ever known. And at the same time, it's hard. There comes a point when you have to decide if it's worth it, if the abuses are enough to make you want to leave, if they outweigh those few moments when you know true pleasure."

It's the word "pleasure" that does it—

It's late and I should go to bed. I shouldn't have hushed conversations with a married man in the near-darkness.

I set my glass on the table, rising—

"Cristina never understood why I couldn't be happy here. Why it wasn't enough. It was what ended our marriage."

I sit back down. "You're separated?"

"Divorced."

"Recently?"

"It depends on your definition of 'recent,' I suppose. It's been two years."

"But she said she was your wife," I sputter.

A short laugh escapes his beautiful mouth. "That sounds like Cristina." There's affection contained in those words, too. He takes another puff of his cigar. "She doesn't like you."

"Why?"

He doesn't speak, but then again he doesn't have to. His eyes say it all—that and the memory of his finger brushing mine earlier on the Malecón.

You know why.

"You thought I was the sort of man who would—"

He doesn't finish the thought, but then again he doesn't need to. We exist in a state of half-finished sentences, the pauses in our conversation filling the inadequacies of words.

"I didn't know."

"Now you do. I'm not."

The sort of man who would hit on women when he's married.

"I should go up to my room," I say.

I don't move.

Neither does he.

"I want to show you something. Will you come with me?" he asks. "I teach a morning class at the university tomorrow; you could attend if you'd like and see the Cuban educational experience in person. And after, I can give you a tour of the island."

"Yes."

chapter fourteen

Elisa

A day passes, then two, without any news from my father. It takes every ounce of strength to keep from asking him about Pablo, to wipe the fear from my face, to maintain the facade that all is well. I pass the days writing Pablo letters, letters I might never have the opportunity to send, letters in which I finally admit the feelings that have been building for so long.

Surely I would know if something has happened to him, if he has passed on?

I think I loved you from the first moment you told me about your passion for Cuba, your dreams for her future. I loved your conviction, your strength, the confidence with which you approached the problem, as though it was your right as a Cuban citizen to demand more, to fight for it.

I wish I had your courage, your convictions. I wish there was more of a fight inside me. I've been raised from birth to continue on, to survive in this dangerous political climate. My grandfather was killed by Machado's men—did I ever tell you that? I think it changed something in my father, in all of us.

And then there's the rest of it. As much as I am loath to admit that my gender limits me somewhat, it does. I've been thinking about what you said to me that night we met at Guillermo's party—about the changes we should demand in Cuba. Perhaps my gender shouldn't limit me.

I read the books you told me about, the ones that inspired you, immersed myself in the words of great men, and I want to believe there is more we can do, more we can expect for our future, but I am also scared. Afraid for you, afraid my family—my siblings—will be targeted by the regime because of my actions.

I wish I weren't so afraid.

Four days after I asked my father for help, he summons me to his study.

"I called in a favor. He'll be released."

My heart pounds.

"You won't see him again."

It is not a question.

I nod.

Another day passes before Pablo is released from jail, before I can see him, my promise to my father buried somewhere beneath layers of guilt. I borrow Beatriz's gleaming Mercedes and drive to Guillermo's house, to the place where we first met, and wait for Pablo, looking over my shoulder the entire time. It was my brother who told me they would be here. I'm not entirely surprised Alejandro knows Guillermo, especially considering Beatriz's interest in attending the party at his house that fateful night. When I received the sealed note from Alejandro telling me Pablo would be released this morning, there was never a question of whether or not I would come. For better or worse, I have taken a stand, not with the rebels, but with my heart. I pray it doesn't fail me now.

I wait as the car pulls into the driveway of Guillermo's house. He's in the driver's seat of the Buick, Pablo beside him, sunglasses covering his eyes, his shoulders hunched over, his face partially obscured.

My heart pounds.

Pablo steps out of the car and stops in his tracks, his hand lingering on the door. He walks toward me, a limp in his gait, a mixture of surprise and what looks to be relief in his eyes. I step into his embrace, holding him gingerly, trying to avoid the bruises, the cuts.

Dried blood mars his shirt.

What did they do to him?

A sob rises in my throat, but I push it down, wanting more than anything to be strong for Pablo.

He breathes into the curve of my neck, his lips caressing my skin, his body sagging against me. In this moment, our roles have reversed, and I am the one to provide comfort, strength. My name falls from his lips like a prayer.

I want to speak, but no words come.

Our bodies shift, our mouths finding each other. I don't even realize I'm crying until tears wet my lips.

"It's okay," Pablo whispers as he strokes my hair. I'm not sure if he says the words for me or for himself. His heart beats against mine, his body shuddering with each breath he takes. "You shouldn't have come," he says, even though he doesn't sound the least bit sorry I did.

"How could I not?"

Pablo's hold on me tightens for a moment before he releases me, as we walk inside the house, Guillermo trailing behind us. Guillermo doesn't speak, but I can feel the disapproval coming off him in waves. Once, it would have bothered me. Now I can't summon the enthusiasm to care. Guillermo gives me a cursory nod before leaving to get food for Pablo, and I follow Pablo into an empty bedroom, sitting on the edge of the bed next to him.

"Do you need anything?" I ask.

"No." His gaze meets mine, and when he speaks his voice is hoarse, as though he's worn it out from screaming. "I met your father."

A moment of silence passes between us before I can reply. "I know."

"You asked him to have me released?"

"I did."

I am unable to ignore the tiny thread of shame that connects my father to the men who did this; my father's clout is a double-edged sword—both the source of Pablo's freedom and a sign that my family is not innocent in the darker side of life in Havana, the brutalities of Batista's regime.

"How did you even know I was arrested?"

"My brother heard about it. He told me."

"And your father? What did you tell him? That you were in love with a revolutionary?"

It's the first time the word "love" has fallen from either of our lips, and hearing it spoken aloud gives it a measure of power I'm unprepared for even as the truth of it resides in my bones.

"I told him you were a friend."

"And he accepted that?"

"My father doesn't concern himself overmuch with the affairs of his daughters." I hesitate. "I promised I would never see you again."

"So this is good-bye, then?"

"No."

I'm in too deep at this point for good-byes, although at the moment, I can't imagine we're destined for anything else. He can't stay in Havana. Not after this. Should I go with him? Take my chances in the mountains? There are other women fighting there, taking up arms against Batista. I wanted more out of my life, chafed at the bonds of family and society, and still—

I'm not ready to join my brother in the ranks of the ostracized and disowned, am not prepared to pledge my allegiance to these causes vying for power around me when they leave a foul taste in my mouth.

Pablo sighs, sitting on the edge of the bed, his head in his hands. "You should go. You don't belong here."

"Of course I do."

"You can't stay. Not with me. This is only going to become more dangerous. They would have killed me, Elisa. They will kill me if they capture me again. I can't stay."

"You're going to the mountains, aren't you?"

"Where else would I go? I don't belong here in Havana."

I don't belong here with you.

"I saw how your father looked at me in that cell," Pablo continues. "We will forever be on opposite sides of this. We are at war; I cannot pretend it does not divide us. Your family will never accept me, and I fear I will never see your father and his friends as anything other than monsters."

"He secured your release."

"He did. And there were eight other men in that cell with me. Men who will face the firing squad tomorrow. Not all of them have wealthy girlfriends whose fathers can protect them."

"We don't have a chance, do we?" I ask, tears building.

"I don't know," he answers.

Pablo takes my hand, brushing his lips against my knuckles. I wrap my arm around his waist, careful to keep from hitting his bruises, my head resting against his shoulder, his heart beating beneath me. I hold on to him even as I feel him slipping away.

He was right when we first met; everything is political.

Where does that leave us?

chapter fifteen

Marisol

The morning after I learn Luis isn't married, I'm up early, dressing to meet him at the University of Havana. I barely slept the night before, the sensation that everything has shifted inescapable. The attraction I've felt for him and attempted to shove in the background of our interactions has reared its head, no longer satisfied being confined to the margins, and what was a crush entirely contained in the safety of my imagination is now a crackling tension between us filled with possibility.

I change my outfit twice before settling on a long black skirt and matching top. I grab a pair of leather sandals and my trusty cross-body bag, my grandmother's ashes a constant presence on my journey through Cuba to the point that it no longer feels unusual to carry her with me. I throw a bathing suit and a change of clothes into a larger tote bag; I don't know where Luis is taking me after his class, but he said it involves swimming.

A knock sounds at the door.

"Come in."

The door opens and Ana greets me with a smile, her eyes twinkling as she takes in my appearance.

"Luis mentioned he wouldn't be working at the restaurant tonight. I take it he's showing you more of Cuba?"

My cheeks flush and I nod. "He mentioned swimming."

Her smile deepens. "It'll be Varadero, then. He's always loved it ever since he was a child." A hint of sadness dims her smile. "He and his father used to go fishing there."

She reaches out, handing me a piece of paper. I glance at the words scrawled there—an address.

"I spoke with Magda last night," Ana says. "She can't wait to meet you."

I look up at Ana, my heart pounding. "I can't believe it. Thank you so much."

"It was nothing. My pleasure. Varadero is not that far from Santa Clara. You could go there after your trip to the beach."

"I feel bad asking Luis to go out of his way." I could probably rent a car or something. Some of the guidebooks I read prior to coming to Cuba mentioned tour buses as well.

Ana practically winks at me. "I don't think he'll mind. Besides, Luis doesn't have classes tomorrow. We can handle his shift at the restaurant."

"I guess I could ask him," I hedge, torn between my desire to meet with Magda and my guilt over asking Luis to play tour guide for another day.

"It's settled, then. Please give Magda my best. It's been far too long since we last saw each other."

I bite back a grin at the decisive way Ana handles things, as she herds me from the room. She reminds me so much of my grandmother.

We part at the bottom of the stairs, Ana heading for the kitchen and the lunch service. Luis's mom is waiting for me in the entryway, a disapproving glint in her eyes.

"Are you ready?" she asks.

I nod.

Apparently, Luis shares his car with his mom, so he asked if I minded if she drove me to the university on her way to work and left his car waiting near the campus while he took the bus this morning. What could I say? It couldn't be more obvious that his mother doesn't like me if she came out and said it herself, and un-fortunately, the ride into Vedado will likely give her plenty of time to do so.

"Thank you for giving me a ride."

She might not like me, but I can't suppress the urge to change her opinion of me, to demonstrate that I'm more than the shallow foreigner she fears will sink her claws into her son.

She shrugs me off. "Luis asked me to."

My cheeks heat as her gaze drifts to the larger bag in my hands, at the implication contained there. I open my mouth to explain that it's not what she thinks—we're going *swimming*—but she doesn't give me a chance. She turns, leaving me no choice but to follow her outside where Luis's convertible sits at the curb waiting for us.

With traffic, it takes us nearly thirty minutes to get from Mira-mar to the University of Havana, and I content myself with staring out the window, watching people pass us by. I attempt a few meager forays into conversation with Luis's mother; my efforts yield the information that her name is Caridad, the general impression that she views me as an outsider, and not much else. I can't blame her; I'd probably dislike me, too, given the disparities between our lives and the fact that my family benefitted from leaving whereas hers suffered for staying.

The question runs through my mind again—what would have happened if we'd never left? If I'd grown up here, alongside Luis? If the revolution had never come? Who would I be if you stripped away the other parts of me and just left me with the identity of being Cuban?

There's a freedom to life here—no need to check status updates, or obsess over someone's posted photos, or spend time crafting a cleverly worded line to share with hundreds of followers and friends. And at the same time, that freedom is an incredible indulgence, the abstention of a life available to me, the choice of it, whereas for the Cubans who live without the barrage of statuses about how much someone loves their spouse or that picture of a friend from grade school climbing Machu Picchu, arms flung out against the backdrop of a fortuitously setting sun, there is no choice. No freedom. Their exile from these things isn't self-imposed; it was thrust upon them by a government that has been in power their entire lives. And so, the beauty of life here—the simplicity of it—is also the tragedy of it.

Caridad drops me off outside the university, handing me the keys to the car to give to Luis as she walks to her job.

My first impression of the University of Havana is of an imposing building, beautiful in its own way. The architecture—like that of so many of the other buildings in Havana—is impressive, the landscape marred by the presence of air-conditioning units hanging outside the windows, marks on the building's exterior.

I climb the steps, staring at the looming *Alma Mater* statue. I walk through the campus, past students sitting on benches, their conversations carrying throughout the outdoor space, the atmosphere reminiscent of my own college experience, following the map Luis gave me until I find his classroom.

Here the differences are more visible—the walls are khaki colored, calling to mind military fatigues, the green chalkboard at the front of the room a far cry from the modern equipment I knew in my university days. Luis leans over a wooden desk in front of the chalkboard, the sleeves of his blue dress shirt rolled up, his long legs encased in darker blue trousers. He's obviously consumed by whatever he's reading, his head bent, his forearms braced against the wood, and I take the opportunity to sneak in the back, sliding into an empty desk chair.

One at a time students filter into the classroom, discussing their evening plans, the lesson they read. Two girls sit in the row in front of me—one of the girls is convinced her boyfriend is cheating on her, and by the details she provides, I'm inclined to agree.

Luis looks up from his desk, his gaze scanning the room—

It settles on me.

He smiles.

That spark is there again, the inevitability of it flaming before my eyes.

Luis glances away, the smile still on his lips and in his eyes as he calls the class to order. Today's lesson deals with a French blockade of Cuba in the sixteenth century, and through the passion in Luis's voice, the French corsair and the struggle of the Cuban people come to life.

The time flies as he lectures, the passion he's expressed discussing Cuba in its modern form evident in his appreciation for its earlier history as well. It's even more interesting for me considering I don't know much about Cuban history before and after the narrow window of the revolution.

There's sadness in the picture he paints of Cuba's origins—the abuse the Taíno suffered at the hands of the Europeans who took their lands, the Spaniards' cruelties. He speaks of Cuba's economy, how sugar has been both savior and damnation—bringing slaves into the country to work the plantations until Cuba followed suit with the United States and abolished slavery in the late nineteenth century.

Luis doesn't use aids when he lectures; rather, he fires questions at his students with an energy that seemingly comes more from excitement than a desire to intimidate. He isn't still when he teaches, his hands in constant motion, his body darting back and forth in front of the green chalkboard. No one watching him teach could doubt how much he loves it, or fail to appreciate his sincerity and passion for the subject. His students are rapt before him, an impressive feat if I remember my college days correctly.

The class flies by with surprising speed, and I don't realize it's over until the students begin pushing back their seats, gathering their books and bags, heading for the door. I linger in the rear of the classroom while a few students approach Luis with questions, his focus intense even in this. That's the most attractive thing about him—not the long, lean build or the mop of dark hair, the close-trimmed beard, the dark, intense eyes. It's his passion, his intellect, his conviction.

And then the students are gone, and it's just the two of us, a classroom of abandoned desks between us.

"So what did you think?" he asks once we're alone.

"You were good. Really good. Knowledgeable. Engaging. I wish I'd had more professors like you when I was in college."

There's that smile again. "They weren't 'engaging'?"

"Not really. A few were, I guess. I went to a huge public university, so my courses were really full—hundreds of students in a class. It made it tough to connect. Plus, I wasn't necessarily the most dedicated student. It took me a while to figure out what I wanted to be when I grew up," I joke.

I majored in communications because I enjoyed most of my classes and it seemed versatile considering I had no concrete plans for when I graduated. My father suggested I work for Perez Sugar handling public relations, but no matter how lucrative the offer was, I couldn't convince myself to join the family fold. I love my family, but all too often these "opportunities" come with strings I'm not ready to commit to.

Our family history includes a sense of obligation. Being a Perez in Cuba meant something once—a legacy and reputation to uphold, a responsibility to never dishonor the family name. When we lost so much in the revolution and my great-grandparents and their children came to America, that obligation continued, growing into a need to establish ourselves in a society where we weren't entirely wanted, where we had to work harder to get ahead, where we had to start over in so many ways. It's a weighty responsibility to carry your family's legacy in every step you take, every decision you make, and one I fear I haven't quite measured up to.

As a Cuban woman my family expects me to cook paella with aplomb, to dress well, marry well, entertain as though everything is effortless. As someone whose family fought to immigrate to the United States, I am supposed to succeed professionally as well, to be both successful businesswoman and elegant housewife.

My grandmother understood, at least, her sense of pride and obligation measured with a healthy dose of pragmatism and love. Was this why? Because she once dared to go against her family's wishes and follow her heart?

"And now you know?" Luis asks, his expression earnest.

I try to smile. "I wish. I'm afraid I'm still figuring it out."

I want my life to mean something, want a job that makes me feel the way he looks when he's teaching, something I'm passionate about that, when I die, leaves the world better than I found it. It's a surprisingly tall order.

"There's no shame in that," he says.

"You've found it."

Luis shrugs. "Don't let appearances fool you. I still have my doubts, still wonder if I am doing enough, if I am on the right path. My family relies on me. I don't want to disappoint them."

"I know a thing or two about family expectations." I offer a wry smile. "It's hard being the future, everyone's expectations riding on you, isn't it?"

"It is."

He reaches out, his fingers grazing my cheek, tucking a stray strand of hair behind my ear, before dropping his hand back to his side.

"So tell me the history of this place," I say, my voice shaking slightly as a tingle slides beneath my skin.

Luis crosses his arms and leans against his desk, his gaze speculative. "You want the history lesson?"

"Isn't that what I came for?"

The history lesson seems safer than anything else. I've felt the attraction between us building since I arrived, but I'm leaving soon, and as drawn to him as I am, getting involved in something that has no future is a terrible idea. And yet here I am.

"Is that what you came for?" Luis asks, his voice soft. He shakes his head at my silence, hiding the smile I hear in his voice with a duck of his head. "The university was founded in the early eighteenth century, was one of the first in the Americas. It was originally located in Old Havana before moving here in the early twentieth century. Batista closed the university in '56 because he was afraid of the radicalization coming out of it. When Fidel reopened it, the university shifted focus and underwent a reformation to be more in line with revolutionary ideology."

He almost delivers the line as though he believes in the merit of such action.

"Speaking of revolutionaries—" I take a deep breath. "Your grandmother got in touch with this woman who lives in Santa Clara. Her name is Magda, and she used to work for my family as a nanny to my grandmother and great-aunts. She might know something about my grandmother's past. Could you drive me to

Santa Clara to see her? If it's too much, I completely understand. I can rent a car or something."

The expression on his face gives me pause.

"Really, it's no trouble for me to see her on my own. I know it's a long trek."

"It's not the distance." Luis is silent for a moment. "You need to be careful, Marisol."

"Do you think it's too dangerous to visit her?"

My great-aunts' concerns come back to me, all those emails with information from the State Department filling my mind coupled with Luis's earlier warnings. Are they right? Am I underestimating the political reality in Cuba? Am I causing problems for him, for Ana? Will I draw trouble to Magda's doorstep?

"I don't know," Luis answers. "On the one hand, you're visiting an old family friend. Of course, if this man is a sensitive subject for the regime, merely searching for him could be dangerous. That's the challenge here. Sometimes you know you're agitating the regime; other times you don't realize they viewed your actions as a threat until it's too late."

"I don't want to bring trouble to any of you."

"I have a feeling taking you to visit your grandmother's former nanny is the least of my problems," he comments. "I'm more concerned about you. You're as much at risk as any of us. Your American citizenship isn't going to protect you here. The regime doesn't look kindly toward journalists."

"Even ones who write about the benefits of color-coordinating your closet?" I ask, my voice filled with exasperation.

"You have a voice and a platform. That's all it takes to terrify them."

"Would you let it all lie?" I ask.

"Me? Probably not. But that's not exactly a vote of confidence."

He rubs his cheekbone, over the bruise there. "How much does this matter to you?"

"I don't want anyone to get hurt because of me, and I don't want to end up in a Cuban prison somewhere. But it's important to me."

Luis sighs. "Then we'll go see her. I was going to take you to Varadero. Santa Clara isn't that much farther. We can go there after we go to the beach." He hesitates. "We could stay overnight somewhere to make the trip more manageable. If that's okay with you."

I take a deep breath. "That sounds perfect."

Luis takes my hand and squeezes it, our fingers threading together. He looks as conflicted as I feel even as he brings our joined hands to his lips, pressing a kiss to my knuckles.

Is this to be a fling? A few stolen moments I'll remember fondly in a month or two—a vacation romance and nothing more? I've always been more of a relationship person, and as I try to picture myself sitting at a table with my friends in Miami, sipping cocktails and telling them about Luis, the image feels wrong somehow. There is nothing in his manner, either, that suggests he's a man prone to flings, his nature more serious than careless.

And yet—

We're both too old to blindly rush into things, to not know the risks involved, how ill-suited we are on paper. Despite all the things we have in common, the reality is that unless relations between the United States and Cuba drastically change, we're starting down an untenable road. A long-distance relationship takes on a whole new meaning in a country like Cuba where the Internet is so heavily regulated, communication thwarted, tourist travel banned by the United States, Cubans' freedom to travel subject to the whims of the government bureaucracy and economic realities. In a country where the government is a terrifying specter towering over its citizens.

How can it be more than just a fling?

"Are you sure it's okay to go see Magda?" I ask again, pushing the niggling doubts about our future from my mind.

"It probably will be fine," he answers, staring down at our linked hands. "If anyone is keeping an eye on you, it'll merely look like you're visiting an old family friend. It's not like they know you're looking for someone."

I still. "What do you mean 'if anyone is keeping an eye on you'? Are you saying the regime is *spying* on me?"

Did it occur to me that they likely monitored Cuban agitators, foreign officials in their country? Sure. But me?

The look Luis gives me is exceedingly patient and a little sad. "They like to keep tabs on things."

"But me? I'm writing a tourism article, not a political piece."

"Yes, and you're also a descendant of one of Cuba's wealthiest and most notorious families. What would you expect? Plus, you're staying here with us . . ." He shrugs. "Like I said, they like to keep track of people."

"Do you think they're following me the whole time I'm here?"

"Probably not. They have limited resources, after all. That said, who knows?"

The notion that someone has been watching me since I arrived in Havana, however innocuously, is terrifying. Were they there when we sat beside each other on the Malecón? Sitting in a pew somewhere in the Cathedral of Havana pretending to pray while actually logging my movements to report back to some government official?

"How do you live like this?" I ask. "Aren't you afraid all the time?"

"You tread carefully," he answers. "And then eventually you become inured to their threats and they lose their teeth. You're still careful, but you test the boundaries and limits a bit more each day, because otherwise you would go mad living in a constant state of fear. And that's what terrifies the regime. If the people don't fear them, they lose their power."

Luis pushes off from the desk abruptly, tugging me forward and closing the gap between us. I tip my head to stare into his eyes. "Ready?" he asks.

Maybe.

I nod.

It takes a little over three hours to get from Havana to the beach in Varadero. Luis stops a few times so I can take pictures of the scenery, as I bask in this side of Cuban life. The space between Havana and Varadero feels off the beaten path, giving me a glimpse of the country that isn't reserved for tourists. It will be different when we arrive at our destination, of course. Varadero is one of the country's most famous seaside resort cities. Of all the places I've wanted to visit in Cuba, this is another that's special to me—a place that meant something to my grandmother.

The water, Marisol. The most beautiful water you've ever seen. The color of that necklace I bought you. You know the one?

Luis's arm drapes around the back of my seat, his other hand tapping the steering wheel, keeping time with the beat of the music on the car's radio. The sun shines down on us, the breeze from the convertible's open top alleviating the heat a bit, but my thighs still stick to the white leather upholstery.

When we finally arrive at the beach, I'm hardly disappointed. Varadero is everything my grandmother said it would be; white sand is cut in fine granules, towering palms loom overhead, the most beautiful clear water my eyes have ever seen lies before me.

It's relatively quiet in this section of beach, and we find a spot off to the side under a palm tree. The nearest sunbather is hundreds of yards away, providing the illusion that we've found our own corner of the world.

Luis sets up a blanket for us in the sand, taking out the hamper he brought from home.

He pulls out tamales and empanadas wrapped in paper and bottled sodas, handing the food to me. I polish off a tamale and an empanada, washing them down with the familiar taste of Materva.

"Do you want to go swimming?" Luis asks once we've finished eating.

The water's impossible to resist.

"Of course."

I pull the dress over my head, wearing the bikini I changed into earlier during one of our stops along the journey, and turn my back to Luis as I stare at the waves lapping at the shore. A fishing boat hovers in the distance, bobbing up and down in the water. Far to the right of me, tiny straw umbrellas pepper the landscape.

This truly is paradise.

I imagine scattering my grandmother's ashes here, making her final resting place in the sand and the sea. And yet—

I'm not ready to part with her; there's an unfamiliar distance between us, the secret of her mysterious romance lingering between us.

You think you know someone, imagine you know them better than anyone, and then little by little, the fabric of their life unravels before your eyes and you realize how little you knew. She was always the constant in my life, and now—

It feels a bit like I've lost her all over again.

I walk toward the water, not waiting for Luis, taking a moment to get my bearings, to calm the racing beat of my heart, to clear my head.

The blue water is like crystal; fish skimming the surface in flashes of colors dart in and out of the waves. The temperature is more a tepid bath than a bracing dip.

The sand slips through my toes.

"Beautiful, isn't it?" Luis asks from his place beside me, his shoulder a hairbreadth from mine.

"It is." I wade farther into the sea, the water undulating against my calves, a fish swimming by. Then another. I go deeper, the water up to my knees, then my thighs, Luis trailing somewhere behind me, giving me space.

The water grows darker and darker before me, until it breaks off, some point beyond the horizon I can no longer see—a home in the United States that suddenly feels very far away.

My fingertips trail against the sea as it caresses my navel. I dive under the waves, and when I pop up again, Luis is there, his back to the sun, watching me.

It feels like a line of dominoes falling into place, like somehow I was meant to end up here, with the grandson of beloved family friends, my feet on Cuban soil, history catching up to me.

I take a step forward. Then another. I stop an inch away from Luis, and our lips meet, the salt from the sea between us, the smell of the ocean filling my nostrils, the sun warming his skin beneath my hands, his beard scratchy against my cheek.

Ages pass before we come up for air.

"Tell me about your family," Luis says.

We've migrated from the sea to the sand, lounging on a worn blanket he brought with him. My lips are swollen from his kisses. I pass the drink we've been sharing back to him and stare out at the water. It's an innocent enough question on the surface, but so very complicated beneath it.

"Why?"

He smiles, his mouth brushing against my temple, his beard tickling my skin. The sight of his injuries makes my stomach clench.

"So I can know you," he replies. "You've met my family—my mother, my grandmother, Cristina. I can't help but be curious about yours. I grew up on stories about your grandmother, your great-aunts. They were like family to my grandmother."

"My family's complicated."

His lips curve. "Aren't they all?"

"True. Perhaps mine seems a bit more so than most because so many of our foibles have played out in gossip columns."

I explain about the rubber heiress, the fact that my grandmother raised me. I've gotten so good at telling this story to people who've asked about my unorthodox family structure throughout the years—why my grandmother sat in the audience at school plays rather than my parents—that I can nearly get through it without a hitch.

"Do you miss your mother? Are you close now?" Luis asks.

I shrug, raising the bottle to my lips once more, the cool drink sliding down my throat. "I suppose I miss the idea of her—what society says the relationship should be—rather than the reality. I never knew her enough to miss her; even now we're more polite strangers than anything else. I've seen her a handful of times in the last decade, usually when we both happen to be in the same place. We get along just fine."

"Still—"

"I had my sisters, my father, my great-aunts. Everyone lived close to one another in Florida, so I didn't lack for family. My father was busy with work a lot, but he still made an effort, was around as much as he could be. Besides, I had my grandmother; that was all I ever needed."

"What was your grandmother like?" Luis asks, his hand drifting lazily across my hip.

Despite the heat, goose bumps rise over my skin.

"Fierce. Unapologetic. Proud. Loyal—to her country and to her family." I pause. "I didn't understand it until now, but there was a sadness in her. A longing. I always thought it was for Cuba, but now I wonder if those times when she grew silent, when she was with us, and wasn't, if those were the times when she thought of him."

"How is the search going? Have you learned anything else about him since last night? Did my grandmother have anything else to add when you spoke with her this morning?"

"No. I'm hoping Magda will have some answers."

He's quiet a moment. "Your grandmother—you said she was all you had. Is that why it's so important to you to find him?"

I nod. "Losing her has been harder than I imagined. I should have realized it would be, but she was always so vibrant, seemed so much younger than her years, and I suppose I took for granted that she would be around a long time. Would see me get married, hold my child in her arms." A tear trickles down my cheek and I bat it away. "I hate that she's not going to be here for all of these moments. That she won't be here to sing 'Cielito Lindo' to my child like she did to me when I was a little girl. There's this giant hole in my heart. I miss her arms around me, the scent of her perfume, the smell of her cooking." More tears well in my eyes, another spilling over onto my cheek. Then another.

Luis's arm tightens around my waist, his lips brushing against my temple

"We had this connection," I continue, the sound muffled against his bare chest. "I could talk to her in a way I couldn't talk to anyone else. And now that she's gone—"

I brush at my cheeks and pull back slightly.

"I have to find him. To try at least. Right now, their relationship is this giant unknown. It sounds like they loved each other, and he was a revolutionary, but beyond that, I have no clue what happened between them. She asked your grandmother to hold the letters for me. She wanted me to come here and spread her ashes. Wanted me to find this. My grandmother knew me better than anyone; she knew I'd have to see this through one way or another."

"Are you worried that what you find will change the way you remember her relationship with your grandfather?" Luis asks, his voice kind.

"Maybe. I don't know. I was so young when he died. My perspective of their relationship was a child's perspective. Who knows what goes on behind closed doors?"

"Marriage is hard," he agrees.

I can't help it. Curiosity has filled me since he first mentioned he was divorced.

"What happened between the two of you—with Cristina?"

He turns his head to stare out at the water.

"It wasn't one thing," he finally answers, and I realize his silence is more a product of his attempt to answer my question as honestly as possible rather than discomfort. "It would be easier to explain if one of us cheated or we had some big fight, but it wasn't like that at all. Each night we went to bed together, and the next morning we woke up and had drifted a little farther apart than the day before. One morning we woke up strangers."

"That sounds painful."

"It was, although, I suppose it could have been worse. Our lives simply diverged. She wanted children. When we married, I thought I did, too. But the more I thought about it, about the world I was bringing them into, the country I was handing off to them, I couldn't do it. That was my fault. She married me expecting one thing and ended up with another. It wasn't fair to her, *I* wasn't fair to her, and that was my mistake. You learn the deepest truths about yourself when you fail at something. When I failed at marriage, I learned I couldn't pretend to be someone I wasn't in order to please another person."

He rubs his jaw, his eyelashes sweeping downward.

"She thought I was too serious. Wanted me to stop holding on to things." He gives a dry little laugh. "I'm not the easiest person to live with."

His words are both confession and warning.

"And yet you both still do—live together. Work in the restaurant together. How do you handle it? How does she?"

"I wouldn't say we live together, exactly. It's not like we share a bedroom anymore. It's different here in Cuba. There's a massive housing shortage in Havana. Cristina wanted to move out, but there was nowhere for her to go. So she's stuck. Thank you, Fidel."

"I can't even imagine how awkward that must be. The idea of living with one of my exes . . ."

"You'd think so, but it's not so bad, really. We've become friends more than anything. Family, in a way. Her parents are both dead. She doesn't have anyone else, and I'm fairly certain she's as disinterested in me as anything other than platonic as I am her. Occasionally she'll bring men home, but I make a point to be out those nights. It's not a perfect solution, but you make do. If things don't look the way you anticipated, you change your expectations. It's an easy way to avoid being disappointed."

"And you never—"

"Bring women home?" Luis grins. "I live with my grandmother and mother. What do you think?"

I laugh. "Fair enough."

"What about you?" He takes the drink from my outstretched hand and raises it to his lips.

"What about me?"

"You never married?"

"No."

"Did you come close?"

"I've never been engaged or anything like that. My longest relationship was in college. We were together for three years."

"What happened?"

It feels so long ago; in the moment, the breakup had been all-consuming, but now I barely remember why we fell apart.

"Just life, I guess. We got to the point where we either had to be more serious or go our separate ways, and neither one of us cared enough to take it to the next level."

"And since then?"

"I date, but I haven't met anyone who's made me want more."

Until now.

"What about your family?" I ask. "Your grandmother mentioned you used to come here with your father. What was he like?"

"Strict," Luis answers. "He was a good father, a good man, but he was a military man, used to giving orders and others following him. He was my hero, though. When he wore his uniform he was larger-than-life to me. When I was a very young boy, I wanted to serve in the military like him."

"What changed?"

"I grew up, I suppose. My eyes were opened to the reality of life around me. Things were easier when my father was alive, when the regime took care of us because he was a high-ranking official in the military. We still received some financial benefits after his death, but my world changed. My grandparents took us in, and my friends were no longer the children of the privileged, but Cubans who suffered. When the government protects you because you are one of theirs, it's not so bad. But ordinary Cubans inhabit a very different reality.

"Still—" He's silent. "My father gave his life fighting in Angola, defending its people and protecting them against the United States' proxies and their intervention in the conflict. Spent his adult life serving the regime. Sometimes I wonder if he would be disappointed that I haven't done the same, that I'm not honoring his memory."

"You've said it yourself—your students are the future of this country. It's clear that you love your job, that your students admire you. That's something to be proud of. Your father fought for what he believed in. You do, too, even if it doesn't involve picking up a gun."

Luis smiles faintly, his lips meeting mine. "Thank you."

He leans back, staring up at the sky. I lay my head in the curve created between his elbow and his neck, pressing my lips there, inhaling his scent, committing something else about him to memory—

For when I'm gone.

chapter sixteen

Elisa

The weeks eke by with agonizing slowness after Pablo leaves Havana, December creeping in, the monotony of life punctuated by the occasional bombing, shooting, random attacks that leave our mother even more convinced we mustn't traipse around Havana on our own. I'm fine with the new rules—I'm in purgatory, clinging to each radio report, every scrap of news about the fighting in the Sierra Maestra. Pablo's letters arrive sporadically, delivered by messengers, ferreted to me by the staff members I've recruited through bribery and cajoling. I live in terror of my mother or father finding the letters, of Magda's condemnation, my sisters' questions.

One afternoon I confide in Ana, telling her I met a man and little else. I want to talk about Pablo, want to share this secret with those closest to me, but each time I begin to speak of him, something inside me rebels. Instead, I content myself with the letters he sends me, the ones I write to him. I hide his letters in my room, reading them over and over again when I am alone, when the connection between us is gossamer thin. I worry my own letters won't reach him in the mountains, that they'll be intercepted, fear I am barreling toward disaster.

Despite the way we left things, the uncertainty of us, I cannot stop hoping our relationship isn't finished.

When the next letter arrives, I rip it open greedily.

There's a stillness in the mountains. A quiet I never found in the city. It's so beautiful—you would love it here. We are drawn to the water, but the countryside has its charms, too. It's so green—we wake up to the sun rising over the mountains, and the view rivals even that over the sea-wall. The clouds are so low it feels as though you could reach up and touch them.

I think of you often. I miss you.

I adopt an intense piety I never possessed before, kneeling in the pews of the Cathedral and praying God will protect Pablo, keep him safe, bring him back to me. And I worry about Alejandro. Constantly.

I'm not sure where God weighs in on the issue of Cuba's future—I fear he created this paradise on earth and left us to fend for ourselves—but I hope he'll protect my brother and Pablo. Hope is all you have to cling to when the world around you evokes every other emotion.

I've taken to spending more and more of my days with Ana. We lounge by the pool, drinks in hand while Maria plays in the water, splashing around. It's hard to reconcile this image of Havana with the one that greets me each time I read my father's discarded newspapers. The news often tells a gruesome tale—bloody pictures of dead Cubans cover the pages. I can't help it—I search the images, the faces, fearing the day Pablo or Alejandro will stare back at me. Batista has been especially prolific lately, purging the streets of anyone he deems a threat. It must be exhausting to have so many enemies, to feel the breath of Fidel Castro against the back of his neck.

Today, Beatriz and Isabel are fighting off boredom by fighting with each other in the living room while I sit on the couch, curled up with a book. God knows where Maria is, probably off chasing lizards in the backyard.

"She's crazy, isn't she?"

Beatriz's voice intrudes on my novel.

"What?" I ask.

"Isabel. She's crazy for saying she'll marry Alberto. Tell her."

Our eldest sister shoots daggers at Beatriz, her gaze turning swiftly to me.

Our parents don't know about the engagement yet. Personally, I doubt Alberto had the stomach to face our father—not that I can entirely blame him. Alberto's father is a doctor, successful and staunchly middle-class, but not exactly sugar baron money; Alberto works as an accountant. He and Isabel met in Varadero nine months ago, and from that moment, she hasn't paid attention to any other man.

He's handsome enough, and he does seem to genuinely care about Isabel, but I'm not quite sure how she feels about him. She's the most difficult one to read of all of us. She keeps her emotions locked tightly away whereas Beatriz lets them fly for the entire world to see. I'd like to think I'm as contained as Isabel, but I fear my heart gives me away.

"If she's happy, that's all that matters," I reply.

Isabel's expression softens, shooting me a grateful look.

Beatriz lets out an inelegant snort.

"If only it were that simple. How long do you think happiness and love will continue once the difference in their circumstances is too much for them to overcome? Do you think it simply won't matter that she was born into all of this and he wasn't?" Her tone gentles as her attention turns to Isabel. "You love him, maybe. You're infatuated with him, yes. But is that enough for marriage?"

"What else is there?" Isabel snaps.

"Compatibility."

Beatriz has an uncanny way of striking at the uncomfortable heart of things.

"We're fine in that department, but thanks for your concern," Isabel retorts.

Beatriz rolls her eyes. "I wasn't talking about sex."

"Beatriz," Isabel hisses, her face reddening.

"Please, like we don't know that's what you mean."

"Perhaps some of us don't believe you must say every single thing you think. That some things are private."

Beatriz shrugs. "I suppose I don't see the point in pretending."

"You haven't any sense."

"Sense? I'm not the one marrying a man who's utterly wrong for me." Beatriz rises from her perch on the sofa, her voice softening a bit. "I love you. I don't want to see you make a mistake. Alberto is a nice enough man for someone. I just don't believe he's right for you, and I want you to be with a man who is worthy of you, a man who is your match in every way."

"Then you presume too much. We are not all you. We do not all have your ambitions. Alberto makes me happy. He is a good man. That is enough." Isabel's gaze narrows. "Is that why you reject every man who proposes, why you play the flirt and keep them at arm's length? Because you don't think they're worthy of you?"

Beatriz shrugs, flashing us an enigmatic smile. "If telling yourself that makes you feel smug and superior about your own choices, then sure."

She leaves us without a good-bye.

"She is impossible," Isabel mutters.

She can be. She also can be too perceptive by half.

A minute later Isabel leaves the room and I am alone with my thoughts, not an entirely welcome place to be. It's been a week since I've heard from Pablo, since I received that last letter, a week of uncertainty and nerves, a week of missing him terribly. Has he simply tired of me or is there something more at play? Has danger befallen him?

I can't help but think of Beatriz's words to Isabel now; is she correct? Once passion fades are we left with compatibility, and if so, will Pablo and I forever be at odds, viewing the world from distinct—and opposing—beliefs?

One of the gardeners walks into the room, his hat in his hands, a look of discomfort on his face. He's one of the staff members I've been bribing for weeks now, using them to carry letters back and forth between Pablo's messengers and me. I'm fairly certain Beatriz does the same thing with our brother.

"Miss Elisa, there's a man to see you. He's in the backyard. He's—"

I leap off the couch, mustering what little decorum I can in the face of overwhelming relief and excitement.

He's home.

In the end, I can't resist the impulse to follow Pablo through the city to the house where he's been staying.

The residence is in the Vedado district, a few streets from Guillermo's home, the site of our first meeting. It's a nondescript place filled with generic furnishings, sparse decor, and a faintly stale scent that suggests it hasn't been aired out in a long time.

"Are you the only one staying here?" I ask when he closes the door behind us.

"For now. I live here from time to time."

The floor plan is fairly open, room leading into room, and I follow Pablo as he walks into the kitchen, my gaze running over his appearance. He looks leaner, and at the same time, more muscular than when I last saw him, as though he's been shaped and molded, chiseled down to the bare essentials during his time in the mountains. His skin is darker than it was when he left, his hair a touch longer than is fashionable. His face is once again freshly shaved; wearing a scraggly beard in Havana these days is tantamount to testing the limits of Batista's self-restraint.

I can't stop looking at him, wanting to pinch myself. This isn't a dream. He's been gone for a month, I've missed him for a month, and now we're here and we're alone.

"Can I get you a drink? Or something to eat? I have a few things in the cupboards." He grins. "I warn you, I'm not the most domestic."

I shake my head.

"Do you want to sit?" He walks out of the narrow kitchen and gestures toward a faded couch shoved into a corner of the tiny room.

To the left of me, Pablo stands in the doorway to the kitchen. To the right of me is another doorway. I can make out the edge of a mattress covered in a navy blue spread, a pair of trouser pants draped across the foot of the bed, this intimate view of his domestic life sending a flutter to my stomach.

I could rationalize my decision by saying there's an uncertainty thickening the air in Havana these days, that each shot, each explosion, each act of rebellion pushes us closer and closer to the edge and I don't know what we'll find when we get there. I could point to my own lack of control in my life, the match that was lit months ago burning strong and bright inside me. I could use so many excuses to justify love, but in the end none of them seem to matter much anymore.

He is here. I love him.

There's nothing else.

I leave Pablo standing in the doorway to the kitchen, my heart pounding as I walk toward the bedroom. My knees tremble beneath my dress.

His gaze heats my skin.

Perhaps this is foolish—it most likely is—but what is there in life if not the ability to indulge in the occasional foolish moment? How many of these indulgences do I have left?

I stop a foot away from the bed, its outline mottled by the dying daylight. I take a deep breath, then another, my back to him, my fingers shaking as I pull my hair forward, draping it over my shoulder, fumbling with the buttons at my nape.

The sound of his feet against the carpet, each inhale and exhale of breath, fills the room.

Pablo stops.

I already gave him my heart, but I can't deny that there's something equally momentous in this, too. Or that I'm more than a little nervous.

His lips ghost across my nape, followed by his fingers at the back of my dress, his knuckles brushing my spine, a reenactment of that first night in the yard behind Guillermo's house. Pablo undoes the line of buttons, the air hitting my back with each one. When he's finished, he kisses my skin, turning me in his arms.

"Are you sure?" Pablo asks, his voice taut.

"Yes."

He leans into me, and I wrap my arms around his shoulders, stroking between the blades, reveling in the feel of him, the scent of him. He rests his forehead against mine, his eyes closed.

"I love you," he whispers.

My eyes slam close. It's silly, really, that saying the words out loud gives them so much power, but it does.

"I love you, too."

· · ·

We lie in bed beside each other, the sheets pooled around our waists. The act of being naked in front of a man, even Pablo, is too novel for me to be entirely comfortable, so I rest on my stomach, my head propped on the pillow, watching him. His hand trails down my back, his fingers walking the length of my spine, the sensation both soothing and ticklish. I bury my head in the pillow, stifling another laugh.

"I give up; I can't take it anymore."

Pablo grins, wrapping his arms around me and pulling me snug against his body, burying his face in my hair.

"Have I told you how much I love you?" he asks.

I turn to face him. "How much?"

A note of seriousness threads through my teasing tone; there are so many differences between us, and I know why I admire him—his passion, honor, and conviction. What does he admire in me?

"With everything I have, everything I am," he answers. "You're the hope in all of this. I've been fighting for so long now that I almost forget what life was like before, who I was when I was just a lawyer in Havana, a brother, a son, a friend. When I'm with you I remember the man I used to be, the man who had hope, a man who wasn't surrounded by death.

"I want to be the kind of man who deserves you. A good man, an honorable man. A man devoted to his country and his family. You are my family now, Elisa.

"You're smart, and you're kind, and you're loyal. You have faith and courage, and you push me to be better, to believe in those things, too. I want to be a man you're proud of. A man you could love."

I want the same things, to be someone he admires, to fight for what I believe in just as he does. He makes me want to be brave.

"I love you," I whisper. "Always."

Pablo takes my hand, his lips running over my naked ring finger.

"I wish you could wear my ring on your hand for everyone to see," he says against my skin.

My heart thunders at the promise contained there. "Me, too."

The keeping of this secret becomes progressively more difficult, a little more painful, and with each day he fights against Batista, protecting him becomes even more important.

Pablo's fingers move to my brow, stroking there, tracing the line, sweeping down to caress my face.

"You're worried," he says.

There's hardly a point in lying to him.

"I am. What happens next? Is this it?"

"This will never be it."

"What else can there be?" I ask, my tone bleak.

"Us growing old together. Raising a family together. Watching our children have children of their own. Falling asleep beside each other at night and waking next to each other every morning."

"Do you really think we can have that?"

"I hope so. If not, what are we fighting for?"

"How bad is it in the mountains? We hear things, but it's impossible to know what's real and what's false with Batista. They say he's censoring more and more."

"That's because we're advancing. We captured one of Batista's garrisons. At some point, morale will play a factor. His military is fighting their own countrymen, have been doing so for years now, and most of them know Batista's not worth dying for. We'll wear them down. And if we don't, another group will. He has too many enemies to survive this."

"How bad is it?" I repeat.

"I don't want to talk about it. I don't want it touching you. I get through the nights in the mountains by imagining you here, safe in the city. Imagining our future together." Pablo grimaces. "War is never anything other than bad, and anyone who tells you otherwise is a liar."

"I worry about you," I confess. "All the time. Wonder where you are, what you're doing, if you're alive. It's so strange to go about my day as though everything is normal, to not be able to tell anyone about you, while I feel like half my heart has been torn from my chest." I take a deep breath. "I worry something will happen to you and I won't know considering we're little more than secrets in each other's lives."

My brother is a conduit of sorts between us, my ears within Cuba's rebellion, but his whereabouts are equally difficult to predict.

Pablo squeezes my hand. "If anything happens to me while I'm gone, Guillermo will find you. It won't come to that, though, because I'm coming home to you, Elisa. Batista himself couldn't keep me away."

"Where will you go?"

"Che is marching toward Santa Clara. He and his men plan to make a stand against Batista's forces."

"And you will join them."

"Yes."

"Are you ever afraid?" I can't imagine the risks he takes, the dangers he faces.

"I was with Latour in the Sierra Maestra at the end of July." He pushes up on his elbow, the sheet falling to his waist, my gaze dropping to his lean chest before returning to his eyes. "We fought the Cuban army. Men died beside me, their bodies crumpling to the ground as their blood spilled over the mountains. Latour was killed. Fidel came to bolster our forces, but we were already surrounded by Batista's army. Fidel had to negotiate a cease-fire—try to, at least—in order to give us a chance to escape. We were a breath away from being wiped out, the revolution, everything we've fought for over. I was afraid then."

"Would that be such a bad thing? If the cease-fire had held? We've been fighting for what? Over five years? What has the rebellion accomplished other than chipping away at us? Batista's still in power."

"He won't be forever. What else is there to do but fight? There is nothing I wouldn't do for Cuba, nothing I wouldn't sacrifice."

Pablo climbs out of bed, walking to where his clothes lie in a pile on the floor, where I stripped them from his body, a sliver of light from the open window highlighting his nakedness. My body is suddenly cold without his warmth.

I never considered that the war would make monsters out of all of them, but I fear it now. There's a danger in the way we live, in blithely continuing on as though nothing is wrong with the society we've created, but there's also danger in the fervor that fills him, the emotion driving all of the bearded ones.

And suddenly, I am very afraid.

"I love you," Pablo says, his voice fierce.

I close my eyes.

"I love you, too."

I've never told a man I wasn't related to that I loved him before today, never had a man say those words to me. It should feel like the beginning of everything, but it sounds unmistakably like good-bye.

Pablo reaches into his trouser pocket, pulling out a tiny box.

I still.

He flips open the box.

His voice is hoarse. "It was my grandmother's."

The ring is beautiful and delicate, the diamonds arranged in a vintage shape.

I swallow, my mouth going dry at the sight of that ring, my heart thundering in my chest.

It's fast. Much too fast.

He's leaving. Revolution is here, knocking on the door.

Pablo swallows, a tremor in his voice. "I don't know what kind of life we'll have when this is over. I probably won't be able to give you the life you're used to. But I love you. Always. I can promise you that."

Tears slide down my face. He slides the ring on my finger.

"Come back to me," I say.

"I promise."

chapter seventeen

Marisol

I check us into a resort on the beach, Luis beside me as I speak to the woman behind the desk, curiosity in her gaze.

We lack the familiarity of longtime couples, and it's impossible to miss the tension between us. Luis shifts from side to side, his hands sunk deep in the pockets of his trousers, his eyes trained to a spot on the wall, near—but not quite meeting—the receptionist's gaze.

I glance around us—we're surrounded by couples, families, all clearly tourists. A man stands off to the side, a folded copy of *Granma* in his hand. While obviously a local, he definitely doesn't look like a guest.

In the research I did before coming to Cuba, I read about the more tragic parts of life here—the flourishing sex trade, tourists preying on the sheer desperation of Cuban men and women who can earn more in a night selling themselves than they will in a year working for the state. Does she think that's what this is? That my expensive clothes and bags, the fat wad of CUCs in my hand, mean I'm here taking advantage of Luis?

I finish the transaction quickly, my gaze now resting on the same invisible point that draws Luis's attention, my heart pounding.

We are an unlikely match, and I have no clue how to bridge the differences between us. I know a thing or two about Cuban pride— is he ashamed that I'm the one paying for the room, that the differences between us are so vast? Will his friends judge him for taking up with a rich American, view him as a sellout or me as his winning lottery ticket?

And how could I explain this to my family? Would they consider Luis a communist because he stayed behind, because his family has served the regime in different capacities? I can't imagine him in my world, and I certainly don't belong in his. Where does that leave us?

Luis carries my bag and his own, following my lead as we walk through the lobby, heading toward the room the woman assigned us. We step into the elevator—blissfully empty—and I stare down at my feet, doubts running through my mind.

I should have gotten us two rooms. This has "bad idea" written all over it. We barely know each other. I came here to lay my grandmother to rest, not to have a fling, however much I gravitate toward him. This is happening too quickly, gaining speed with each moment we spend together, with each kiss—

"Marisol." Luis takes my hand, his fingers stroking my wrist. "For most of my life, it was against the law for Cubans to stay in hotels like this. Now we can, but only the smallest percentage of Cubans can actually afford them. I'm sorry if I'm a bit"—he pauses as though he's searching for the right word—"uncomfortable," he finishes. "It's not you; it's simply the way of things."

I can't imagine the lack of freedom he describes, not to mention the feeling that Cubans are treated as though their country isn't even theirs, as though their wants, their needs, their lives are subservient to the foreigners who come and go at will, when they themselves have little to no control over their own movements.

"I've never done this before," he adds.

"No American tourists?" I ask, my heart thundering in my chest as I struggle to keep my tone light.

"No tourists at all." He leans into me, his lips brushing my cheekbone. "This means something to me."

"This means something to me, too," I reply.

The elevator pings, and the door slides open. Luis holds his arm out while I walk into the hall, following the sign to our room.

There it is.

610.

I fumble with the key, my fingers shaking as I try to turn it in the lock. Once. Twice. The key scrapes against the metal, my palms damp.

Luis steps up, his chest against my back, his hand covering mine. He takes the key from me, slipping it into the lock, turning it in one fluid motion.

Goose bumps rise over my skin.

His free arm snakes around my waist, holding me against him, his breath on my neck, his face buried in my hair.

The door opens, revealing our hotel room. It's small, but clean. Certainly not opulent, but enough.

We cross the threshold, Luis's arm still around me, and the door closes behind us with a click.

We're finally alone.

I set my bag on the floor near the door, my gaze on the bed. It overshadows everything else in the room, the implication contained there setting off a whole new set of jitters. Is this really about to happen?

I take a deep breath, then another, attempting to sift through the emotions tumbling around inside me. A part of me wants this desperately, has wanted it from the beginning, the desire intensified by our kisses on the beach, by each moment I spend with him. The other part of me is still mulling over the impossibility of us, guarding my heart as I listen to my head. A little caution seems prudent in this situation, even as my willpower crumbles with each second that passes.

"What are we doing here?" I ask, staring at the bed, the floral bedspread, the two pillows propped against the headboard. I imagine us lying there, limbs entwined.

"I don't know," Luis admits as he takes a step closer to me. Then another. "You are entirely unexpected."

"Is that a bad thing?"

"No. Just complicated." He takes a deep breath. "I thought you were beautiful when I watched you walk out of the airport. You looked so vibrant and excited, your hair blowing in the breeze. I hoped you were the one I was there to pick up, and then you walked toward me and I thanked whatever power it was that brought us together."

I turn, facing him, the uncertainty in his expression surprisingly reassuring, the desire in his eyes sending a thrill through me.

"I thought you were laughing at me," I confess.

"I thought you were charming," he says. "And yes, you made me laugh, but not at you. And then I drove you through Havana, took you to your family's house and saw the way you looked at it, heard the way you spoke of your family, of what being Cuban meant to you, and I knew."

"Knew what?"

"That you were here for me."

"How? How can this work? I don't know what I want here," I say, my voice barely above a whisper, the caution and control I clung to slipping away. "In this moment, I want you. But after that—"

"Then maybe we just have this moment."

"Is that enough?"

He smiles, a tinge of sadness on his face. "I have a feeling there will never be enough moments with you, Marisol."

If any other guy said that to me, I would dismiss it as another line, a move in the dating game, but there is something eminently trustworthy in him, and the sincerity I saw in him from the beginning, the solemnity in his expression, the truth in his words removes any doubt. He is not a careless man, and whatever the future holds, I know he will be careful with me.

My legs quiver as I sink down on the edge of the bed. My fingers fist the bedspread beneath me as I stare at the bright pattern—the garish colors blending together into a kaleidoscope before my eyes, my heart thundering in my chest.

How can someone be so comforting, and yet, utterly terrifying at the same time?

When I look up, Luis is standing next to the edge of the bed, the leg of his trousers brushing against my knees.

He doesn't speak, but he doesn't have to. There have been moments when I've found him to be impossible to read, but in this moment, in this hotel room, his guard is down, his emotions etched all over his face, in the tremor in his hand as he reaches out and strokes my hair, as I curl into his touch, as he skims the curve of my cheek.

My eyes slam closed.

I wait for him to kiss me, to lever me back onto the mattress, his strong arms wrapping around my waist, pulling me against his sinewy frame. I wait for a moment that stretches on and on, until I can't wait anymore, the anticipation building inside me, the spark that was lit burning fierce and strong.

In the end, I'm the one who moves. Because while I don't have the answers to any of the questions filling me with doubt and uncertainty, I know this—

If I don't close the distance between us now, I will regret it for the rest of my life.

I lean into the arc of his body, pulling him down to meet me, catching him on an exhale, my mouth pressed against his, his breath becoming my breath, my hands taking over, my body colliding with his as the last of my misgivings retreat.

Luis bends me back, taking over the kiss, lowering me to the mattress, the comforter rough against the bare skin above my dress, his body firm against mine, a hint of breeze blowing across my skin from the ceiling fan rotating overhead, the distant noise of guests in the hall intruding on our privacy.

He whispers endearments to me in the language of my heart, his lips ghosting across my earlobe, his hands roaming over my curves, his fingers unhooking and removing clothing in a tangle of limbs, as I fumble with the buttons of his shirt, his belt, our shoes falling off the edge of the bed, our movements punctuated by the occasional bout of laughter, by a sweeping wave of desire that binds me to him with each moment that passes, until the rightness of this—of *us*—simply eclipses all else.

Afterward we lie in bed, naked, my head resting on his bare chest, his hand stroking my hair.

Minutes pass. The only sound in the room is the inhale and exhale of breath. What comes next?

His fingers walk across my skin.

I tip my head toward him for a kiss.

"I wasn't expecting this when I picked you up at the airport," Luis whispers against my mouth.

"I wasn't expecting any of this," I admit. "I came here planning to write an article about traveling to Cuba, and instead of *paladares* and sightseeing, my notepad is filled with politics."

"Cuba is rubbing off on you," he says, pride in his voice.

"I guess it is."

"You could write an article about politics once you're home, you know."

"Cuban politics?"

"Why not?"

"Politics aren't really my thing. I write about accessible topics—the best restaurants to eat at when you're in a particular city, a skin-care regimen that will help keep wrinkles at bay, the ideal way to pack your suitcase to maximize your storage space."

"And politics aren't accessible?"

I turn onto my side, facing him. "I suppose I've never seen my-self that way. I'll leave things like revolutions to people who are well versed in what they're talking about. I'm not exactly known for being serious." I offer a wry grin. "I'm sort of the flighty one in the family."

Luis makes a disapproving noise in his throat. "You can write about revolutions and the best way to pack your suitcase. One doesn't make you less than the other."

I laugh. "If only it were that simple."

"Why isn't it?"

"Because my family expects things of me, because my last name carries a weight of responsibility and I've never quite measured up. I doubt anyone cares to hear what I have to say about politics. Every family has that one person who doesn't fit; that's always been me."

Except for my grandmother. She adjusted to the curves and shifts of my life with agility and understanding, and occasionally, a plate of *merenguitos*.

"It can be simpler than you think," Luis replies. "You can't live your life to please others if you're not proud of yourself. I saw the man Cristina wanted me to be, and no matter how hard I tried to pretend, I simply could not be that sort of man—the type who turned a blind eye to injustice and cruelty—and still retain some semblance of pride."

"Are you happy now?"

He smiles. "Am I happy in this very moment? Right now, in bed with you?"

I grin, burying my head in the curve of his neck. "Yes."

"Yes," he echoes.

I look into his eyes, my fingers skimming the bruise on his cheekbone, his expression sobering. I open my mouth to speak—

"I don't know—"

"—Things are complicated right now," he says, finishing the thought for me.

"Yes."

I'm leaving in a few days, and he'll remain here. Even as things are slowly, subtly changing, a wall exists between our countries—an ocean of differences—and I don't know how to navigate it.

Luis sighs, his chest heaving with the effort. "These are difficult times in Cuba. Right now my fortunes are hers, and unless things radically change they're on a decidedly downward trend." He's silent for a heartbeat. "I don't want them to be yours."

"Is it better for anyone? Than it was before?"

"Is the status quo better for some? Perhaps," Luis answers after a beat. "For those involved in the upper echelons of the regime, sure. The military, for one. I saw that firsthand. For certain members of the artistic class, their art shields them from that which most Cubans experience. They can travel, tout their talent and the impression that it was nurtured in a Cuba that prizes education and art, making Cuba look good. Same for the baseball players and other elite athletes."

"And for those who don't agree with the regime?"

Luis grimaces. "Then it is very bad." He sits up, pulling away from me, leaning back against the headboard. Gone is the man content to languish over my curves, interspersing his caresses with laughing kisses.

"It's a bit better for the farmers, I suppose, for those living in the rural areas," Luis continues. "They were pushed to the fringes of Cuban society under Batista. Under Fidel, they at least had the ability to feed themselves off the land, even if they risked imprisonment to do it. When we were hungry, life in the city became a curse.

"When I was a boy, we went to the country and a family friend gave us meat from one of his animals that he had killed. It was illegal for us to have it, but food was scarce then and we were so hungry. On the way back to Havana, our car broke down, the same one I am driving now, and I will never forget the fear in my grandmother's and mother's eyes as men came and helped us get it working again, as they worried someone would discover the meat in their trunk."

"What would have happened?"

"Life in prison."

I gasp.

Luis shrugs. "When you're so hungry you fear you will die, you're willing to risk it. It wasn't always like that in Cuba, but there were too many times when desperation was all we knew."

"Your mother and grandmother must have been very strong to survive on their own like that. To raise you amid such tumult."

Luis smiles, love shining in his eyes. "They're amazing. Two of the strongest people I've ever known. My grandmother is all smiles and welcomes everyone. My mother is more guarded, but she's always been there for me."

"Did your mother ever think of leaving Cuba with you?"

"We never discussed it," Luis answers. "When my father was alive, there was no need. Life was relatively good as an officer's wife, as an officer's son. And I think my mother was more open to the regime back then. Her family believed in Fidel's reforms; it was a passion she and my father initially shared, although I imagine that passion has all but disappeared after she's seen the future the revolution promised."

"I can't believe the regime has lasted so long given the life you describe."

"It would be narrow-minded to say the entire country feels as I do, but many do," Luis replies. "And even though we cannot wear that banner proudly, I believe there are enough of us to change things."

He delivers the words with such conviction that I almost believe it possible.

"Did any of Fidel's reforms succeed?" I ask.

"The social ones fared far better than the economic and political ones, for sure. Look, it's not all bad. I agree with some of the things he's done or attempted to do. Being black in Cuba is a bit better than it was in 1959—on paper, at least," Luis adds. "But is 'a bit better' enough? It's been nearly sixty years. How much has the world changed in that time? Race still matters here even though the regime says it does not. The majority of the exiles who send money back in the form of remittances to their relatives are of European descent. My black friends face difficulty getting hired to work in the tourism sector. Without remittances, without access to CUCs, the deck is stacked against black Cubans. And how can we measure racial inequality when the regime willfully ignores it?

"Men and women are 'equal' under Fidel's government, but what does that mean? 'On paper' tells a far different tale from the reality of everyday life. This incremental progress where we exalt Fidel for the fact that things have gotten just the tiniest bit better in nearly sixty years is not enough. Fidel was good for Fidel and his cronies. The rest of us deserve more . . ."

He makes a sound of disgust.

"This island will break your heart if you let it."

I think of my grandmother dreaming of a country just removed from her grasp, ninety miles that stretched on to eternity, of all the refugees and exiles in Miami and throughout the world, and I can't disagree with him.

"Would you ever want to travel to the United States? If things changed and opportunities for Cubans increased?"

The question fills the air around us, the divide between our circumstances the elephant in the room.

"I don't know. I got my passport years ago when they finally made it legal to travel. It seemed safe to hedge my bets even if the cost was prohibitively expensive. Without the *paladar*, I never would have had the funds. In Cuba, your passport is issued for six years, but it costs about two hundred dollars to perform the mandatory renewal every two years. Nearly a year's salary every two years to just hold a passport. Add in the cost of travel and it seems like a very distant dream unless you have an outside benefactor or access to CUCs.

"And the United States?" Luis sighs. "It's complicated. Within Cuba, there are different views on our relationship with the Americans. Some believe the United States is the source of our problems; others dream of moving there so they can earn enough money to send back to their families and eventually bring them over, too. And some think the reality lies in the middle."

"Where do you fall on the United States?" I ask, half afraid of his answer.

Is it possible to separate your political views from your personal ones? To love someone who represents something you don't agree with? I am American. Does he see me as an extension of my country's at times flawed policies?

"We've paid the price of politics over and over again," Luis responds. "The embargo is ridiculous. It's hurt the Cuban people, not Fidel and his cohorts. It doesn't work."

"True. But to some it isn't merely politics. For the most part, there's a generational divide on the embargo. My grandparents' contemporaries hate the idea of giving Fidel anything after he took everything from them. They had family members that stood before those firing squads, whose blood spilled on the ground, who were imprisoned for speaking out against injustice. Families were torn apart. They were separated from their loved ones, their memories, their legacies. Everything they had was seized by the government when they left. Their thoughts, emotions, lives were regulated by Fidel *before* they left. They watched the country they loved change into something they no longer recognized.

"The anger among the exiles is legitimate. It's lessened with each subsequent generation, but there are real reasons for the anger. The revolution didn't happen nearly sixty years ago for them. They live the revolution over and over again with each day they are in exile, with each hour they are reminded that they cannot go home."

"And those of us who remained?" Luis asks. "In some cases perhaps those Cubans were made to leave, but for the most part you seem to forget that they had a choice."

"Did they, though? How can you live in a place that seeks to eradicate your existence? That offers so little and takes so much?"

"I don't have the answer to that. But you've seen the people suffering here. What do you think of the embargo?"

"The embargo hurts the Cuban people and fails to target the regime," I reply. "But I didn't lose a loved one to Fidel. My whole life, everything I worked for wasn't taken from me. My generation is less inclined to hold on to the anger, but I am loyal to my grandmother, to my great-aunts. For the exiles, being Cuban means you're born with a loathing for Fidel even after his death."

Luis smiles ruthlessly. "That might be another trait we share."

"Where do you stand on all of this?" I ask again.

"I love my country," he replies. "I am Cuban. I will always be Cuban. Go to America to visit? Perhaps. But my home is here. My loyalty is with my country."

"Is it really that simple, though? Not everyone has the luxury of tying their Cuban heritage to a place. For many being Cuban is something they carry with them in their hearts, something they fight to preserve even when all they have are their memories. When they left, they couldn't take anything with them. No photographs, no official documents, no family heirlooms or mementos. That kind of exile makes you angry."

"You're right. Both sides love Cuba, they just do it in different ways. Some love it so much they can't leave; others love it so much, they cannot stay."

Luis takes a deep breath. "I write. Under a pseudonym. Online."

The words would be innocuous anywhere else. I know quite a few people who blog on a wide range of subjects. But Luis doesn't say the words like they're innocuous; rather, as if he's entrusting me with a secret—a deadly one. There's an earnestness there, too, as though he wants me to know him, and this is the most intimate part.

"What do you write about?" I ask, even though I already know the answer. Politics. He's been hinting at it the entire time, and now that I know him better, it's not shocking, really. He has a strong sense of justice coupled with an appreciation for history, and there is an abundance of injustice around him.

The look in his eyes—the fury blazing above a fading bruise on his cheekbone—says it all.

"What would they do if they found out?" I ask. "That's the reason for the pseudonym, isn't it?"

"Yes. I wanted to protect my family. They didn't sign up for this, and it didn't seem fair that they would suffer for me speaking out."

"What would they do?" I ask again, a chill sliding down my spine as my gaze drifts back to the hints of violence on his face.

"It depends on how big of a threat they determined me to be, and given that I'm a professor teaching at the university, where I possess the power to subvert my students . . ." He sighs. "They could see me as a significant threat. They could block my site. Fire me. Fine my grandmother's business to the point where it would no longer be viable or simply shut it down altogether. They could pay my neighbors and colleagues to spy on me. Hire men to rough me up. Throw me in jail. Arrange for me to meet with an untimely accident—a car crash or something similar. Perhaps a mugging in one of the less savory parts of the city."

He delivers the words in a calm tone, yet with each deliberate pause, it's clear how much he's thought about this.

"That night we shared the rum on the veranda—you weren't mugged, were you?"

"No."

"So they already know who you are. They want you to stop."

"Yes."

"And the roughing-up was what, exactly?"

"A warning."

"Has this happened before?"

"No. I wasn't on their radar before, but now I appear to be."

"What changed?" I ask.

"I don't know."

I don't believe him for a second. He's not a man predisposed to deceit, and the false note in his words rings true in his voice and in his eyes.

"What changed?" I repeat.

"I don't know for sure. They were more concerned with their fists connecting with my face than conversation, but if I had to guess . . ."

No.

"Me."

His silence is all the confirmation I need.

"Oh my God."

I'm going to be sick.

"It's not your fault," he adds quickly. "But you're here as a journalist—tourism article or not—and no doubt they checked up on us when they learned you would be staying with the family. Perhaps the closer inspection was all it took." Luis rubs his jaw. "It was only a matter of time before they found out. I knew when my grandmother mentioned you would be staying with us that it might draw the regime's attention. It was my decision to make, my risk to take. I don't regret it for a moment."

"I am so sorry. I never wanted to bring trouble to your family, never wanted to be a burden. I could have stayed at a hotel or—"

"No. I am tired of worrying. Tired of hiding. I don't want to endanger my family, but at the same time I knew the risk I was taking when I began blogging a few years ago. This was my choice, and I'll deal with the consequences."

Yet now that he's told me the dangers he's faced, I am filled with worry.

"How did you get started?" I ask.

"In the beginning, the blog was more for myself than anything else. It was an outlet, a way to express myself when the walls felt like they were closing in on me, when I choked on all the things I wanted to lecture about in the classroom and couldn't speak of. I had friends who helped me. I would email my thoughts, and they would arrange for others to post them, often from overseas. It's dangerous, but one of my friends—"

His voice breaks off before the name slips from his lips. I've no doubt he's the sort of man who would die before spilling someone else's secrets.

"He's good with computers and feels the same way I do. I couldn't do it without him. And still—" Worry enters his gaze. "He has a wife. Children. We're all at risk here. My audience was small enough that I was probably able to operate below their notice for a long time, but it has grown each year. Who knows? With Fidel's death the government seems to be cracking down even more."

"What will you do? Are you going to stop? That's what they want, isn't it?"

Luis won't meet my gaze, and once again his silence is answer enough.

"Is it worth it? Truly?"

"It depends on how you measure that, I suppose. Have my words connected with some? Made them think about our government? Our way of life? I hope so."

He gives a self-deprecating laugh.

"On good days, I am hopeful. On bad days, I wonder why I bother. But isn't that the point? They've created a system to wear you down so you're so tired from the weight of it, fighting lines and bureaucracy and the things you need to make it through each day, you don't have any fight left." He takes a deep breath. "It's difficult spreading your message when the government censors certain words in communications. I don't know how many Cubans read what I write. I'm speaking in the hopes someone will hear me, that those outside Cuba will understand what life is like for us. I speak to remind myself I exist.

"I don't know how to give up. How to not fight for Cuba, to not challenge myself and others to be better, do more, speak out against injustice." He pauses. "Yes. It is worth it."

"Does your family know?"

"We don't speak of it, but I imagine my grandmother and mother suspect. Cristina, too. I've held these opinions for a long time even if blogging has become a fairly recent development. Cristina worried about my beliefs. She wanted me to keep my head down when we were married, to not agitate the regime. She'd already lost far too much.

"I feel like a coward blogging under a secret identity when others are so brave—like the Ladies in White taking to the streets to protest—but I love my family and I wanted to protect them. Besides, when the odds are as stacked against you as they are here in Cuba, you don't play by the rules. The government certainly doesn't."

Was this what my grandmother felt? This fear? Did her wealth and privilege keep her removed from the revolution until it was in front of her and she couldn't look away anymore?

"What happens now?" I ask, watching the fan turn, the blades going around and around again. Regardless of what he says, I hate that my presence here put him in the regime's crosshairs, that he's now under increased scrutiny because of me.

"I don't know," Luis answers.

For the first time in my life, I know true, bone-chilling fear. For the first time in my life, I understand the precarious frailty of freedom.

chapter eighteen

Elisa

Pablo is gone with a kiss and a good-bye, gone to fight, and I am once again alone, the engagement ring on my finger when I am in private, on a chain under my clothes when I am not.

We hear bits and pieces about the fighting, but there are no letters, no surprise visits to Havana. He has gone to war, and I am left at home to wait for his return. They're fighting in Santa Clara now, and without his letters, I'm greedy for any news I can glean. I attempt to overhear my father's conversations, scanning the newspaper for any mentions of the battle. My brother is absent as well, and I shudder to think of the trouble he could be in, of the danger that faces them both. Should I have left with Pablo? I can't imagine myself in the countryside, and at the same time, I miss him terribly. I am torn between my heart and my head, between love and loyalty.

We celebrate Noche Buena with our usual feast—a whole roasted pig, yucca, black beans and rice, flan for dessert—the champagne flowing freely, conversation veering from politics, from anything too controversial. The extended family gathers—aunts, uncles, cousins, grandparents—a house full of Perezes. We line up on the giant marble staircase in the entryway, the four of us in the front row in our best dresses, our parents beaming with pride despite the gap in the photo, the missing sibling who should be photographed beside us. The next morning my sisters and I crowd in front of the Christmas tree and open presents while our parents sip coffee and smile indulgently.

I've always loved Christmas; no matter how old I am, Christmas feels like magic, a cleansing of sorts that wipes away the slate for the year, heralding the beginning of good things to come. This year—

They are fighting again. While I feast on roast pork and my family sips French champagne, Pablo and Alejandro are—I don't even know where. Santa Clara? Somewhere out there, in the mountains, on the coast, in the countryside.

When we attend Mass for Christmas, I sit in the pews of the Cathedral of Havana, my head bent in prayer, my fingers steepled together. I'm not even sure what I'm praying for anymore—for the rebels to succeed? For Batista to fall? For the rebels to lose and for things to remain as they are? The only constant in my prayers, the only words that fill my head, are for them to be safe. I think I could bear anything else, if God or whoever is up there keeps Pablo and Alejandro safe.

It begins with a murmur after midnight, spreading throughout the New Year's party. We're at a family friend's house in Miramar, the ballroom crammed with Havana society save for a few missing this evening.

"They're saying on the radio that Guevara's forces have taken Santa Clara."

I jerk, the untouched champagne sloshing in my glass. Beside me, Beatriz stills.

We're dressed in designer gowns our mother ordered us from

New York months ago, our organza skirts gliding across the dance floor, the light from the sparkling chandelier above our heads making our jewels glimmer and shine. Isabel dances with Alberto; Maria is off in the corner with some of her friends; Ana stands next to Beatriz.

The murmur grows. "Someone saw cars loaded with suitcases on the road to the airport."

Beatriz grabs my arm, her nails biting into my skin. My gaze darts to my parents, standing at the opposite end of the room, some intrinsic need to search for reassurance driving me, as though I am a young girl once more and they will tell me all will be right in the world.

My mother's face has gone white; my father's expression is grim.

"Batista announced his plans to leave the country," another person proclaims. "He's taking over a hundred of his advisors and friends with him."

And suddenly, the absences make sense, the men and women who should be here, the children I've played with who are not. And more than anything, there's a sharp stab of panic, the realization that if what they're saying is true, we have been left behind.

The murmur transforms into a shout.

"President Batista has fled the country! Long live a free Cuba!"

The evidence of how divided we are as a country could not be more terrifyingly obvious than at this moment. For some the news that Batista has fled, abandoning us to Fidel and his men, is met with the kind of exuberance that suggests they've been pretending all along, their bodies bowed in obeisance as hatred filled their hearts. For the rest of us, a deathly calm has settled over the crowd; it is fear. Bone-deep fear.

My mother is the first to move, organizing us until we stand in a huddle of Perez girls, our pastel gowns crushed together.

"We need to go home. Now."

It's the first time I can ever remember my mother commanding my father to do anything, but there's no question now that she's in charge.

None of us speak as the band begins playing, people cheering and dancing, champagne flutes rising in the air. I follow behind Isabel, Maria's hand in my free one, my stomach pitching and swaying with each step. It takes a few minutes for us to push our way through the throng, the alcohol and news loosening everyone's limbs. It's as if they've decided that for a few hours—the space between Batista leaving and Fidel reaching the city—Cuba is without a ruler and they are determined to make the most of it.

With every step, though, my gaze connects with someone else in the crowd wearing an expression I fear mirrors my own.

What will become of us now?

chapter nineteen

Marisol

The next morning, I'm equal parts nerves and anticipation. We're headed to Santa Clara today, and I can't wait to meet Magda. Earlier as we lingered over coffee in the hotel room—our hands linked, Luis's lips brushing against mine, his free arm wrapped around my waist—I called to let Magda know we were coming, a lump forming in my throat at the emotion in her voice. I can't believe I'll finally meet her.

I follow Luis outside to his car, waiting while he holds the door open for me, as he walks to the driver side, uncoiling his long frame into the front seat. The engine comes to life in a series of fits and starts, a few whispered prayers from Luis, the caress of his fingers against the dashboard.

"Are we going to be okay to get to Santa Clara?"

He grins and shrugs. "We'll find out."

After a few words for the Virgin Mary the car settles into a rhythm, the engine plugging along as we pull out onto the road.

I struggle to push aside my worry over our future. Over the risks Luis is taking with his writing. The danger I've brought into his life.

"So what answers are we looking for here?" he asks, our bodies tucked against each other.

One night has changed so much—the brush of skin against skin, the mingling of breaths, has rearranged space and time. Our hands are linked, resting against the convertible's worn leather seat, our bodies as close as the car's interior will allow. It's the most natural thing in the world now to accentuate our drive with casual touches—his hand running through my hair, my head on his shoulder, our legs against each other.

"I don't know," I answer. "I'm hoping my grandmother trusted Magda, confided in her. And I'm excited to see Santa Clara. He fought there. At least, I think he did. His last letter mentioned he was joining Che."

"In the Battle of Santa Clara?" Luis asks, his tone laced with interest, the history professor back in full force.

"Yes. What do you know about it?"

"It's romanticized and vaunted as the turning point of the revolution. Batista had three thousand men in Santa Clara. They had tanks, machine guns, mortars. There were three hundred rebels."

And my grandmother's love was one of them.

"By all accounts, the rebels should have been annihilated. They were outgunned, outmanned. Batista knew the importance of defeating the rebels once and for all, and this was supposed to be his chance. Instead, it became his Waterloo."

"What happened?"

"In the end, it wasn't the guns that decided the victory, but rather the spirit of the men. At least, that's what the history books say." Luis shrugs. "The Cuban military was tired. They'd been fighting their own citizens in skirmishes for a very long time. And it was difficult to ignore the abuses of Batista's regime. The rebels simply wanted it more. And the locals helped the rebel forces."

"Did anyone die?"

"Yes—although that is disputed. There were injuries and some deaths, but as with so much involving the government, the truth has been obfuscated. Truth in Cuba is constantly being redefined so much so that it is now meaningless."

"Are there sites to see surrounding the Battle of Santa Clara?"

Maybe I'll include it in my completely neglected travel article.

"You can visit the train tracks where the battle took place, the box carriages and bulldozer that derailed the train. Santa Clara is a shrine to Che. There's a museum in the city, and he's buried in a mausoleum under a giant bronze statue of himself. The last, most important battle of the Cuban Revolution, and he was the one to lead it, not Fidel."

"That had to burn."

Luis laughs. "Yes, I imagine it did. You can see why there's so much speculation about rancor between the two, concerns that Che's legacy would overshadow the bearded one's, suspicion that Fidel played a role in his death in Bolivia."

"I would like to see it, if we can. Visit the town, get a feel for the place where they fought."

"This isn't just about finding the perfect resting place for your grandmother, is it? You're looking for something for yourself, too," Luis says, glancing at me again.

"I guess I am." I stare at the countryside surrounding us. "I came here to learn about my family's history, to find the perfect place to spread my grandmother's ashes, but now I'm more confused than ever. When my plane touched down, I thought I'd come home. I'm as Cuban as I am American, as I am Spanish, and yet, until now I'd never been here. I don't have a tangible connection to this place; my grandmother, my great-aunts kept Cuba alive for me, and now my grandmother's gone, her sister Isabel deceased, my remaining great-aunts growing older, and my sense of being Cuban is slipping through my fingers.

"Yes, there's a strong Cuban community in South Florida, and I speak Spanish, and ring in the New Year with grapes and a bucket of water, and eat *lechon asado*, and listen to Celia Cruz, but there's an aimlessness to it all. I'm not grounded in anything; my feet didn't touch Cuban soil until I was thirty-one years old. And now that I'm here?

"You've all moved on. There's a modern Cuba now with a rich history, and emerging cultures, and experiences. And I'm not part of that. None of my family are. We left, and we haven't been able to return, and we're stuck in stasis in the United States. Always waiting, always hoping, wondering, praying that we would wake up and see a headline on the news that Fidel had died, that the government has admitted this was a terrible mistake, that things will go back to the way they were. As exiles, that hope is embedded in the very essence of our soul, taught from birth—

"Next year in Havana—

"It's the toast we never stop saying, because the dream of it never comes true. And if it does one day, what then? There are Russians in the home my ancestors built. What will we return to? Is it even our country anymore, or did we give it up when we left? I'm trying to understand where I fit in all of this."

I take a deep breath, the pressure building in my chest.

"I walk down these streets, and I look out to the sea, and I want to feel as though I belong here, but I'm a visitor here, a guest in my own country."

Luis takes my hand.

"Then you know what it means to be Cuban," he says. "We always reach for something beyond our grasp."

· · ·

We make good time, arriving in Santa Clara an hour before Magda expects us. We head first to the Tren Blindado—the monument to the turning point in the Battle of Santa Clara when Che and some of his rebel forces derailed the armored train containing reinforcements for Batista's forces, ultimately defeating them.

"There were two major efforts in the Battle of Santa Clara," Luis explains. "The battle led by Che to take the train involved a small group of his men. The larger contingent fought near Capiro's Hill."

We pay the entry fee and take a quick tour. I snap a few pictures—the infamous yellow bulldozer that derailed the train, the railroad cars lying around like broken dolls.

I try to envision the man from my grandmother's letters here, holding the mortar in his hands that's now affixed to the wall, contained in a glass case. Did he think of my grandmother as he fought? Did he know how much this battle would determine Cuba's future?

We bypass the museum and mausoleum where Che is buried, although his statue is impossible to miss, looking down at us, a colossus in bronze.

We make our way to the Loma del Capiro, the infamous hill where the second prong of the battle took place. It has the added advantage of looking down over the city, providing a panoramic sweep of Santa Clara.

Two flags fly—the Cuban flag and the flag of Fidel's 26th of July Movement. Below them lies the city where the revolution took place—

It looks like it's been forgotten and neglected, the buildings in a state of disrepair.

Tourists mill around, snapping pictures and chatting in different languages.

"The events here happened almost sixty years ago, and yet, it feels so personal," I murmur to Luis, ducking my head to avoid the crowd.

I look into his eyes, searching there, trying to read the emotions in his gaze. He's so guarded at times, adept at hiding what he thinks and feels. I suppose in a country like this, that shield is a necessity— the difference between life and death. But there are hints—no matter how good he is, his feelings lingering beneath the surface, the passion and conviction in his voice unmistakable.

He yearns for a different Cuba, too.

Magda Villarreal lives in a small apartment near the Parque Leoncio Vidal. Her home is one of many stacked on top of one another and smashed together in a squat building with a crumbling facade. We climb the stairs to her floor; her living conditions are a stark contrast to the Rodriguez home in Miramar.

It's loud, even in the hallway, the walls offering little privacy between residents. There's a faint odor in the air, damp lingering in the floor, ceiling, and walls. Trash litters the stairwell. The railing is cracked and broken in places, the steps chipped, tile chunks missing.

"Is it—"

"Like this in most Cuban apartments?" Luis finishes, his tone grim, his voice low.

I nod.

"It's even worse. By Cuban standards this isn't bad at all."

Even in a country where everyone is supposed to be equal, there are clear disparities between those who have little and those who have less.

Luis knocks on the door to Magda's apartment, and we wait, the sounds of her footfalls padding across the floor growing louder and louder until they stop. The door swings open, and a short woman with dark skin and dark hair sprinkled with gray greets us on the other side.

I've never seen pictures of her, none remain, but there's that same sense of recognition I had when I saw Ana Rodriguez for the first time.

Magda's eyes well with tears.

"Elisa's little girl, come to see me."

Her hand shakes as she takes mine, her frail fingers gripping me, a tremor in her grasp, the bracelets on her bony wrist clanging together.

"I never thought I'd see any of them again, and now you're here." Her lips curve into a smile. "You have the look of your grandmother." Her eyes twinkle. "And perhaps a bit of Beatriz."

I laugh, the sound muffled by the emotions clogging my throat. "I've heard that. Thank you so much for inviting us to your home."

Magda ushers us into the tiny apartment, motioning for us to sit. She chats with Luis for a moment, asking about his grandmother, the affection in her voice obvious. I look around the apartment as they talk; the space is filled with framed photographs of her family and friends. A small table covered in a white cloth sits in a corner, painted figurines atop it. They share the space with a few photographs, a crucifix, rosary, several candles, and a cup filled with what looks to be water.

Despite Castro's desire to ban religion in Cuba, people have found ways to honor their faith, both in the pews of the Cathedral of Havana and here, with this offering to the Santeria gods and goddesses. It's a quiet act of defiance, but a powerful one all the same.

Magda excuses herself for a moment, returning with drinks. She settles on the chair opposite us, the fabric fraying at the edges. By looking at her, I never would have guessed she's as old as she is, and her manner is that of a woman a decade or so younger.

In all the stories my grandmother told me of Cuba, she always spoke of Magda as the woman who raised her, a surrogate mother of sorts, and now I understand that was another thing my grandmother and I shared—our lives were shaped by strong women who raised us as their own.

I answer Magda's questions about my great-aunts, my grandmother, telling her the story of my grandmother's ashes. The emotion that snuck up on me before, the grief, is absent in this little room, and instead I am filled with joy talking about my family. I can easily imagine my grandmother next to me, interjecting throughout this conversation, sharing confidences and stories. I hear her in Magda's voice, see her in Magda's eyes. That's the thing about death—even when you think someone is gone, glimpses of them remain in those they loved and left behind.

Luis sits beside me, sipping his espresso, his knee resting against mine, his presence reassuring. An hour passes as we catch up on each other's lives, and then I ask Magda about the letters.

"I have some questions about my grandmother. Ana thought you might be able to shed some light on them."

"Of course, what would you like to know?"

"I found a box of my grandmother's things." I tell her about the letters. "Did you know about him?"

"Yes."

I lean forward in my seat.

"Well, I knew some of it," she clarifies. "Those last days—their last days in Cuba—were heartbreaking for Elisa. The last day I saw her—"

A tear trickles down her cheek.

"What happened?"

Magda sighs. "The family left. It was a terrible day. We weren't supposed to know, of course. They pretended they were going for a trip. They would do that—your great-grandmother and the girls.

Go to Europe or America to shop. They were careful; all it took was the wrong word overheard and repeated to the wrong person. Especially for a family like the Perezes."

She makes the motion of a beard over her face.

We all know who the bearded one is.

Fidel.

"I knew, though, when I looked in my girls' faces. Isabel took it the hardest at first. Her fiancé stayed behind. Isabel was never one for talking about her emotions. Eventually her sisters would pry whatever was bothering her out of her and she'd open up to them, but it took time.

"Beatriz was angry," Magda continues. "She was always fired up about something. Your great-grandfather loved her best; no matter how hard he tried to act like he loved his girls equally, you could tell. She drove him crazy, but he loved her. They got into a fight in his study the night before they left. I wasn't trying to eavesdrop, but you couldn't help but overhear—the whole house listened to them carrying on. She didn't want to leave, didn't want to give Fidel the satisfaction of winning."

That sounds like Beatriz.

"Maria was the baby, of course. The girls all tried to shield her as much as they could. Alejandro—"

Her voice breaks off as she makes the sign of the cross over her body.

A lump swells in my throat. I've grown so used to my great-uncle's name evoking that same reaction among his sisters.

"Your grandmother was my favorite," Magda whispers conspiratorially. "I didn't have children then; I hadn't met my husband yet. Elisa was mine as much as she was your great-grandmother's. In those days, the nannies raised the children. Not like now. I dried Elisa's tears. Held her when she was in pain. And after what happened with that boy—"

My heart pounds.

"The revolutionary?"

"Yes."

"Please. What did she tell you about him?"

Magda's expression darkens. "He was trouble; I knew it from the first moment she mentioned him."

"Did she tell you his name?"

"No. She never did."

Disappointment fills me. We've come this far in our search only to be back where we started.

"She didn't want to tell me about him at first, of course, but then she didn't have much of a choice," Magda continues. "She was scared, and she needed help with the baby."

It takes a moment for her words to register, to hear them over the white noise rushing through my ears.

"I'm sorry, what did you say?"

She blinks. "I assumed that was why you wanted to know about him, because of the baby."

"What baby?"

chapter twenty

Elisa

It's strange how the world around you can change in the blink of an eye, how the difference between a few hours can mean everything. In one moment it was 1958 and the world was one thing; minutes passed and then it was 1959, and the world as we knew it disappeared.

The morning light confirms what we learned last night. Batista has fled and left us in the hands of the men marching into Havana from the countryside, the Sierra Maestra. Is Pablo with them? What will become of my brother? Their return is the only glimmer of hope in all of this, and I cling to it now.

Gossip filters in throughout the day. The neighbors are out, Ana's parents stopping by, everyone gathering around the television and radio, attempting to discern what will happen next. They say the fighters are coming back, pouring in from the mountains, carrying weapons and dressed in olive green fatigues, flaunting long, scraggly beards. It appears as though the victory has caught them nearly as off guard as it has caught the rest of us. Batista seemed like an inevitability we would always suffer. Fidel is a looming unknown.

I sit in the house with my parents, my sisters, making idle conversation.

No, I didn't realize the Mendozas fled with Batista. What a shame we didn't get to say good-bye.

Workers are striking, the city celebrating, but our street in Miramar is eerily quiet except for the trickle of neighbors. Everyone cites a friend of a friend when they give their information; everyone speaks with an air of authority as though they possess a map for the future.

By the afternoon, I can't take it anymore. My stomach is in knots, dizziness hitting me in waves, and I crave the fresh air. The atmosphere in the house is like being closeted in a sickroom. I flee to my room, changing into a pair of trousers and a cotton blouse, sliding my most serviceable pair of sandals onto my feet.

A knock sounds at my bedroom door, and Magda walks in just as I am finishing dressing, her eyes widening as she takes in my appearance.

"Absolutely not."

I don't bother denying my intent; she knows me too well for that.

"I want to see what the streets look like."

I want to look for Pablo.

Her mouth tightens in a firm, disapproving line. "I can tell you what they look like. The same as they did with Machado. You don't want to be out in that mess."

"Just for a moment. Please don't tell my parents."

"What is this about? Really?"

I want to go to the house where Pablo stayed the last time he was in the city. I want to know if he's returned to Havana. I *need* to see him.

"I have a friend. He was fighting in Santa Clara."

"Elisa—"

Only Magda could say my name in such a way that I felt compelled to confess all my sins.

"He's more than just a friend," I whisper.

"What have you done?"

It's the worry in her voice that tugs at me. With my parents, I would expect condemnation, but with Magda I only find concern. The knot in my stomach tightens. "I fell in love."

She closes her eyes, her lips moving as though in prayer.

"He's a good man," I protest.

"You play a dangerous game. Your family—"

"I know. I only want to see that he's back safely. That he's alright."

I don't tell her the rest of it; there are some things I'm not ready to share.

She shakes her head, making the sign of the cross over herself. "May the saints preserve us."

I walk down the Paseo del Prado, Magda beside me, her arm tucked in mine, a worried expression on her face. No matter how hard I tried to convince her to stay home, she wouldn't be dissuaded. No one even noticed us leaving—they were so thoroughly engrossed in the tale of Batista's exodus.

Magda's strides quicken with each step, her gaze sweeping around. The streets are crowded, people talking and laughing, evidence of the strike everywhere you look. They are clearly ready to give Fidel a hero's welcome. I overhear pieces of conversations—someone let pigs loose in one of the mob's casinos.

My heart pounds as we turn down street after street until we reach the building where Pablo was staying. Two children sit on the front steps throwing a ball around, a dog lying beside them. Magda follows me inside, refusing to leave me when I climb the stairs to the second floor.

A wave of dizziness hits me again, and I regret not eating the lunch my mother served at the house earlier—after one bite it tasted like sawdust in my mouth. My hands tremble when I reach Pablo's front door, as I knock on the wood.

Magda's disapproval over the condition of the apartment building is stamped all over her face.

No one answers.

I knock again this time, louder, my knuckles moving in desperation. The door opposite Pablo's opens, a woman sticking her head out, her gaze running over Magda and me.

"What do you want?" she demands.

"I'm looking for the man who lives here."

Her gaze narrows, clouded with suspicion. "No one has been around for weeks."

Disappointment fills me. "If he comes back, will you tell him a woman was here looking for him?"

She shrugs before closing the door behind her, the sound of a child's cries filling the hallway.

I sag against the wall.

"Are you ready?" Magda asks. "This is not the kind of neighborhood you want to be in once the night comes."

I nod, my eyes welling with frustrated tears.

We leave the building, walking down the street, heading toward our car. The crowd appears to have swelled since we first entered the apartment, more and more people clogging the streets, their voices growing louder, the frenzy magnified.

I curse my stupidity, the foolishness that had me taking to the streets looking for him.

My voice is strained. "We need to get home."

I've never seen the city like this—it's a jubilant madness, but madness just the same. A man wielding a bat in his hands runs up to one of the parking meters, smashing it over and over again, his face contorted in fierce determination.

Whack. Whack.

The change inside clangs together before the machine tips over, smashing to the ground, coins spilling all over the concrete sidewalk. People swoop in—children, their parents—scooping up the money.

What surprises me most, what terrifies me most, is the anger. It's as if they've kept a tight lid on their emotions, letting the fury fester for years, contained by Batista's policies, Batista's injustices, and now that he's gone their anger has shifted, threatening everything in its path.

Magda's grip on me tightens as our strides lengthen, the mob swelling.

How long before they turn their attention from the parking meters to us?

My heart pounds when we reach the car, my hands shaking as I struggle to open the door. It takes two attempts for me to wrest the handle and pull the door open. My fingers tremble as I sit in the driver's seat and start the car.

"I'm so sorry. I should have never tried to go out today. I had no idea it would be like this."

"It was like this in '33, with Machado," Magda says, her voice grim. "It will get worse before it gets better."

I'm afraid she's right, and the anger bubbles up inside me, threatening to overflow. I'm angry at the men on the street, angry with Batista, Pablo, my brother. What did they usher into this country?

We're silent on the drive back, and it's only once we're in the safety of the big house, behind the gates again, that I feel some semblance of peace, and even that is short-lived. How long before the violence comes here?

Magda follows me to my bedroom, sitting beside me while I sink down onto the bed.

"Promise you won't go out like that again."

I nod, a wave of nausea hitting me. "I promise."

"That boy—"

I've been carrying this secret for far too long, and I need to tell someone. The words tumble out.

"I'm pregnant."

It is a truly bizarre thing to know your body for nineteen years, to grow used to it, its habits and quirks, and then to have it change on you so unexpectedly.

It began slowly a few weeks after the last time we saw each other—an urge to nap during the day, a bitter taste in my mouth, nausea constant. I eschewed my favorite foods for things I never enjoyed before, my emotions heightened. By the time I missed my period, I knew. I was late, and I was never late, and my body erased any doubt from my mind.

Magda hovers over me now that she knows about the baby, feeding me more food than I can possibly eat, encouraging me to nap, stroking my hair, praying beside me.

Even as I worry about the baby, about the uncertainty of my future, the troubles in Cuba's future loom large. Fidel has named Dr. Manuel Urrutia Lleó as the provisional president, but everyone says Castro will be the one pulling the strings anyway. The airport has been shut down; no one can get flights out of the country. Our driver reported seeing American tourists sitting on the front lawn of the Hotel Nacional, their suitcases in hand, fear and anger etched on their faces. They were finally evacuated by ship to Key West.

And it's not just the airport—the whole country is under general strike. Our father's been making angry phone calls all morning, trying to figure out what's happening with his workers.

Mobs have opened the doors at El Principe, letting the prisoners escape. Havana has descended into madness.

I'm back in the house, perched on a silk couch in our elegant sitting room, surrounded by paintings in heavy gold frames.

"They ransacked El Encanto," my mother says, her lips pursed in a tight line. There is no greater sin in her mind than the destruction of haute couture.

I imagine all those dresses we used to try on, now in apartments throughout Havana, worn by those who admired them in magazines. We used to find a little bit of magic in those dresses; will that same magic rub off on their new owners?

"They got the casinos, too," my father says. "No one is doing anything to stop them—the military, the police, they've all simply given up. They're giving our country away without a fight," he thunders.

"Are they going to come here? For us?" Maria asks.

My mother pales. "Don't say that. Don't ever say that," she snaps.

"What?" Maria looks bewildered. "They want money, don't they? We have money."

My father ignores her.

"They're patrolling the streets now. They say the 26th of July has pushed the police force out." His face turns red. "People are hanging signs outside their houses thanking Fidel. For what? Do they really think he is on our side? He preaches peace and democracy while he prepares to feast on the carcasses of his enemies. He has made fools of all of us, mark my words, and I fear far worse before the month is out."

chapter twenty-one

They swarm into the city in a steady flow of green uniforms and beards. They carry guns in their hands, and I cringe at the cold black metal, at the manner in which they survey their surroundings as though Havana belongs to the 26th of July. They're good-natured in their victory, but then, victors can always afford the luxury of happiness. For the rest of us—

I scan each face looking for Pablo, searching, equal parts hoping to find him, equal parts afraid I will.

I fear it would break my heart to see his face, his body in those odious fatigues. And yet, the absence of him brings its own pain. Surely, he'll come to me? And my brother—no one knows where Alejandro is or what he's doing. Has he aligned himself with the 26th of July? Is he their enemy?

We are inundated with images of Fidel marching toward the city, taking his time, prolonging the six-hundred-mile journey like a predator savoring his kill. The nauseous feeling in my stomach doesn't subside.

"They've recognized Fidel's government," my father says.

"They?" my mother asks.

"The Americans."

"And the elections?"

"In eighteen months or two years." My father's mouth tightens. "In the meantime, the president—controlled by Fidel—has removed all political figures appointed by Batista. Some of his cabinet members have sought asylum in foreign embassies. Others have been arrested."

He doesn't say the rest, but I know—

Others have been executed by firing squad.

My father rattles off a list of names, men who came and dined at my mother's infamous Parisian dinner table, who gave us mints and sweets when we were children, men whose sons I danced with, whose daughters I knew well. My mother's cries drown out the rest of the names.

My hand drifts to my stomach, my palm resting protectively against the silk fabric. What world am I bringing this child into?

"They've frozen the assets of Batista's officials," my father says.

My mother's eyes widen with alarm. "And our investments?"

"They can't touch the money overseas. That's something, at least. The president of the National Bank is gone. Same with the Agricultural and Industrial Bank."

More friends of my father's.

"They say Batista is in Santo Domingo now, taking refuge with Trujillo."

He's in good company, then. The Dominican president is a longtime friend of Batista's and as much of a tyrant.

"Many of Batista's closest advisors are with him, waiting this thing out until it is safe to return."

My father doesn't say more, but I hear the unspoken worry in his voice, the push and pull. Should we leave or should we stay?

We gather in front of the television that evening, the room silent as we watch Fidel speak in front of the crowds at Camp Columbia, the military barracks in Havana. There must be thousands of people there, tens of thousands, hundreds of thousands. He's surrounded by a sea of Cubans looking to him as though he is the answer to everything they've ever hoped for, prayed for.

A week ago a different man stood there, sneaking out of the country he controlled for many years. Leaving us with this. Earlier, tanks and trucks rolled through the city as though we're being occupied by an invading army rather than liberated by one of our own. They've opened Camp Columbia's gates, and the space is filled with Fidel's compatriots, with ordinary Cubans. They come to see Fidel—their messiah. He is still relatively unknown throughout Havana, a Robin Hood figure of sorts, but they know one important thing about him—

He is not Batista.

They hated Batista.

But it is clear that Fidel is no savior, either.

There are no saints in Havana.

I wake the next morning, and the sky is duller, the air thick and cloying, last night's spectacle casting a pall over the entire city.

I join my sisters in the dining room for breakfast; our parents have disappeared somewhere in the house. The more Fidel inserts himself into Havana, the more my parents retreat.

What would the corsair have done? Would he have taken up arms and fought? Or would he have taken his pretty French wife and their child and hied off in his great big ship for better lands?

More people are leaving each day—friends of my fathers, friends of Batista's. Fidel and his cohorts are obsessed with purging the country of anyone tied to the old regime, but what happens when they've spilled all the Batista loyalist blood there is to spill? Who will they come for next?

The food tastes like sludge in my mouth, my stomach and the

babe rebelling, but I force myself to swallow, shoveling the rich breakfast down my throat.

It is entirely too quiet in the house. Our silverware scrapes across bone china. Only Maria seems content to sit in silence, stifling yawns between bites of her food. The rest of us look shell-shocked. On the streets people celebrate, the mood of the country jubilant.

In our house and so many others like it, we're afraid to venture out, fear the knock on the door, worry they'll eventually get to our family's name on a list somewhere. Afraid to leave, afraid to stay.

"Miss Elisa?"

Our maid Charo stands in the doorway to the dining room, her eyes wide. "There's a man here to see you," she whispers, her gaze darting around, no doubt looking for my mother.

I hear the word "man," and everything else disappears. My sisters ask me questions somewhere in the background, but I don't hear them. I don't even hear the rest of what Charo says before I'm pushing back from the table, walking—nearly running—through the house.

He's home. Everything will be fine now. He's safe. He's alive. My hand falls to my stomach, caressing our child, my other hand opening the front door, eager to see Pablo, to collapse into his arms.

The sunlight hits me first, so bright it's nearly blinding, deigning to break through the clouds and show its face. The sound of people cheering somewhere off in the distance is a dull roar, but that, too, fades away.

A man stands near the front gates, his head ducked, wearing olive green fatigues and a matching cap, a beard covering the lower half of his face.

My heart pounds.

I walk toward him, my feet moving more quickly now, kicking up stones in the front drive.

He's home. We will be married now. He will be so happy about the baby. We'll sort out the rest of it.

He's home and that's all that matters.

He looks up as I approach, his dark gaze solemn, and I stop in my tracks, confusion filling me. The eyes that stare back at me aren't Pablo's. It takes a moment for me to recognize the face, another moment still for the words to come to me, bursting through the recesses of my memory.

If anything happens to me while I'm gone, Guillermo will find you. It won't come to that, though, because I'm coming home to you, Elisa. Batista himself couldn't keep me away.

I stop a foot away from the gates, tears filling my eyes, my knees buckling beneath me.

"I'm so sorry," Guillermo says, and then I can no longer hear the rest of his words for the white noise rushing through my ears, my body collapsing against the earth.

Pablo is dead, and Havana is dead, and I am dead.

chapter twenty-two

Marisol

I sit in the passenger seat, staring at the palm trees waving in the breeze. I don't speak. Magda has taken everything I thought I knew about my family, about my grandmother, about myself, and turned it upside down. The man I knew as my grandfather, who my father believes is his father, isn't really at all. Instead, my biological grandfather is—was—one of Fidel's men, a man who died fighting in the Cuban Revolution, who gave his life for everything my family stands against. The sheer fact that my grandmother loved a revolutionary was difficult to wrap my mind around, but this—

"Do you think your grandfather knew?" Luis asks. "About the baby?"

I try to remember the times I saw them together, how he treated me and my father, my sisters, the love he showed all of us.

My grandfather was one of the first people my grandmother met when she arrived in the United States; his family was involved in the early days of the Cuban exile movement, assisting new arrivals to acclimate to life in the United States after Castro took power. His parents—my great-grandparents—left during the Cuban

Revolution of 1933, which ousted then President Machado, a general who'd fought against Spain in the War for Cuban Independence.

My grandfather was born in the United States, and his stories weren't of Cuba, but rather watching Florida grow and change throughout the years. When Great-Grandfather Perez died he left his sugar empire—resuscitated from its near demise at the hands of Fidel Castro and his compatriots—to my grandfather to run. And so Perez Sugar was for the first time since its inception in the late 1800s run by a Ferrera and not a Perez.

According to my grandmother, theirs was a whirlwind courtship. He fell in love with her the first moment he saw her sitting in the living room of a family friend's house in Miami. It took him a month to wear her down, and once he did they eloped in a simple ceremony in City Hall. I asked her once if she regretted missing out on the big, splashy wedding.

Those were difficult times, Marisol. We weren't thinking of gowns or parties anymore. We were mourning—the loss of our country, our family, our friends.

And now I understand my grandmother's urgency a bit more. She was pregnant and unmarried in a time when she would have caused a huge scandal and likely added to her family's grief.

"He had to have known," I answer. "She wouldn't have kept it from him. Not something like that. Besides, my father was born months after they came to the United States. My grandfather would have suspected based on when the baby was conceived."

Magda told me how much my grandmother grieved when she discovered her lover died in Santa Clara. I can only imagine what it must have been like for my grandmother—nineteen, pregnant, caught in the midst of a revolution, learning the man she loved, the father of her child, was dead. Who could my grandmother have trusted with her secrets after something like that? She'd been forced to leave her best friend and the woman who'd practically raised her in Cuba. My great-grandparents no doubt would have been angry and ashamed, especially given the identity of the baby's father. No wonder she'd ended up with my grandfather. Did he ask her to keep the secret of my father's paternity or did she choose to do so on her own?

"I wish—"

My voice breaks off, and I can't finish the thought, the emotions pummeling me.

I wish I'd known the truth. I wish I'd had a chance to know my biological grandfather, to hear how my grandmother felt about him in her own words.

I loved my grandfather, and while I don't remember him well, my memories are of a good man, my memories of my grandparents' marriage a loving one. But this need to know, to understand where I came from, is a powerful urge.

Luis starts the car's engine and pulls out onto the road. I glance back at Magda's building; we exchanged information and plan on keeping in touch.

"Your grandmother must have been very brave to survive so many losses," Luis says, his voice gentle.

And at such a young age, too.

"She was."

"You should be proud of that. And of him. For better or worse, strong blood runs through your veins. You read his letters to her. What sort of man was he?"

Can you take the measure of a person based on ten or twenty letters? I don't know. As a writer, I know better than anyone how easily words and emotions can be manipulated. But I do know my grandmother, and I cannot believe she would love a man who wasn't worthy of it.

"He was a good man." I recall the words he wrote her, the passionate strokes of his pen across the page. "A dreamer. A fighter."

"Then he is an ancestor you can proudly claim."

Is it that easy? Was his legacy saved by death? Had he lived through the events of the revolution and everything that came after, would he have spoken out against Fidel's abuses or would he have turned into a monster himself?

The line between hero and villain is a precariously fragile one.

"I'm sorry he died," Luis says. "That you weren't able to find him like you wanted."

"Me, too."

This is it. There are no more answers to be found, only questions. I will never have a chance to know the man whose blood runs through my veins. This part of my family is gone now, too, just like my grandmother.

When I was searching for her lover, there was still hope, a sense of purpose to my trip here beyond finding her final resting place. Now there's just the unknown, and of course, the uncertainty of my relationship with Luis.

He brings our joined fingers to his lips, kissing my knuckles. "Everything is going to be okay," he says, as though he can read the thoughts going through my mind.

"Will it?"

"*Ojalá.*"

I smile, the spirit behind the word something so quintessentially Cuban, something incrementally beyond hope that exists entirely out of our hands.

"This means something to me, Marisol," Luis says, echoing his earlier words in the hotel elevator.

A little crack forms over my heart. "This means something to me, too."

I spend the rest of the drive back to Havana with Luis's arm wrapped around my shoulders, his lips occasionally brushing my temple, our legs pressed against each other, studying his profile.

"Let's go out tonight," he suggests as we near the city. "Let's do something to take your mind off all of this."

"Like a date?"

He laughs. "Yes, a proper date. Somewhere along the way we've gotten things turned around a bit. I'll pick you up and take you to dinner—nothing fancy, but I promise the food will be perfection." He winks at me. "I happen to know a few good *paladares*. Afterward, we can go dancing."

I grin. "You dance?"

Somehow I can't quite imagine formal, slightly serious Luis dancing. Then again—

"Occasionally," he says with a small smile. "Don't tell anyone, but my grandmother taught me when I was a very little boy."

"Mine, too. She used to play old records in her living room, and we'd dance together. I was terrible at first," I confess.

"And now?" he teases.

"I have a few moves."

"I'm even more intrigued. I need to help my grandmother get ready for the dinner service since I missed yesterday, but perhaps we can go out afterward?"

"I would love that."

When we arrive back at the house, we part ways, and I set my bag down in my bedroom and head to the heart of the house—the kitchen—where Ana is preparing dinner for the *paladar*'s guests.

She smiles when she sees me.

"How was your trip?" she asks, greeting me with a kiss on the cheek.

"Beautiful," I answer. I'm not ready to tell her what we learned from Magda, am still processing the news myself. "Can I help you prepare dinner?"

Ana waves me off with a cluck of her tongue. "No, no. I have it. It's almost done. We have paella today."

I can smell it, the aroma of yellow rice and seafood filling the tiny space. She has the same style of enormous pan my grandmother used to cook her paella sitting on top of the stove.

"How do you decide the menu each day?" I ask.

"It depends on what I can get at the market. If I can find chicken that day, we eat arroz con pollo. If they have seafood, I make a paella. We're limited by the shortages, of course, but we make do."

"That has to be challenging."

She smiles. "I like a bit of a challenge. It helps me to be creative with the menu, and it keeps the guests happy because there's always variety. It's not an easy business; when the government opened the *paladar* system, many tried and many failed. The taxes and license fees can bankrupt you. Not to mention, you can create a menu only to have it fail miserably when you can't find the ingredients. You can spend days searching for something as simple as eggs or milk.

"Many of our guests, the tourists who come, don't understand the challenges we face. They judge our restaurants by the standards they are used to in their home countries, but we make do with Cuban ingenuity."

She winks at me.

"It doesn't hurt that we have Luis playing 'La Bayamesa' on the saxophone. We hang the photos my husband took in the revolution's early days on the wall, serve our guests on what's left of my grandmother's finest china. They come here for the romantic Cuban experience, and we give it to them."

Was that what I came here for? The "romantic Cuban experience"? I'd be lying if I didn't admit I'd had an image in my mind of what it would be like here. I'd told myself I'd be open-minded, that I wouldn't let the stories I'd heard, my family's perspective of exile, cloud my impressions of the real Cuba. I'd been convinced I'd find two narratives here—ours and theirs, and that the truth would lie somewhere in between. But I didn't realize how bad it would be. In all the discussions of opening relations with Cuba, of eradicating the embargo, the focus has always been on the island as a tourist paradise, perpetually frozen in time. I didn't realize how much people still suffered, didn't understand the depth and breadth of the problems facing everyday Cubans.

Ana gives me a sidelong glance.

"Speaking of Luis—" Her voice trails off for a moment. "Elisa and I used to talk about our lives when we grew older. We imagined being bridesmaids in each other's weddings, raising our children together, becoming grandmothers together. We used to imagine our children playing as best friends, perhaps even falling in love. It's good to see the two of you together."

"We're not—"

I'm not even sure how to finish the sentence. Not together? Not in love?

"I don't know how we can be together," I say instead.

"Have faith, Marisol. You could be good for each other. It might seem impossible now, but trust me, you never know what the future can bring."

Luis walks into the kitchen at the tail end of her speech, greeting his grandmother with a hug and kiss. I busy myself with the paella, mindlessly stirring to occupy my hands, my cheeks burning. There are some things we've yet to speak of, conversations I'm not ready to have. I leave soon—what will happen when I do? Will we keep in touch or will this connection between us peter out once we return to our normal lives?

Ana leaves to visit the guests, and we're alone once again.

Luis closes the distance between us, kissing my forehead. He smiles at me as I pause mid-stir.

His fingers stroke my nape. I flush again.

"You're nervous," he says, sounding amused by the notion.

"Yes."

"Why? You weren't nervous before."

"I was always a bit nervous, but it feels strange in this house, with your grandmother here, Cristina, your mother. I don't want to step on anyone's toes. And then there's everything else. I don't want to start something I can't finish; I don't know what I'm doing here," I confess. "I came to bury my grandmother, and now everything is mixed up. I have a grandfather I never knew I had. And you—"

I came here to write an article about tourist locales, and now my mind is full of policy and injustice; I came here single and carefree, and now I risk leaving my heart behind. It's as though Cuba has awoken something in me, and I can't—don't want to—shut it off.

"I know." Luis steps back with a sigh. "Things are complicated."

"Yes."

I turn, looking into his dark eyes, searching—

"You're good at that," I murmur.

"Good at what?"

"Hiding what you're feeling, thinking. About some things, you're an open book, but with others . . ." My voice trails off. "You're difficult to read."

"Is it really a mystery, Marisol?"

I close my eyes at the sound of my name falling from his lips, as my pulse accelerates, at the flutter in my stomach.

When I open my eyes, he's still there, his gaze boring into me, his expression as inscrutable as ever.

Luis steps forward, closing the distance between us, his lips caressing my forehead, his fingers running through my hair.

He takes a step back and gestures toward the stove. "Dinner is almost finished. Can you be ready in an hour?"

I open my mouth to answer him—

Luis's mom, Caridad, walks into the kitchen, setting a stack of plates down on the tiny counter space with a thud.

Luis's hand drops to his side. My cheeks flame as I take a deep breath, the air whooshing through my lungs.

"Do you want to leave in an hour or so?" he asks again, his voice low.

I nod.

Caridad's gaze follows me from the room.

chapter twenty-three

Elisa

He died in Santa Clara. He fought valiantly. There's little else I have to remember him by besides the memories I cling to now, the letters, and the few tangible signs I have that he was real and that he loved me.

And then there's the baby.

I spend two days in bed. My sisters cover for me; they don't ask any questions, but their worry is a palpable thing. Only Magda knows the truth; only Magda knows the full extent of my fears, and my heartache. She sits beside my bed, stroking my hair, attempting to convince me to eat and drink.

"For the baby," she whispers.

I exist in shadows, the sunlight flitting and disappearing, the noise of the household around me, the sounds of the street I've come to loathe.

Several days after my world is ripped apart, I'm forced out of bed. We have a new crisis to contend with—revolutions don't care much for broken hearts and shattered dreams.

They've finally reached my father's name on the list.

My mother is sobbing on the couch when I come downstairs, Isabel and Beatriz sitting beside her. Maria is in her room with Magda. It's becoming more and more difficult to shield her from all of this.

"What happened?" I ask. I always feared it would be Alejandro who drew their notice, Alejandro who wasn't afraid to denounce Fidel, who danced far too close to the flames. But our father—

Beatriz answers me. "Che went by his offices."

Oh, how I hate the Argentinian. It's bad enough to see Fidel behaving as though the country is his for the taking, but Che isn't even Cuban, adding insult to injury.

"He took him to La Cabaña," Isabel says, her expression grim.

Batista's prison has been converted to Fidel's prison. Some revolution.

"When?"

"This morning," Beatriz answers, her face pale. "That's all we know."

Under the new freedom and democracy Fidel is bringing to Cuba, they can hold him for however long they like, do whatever they'd like to him.

Progress.

I fear the anger inside me will simply erupt one day, no longer contained by silk gowns and gloves.

"They will kill him," my mother whispers.

"They won't," Isabel says, her words lacking conviction.

They might kill him.

A tear trickles down my cheek, then another, piercing the haze that surrounds me. My grief over Pablo's death is suddenly a luxury I cannot afford.

"What will we do?" my mother asks.

Leave Cuba.

The thought surprises me, but there's logic behind it, the image of the crowd knocking over the parking meters, looting, filling my mind once more. This is no longer a safe place for us, and if they are after our father, how long before they come after all of us? How safe will my child—all that I have left of Pablo—be in this version of Havana?

Where is Alejandro?

"We wait," Beatriz says instead, her voice grim.

Time moves differently now that Batista is no longer in power. I used to complain that my days were filled with parties and monotony; now they're filled with terror, and I long for the days when my biggest worry was which hat suited me best. Our father remains in La Cabaña, and each day brings more executions and no word from Alejandro. More and more of my parents' friends are leaving the country, heading to the United States, to Europe. More and more people leave, yet we wait, waiting to hear what will come of our father, waiting for a message from our brother, waiting, waiting, always waiting.

Our mother's uncle visits our father, passing on the news that he is still alive, confined to a dank, dark prison cell. Isabel and Beatriz sit next to our mother, holding her hand while our great-uncle delivers an update on our father's condition with a grim expression on his face.

Days pass, a week, until waiting at home becomes as distasteful as the alternative and we find ourselves in the belly of the beast.

The prison was built as a fortress in the eighteenth century to guard against English pirates and later converted to a military barracks. It is being run by the Argentinian—Che Guevara—the very man Pablo once spoke of to me. His friend, his brother in arms.

The stone fortress looms in front of us, Beatriz's hand clutched in mine.

"This is a bad idea," I whisper, my hand drifting to my stomach. I catch myself mid-motion, allowing my arm to dangle at my side. The nausea is back in full force, this morning's breakfast already reappearing.

The sun beats down on us, unrelenting.

"Would you rather have stayed in the house?" she asks.

No, but it isn't only me anymore. I should have refused when Beatriz asked me to accompany her.

She squares her shoulders, her gaze on the looming stone fortress, a familiar expression on her face—Beatriz on a mission is a dangerous thing.

"Wait for me here."

"Are you crazy?" I hiss. "You can't go in there on your own."

"What would you suggest I do?"

"They're killing people, Beatriz. With frightening regularity."

Anger blazes in her eyes; Beatriz's rage just might be a dangerous thing, too.

"There's someone who might help me," she says.

If Beatriz has connections in La Cabaña . . .

I grab her arm, pulling her toward me. "Are you involved with the 26th of July?"

"Of course not." The words drip with contempt. "But I know someone who is."

"A friend?" My voice lowers. "A lover?"

"Not even close." Her gaze returns to the stone fortress, as though she's steeling herself for an unpleasant task.

A shiver slides down my spine at the ferocity in her expression. There will be no dissuading her.

"It's been days, nearly a week. Who knows where Alejandro is?" Her voice breaks. "Who knows if he's even alive? And our father—what else are we to do? I have to try."

"Beatriz—"

"Please."

I let her go because there is no other option—if I don't let her go in today, she'll just come back and try again tomorrow. Reason has fled all of us, and yet I no longer have the luxury of making reckless decisions myself. My baby has already lost one parent to this revolution. It's up to me alone to keep our child safe.

I stand in the shadow of La Cabaña, watching as my brave, beautiful, headstrong sister walks into the fortress. I almost envy Beatriz her independence, her courage, her audacity. For the first time the full impact of my pregnancy hits me. I was so focused on Fidel, and then Pablo's death, and now my father's imprisonment, that the baby has been an abstract concept.

But I am to be a mother now. To raise this child on my own.

It is both a terrifying responsibility and a tremendous joy.

Soldiers pass by me, their green fatigues ragged, their gazes first on me, then drifting to Beatriz's retreating figure. Their laughter echoes in the air.

The nausea makes another untimely appearance.

I pray, words from childhood, words I've used more in the past several months than in the totality of my life combined. I pray for Beatriz, for my father, for my brother, for my unborn child, for all of us now.

Minutes pass, an hour. The stark reality that I may have lost Beatriz, too, that our father might never be returned to us, hits me with an intensity that grows with each ticking moment. How are we to provide for our family without him? Will my great-uncle take us in? Another distant family member? How will we survive this?

And just when my panic reaches an unbearable level Beatriz walks out. It's impossible to tell if she was successful or not; Beatriz walks the same in victory and defeat.

She stops a foot away from me, her expression grim.

"I wasn't able to get him out. I was able to see him, though. He's injured but fine. Furious with me for coming." She swallows. "They shoved him in a cell with ten other men. Like animals."

"What are they going to do with him?"

"I don't know." Her silence tells a different tale.

"Beatriz."

"They're shooting people. Three times a day. Like clockwork." Her expression turns murderous. "Che likes his schedules."

This time I do throw up, the contents of my breakfast landing on the ground beneath me.

Beatriz is there in an instant, silent, stroking my back, pulling my hair away from my face.

"What's going on with you?" she asks, her gaze sharp once I've righted myself.

I shake my head, wiping at my lips with the handkerchief I pull out of my bag, an acrid taste in my mouth. "It isn't the time."

Soon it will be, though. How much longer can I hide this secret? How much weight can we bear on our shoulders before we collapse?

Beatriz seems to accept my answer for the moment, but her gaze is searching.

The corner of her mouth is smudged, bright red lipstick marring her face.

I shudder. "What happened in there?"

She shakes her head, her gaze shuttered. "I'm fine. It isn't the time," she says.

I wrap my arms around her, needing this moment of comfort. "What do we do now?" I ask her.

"We go home. And we wait."

We lock arms, turning away from the fortress. My legs shake.

Behind us, the sound of gunshots fills the air—

One, two, three, four, five, six, seven, eight.

I count them as tears rain down my cheeks.

For the first time in my life, I know what it is to truly hate, the emotion filling me entirely, annihilating everything else in its path. And then the hate is gone, as swiftly as it came, leaving me with new emotions I'm not equipped to deal with.

There are dozens of ways you can betray your country—broken promises, failed policies, the sound of a firing squad pumping bullets into flesh. And then there's the silent betrayal—the most insidious one of all. We thought we were being smart by merely enduring Batista. We thought we were playing the long game, cozying up to power so we could keep our grand homes, and our yacht club memberships, and our champagne-filled parties. We thought the indignities of his regime wouldn't touch us.

I told myself being a Perez meant more than being Cuban, that my responsibility to my family, to do what was expected, to be the woman my parents wanted me to be meant more than fighting for what I believed in, for speaking out against Batista's tyranny.

And the whole time we were pretending our way of life was fine, the "paradise" we'd created was really a fragile deal with a mercurial devil, and the ground beneath us shifted and cracked, destroying the world as we knew it.

Fidel has shown us the cost of our silence. The danger of waiting too long to speak, of another's voice being louder than ours because we were too busy living in the bubbles we'd created to realize the rest of Cuba had changed and left us behind.

I feel guilt and shame.

chapter twenty-four

Marisol

That night I dress for dinner with Luis, counting down the few days—three—we have left together in my mind, wanting this evening to be special, to make the most of our time together. Luis knocks on my door just as I'm finished changing into my red dress, the scent of the perfume I've spritzed lingering in the air.

I open the door and am greeted by the sight of Luis standing outside my room, smiling at me, his gaze running over my appearance, a bouquet of sunflowers in his hand.

We walk from the Rodriguez house to the Malecón, our hands joined, fingers linked. When we reach the water's edge, he buys two bottles of Presidente from a cart vendor. We take a seat on the stone ledge, our feet dangling over the water as it crashes against the rock, the sea spray hitting my bare calves.

The sunset rolls in, transforming the landscape as the locals come out of the crumbling buildings lining the promenade, carrying music and laughter with them. Luis hooks an arm around my shoulders, bringing me closer to his body, my head burrowed in the crook of his neck. My lips slide over the skin there, tasting the salt from the water. My hair whips around me in the wind.

"I'm going to miss this," I say, turning away from him and staring out at the sea. It feels like I just got here, and now there's not much time left. I've been thrust into this unexpected world, its impression lingering. I no longer wish to write about Cuban restaurants and foods; I long to write about revolutions, exile, loss. I ache to write about Cuba's future. I yearn to return.

How can I return to Miami and resume the life I lived before now that everything has changed?

Luis's grip on me tightens, a sharp exhale escaping his mouth. He doesn't answer me; what is there to say? I hope I can return soon, hope relations will continue to improve, pray the barriers between our countries will lessen with time. Who knows? We are just a small country in a world full of tragedies.

I want a chance to learn about my grandfather, to see Ana again, to explore the parts of the island I've yet to see. And of course, there's Luis.

He tips my head toward him, capturing my mouth in a fierce kiss. My hand rests over his heart, my fingers gripping the fabric of his shirt.

I've been with enough men, am old enough to recognize that this thing between us is different than any time before, that my heart is engaged in a way it never has been. I've never felt this instant connection with someone, this sense of recognition, the audible click of two pieces fitting together.

Behind us someone laughs and cheers, the sound filtering to background noise, my world narrowed to this.

I love you.

The words seem unfair, a burden to place on him, a tether with far too many commitments attached. Our lives couldn't be more different, and I struggle to imagine him inhabiting my world as much as it's impossible to envision myself living here. The part of me that yearns to feel a connection to this place wishes I could ignore the realization that this is not my home. It's the land of my grandmother, the legacy that shapes me, but the modern iteration is something else entirely, something I can't quite identify with no matter how badly I wish it were so. My family's fortunes have changed, and while this is our past—and hopefully, our future—it cannot be our present.

And yet this is where my grandmother wished to rest, the country that held such a fierce hold over her heart—was it the country or the man? Or did the memory of both become so inextricably linked, tangled up in each other, that it became impossible for her to tell where one ended and the other began? She fell in love with him here, on the Malecón, the words they whispered carried on the air, their eyes cast toward the sea.

"What are you thinking about?" Luis asks.

"My grandmother. Her life here."

"You don't have much time left to decide where to spread her ashes."

"I know."

I look out at the water, the sun making its final descent.

"I can't help but wonder what would have happened if he never died, if they'd had a chance at a life together. Would the revolution have kept them apart or would they have loved each other enough to make it work?"

Luis brings our joined hands to his lips.

"I don't know."

Neither do I.

We walk into Vedado, down darkened streets, the tourists ensconced in their hotels, the locals out in full swing. Without the kitschy-themed bars and the state-run restaurants in the more touristy parts of the city, Cubans make their own fun, impromptu dance parties breaking out on the sidewalk, kids gathered in circles, playing games, their laughter ringing in the night.

Luis grins at me, my hand in his. "Now you're getting the authentic Cuban experience."

"Where are we going?"

He's vacillated between playful and serious all evening, and these moments when he's happy and teasing are my absolute favorite.

"You'll see," he answers with a wink.

A car turns down the street, bathing me in the glow of two bright headlights.

It stops.

Luis brings me to his side, putting his body between the vehicle and me.

It's not a vintage car like the ones I'm used to seeing in Havana now—chrome, leather, bright colors, and rolling lines. This one is black, boxy, ugly, old in a way that's neither glamorous nor nostalgic.

Luis's hand on my waist tenses. It drops away.

Two men step out of the car.

They're dressed casually, nondescript clothes that wouldn't draw my attention under normal circumstances. They walk as though they're in uniform, though, with the kind of purpose that comes with the sanction of official power. They might not approach us flashing badges, but it makes no difference. They are important. They are powerful.

Even though he is in the grave, there is no mistaking it—they are Fidel's.

It happens so quickly—the flash of headlights, the sound of heavy metal car doors opening, slamming shut, the footfall of shoes on the cracked sidewalk, Luis's voice saying my name, the warning contained there a scream wrapped in a whisper.

"Marisol—"

He steps away from me, leaving me standing on the sidewalk alone, my hand dangling at my side. It's only a few steps, but he might as well have shoved me away from him. We were together, and now we're not. I am Cuban, and I am not.

Luis's back is to me, but tension is evident in the set of his shoulders, in the distance between us. The perimeter surrounding him and the men walking toward him might as well be contained by an electrified fence—no one on the street pays us any attention, their gazes anywhere but on Luis and the men, on me, their gaits growing more rapid, their feet carrying them far away from the danger surrounding them. The effort they exert not looking toward us is a palpable thing.

The men stop in front of Luis. Their voices are low, and I can only make out bits and pieces of the conversation, but it's enough—

They're taking him with them. I don't know where.

Luis doesn't look back at me as he gets in the car. Doesn't turn around and beseech me to tell his grandmother and mother where he's gone, doesn't ask for me to call an attorney on his behalf. He doesn't protest or attempt to fight them off, as though he's resigned himself to the inevitability of this.

The car drives away in a squeal of tires, and he's gone, the dark vehicle making its way down the Havana street, leaving me behind, wondering when—if—he'll return.

My heart pounds, the passport in my purse burning a hole there. Should I go to the American embassy? Or return to the Rodriguez home and let Ana and Caridad know what has happened? Minutes earlier, I felt safe, happy here in Havana with Luis. Now I'm terrified.

The streets in Vedado no longer look so friendly, the evening growing dark, and I doubt I could find my way back to Miramar without assistance. Should I hail a cab? Check into a hotel and ask for help?

Another car pulls up alongside me. I grip my bag, holding it to my body, trying to remember the lessons I learned in the self-defense class my grandmother made me take nearly a decade ago.

A single girl living alone in Miami can never be too careful, Marisol.

A man with a thick neck and hulking shoulders gets out of the car. He looks like the sort of man women take note of in parking garages, on elevators, the sort of man you instinctively fear.

For a moment I freeze, my brain attempting to reconcile the fact that he's walking toward me. He reaches out, his hand gripping my arm, pulling me toward the car, and I explode, my arms and legs hitting him, a scream torn from the depths of my throat.

Will anyone help me?

And then there are more hands on me, and they lift me, limbs flailing, and dump me in the back seat of the car.

chapter twenty-five

Elisa

As quickly as they grabbed him, the regime returns our father to us, battered and bloody but alive. We exist in a state of nervous détente; no one knows why Fidel chose to toss him back like a fish too small to be gobbled up by the regime, but we're on tenterhooks, waiting to see if they will come for him again. Perhaps Fidel's too busy, his attention on bigger things.

We've gone from private firing squads under Batista to public trials and executions courtesy of Fidel. I can just summon up the bare minimum amount of rage, the smallest dollop of horror. I'm numb on the inside—it's been two weeks since Guillermo came to our door and told me Pablo had died, and it still feels like I'm living a nightmare. At night I read Pablo's letters over and over again, as though they could conjure him up, the words on the page transforming into flesh-and-blood man.

No one warned me love would hurt so much.

We gather in front of the television, in a routine that is now becoming all too familiar. Indeed, this is a family affair; even my mother is here watching. As much as the whole process repels her—the very idea of the masses judging the elite is anathema to her—there's a morbid curiosity that drives us all. Is this what they felt in France as they watched the guillotine's blade be judge, jury, and executioner?

All it takes these days is an accusation, even the word of a child, to commit a man to death. Fidel says these spectacles will bring transparency, that he has nothing to hide, and he isn't wrong—the horror of what has befallen our country is indeed on display for the world to see.

When will someone come to our aid? When will the rest of the world condemn him?

In the end it's too much to watch, the television's harsh glare doing nothing to dull the travesty before us. We sit slack-jawed and appalled, unable to speak, unable to move. How many of our countrymen have died since Fidel took power? A thousand? Two? Their names are whispered, and then forgotten, left to linger in the air before they disappear forever.

Finally, it's Beatriz who breaks the spell.

"Turn off the TV," she snaps at Maria.

She should not be seeing this. What are my parents thinking? We should all be working to preserve the fiction of her innocence, to protect her from all of this. *They* should be protecting her. But ever since Fidel marched into Havana, ever since Batista left and everything changed, my parents have devolved into a state of inaction.

Maria's eyes widen at Beatriz's tone; she's enjoyed a sanctuary of sorts as the youngest. We've all tried our best to be patient with her, gentle with her. But these are challenging times.

I turn my gaze toward the flickering light on the TV before it goes dark completely. They're trying Batista supporters, those who served in the military, as war criminals in the Havana sports stadium. Tens of thousands sit in the crowd cheering and jeering, eating ice cream and peanuts, roaring as they call for blood. We are

Rome, and this is the Coliseum, the lions' teeth sinking into Cuban flesh for vengeance and blood sport, televised for the entire nation to watch—a cautionary tale of sorts.

Will I see my father's face on TV next? My brother's? I've already lost the man I loved to this madness. When does it end? This is not a trial. This is not justice. And I think of Pablo now, of what he fought and died for. The man I knew, the man I loved, would not have wanted to see us reduced to this. Where is the constitution we were promised? The end to Batista's cruelty? We have replaced one dictator with another and still my countrymen cheer. They chant "to the wall" now, quite literally calling for the deaths of those who supported Batista, those they believe have slighted them, those they wish to stand before a firing squad.

At night when I dream it is a strange mix that assails me— Pablo's blood-soaked hands, Fidel's roguish smile, maniacal white doves heralding disaster, crowds chanting, calling for our heads, setting Havana ablaze. Magda says it's the baby causing the dreams, that it's normal for my emotions to run high. She burns candles and offers prayers to the gods, but neither Changó nor Jesus appear concerned with saving Havana.

The events at the stadium affect the tenor in the city as the weeks drag on and January becomes February. My parents have snapped out of the fog that surrounded them, and they speak in hushed voices late at night, long after they think my sisters and I have gone to sleep. The household dynamics have shifted—there's an undercurrent now as though the staff is holding its collective breath, waiting for the other shoe to drop.

Magda senses it, too, mediating the tension between the family and the staff, taking care of all of us.

She prepares a bath for me, filling the water with herbs and perfumes, a dash of holy water smuggled out of the Cathedral of Havana.

"It will protect you," she says as I sink into the water.

The clock is running down on my ability to keep the pregnancy a secret. My clothes still fit, but it's only a matter of time, and I can't help but think that if we lived in different times, if the world as we know it wasn't falling down around us, my parents would have noticed that something is wrong by now.

It's perhaps the only favor Fidel has done or ever will do for me.

I never knew it was possible to hate someone as much as I hate him. Every glimpse of him is a slap in the face. Why couldn't he have died instead of Pablo?

Tears run down my cheeks, spilling into the bathwater, mixing with the holy water, the items the santero suggested Magda use.

"Shh."

She strokes my hair, singing to me in her soothing, deep voice, and I'm at once a little girl again, safe in her embrace.

"Will you sing to the baby?" I ask her.

Magda smiles. "Of course. Just as I sang to you and your sisters." She squeezes my hand. "I will teach you my songs."

That night I don't dream of blood, or Pablo's dead eyes, but of a little girl, her tiny hand clutched in mine, her long hair flowing behind me. I brush her hair until it gleams, braiding it, and she asks me to tell her stories, of Cuba, of my family. She listens intently, as I give her our history, as I kiss the top of her head. She is content to sit with me, until I wake the next morning, the overwhelming sense of loss surprising me when I find her gone. I'm not sure how I know, but I do—

She needs me. Desperately.

Perhaps it was the bath or simply the product of a good night's sleep, but I climb out of bed feeling better than I have in a long time. I dress quickly, making my way to the dining room.

One of the maids is listening to Fidel on the radio in her room; it's jarring to hear his voice from the back of the house, the sensation that he has invaded our sanctuary inescapable. I've had enough of his stupid speeches, enough of Fidel and his promises that will never come true. Empty words from another king of Cuba, replacing one tyranny with another. I want to tell her to turn it off, but in this climate no one can afford the luxury of shutting one's doors to Fidel. He is in all our homes now whether we want him here or not.

Pablo's dreams of reinstating the 1940 Constitution are just that—dreams. Instead, Fidel gives us the Fundamental Law, if it can even be called that. Under this farcical piece of legislation, Fidel has the power to hold prisoners without charge, but this threat pales in comparison to the macabre spectacle at the stadium.

How do they not see? The same people who cheer Fidel's cruelty vilified Batista for his. Is it only accepted because they hate us? Because they coveted our way of life? How long do they think Fidel will continue to operate as a piece of fiction—a benevolent Robin Hood? He steals from the rich and gives to the poor, but what will happen when all the money has been driven from Havana? Will he stop or will he continue to take and take?

Serving in the military under Batista can get you executed. Supporting Batista in a climate where supporting Batista wasn't an option can get you executed. What else will Fidel use as an excuse to eviscerate his opponents?

My sisters are sitting at the dining room table from Paris, eating silently when I enter.

"Where is Beatriz?" I ask, noticing her seat is empty.

Isabel's brow furrows. "I don't know; she was already gone when I woke up. Are you feeling better?"

Does she suspect?

"I am, thank you."

I stare at the ring on her finger, watching the diamond catch the light, thinking of the ring hidden in my room, the one I wish I had the courage to wear. I want to tell them. I want to tell them, but I am a coward, and I fear in their eyes a traitor. I'm afraid I will break their hearts. I'm afraid they will cast me out for betraying our family.

I'm afraid.

Pablo died for the very forces that are now destroying our country, the people who threw my father in prison, who beat him, who treated him worse than one would an animal, who very well might come back and kill him. Men who kill for blood sport and entertainment.

How do I tell them that?

"Isabel, Elisa—Beatriz—" Magda runs into the room, her eyes swimming with tears, her voice shaking.

Ice fills my veins as I look at her, as her face falls before me, as her body simply crumples to the ground.

Isabel reaches her first, grasping her arms, holding her up. "What's wrong? What's happened?"

A low, keening sound erupts from Magda, and my world simply shatters.

Not Beatriz. I can't lose my sister, too.

"Where's Beatriz?" I ask, my voice calm compared to the terror racking my limbs. Perhaps some part of me has simply become inured to the violence. Did Beatriz return to La Cabaña? Is she in prison now, too?

Magda takes a deep breath, her body quaking. "She's outside. She . . . she found him." A sob escapes her lips.

Now Isabel is the calm one. "Who?"

I don't wait for her answer, my legs carrying me out the door, running to the front gates. I kick up gravel beneath my shoes once I reach the path in the front entrance. A crowd is beginning to form in front of the house—gardeners, staff—someone calls my name behind me, but all I can think of is Beatriz—

My steps slow.

She's sitting on the gravel floor, her gown—one we bought together not too long ago when our world was a simpler place—pooling around her. If not for the incongruous setting, she'd look like a debutante posing for a society photo; if not for the blood splattering her dress, staining her palms, or the body cradled in her lap.

I know the moment she looks at me. How could I not?

I sink to the ground beside her, my legs rubber. I know I'm crying because my cheeks are wet, but I feel removed from my body, as though I've left it and floated up to the sky, looking down on all of us, praying for our souls.

"They dumped him," Beatriz babbles. I reach out and grasp her free hand. "In front of the gate. A car—it sped by and then it stopped." Tears stream down her face. "The door opened and I saw him—he's so skinny, isn't he? Like he hasn't been eating for a while." Her fingers shake as she strokes the face that looks so very much like hers. "He was already dead when he hit the ground. I tried—"

I focus on her, because I can't look down, can't look at him.

The crowd around us grows, the servants shrieking, Isabel and Magda crying. Our parents should not see this. Maria cannot see this.

Beatriz's gaze meets mine, the wet sheen there covering steel. "One day they will pay," she vows.

"Yes, they will."

I look down into my dead brother's eyes.

chapter twenty-six

Marisol

When they remove the hood from my head, I'm in a room—gray, nondescript, vaguely residential in nature—there are two armchairs, a table in the corner with a lamp, the light casting a yellow glow around the room, a lumpy couch shoved into another corner. A frayed rug covers a dirty ground.

My hands are unbound.

The man who grabbed me off the street stands before me, and I open my mouth to plead for my safety, to ask about Luis, a million words and protestations pushing to escape, but before I can cobble together my jumbled thoughts, before I can make myself *move*, he is gone, shutting the door behind him with a firm thud, and I am alone.

Are they going to question me? Rape me? Kill me? How long are they planning to hold me here? Will anyone realize what happened to me?

A tear trickles down my face. Then another.

The door opens.

Another man walks into the room, this one much older, his steps slow, an elegant cane in one hand, wearing a neatly pressed guayabera and crisp trousers. His black leather shoes gleam. Whereas the first man screamed "danger," this man screams "power."

The door shuts behind him with an ominous thud.

For a moment we stare at each other, sizing each other up. He's tall and lean. Distinguished, his hair a steely gray, his face defined by thin lines and wrinkles, his eyes dark, his gaze hooded.

He takes a step forward. "We're not going to hurt you," he says in Spanish after a moment, his tone surprisingly gentle for someone who exudes such influence, as though he is the sort of man positioned to send another to his death with the stroke of a pen.

I almost believe him and then I catch myself. Is that part of their game—lulling their enemies into complacency and then attacking?

"And the man I was with? Are you going to hurt him?"

Are they hiding Luis somewhere here, too? In another room?

"I'm not. But I'm afraid I cannot speak to Mr. Rodriguez's whereabouts."

My stomach sinks as Luis's last name falls from his lips. This was the threat Luis warned me about from the beginning. Was roughing him up on the street the other night a precursor to this? Will I leave this room alive?

"Can't? Or won't?" I ask, a tremor in my voice.

"Can't."

He speaks with the care of a man who parses each and every word, and for some reason his gentle tone strikes a chord of terror deep within me, the kindness in his voice incongruous with the evening's events. What is his role in all of this?

I struggle for calm, reaching for the courage I hope lies somewhere inside me. "Then why am I here? What do you want with me?"

He doesn't answer, but instead walks toward an empty chair in the corner, dragging it in front of me. He takes a seat, crossing his ankle over his opposite knee, in a pose that tugs at my memory. He looks down at my hand, his gaze settling on the ring there.

My fingers curl into a protective ball, my knuckles resting on my thigh.

"Marisol Ferrera."

A chill slides down my spine as my name falls from his lips. So it's not just Luis on their radar—do they think I've been involved with his blogging? That I'm helping him? One of the people posting his blogs overseas? Or is this because I've been going around the country asking questions?

The man's gaze moves from the ring, to my face, and back to the ring again.

"Were you hurt? I told them to be gentle with you."

Are all Cuban kidnappers this polite? Somehow I doubt it. Still, his words resonate. *Told*, not asked. Yeah, he's the one in charge.

"You grabbed me off the street. What did you think would happen?"

What looks startlingly like regret flickers in his dark brown eyes. "I know, and for that, I apologize. I didn't know what else to do."

"Why? What do you want with me?" I ask again as Luis's earlier words come back to me now. Have I been followed the entire time I've been in Cuba?

"You have caught the government's attention—they were already watching Mr. Rodriguez thanks to his extracurricular activities, and then you came to Cuba as a journalist. Your family is known here, on the government's radar, known for supporting efforts against the regime in the United States. Once you arrived in the airport, they were made aware of it."

They?

"And you? Are you not part of the government?"

He inclines his head in a subtle nod, acknowledging my point.

"Not as much as I was in my younger years, but I still have a few connections. Your presence here was brought to my attention as well."

Why? How am I going to get out of this? These people don't play by any rules I'm familiar with, and even for someone with a last name that normally draws attention, this is an entirely different and far more terrifying microscope to be under.

"You've been watching me?"

He almost looks embarrassed. "I've been trying to protect you. When I saw your name, I asked some of my men to look after you, to make sure no harm came to you while you were in Havana. My reach did not—could not—extend to Mr. Rodriguez. His name had already made it up the ranks."

How far up? What does the hierarchy even resemble in a country such as this?

"Why were you interested in me? Did you know my family before they left Cuba?"

He's too young to be a contemporary of my great-grandparents, a bit older than my great-aunts, my grandmother . . .

His hand shakes as he shoves it in his pocket, and something about that motion, his posture in that chair—the casual elegance of it—is so familiar—

When he speaks again, his voice is strained, the emotion there answering the question in my mind.

"You look like her."

The final puzzle piece slides into place as a lump forms in my throat.

Of course.

I see traces of my father in him: the eyes, the mannerisms, the build.

"Yes, I do." I take a deep breath. "You're the man from the letters, aren't you? My grandmother loved you. You loved her."

A look of surprise flashes across his face, and he nods.

The evening's events crash over me again and again, and it takes a moment for me to gather my thoughts, to deal with this new twist; this trip to Cuba throws me more and more off-balance with each day that passes. I've gone through emotional whiplash—my grandmother loved a revolutionary once, the man I spent my whole life thinking was my grandfather isn't my biological grandfather after all, my biological grandfather is a revolutionary, one of Fidel's men, and now he's alive and sitting across from me.

Does he know the rest of it? Does he know my grandmother was pregnant? Does he know he's my grandfather?

"I didn't know your name. The letters were unsigned. I thought you were dead. But I—I've been looking for you."

"My name is Pablo Garcia," he replies.

My grandfather's name is Pablo Garcia. Such a simple thing, but suddenly, it feels like everything.

"Why me?" I repeat, my tone softer as I study the man I now know is my grandfather.

"Because I failed Elisa once, and I couldn't fail her again," he answers. "I've waited and wondered if I would hear something about your family over the years. I've kept an eye on Ana Rodriguez and Magda Villarreal because they were important to your grandmother. Like I said before, when you came into the country, your name was flagged. I still have friends in the government, and they brought it to my attention. How could I not watch over Elisa's granddaughter?

"I apologize for the circumstances of our meeting. I never intended to disturb your trip here, only to make sure you were safe, but when I saw the police were planning to grab Luis, there was no other option. I didn't want them to take you. The best I could do was arrange for my men to intervene."

"Do you know where Luis is?" I ask again.

"He's alive. They're merely questioning him for now. If something happens to him, I will know."

"What can I do for him?"

"At the moment? Nothing. I am doing everything I can, but these things take time. You getting involved will only complicate things for Luis—if they suspect him of espionage, of colluding with an American." Pablo clears his throat. "Perhaps while we wait, we can get to know each other a bit. If you would permit me, I would like to know more about you. About your grandmother."

A moment passes while I study him, searching for some sign, a flash of intuition that tells me he is a good man.

"You're asking me to trust you."

"Yes."

"I don't even know you," I protest. "All I know is that my grandmother loved you decades ago."

And the letters. Is that enough to go on?

"I know. Please give me a chance."

Isn't this what I wanted all along?

He looks up to the ceiling for a moment, and when he glances back to me, his eyes swim with emotion. "How is she? Your grandmother? Elisa."

I say the words quickly, like ripping off a bandage, for his benefit and perhaps, a bit, for my own. "She passed away. Six months ago."

His eyes close for a moment. When they open, there's a wet sheen there. "I'm sorry to hear that. What happened? Was she sick?"

He asks the question with the resigned tone of someone who has already watched loved ones succumb to a variety of illnesses and with an earnestness that tugs at my heart.

"No. It was sudden. They say she didn't feel anything, that she went quickly and painlessly. A heart attack in the night."

Her longtime housekeeper found her in bed the next morning.

"At least she was spared pain," he says. He coughs, his hand on his chest, his fingers curled into a fist over his heart. "Why did you come to Cuba?"

"When my grandmother died, she left a note behind asking to be cremated and to have her ashes spread in Cuba. She always wanted to come back here after Castro—"

I'm afraid to finish the sentence, not sure if I'm speaking to the man my grandmother loved or Fidel's loyal follower.

"That is a sentiment shared by many in Miami, I'm sure," Pablo comments, his tone dry.

Did he know my grandmother lived in Miami, or was that merely an accurate guess? He's had eyes on me since I landed in Havana. What else does he know about me? How did he know her married name?

"And you decided to stay with Ana?" he asks.

I nod.

"Elisa spoke of her often," Pablo continues. "We never met, but I felt like I knew her through Elisa's stories. She loved Ana very much. The combination of your last name with Ana's name and address was enough for me to know you were Elisa's. But how did you know who I am?"

"Ana mentioned my grandmother had buried a box in the backyard of her parents' house. I found your letters. The ring."

His gaze darts to my hand, lingering there.

"Ana gave me pieces of the story. Then she told me about my grandmother's nanny, and Magda filled in more. But I don't understand—Magda told me you died in the Battle of Santa Clara on New Year's Eve.

"My grandmother never spoke of any of this to me," I add. "We were close; she raised me. I would like to know this part of her. I'm trying to fill in the rest of it. Trying to understand what happened. Magda said your friend Guillermo told my grandmother you'd died."

"I almost did die. Santa Clara was chaotic. I went with Che and his forces to the city at the end of December."

"Were you and Che friends?"

"I wouldn't say we were friends. Compatriots by circumstance rather than birth. He came here from Argentina looking for a fight. He wanted to revolutionize the world one country at a time."

"He was beloved by many, though, wasn't he?"

"He was. He had charisma, and his fighters looked up to him." Pablo shrugs. "I cared more for Cuba than I did about revolution. I dreamed of freedom in those days. Freedom from Batista's tyrannical ways, from our position as America's playground. I wanted the island to be democratic and independent; I wanted the Cuban people to determine their own future. Sometimes I wondered if Che merely liked the fight."

"Yet you fought beside him."

"I did. We were brothers of sorts. You don't always like your brothers, don't always agree with them, but you take up arms and fight beside them. In those days, it was the right thing to do."

"So you went to Santa Clara."

"I did. Elisa didn't want me to go. She was afraid something would happen to me, to Cuba, to us. And I didn't want to leave her. But after I got out of prison, after Elisa—and your great-grandfather—helped get me out, my days were numbered. Batista was determined to make an example of the rebels, and it was only a matter of time before I ended up in front of a firing squad."

"Were you scared?"

"Terrified. In my younger years, I would have told you I was ready to die for my country, that I was brave, but it's the prerogative of old men to tell the truth. I was afraid I would die. Afraid I would be wounded. Afraid I'd never see Elisa again. Afraid we'd lose and all we'd done would be for naught.

"But on the way, that fear changed. On the way to Santa Clara people came out of their homes, from the fields where they worked and cheered us along. Their shoes were worn, their clothes dirty, but there was hope in their eyes. They saw us as their future. Cuba's future. And it was impossible to not feel proud on that march, to not feel like we served something greater than us, to not feel some sense of purpose that if we faced death, it would not be in vain. Young men dream of nothing more than becoming heroes, and we knew that whatever happened in Santa Clara, we would be remembered as heroes or martyrs."

"Why did you decide to fight?"

"I met Fidel when I was studying law at the University of Havana. We had a class together, and we went out for drinks one night after a lecture. He was so passionate back in those days; it was easy to get swept up in his words, in his enthusiasm for change. We were consumed by the idea of dethroning Batista, so caught up in the spirit of the fight that we didn't think as much about the future as we should have. We agreed Cuba should be free, but we didn't realize at the time that we had different views of what that freedom would look like, that the reality would be different from the one we spoke of when we were just kids playing at revolution."

I'm surprised by the candor in his voice, by the thread of regret beneath it all.

"What would you have done differently?"

"Everything. Nothing. Who knows how much would have changed?"

"What happened that day in Santa Clara?"

"I was shot at Santa Clara. There were a few hundred of us. Some went with Che; others, like me, armed with grenades, were sent to capture the hill. El Vaquerito led us."

"El Vaquerito?"

"Roberto Rodríguez Fernández. He died at Santa Clara. He was only twenty-three."

He delivers the words in a matter-of-fact tone of voice, as though he is too familiar with men dying in war.

"Batista's army had nearly four thousand soldiers, tanks, planes. We were outmatched and outgunned."

"But you won. I saw the memorial, the train."

He seems pleased by this.

"We did. Batista's forces were tired of fighting. When we captured the train Batista sent with reinforcements, it was all over. Batista fled during the early hours of New Year's Day, and everyone marched toward the city. I lost a lot of blood, and my wound became infected. I nearly died; the doctors didn't think it was wise to move me. So I stayed and recovered in a house nearby. In the confusion, Guillermo thought I'd died.

"By the time I was well enough to contact Elisa, Batista was already gone and Fidel had taken power. There were strikes throughout the country, and everything descended into a state of chaos. I had to be careful; her family never would have approved, and at that time, I had nothing to offer her.

"I went to Havana to see her. Before I had a chance, I learned her father was in prison. They were after anyone who supported Batista in those days, and already the regime was discussing taking the plantations away from the elite. The Perez family was an attractive target."

I'm struck by the way in which he describes the regime as separate from him, as though Castro's revolution was almost, but not quite, his.

"He was in La Cabaña," Pablo continues.

A chill slides down my spine as I remember the sight of the prison in Havana looming on the horizon.

"Che had him. I had a few cards to play, and I knew how much Elisa loved her father, that it would have broken her heart to have lost him, that the family depended on him. In the end, it wasn't enough—"

This is the part of the story I didn't get from the letters, Magda, or Ana, the missing piece to the puzzle.

"I met with Elisa's father, your great-grandfather, before he was released, and he promised he would tell her I was safe, that I loved her, that I would come for her when I could, when I had something to offer her. I gave him a letter to give to her. He seemed grateful to me for getting him out, but at the same time, I saw the way he looked at me. I was just another criminal in green fatigues in his eyes. And still—I had hope. That the dream of Elisa, of a future of us together, the one that had sustained me through prison, my time in the mountains, would eventually come true.

"And then they killed Alejandro," he says, sadness in his gaze. "After everything, I couldn't save him."

"What happened?"

I grew up knowing that once, my grandmother had a brother, but the mention of him was always too painful for her and her sisters to discuss.

"I didn't know him personally, only what I heard through the rebel circles and my relationship with Elisa. He was well-liked, charismatic, well-placed to influence Cuba's future. He was a threat, and someone took that threat seriously enough to kill him."

"He wasn't with the 26th of July?"

"No, he wasn't."

Those words seem particularly ominous.

"As soon as I learned Alejandro had been killed—I wanted to see Elisa, to comfort her. And at the same time, I worried my presence would be a slap in the face for all they'd lost. So I stayed away for a while, thinking it was the honorable thing to do. Eventually,

I realized your great-grandfather never told her I was alive, never gave her my letter. I learned Guillermo told Elisa I was dead, that she thought I was gone. I don't blame your great-grandfather, not after all he'd lost. My own family disowned me for joining Fidel. The last words my father said to me were that he was ashamed I was his son, that I had betrayed my country, my people. I didn't want Elisa to feel the same way, couldn't bear the thought that I'd destroyed what she loved, too.

"I went to her house to see her once I learned Guillermo had told her I died, once it became clear your great-grandfather didn't tell her I was alive, once some time had passed. I asked one of the gardeners about the family, and he said they had gone, fled to the United States. He didn't know when they would return. That was in March. I told myself she was safer there. You can't imagine the fear we lived with during those days, even those of us close to Fidel. Perhaps those of us close to Fidel more than anyone. It took nothing to sentence a man to death. You learned to survive by following his orders, by agreeing with everything he said. Men who didn't, good men, well—" His voice cracks, and I see the man my grandmother loved, the earnestness there and the immense sorrow at all that goodness and hope being twisted into something else entirely. "The firing squads, the blood—"

His eyes close.

"It wasn't what I believed in. Wasn't the future I had fought for. But I couldn't give up. We'd come too far for the country to fail. The problem was no one really understood what it would take to make the necessary changes in Cuba. And there were so many problems to be addressed. So I stayed behind and I worked. I wanted to help with legal reform. One of the goals of the revolution was to restore Cuba to the 1940 Constitution. Of course, instead we had the Fundamental Law.

"I worked every day. I saved. And I made plans. Fidel traveled to New York in September 1960 to address the United Nations, and I was part of the delegation that accompanied him. I went with the hopes that once I was in the United States I could find Elisa. I knew she was in Florida. I didn't know where she lived, but I found the headquarters of your great-grandfather's sugar company in Palm Beach.

"It took most of my savings to get there, and when I did, he met with me in his office. From the beginning, some part of me knew Elisa didn't belong with me anymore. She'd never cared about the money, but in having money I now saw a security I couldn't provide for her. Cuba was in such a state of unrest that it would have been a challenge to protect her, to give her the kind of life she deserved. And I worried. Worried about her being a Perez in a country where it was no longer prudent to stand out for having more than everyone else. Your family was known in Cuba. Elisa and her sisters were known in Cuba. Those were dangerous times to be one of the elite. Fidel had nationalized Cuban industry—the sugar fields. Privately, he was talking about the government seizing the property of those who left.

"And then your great-grandfather told me the news—that she'd married. He wasn't cruel about it; quite the opposite, really. He showed me a picture of your grandmother in a wedding dress, standing next to her husband."

Pain fills his eyes.

"She looked happy. Safe. He said they'd fallen in love quickly, had married quickly. They had a child already.

"What was I supposed to do? She was happy. She had the life she had always wanted—to be a wife and mother. Meanwhile I fought for a country that was falling down around me. I wasn't the kind of man who would disrupt her life when I had nothing to offer her. There was no honor in such action.

"So I came back. I worked with Calderío to reform the legal

system. Later on I worked with the law school to shape the new curriculum." He smiles. "I met my Julia, and we married. Had children of our own. Six grandchildren now. It's not the life I imagined for myself, the one Elisa and I dreamed of, but the older you get, the more you learn to appreciate the moments life gives you. Getting them certainly isn't a given, and I feel blessed to have carved out a life here where I could be happy even if it wasn't quite the happiness I envisioned, if the things I dreamed of never quite came to pass."

I have a feeling he's not just talking about my grandmother anymore.

He gestures toward my hand. "May I?"

I nod, sliding the ring off my finger and placing it in his hands.

Emotions swim in his eyes.

"It was my grandmother's." He smiles again. "I didn't have much money back then, but I wanted to make Elisa a promise, one she could believe in, so I gave her my grandmother's ring. Elisa couldn't wear it on her hand, of course, so when we weren't together, she wore it on a chain around her neck, near her heart."

"Would you like it back? If it's a family heirloom—"

He shakes his head, placing the ring back in my palm. "It was meant for you." He's quiet for a moment. "You don't just have the look of Elisa, you know. I see my mother in you, too."

I still, my heart thudding.

"When did you realize?" I ask.

"When I saw the ring. Then I recognized my mother in your face." A tear trickles down his cheek. "Do I have a son or a daughter?"

"A son."

"Tell me about him. Please."

So I do. I tell him about my family, half of my heart here, half of it with Luis, praying for his safety, waiting for Pablo's man to come tell us what's to become of him.

"Will you tell them about me?" Pablo asks once I've finished, and I sense the hesitation behind the question, recognize his fear that he won't be accepted because of his political allegiances.

The revolution has divided so many families; it's wrecked ours enough.

"Yes."

"Do you think they'll want to know me?" he asks, the uncertainty in his voice tugging at my heart.

"I do."

A knock sounds at the door, and Pablo excuses himself. He opens the door and exchanges murmured words with the man from earlier. When they're finished, he returns to me.

"It's safe for you to go back to Ana's tonight. They're still questioning Luis, but I'm working on getting him out. I need to meet with a friend who might be able to help us."

The word "us" is incredibly reassuring.

"Do you think you can secure his release?"

"I hope I can. I promise you, Marisol, I'll do everything in my power to make it happen."

chapter twenty-seven

I take a cab back to Ana's in a daze, relaying the events to her, Caridad, and Cristina. They receive the news of Luis's arrest with resignation and a sense of calm that would have shocked me if I hadn't grown used to this Cuban pragmatism. I tell Ana privately about Pablo, that he's my grandfather, my hope that he will be able to help Luis.

"What do we do?" I ask once I've finished the tale.

"We wait," Ana answers, her expression grim.

The next morning, Luis is still not back with us, and I walk to my grandfather's house in Miramar, to the address he gave me the previous night, worry in my heart as I approach his home. What if he's not here? What if he can't help me or he changed his mind once he realized the precariousness of Luis's position? I'm staking a lot on the letters, on the fact that my grandmother loved him, the time I spent in his presence, on the hope that he'll be able to do something to get Luis out of this mess.

A mere block marks the difference between Pablo's house and the one my grandmother grew up in. He must drive past the old Perez estate every single day; does he think of her often?

The house is ahead of me, the well-manicured lawn, immense palm trees swaying gently in the breeze, and elegant exterior a surprise. My grandfather's stature in life seems to have changed quite a bit from that of the staunchly middle-class lawyer described in his letters, and his home is in far better condition than its compatriots.

Some are more equal than others.

I press on the gate, the iron creaking as it swings open. The sound of the ocean mixes with the noise of children laughing and yelling somewhere on the property's immense grounds; there's an entire family out there I never knew.

I continue forward, my sandals slipping against the rock driveway, my legs wet noodles. I reach the front steps and hesitate. I close my eyes, offering a silent prayer to the heavens and the one person I know absolutely has my back up there as I knock on the heavy wood door and wait until it opens, revealing an elderly Cuban woman in a flowered dress.

"May I help you?" she asks.

Is this his wife?

I swallow. "I'm Marisol Ferrera. I'm here to see Mr. Garcia."

She's silent for a moment, her gaze assessing.

"He's sitting out on the back porch. I'll show you the way."

I follow her through the house, my gaze on the paintings on the wall, the furnishings. Nothing is in luxurious condition by American standards, and yet, the pieces have clearly fared far better than at the Rodriguez home. Does my grandfather have someone else's family legacy hanging on his walls?

The woman leads me to a covered outdoor area with a breathtaking view of the sea and sky, a storm out over the water. She asks me if I would like a drink, and I decline.

My grandfather sits in an oversize chair under the covered space smoking a cigar, a glass of amber liquid in front of him. He wears a sharp panama hat, another guayabera, the hem of his shirt blowing in the breeze, and black pants.

Pablo sets his glass down.

He rises from his chair, his hand gripping the arm, his eyes on me as he exchanges affectionate words with his wife before she's gone, closing the doors and leaving us alone on the patio overlooking the sea.

The rain slaps the tile patio beyond the covering.

"What's happening with Luis?" I ask.

"They're attempting to charge him under social dangerousness," my grandfather replies.

"What does that mean?"

"The people who have been tried under the charge have been imprisoned for several years. Occasionally, the government will go for something a bit lighter, like house arrest, but in this instance that's best case. The law allows the government to detain someone if they think they may commit a crime in the future. They have applied it against dissidents in the past, and that's what they're aiming for in this case.

"Because he works at the university, their concern is his influence over his students, his opportunity to organize them, to create a movement against the government." My grandfather sighs. "At the moment he's being held in a cell alone, but when he's in prison, things can happen. He's not safe there. I had hoped he would be released by now, but I fear things are worse than I imagined."

"What can happen to him?"

"People get into fights, people are killed. Even before he's in prison, things will be dangerous." His voice lowers to a whisper. "People disappear. Have the misfortune to be involved in a car accident on their way home. This is not America. Once you are in the regime's sights, you are not safe. If they think he's dangerous enough, they will do whatever they have to in order to silence him."

"What do I do? Get him a lawyer? Get the Americans involved? Human rights groups? Who can help him?"

Will they even care, or is he just one Cuban in a long line of human rights abuses?

"I'm waiting to hear back from a few friends well-placed in the judicial system. I'm trying to get him out, but it's complicated, and we must be very careful in how we handle this. I know you're scared, but, Marisol, you also need to be careful. If they think you're involved, if they can create a connection that makes it appear as though you're involved, they can try you as a spy; you can get caught up in this, too. These are dangerous times, and your nationality will only afford you so much protection."

My great-aunts' earlier warnings return to me now.

"I know you want to help, but you have to understand that there are limits here," Pablo adds. "You must be smart about this. Wait at Ana's house, and when I know something, I'll come to you. There's nothing you can do to get him out until then and your intervention will only make things worse. Promise me you'll wait."

It's a hard pill to swallow, but the logical, rational part of me knows he's right. And if Ana, Caridad, and Cristina can be stoic about this, I must be as well.

"I promise."

"This man—he's important to you, yes?"

"He is." I swallow. "Will he be okay?"

My grandfather's expression is grim.

"I hope so."

The next few hours creep by with agonizing slowness. Life doesn't stop because Luis is in jail; the Rodriguez women still prepare meals, taking in guests, the kitchen quiet as a tomb save for the occasional piece of silverware scraping against a plate, a pot banging against the stovetop, the hiss and boil of water.

The urge to cry is a battering ram weakening my defenses, and yet, there is an unspoken agreement here. Luis's grandmother, his mother, Cristina—none of them break. There's a tremor in their hands, the occasional hitch in their throat, but they don't cry.

No one objects when I join them in the kitchen, helping to make the picadillo for the evening meal. The *paladar* is full tonight, the tables packed with tourists—Canadians, two Australian couples, and a French family. Cristina and Caridad serve the guests with somber expressions and trays laden with food.

I worry most about Ana.

When the other two women are out serving guests, she allows the facade to slip a bit, murmuring prayers and rubbing the bracelet on her wrist as though it's a rosary.

"Would you like to lie down?" I ask.

My cooking skills aren't on par with Ana's, but picadillo is a staple in the Cuban diet. I've helped my grandmother make it hundreds of times, and it's one of my few culinary achievements.

"Thank you, but no. It helps me to stay busy—to keep my mind from wandering."

"Me, too."

She reaches over and squeezes my hand. "He'll be okay," she proclaims, her hand drifting to her chest, a beat above her heart. "I feel it here."

We cook in silence, working in tandem to create the picadillo. When I press Ana to eat some herself, she waves me off and says I should eat instead. My stomach is too full of nerves and worry for me to bother with food, and we continue on in the tiny space.

Cristina and Caridad drift in and out of the kitchen, returning to serve the guests.

Someone pounds at the front door.

We both still. Ana's gaze darts toward the kitchen entrance and back to me.

Her hands drift to the bracelet again, her fingers flying over the beads. "Will you come with me?"

I nod, the words stuck in my throat.

I take her hand, and we walk toward the door together. When we reach the front door, I pause. "Do you think we should—"

Wait? Get help? A litany of objections runs through my mind before I remember this is Cuba, and the rules here work differently. There is no media to highlight these abuses, no government to complain to, no friend or neighbor to call upon to aid us. We are really and truly alone with only ourselves to rely on.

Ana straightens, pushing her shoulders back, her fingers fumbling with the lock on the door. She swings it open.

Luis and my grandfather stand on the other side.

The sight of Luis is a shock, even more so because of the condition he's in. His lip is swollen, a fresh bruise on his cheekbone, a cut near his jaw, his beard matted with blood. His arm hangs at his side, his torso hunched over as though damage has been done there, too.

They cross the threshold and Ana closes the door behind them.

I step forward, wrapping my arms around Luis, careful to keep my touch gentle, to avoid doing further injury to him. I pull back, searching his expression, my gaze running over his face for more injuries I might have missed.

"Are you okay?" I ask. "What happened?"

"I'm okay," he answers, his voice weak.

I step back while Ana hugs him, her voice full of worry and love.

"Did you get him out?" I ask my grandfather. When I went to him for help, I didn't expect such quick results.

"For now. Is there somewhere we can talk? Somewhere private?"

Ana nods and takes us to the small sitting room off the entryway.

When the door shuts, my grandfather fills us in on the rest of it.

"Officially, it'll look like he was accidentally released. It happens—clerical errors, overcrowded jails and prisons, people get lost in the shuffle. It's not going to buy much time, though."

He turns his attention to Luis. "You have a passport, yes?"

Luis gives a clipped nod in return. "I thought it was a prudent move when they removed the ban on foreign travel."

I don't miss the way he says "they" or the look he gives my grandfather when he says it. At the same time, there's a wary trust in Luis's eyes and I've no doubt my grandfather told Luis about his relationship to me.

"Good," Pablo answers. "Then you can go from Havana to Antigua. Buy a return ticket—Marisol can help you. The fare will be high, but they won't require you to have a visa to get into the country. There's no time to get you a visa to fly to a country that will require one. Hopefully, at the airport they will think you are going on vacation."

"Won't they flag his passport at the airport, though?" I interject.

"At the moment, there's nothing to flag. You've disappeared from their records. It won't last long, though.

"Once you're in Antigua, you'll want to get a plane to the United States," Pablo continues. "That will be difficult, but with enough money, not impossible."

He turns to me. "Marisol will need to help you with the rest of it. You'll need to charter a plane to take you from Antigua to Miami and to sort out his entry into the United States. Can you do that?"

Honestly? I have no clue. But at the moment, we seem to have few options available to us.

"I think so. My father's company has a plane he uses for business. My family will help."

Once, it was enough that if we could get Luis to the United States, he would be offered refuge. Under the decades-old wet foot, dry foot policy, Cubans who were captured in the water were sent back to Cuba by the Coast Guard; Cubans who reached American soil could stay.

Now, thanks to recent politics, things are more complicated.

My grandfather's expression turns grim. "You need to understand something, Marisol. They can arrest you on suspicion of even helping Luis leave the country. They know you're here as a journalist. That you're staying with the Rodriguez family. You could be in just as much trouble as Luis. And if you aren't successful and they catch you, they can throw you in prison for a very long time. There are few offenses the government takes more seriously than helping a Cuban leave the country illegally."

I don't take lightly my grandfather's warning or the risk he's taking himself by helping us, but at the same time, how can I not help get Luis out of Cuba?

"We're not doing this. She's not doing it," Luis interjects. "She's risking her freedom and her life. No."

"You don't get to make that decision for me," I protest.

"If we're caught—"

"Then we won't get caught." My heart pounds. "There's no way I'm leaving you here to die. Part of why you're in this trouble is because I helped bring your work to their attention."

"Bullshit," Luis snaps.

"You need to think about this, Marisol," my grandfather cautions. "Luis is right; it's a risk. A dangerous one."

"Aren't you putting yourself at risk as well?" I ask my grandfather.

"I'm an old man. How many years do I have left? I've served the regime well for a long time, and I've accumulated enough influence." His smile is wry. "It's the right thing to do."

"Then don't expect me not to do the same."

I came here searching for my family's legacy, and now I know what it is.

I grew up on their stories, but it was different hearing my grandmother and her sisters recount their experiences. They spoke of their own bravery in a matter-of-fact tone as though it was something they did that anyone would have done in their position. But now I've seen a sliver of what they lived through up close, the grace with which they bore their suffering, the strength with which they carried our family and our future on their backs. They sacrificed and risked their lives for those they loved, for their country. They were brave when it mattered most.

How can I not honor their legacy?

"Marisol—" Luis interjects.

"We'll talk about it later," I answer. I turn toward my grandfather. "You think this could be successful?"

"There's no guarantee it will work, but it's the best chance you have," my grandfather answers. "But we need to move quickly. Luis will be back on their radar soon. These things can only be covered up for so long. They've had people keeping an eye on you since you arrived in the country, Marisol. I had them momentarily reassigned, but it will only buy you a day or two at the most."

"And my family? What about them?" Luis asks, his mouth in a tense line.

Our earlier conversations come to mind, his reluctance to leave, his fear that his actions will put his family at risk.

"These are difficult times for the regime," my grandfather answers. "There is international scrutiny that wasn't there before and also an element of unpredictability in their relations with the United States. They need to have a better relationship with the United States; you know this as well as I do. Things will not change overnight; human rights will not change overnight. But Raúl is not stupid. Cuba needs to make some semblance of overture to the United States. The government needs to be careful about which battles they choose to fight, and given Luis's grandfather's prior relationship with the regime, his father's heroism in Angola, and Marisol's connections in the United States, they can't afford for this situation to become exacerbated.

"I've spoken to some friends in the government and impressed the gravity of the situation upon them. Your family will not be harmed, Luis. I give you my word. I've called in all the favors I can to assure it. But you have to leave. The more you push, the harder they'll push back. If you disappear, they will move on and forget you. But if you stay—"

"How can *you* stay?" I ask Pablo. "How can you support what they're doing?" I'm grateful for his help, but I can't reconcile the man who seems to have such a good heart with a government official involved in such corruption. "You have to know this is wrong."

"Is it better to stay and become part of the system or leave and be considered a traitor?" my grandfather replies. "A worm? I do not know. If I leave, what will change? If I stay, what will change? I have tried to be a counterbalance to some of the more extreme notions that have arisen over the years. Tried to preserve the rule of law. This is my home, imperfect though it is. I have to believe—hope—there is still some good I may do, some change I may effect to help Cubans. That has to be enough now. I do not begrudge those who live abroad now, who found the situation such that they could not stay. Please do not judge me for the fact that I cannot leave."

"You're still fighting."

"I am. Revolutions are for the young. When I could, I fought for what I believed in. But I'm an old man now. The older you get, the more you realize that change—meaningful, lasting change—doesn't always come with violence and bloodshed, but with reform, however slow, however gradual. When I was young and rash I believed the only way to defeat Batista was to kill him, to take his country and government away from him by force. But now?

"The problem with revolution, with the wave of violence it carries with it, is that it's like a flash flood—it sweeps everything away, and nothing looks the same as it once did. And you think this is good, change was what you wanted in the first place, change was what you needed. But suddenly you have a country you must govern, people whose basic needs must be met. You must stabilize a currency, and create a legal system, and reform a constitution. Those are not the things young men dream of. They dream of dying for their country; dream of honor in battle. No one dreams about sitting at a desk and arguing over phrases.

"But those words, those laws, that infrastructure is everything. Without them, no government can succeed. I am not blind to what my countrymen are suffering, Marisol. Or the problems that exist. But I am here, with my pen. The revolution we need now will be fought by those arguing over words, phrases, passing legislation and loosening restrictions. Men willing to sit at a table and discuss the things we've been afraid to address for many, many years. I am meant to be here, to finish what I started, and hopefully, to be part of that change. For my family, for my country."

That's the gap between him and my grandmother. She could not have lived in this world he created, and he could not leave it.

He turns to Luis. "The longer you stay, the less I'll be able to do for you. The more restricted your movements will become. The more danger to Marisol. You need to leave tomorrow. Marisol can get you a flight, and I have all the exit paperwork sorted out for you. We have a small window of time in which we can blame your release and departure as a clerical error, the product of departments not speaking with one another. The longer you wait, the greater the chance that you will be picked up by the police, that you will be prevented from leaving the country. If you're picked up again, I can't help you. You will be dealt with swiftly and mercilessly."

"He's going," Ana replies, speaking for the first time, her fingers on the bracelet again.

"Abuela—"

"We'll discuss it later," she says, her tone firm. Her gaze turns to my grandfather, tears welling in her eyes. "Thank you. Thank you for what you have done for my grandson."

He bows. "Of course. If you'll excuse me, I need to get home. My wife will be worried." He turns to face me. "Marisol, I would very much like to see you before you leave."

The reality that we're leaving so quickly hits me. I thought I would have a couple more days here, but now it's all unraveling.

"Will you meet me at the Malecón tonight?" I ask him. "There's something I need to do."

"Of course."

chapter twenty-eight

After my grandfather leaves, Luis and I retreat to his bedroom with a makeshift first aid kit in hand. My fingers sweep across his face, careful to keep from hitting the bruises, the cuts near his eye. He unbuttons his shirt, his knuckles scraped and bleeding.

I suck in a deep breath. "What did they do to you?"

His hands tremble over the buttons. "Trust me, you don't want to know."

He shrugs off the shirt, the bloody fabric hitting the floor.

I gasp.

Bruises mar his torso, a particularly nasty one dangerously close to his kidneys.

"You could have been killed."

"I'm fine."

"You're not fine. They could have killed you, and there's nothing we could have done about it. Nothing you can do about it. Do you realize how crazy that is?"

"They just wanted to scare me a bit. If they'd wanted to kill me, they would have."

"And the next time? You heard what my grandfather said. You have to stop. What you're doing is dangerous. It's going to get you killed. Is it worth it?"

"Of course it is." Whatever they hoped to beat out of him, I fear they've only made it stronger. "It has to be."

It's one of those moments when blinding clarity hits me and two halves cleave together.

Like my grandmother before me, I've fallen in love with a revolutionary.

I feel the same helplessness she must have felt, the same sensation that we're on a train hurtling off the tracks and there's nothing I can do to stop it. I don't know what to say anymore, how to convince him he has to leave.

I can't fathom living in a world where you have no rights, where there is no oversight, no accountability. The United States isn't perfect; there's injustice everywhere I turn. But there's also a mechanism that protects its citizens—the right to question when something is wrong, to speak out, to protest, to be heard. It doesn't always work, sometimes the system fails those it was designed to protect, but at least that opportunity—the hope of it—exists.

The ability to crush a voice is staggering here.

"Do you really think you can change the government? That they're going to let you?"

I dab at the wounds on his face with the antiseptic.

Luis hisses as I touch the cut near his cheekbone.

"I see the hope for change everywhere I look, the undercurrent of it running through Cubans' daily lives," he says. "They know this *isn't* enough, that we deserve more. They dream of little changes that would make their lives easier, make their children's lives easier. Most of us remember when things were really bad, when it was a challenge to get enough to eat, and we remember the desperation we felt, the gnawing hunger in our bellies, the weakness in our muscles, in our bones, and the willingness to break the law because otherwise we would quite simply die. We're dying a different death now, one that isn't physical," he continues. "We need to keep putting pressure on the government, keep pushing for change, demanding they do better. They should fear us. We have a generation now that looks ahead and isn't pleased with what they see.

"My students—the future of this country—they care about technology, what little they're able to access through legal means or not; they care about popular culture, which is smuggled to them through flash drives and in foreigners' suitcases. They're pragmatic in their desire for change, for more. For now, they're occupying themselves with the fight—with gathering all they can on the black market, with changing their own realities. But what happens when they've exhausted their limited resources? What then?"

Isn't that what I admire most about him? What attracted me to him in the first place? The passion, the commitment, the absolute dedication and love for his country. The men I know in Miami are obsessed with what kind of car they drive, or the brand of watch they wear, what club they're going to on Saturday night. Luis lives for Cuba, and I love him for it; but now I fear Cuba will kill him.

I continue patching his wounds, soothing his bruises, struggling to keep the worry from my voice, to stifle the fear. "I understand that you want to make those changes. I admire your passion. But what if the limitations imposed by the government are too stringent for you to accomplish those goals?"

"I don't know. But what you're asking me to do—it's not in my nature to give up. To run. And I don't want to risk you in order to do it."

"It's too late for that. In their eyes, I'm probably already a threat. And don't consider it giving up or running. Call it a strategic retreat."

"I'm abandoning my country, my family, my people. My father died fighting for what he believed in. And I'm running away to save myself. How can I live with that?"

My heart breaks for him, because I understand the responsibility he carries with him, the desire to honor his family and to live up to the sacrifices they made. And at the same time, the chasm between us has never felt greater than it does now, the sand stretching on to an infinitesimal length, the sea boundless. Ninety miles feels like an impassable distance.

"If you die, things won't be better. What will your family do then? At least if you're alive, you can send them money, more than they would make here; you can make a difference from outside of Cuba. Perhaps more of one than you would make inside the country with all the restraints the government imposes upon you."

"You want me to go with you."

"I do."

"Because you love me or because you think it's the right decision?" Luis asks.

How has he known this when I only just worked it out myself?

"Because I love you and I think it's the only decision."

His eyes close for a moment when the word "love" leaves my lips as though he's absorbing the force of that word, as if I've hit him with a physical blow.

His eyes open. "I'm not afraid to die for what I believe in."

"Maybe not, but what does your death accomplish? You wouldn't be the first one, and you won't be the last, and what changes? Nothing. I would rather you be alive in the United States than dead in Cuba."

He makes an impatient noise. "You don't understand. You speak as though Cuba is just a place to live, as though it's nothing more than taking a few boxes and moving them from one house to the next. It's not. This is my home. My country."

"How can you love a country that does this to its citizens? A government willing to throw you in prison for speaking out against their abuses. I came here wanting to love Cuba; I told myself I would look at it through clear eyes, that I wouldn't be swayed by

Miami's view, that I would judge it on its merits and not through the lens of the exile. But I can't. I'm Cuban, too. Perhaps I wasn't born here, but my blood is Cuban. How can you fight to stay somewhere where you are not wanted, in a place that will get you killed? You're a smart man; it makes no sense. Where is the logic?"

"Ahh, but love is not logical. It is my weakness, perhaps, but it is my country. How do I not love it?"

"But at what cost?"

"When you love something you don't count the cost."

"And me?"

Luis smiles sadly. "You know I love you, Marisol. Do not ask me to choose between who I love and who I am. I fear it would not reflect well on either one of us."

"I'm not asking you to choose. There is no choice. They've made the choice for you. You cannot stay here and live; and death is not a continuation, it is not a way of fighting them; your death will mean nothing. You can do more good alive in Miami than dead in Havana."

"The exile's refrain."

"So what if it is? At least we've preserved a version of Cuba that does not exist in this place. We're the only ones who've preserved it."

"You cannot live in a museum, Marisol. The problem with your 'preservation' is that it fails to account for the fact that there is a real Cuba. A living, breathing Cuba. You're all so busy fighting imaginary ghosts in Miami while we're here, bleeding on the ground, dealing with real problems. Your exile community isn't concerned with the black market, or the housing shortage, or the very real flaws in the much-touted education system, or the fact that racial discrimination occurs on a daily basis. You're still pissed because your grand mansions were taken away and are now occupied by the very men you hate the most. The rest of us are caught in the middle, worrying about how to survive."

"So teach us. Come to Miami. Get involved with the movement there. Change the narrative. The discourse is changing. Fidel is dead. The enmity toward the regime is turning to a very practical approach on Cuba. We're on the cusp of a new era in Cuban-American relations; perhaps there is an opportunity for something better. That article I'm writing? What if it wasn't about travel? What if it was about contemporary Cuba? What if you told your story? Help us. Teach us about the problems facing Cuba now."

"It still feels like I'm abandoning my country."

"It's already abandoned you. This isn't your country. Or your grandmother's. It's Castro's. And now, his ghost's. It was supposed to be yours. That was the promise of '59. But they broke that promise almost from the beginning. This version of Cuba belongs to the regime, but that doesn't mean the future has to.

"Retreat is a victory of sorts. You can't win this battle, not like this. You're not giving up, just giving yourself a better chance to change the system in a world where you don't have to play by their rules."

He shakes his head. "Marisol." His tone is resigned, but there's a gleam in his eyes that wasn't there a few minutes ago.

"You know I'm right."

"Perhaps," he acknowledges.

"We have to make do with the opportunities that present themselves. We have a chance to get you out. We need to take it."

He's quiet for a long beat, the only noise in the room the sound of our breathing, the whirl of the ceiling fan overhead. And then—

"I know."

I run into Cristina on my way out. She's sitting on the steps, smoking a cigarette, staring out at the rusted metal gate at the entryway.

"You want him to leave with you," she says, her tone flat, not bothering to glance at me.

I guess Ana filled Cristina and Caridad in on the conversation with my grandfather. I'm exhausted from my talk with Luis, with the events of the last few days, my grandmother's ashes a weight in my bag, and more than anything, I don't have much fight left in me.

"Yes."

She takes another drag of her cigarette, the smoke billowing in the air.

"Why? Because you love him?"

There's no anger in her voice; the words are delivered in a flat, unemotional tone.

"Yes. I'm sorry," I add, knowing as soon as the apology leaves my lips that it rings hollow and inadequate, even as it's all I have.

Love feels like a luxury here in this world where divorced couples are forced to live together because there is no housing, because the government makes it so. Love feels like a luxury in a world where so many struggle for the basic things I take for granted.

"Do you?" I ask.

"What? Love him?"

I nod.

"He is a good man. Kind. Hardworking," she answers.

"What alternative do I have?" I ask, the doubts creeping in. Am I being selfish? Or is leaving truly the only answer available to him? "They'll kill him if he stays. I love him, yes. But this isn't about me. It's about his future."

She scoffs. "It must be so nice for him to have a wealthy American woman who's willing to make his life easier." Her gaze pins me. The condemnation in her eyes strips me bare. "Do you think this is the first time I've heard this story? Do you know how many of my friends have dreamed of a man who would take them away from this? Have ended up pregnant and abandoned or worse? Perhaps the roles are reversed, but you're just another rich foreigner making promises. What will he know of your world? What will your rich American friends think of him?"

"It's not like that," I protest.

Are the differences between us simply insurmountable?

"Isn't it, though? Isn't it exactly like that? You come here, and you spend a few days in Cuba, and tell yourself you've fallen in love, that you're 'saving' Luis. And then you return to your nice, safe life in America, far away from all this. You say you want to be Cuban." Her hands wave in the air, the cigarette dangling between her fingertips, ash falling to the ground. "This is what it means to be Cuban. To be a woman in Cuba is to suffer. What do you know of suffering?"

I don't. Not like this.

"What would you have me do?" I ask.

"Nothing. I wouldn't have you do anything. But you're all complaining about how you lost your country, and the reality is you didn't lose your country; you left. You left the rest of us in hell. And now he's leaving right alongside you."

"Would you rather him stay here and die?"

My frustration isn't with Cristina, it's with this whole situation, but at the moment she's voicing the things I fear the most.

She takes a drag of her cigarette. "No."

"Then what would you have me do?" I ask again. "You don't want him to leave, but he cannot stay. So what solution is there?"

Her smile mocks me. "Is that what it's like in your world? Do things get wrapped up in pretty little bows and happy endings? You go back to America with Luis. You get married and have children, and have your perfect little life together. But deep down, you have to know you won't have all of him. I tried to make him choose between me and Cuba, and he chose Cuba every single time. No matter how much you love him, how much you think he loves you, a part of him will always be here. And a part of him will always resent you for taking him away."

Maybe. Maybe the parts of him are enough; maybe things will change and it won't have to be a choice anymore—

I stand there, looking down at her sitting on the steps, the straps of her sandals worn, her expression hardened to steel.

This island will break your heart if you let it.

"You could leave, too, you know."

She laughs, the sound unvarnished and raw.

"Find some nice man who tells me he wants to take me away from this place and leaves me with a swollen belly and a disease or two? No, thanks."

"We could try to get you out. All of you."

Scorn fills her gaze. "I tried once. Did Luis ever tell you that?"

"No."

"I was six. There were twenty of us in a raft. My parents and fifteen others died. We spent a week floating in the water, starving, exhausted before the Coast Guard picked us up and brought us back to Fidel. The adults were thrown in prison. I was sent to live with my grandmother. I'll take my chances, thank you very much."

I'm rooted to this spot, some part of me wanting to stay and convince her, another part of me already gone.

"I have to go."

My grandfather is waiting for me at the Malecón.

"Then go."

When I reach the gate, I turn around, watching as she snuffs out the cigarette on the steps of the house, her gaze trained somewhere out to the sea.

What does it say about a place that people will risk certain death to leave it?

I walk from the Rodriguez house to the Malecón, my conversation with Cristina running through my head on repeat. Luis is with his mother and grandmother, discussing the logistics of him leaving. And I'm here, finally fulfilling my grandmother's last wishes, the reason I came to Cuba. Waves crash against the rocks at El Morro, the sun setting on another Havana day.

My grandfather stands next to me, staring out at the sea, and I wonder how many times he did this and whether he searched for her, somewhere beyond the horizon, when he did.

I don't realize I've asked the question aloud until he speaks.

"I imagined her there. America. As a wife. A mother. With the life we always dreamed about—a house full of kids somewhere with a palm tree in the backyard. I imagined her aging as I have. Each year that passed, I thought of her." He sighs. "It was enough to hope that she was happy."

I hate that their story doesn't have a happy ending, that ultimately, this is yet another thing Fidel took from them.

"It feels incomplete," I murmur.

"Life so often is. It's messy, too. This isn't the ending, Marisol. When you're young, life's punctuation so often seems final when it's nothing more than a pause. When I learned Elisa had married, I thought our story had ended. Accepted it. And now, almost sixty years later, you're here. I have a granddaughter. A son, a new family. A piece of Elisa.

"You never know what's to come. That's the beauty of life. If everything happened the way we wished, the way we planned, we'd miss out on the best parts, the unexpected pleasures." He shrugs, gesturing around him. "We all had a vision; we had a plan. Fate, God, Fidel, they all laughed at that plan. I thought I was on one path, and it turned out to be something else entirely. That doesn't mean it's all bad, though."

He smiles, wrapping his arm around me, bringing me against his side.

"I'm glad we found each other," I say.

He stares up at the sky, a gleam entering his gaze. "I like to think Elisa's up there smiling down at us, that she brought us together because she wanted us to meet, wanted you to be part of my life."

He begins speaking as if his words are the continuation of a conversation he is having with himself, a memory.

"She was wearing this dress." He smiles. "White. It had this full skirt, and it swayed when she walked. I couldn't stop watching her hips," he confesses with a look in his eyes that makes him appear decades younger.

I laugh.

"I brought her a white silk rose. I'll never forget her smile when I gave it to her. We were both so nervous. I kept shoving my hands in my pockets because I didn't know what to do with them, because there wasn't anything I wanted more than to take her hand in mine and never let go. The night kept growing later, and I knew we'd have to part soon, and I didn't want to leave her. Didn't want to ever let her go."

"Did you fall in love with her here on the Malecón?"

"Perhaps. Perhaps I fell in love with her that first moment I saw her standing on the fringes of Guillermo's party, her expression so earnest. Once Elisa burst into my life, there wasn't a moment when I didn't love her. She was a bright spot in years that were filled with violence and bloodshed. She gave me hope."

"What was she like when you knew her?" I ask him.

"Fierce. Passionate. Loyal. Brave. Smart. She cared about people, and she cared about her country. There was a kindness to her; she always wanted to see the best in everyone around her."

So little changed between the girl he knew and the woman who raised me.

I reach into my bag, removing the container of ashes, my fingers leaving shadowy prints on the cool metal.

I would be lying if I didn't admit that this feels a bit unsettling, the act of holding my deceased grandmother in my hands a bit macabre. And at the same time, a weight rolls off my shoulders, as I cast off the mantle of grief that has lain there for so long.

I will always miss her, but I've been given a new chance to know her, and through her, a whole new family. A pause in what felt like an ending.

And this, too, is right—her reunion with the man she loved and the country that forever held her heart.

I pass the container to my grandfather.

A tear slips down his weathered face as he strokes the metal, a tremor in his fingers.

"Are you sure you don't want to do this?" he asks.

I shake my head, understanding what was missing before, why I couldn't come up with a final resting place that felt *right*. It wasn't a place; it was a person. I brought her back to Cuba. The final steps should be his.

Pablo's hands shake as he unscrews the lid, as he tips the container out over the sea, into the wind. It's not as romantic as I imagined it; bits of bone fragments sail through the air. But then again, what is?

It's the after, though, that means the most. We stand side by side, staring out at the ocean, at some point we can no longer see.

Ninety miles. Ninety miles separate Cuba from Key West, the southernmost tip of the United States. Ninety miles that might as well be infinite.

How many souls have been lost in these waters by people risking everything to find a better life? People like Cristina's parents—filled with desperation, stretching out for hope? How many people on both sides of the water have stared across the ocean, yearning for something they can't have—a family member, a lost love, the country where they were born, the soil where they took their first steps, the air they first breathed?

"Will you come back?" my grandfather asks. "Will you bring them? My son, my granddaughters? Will you meet your cousins?"

"Yes."

"Then I will wait." He reaches into his pocket, pulling out a packet of letters tied together with a faded string. I recognize the handwriting on them instantly.

He smiles. "I think she would have wanted you to have these."

chapter twenty-nine

Elisa

The days, weeks, after Alejandro—I cannot finish the thought—run together as February passes on until it is nearly March. The wave of grief hits all of us, even our parents—our father who once declared him "no son of mine" for attempting to assassinate Batista so long ago. Alejandro's funeral is a somber affair—only family. I cannot bear to think of his mangled body lying in that casket.

Did God heap all of our losses together in one fell swoop so we could bear them more easily, drifting from one death to another, vacillating between heartbreak and despair? Would it be crueler if they were stretched out over years, or is the sheer avalanche of loss our punishment for our sins?

I no longer know.

I am sick, mostly in the mornings, but every once in a while my body likes to surprise me with an afternoon malaise. I possess a newfound respect for my mother; she did this five times—four healthy pregnancies and a baby who went to live with the angels.

Magda clucks over me, my sisters sneak suspicious glances my way, and my belly swells with each day, but the dawn of new life is shrouded in the death that shakes us all. Still—how long before I can no longer hide the changes beneath my gowns? I hold my breath, waiting for my parents to say something, for my mother to notice the differences in my appetite, but she does not, her grief consuming her, her whispered conversations with our father becoming more frantic. And then our parents usher us into our father's study and the reason for their distraction becomes clear.

I sit next to Beatriz and Isabel on the couch in the corner of my father's study, praying my stomach can make it through this family meeting without giving away my condition. Maria and my mother sit in the chairs opposite his desk, my mother in the very chair where I once sat and begged for my father to intervene and save Pablo's life.

I thought I was saving him by sending him to the mountains, but it was all for naught.

And Alejandro—

A lump forms in my throat. Beatriz tenses beside me when our father begins speaking.

"The situation in Cuba is changing. There are rumors that they're going to pass an act to reform the amount of land an individual or company can own. Small farmers will be fine, but for those with more than a thousand acres, the plantations . . ." My father swallows. "They say Fidel wishes to take those away."

Fidel's initial desire to abstain from government has been obliterated. José Miró Cardona is out, and Fidel is prime minister now. Manuel Urrutia Lleó is Fidel's creature. We are all Fidel's creatures.

Fidel killed my brother—or gave the order, at least. I am certain of it.

"It's hard enough with the labor problems," our father continues. "But if Fidel gets everything he wants? They treat him as though he is a god; there is no stopping a god, no reasoning or negotiating with one. He will destroy everything in his path." His voice breaks over the words. We do not speak of it, but we all know. "The people will let him, they will cheer him on, fueled by their anger and their thirst for blood, and they will tear those of us who prospered all this time from limb to limb."

My mother pales—

The French Revolution has come to Cuba.

His voice lowers; in Havana now, the walls have ears.

"We will go."

"Emilio—"

"Quiet."

My mother falls silent.

"We will go," he continues, "because it is no longer safe for us to stay. We will go until it is safe for us to return."

We will go because they are killing Perezes in Havana.

"Where will we go?" Beatriz asks, a defiant gleam in her eyes.

I close mine, offering a prayer that she will accept this, that we can get through this with minimal discord. I have nothing else left inside me. Whereas Alejandro's death has drained me, it has filled her with a righteous fury the likes of which I have never before seen.

"To the United States," he answers. "I have some friends in Florida who will help us. There's sugar in South Florida. I have some land there."

I'm not entirely surprised. My father is the sort of man who always has a card up his sleeve, who has a contingency plan in place.

In contrast, my mother looks like she might faint.

"Who will watch the house while we are gone? Our things?" she asks.

I feel a pang of sympathy for my mother; my father isn't interested in her opinion, her concerns, her fears. He has decided we will go to America, and he will brook no argument over the matter.

"The servants will," he answers. "Your aunt can come stay for a bit. It will be no different than when we've left the country for a trip. This one will simply be longer, give some time for the country to sort itself out. This insanity cannot continue forever; at some point, the people will come to their senses.

"Fidel does not offer any real solutions for Cuba. He has no experience governing, doesn't have what it takes to lead this country. They flock to him now because he removed Batista, but mark my words, there will be another leader whose name they're chanting sooner rather than later. Perezes have shaped Cuba's future for centuries. Sugar is this country's foundation. We will always have a home in Cuba."

I want to believe his words. I want to believe in something when I fear I no longer believe in anything at all.

Tears spill over Isabel's cheeks. Beatriz looks like she wants to slap someone. My mother and father appear slightly shell-shocked as they run through his plans, their voices hushed to prevent any of the staff from overhearing.

The staff—

What will happen to Magda in our absence?

What will I tell Ana? The rest of my friends?

"Nothing," my father says when I ask the question aloud. "You are to say nothing to draw attention to us." His words are directed toward all of us, but his gaze rests on Beatriz.

Maria appears caught between excitement and fear—to be thirteen again.

My hand drifts to my stomach, to the life beneath my palm, that tiny life fluttering inside me. I can't hide the secret much longer. Once we're settled in the United States, I'll have to tell my family about the baby, need to face this additional change in my life. But not yet—

Not until we make it through this next challenge, this next shift in fortunes.

So now we will go and inhabit the country that has shaped our destinies whether we wanted it to or not. There's an irony in the fact that our casinos and hotels are filled to the brim with Americans, and now we will flood their country in a similar fashion, looking for some sanctuary from this mess we've gotten ourselves into.

"We leave tomorrow," my father decrees.

My sisters are crying now, attempting to muffle their tears, to keep the rest of the house from knowing our plans.

"We will go as tourists. It is the only way. You will treat this as a trip abroad; you can each take one suitcase with you. Anything valuable will have to remain behind."

"What will we do when we get to America? Where will we stay? How will we live?" Isabel asks.

Is she thinking of her fiancé? Would I leave if Pablo were alive? I don't know. I share my father's fears, the sense that we are no longer safe or welcome in our own country—my brother's dead body lying on our doorstep is a testament to that. I am afraid to bring my child into this world—our child—afraid of what the future holds.

America is an unknown looming before us, but it can't be worse than this.

The house is silent for the rest of the evening. My parents have retreated to their bedroom, Maria has gone to bed, and I'm fairly certain both Beatriz and Isabel have snuck out of the house, perhaps to say good-byes in their own fashion.

I pack a suitcase, surprised at how easy it is to condense one's life into a small container. Of course, it's much easier when one's valuables must be left behind. Once I've finished, I change into my nightgown and robe. My jewelry box full of every single piece of jewelry I own save for one rests on top of my dresser.

A few minutes later, Magda enters my room.

"I see Beatriz and Isabel are out and up to no good," she complains.

I can't help but grin at her indignant tone. The city is falling down around our heads, but she's concerned about my sisters' reputations.

I don't think I've ever loved her more.

"How are you feeling?" she asks, sitting next to me on the bed and rubbing my back like she used to when I was younger.

I rest my head on her shoulder, my hand settling over my stomach. I've noticed myself doing it more and more, catching myself mid-motion when I'm out in public or around others. I tire of all the secrets I keep locked up inside me.

"Better. Thank you."

I can't cry.

I take a deep breath, steadying myself. "I would like to give you something." I walk over to the dresser. My fingers shake as I hand her the jewelry box. This will be one of our secrets, like so many before it.

"We're going on a trip tomorrow. To America." My father will likely tell the staff tomorrow morning, but I've never thought of Magda as anything other than family.

She takes my hand, her fingers trembling. The timing of our trip is clearly not lost on her.

"We might be gone for a while." I *cannot* cry. "And I'm not sure when we will return. I would like you to have this."

Magda shakes her head, tears welling in her eyes. "I couldn't."

I attempt to paste a smile on my face, try to hold back the emotions threatening to spill over the floodgates.

"I want you to." I take a deep breath. "I want you to take it and go to your family. They're in Santa Clara, aren't they? I want you to use it to get out if you need to. To take care of yourself and your family. One day Fidel and his men might come for this house, for everything in it, and if they do, I want to know you are safe. That you have the freedom to do as you please."

"Absolutely not."

"Please. Please take it. I will worry about you the entire time I am in America if you don't. These are troubled times, and I want to know you have security in them. Please."

Tears spill down her cheeks. "This is everything. This is far too much."

"It's not nearly enough."

There is no price you can put on all the nights she rocked me to sleep, the times she held me when I was sick, wiped my tears, held my hand. There is no price I can put on the nineteen years she has loved me, stood beside me, been like a mother to me.

I wrap my arms around her, holding her close, as she has done so many times to me, while her shoulders shake, while my heart aches.

"I love you," I whisper.

"I love you, too," she says. "And one day I will hold your baby in my arms, just as I held you when you were a young girl."

It's hard to let go.

"I need help," I say over the line.

"What do you need?"

I think if I told Ana I had to bury a body in the backyard, she'd bring a shovel.

"Can you come over?" I ask.

"Of course."

Thirty minutes later I meet her in my backyard, beneath the enormous banana tree we've played under since we were little girls. We're both dressed in our nightgowns and robes. It isn't the first time we've had a late-night adventure such as this one, although in our younger years our exploits were limited to sharing secrets about boys we liked. Now I'm asking her to be the guardian of the box holding my greatest secret.

"Is something wrong?"

"We're leaving tomorrow," I whisper. "Going to the United States."

I don't say the rest, some words simply too painful to utter—I don't know when we'll return.

Tears well in her eyes. "Elisa."

I swallow. "We can't stay."

She nods, her knuckles white as she clutches the lapel of her robe. Everyone knows what happened to our brother now.

"I'm not entirely surprised. You certainly aren't the only ones."

"Your parents?" I ask.

Ana shakes her head. "They want to wait, see what happens in the next few months."

I can't blame them for that. It's hard to leave everything behind you, not knowing what will greet you when you return.

"I will miss you," she says.

My throat is hoarse. "I will miss you, too."

She hugs me, and the familiarity of it is both a balm and salt in an open wound. This is home. How can I leave?

Ana releases me, and I wipe away the tears that have fallen on my cheeks. Her gaze sweeps over the box behind me, the makeshift shovel I stole from my mother's flatware collection. This isn't a wholly original idea—two hours ago I watched from my bedroom window as my father crept out in the night and buried items a hundred or so yards away from the palm tree—but it's the best one I could come up with on such short notice.

"So what are we doing?" Ana asks, a sad smile on her face. "Digging for buried treasure?"

It's exactly the sort of trouble we would have gotten into when we were younger, digging up my mother's prized flowers and pretending we were pirates—I blame the French corsair for the inspiration.

"No, burying it."

I pull out the box I pilfered from my father's study—inside I have placed my most treasured possessions, my memories, the only pieces of Pablo that remain.

"If something happens, will you dig this up for me? I don't know what else to do with it, and I don't want anyone to find it. Can you keep an eye on it for me?"

I could give it to Ana to hold on to, but who knows where her family will end up, how the winds of change will eventually affect them, too. If the madness of this revolution has taught me anything it is that the affairs of men are impossible to predict; I prefer to rely on the constancy of the earth beneath our feet. It doesn't care whose blood spills onto its soil or whose boots march upon its grass—it is Cuba, impervious to those who profess to control it. The earth cares nothing about revolutions.

"Of course," she replies.

Ana grabs one of the instruments, a laugh escaping from her lips. "This is one of your mother's serving spoons, isn't it?"

"It is."

I almost laugh at the absurdity of it. Two Havana debutantes in our robes, using my mother's finest silverware to dig in the dirt in our backyard. And at the moment, I can't think of a better use for it. This seems to be a year for the tragic and the absurd.

We speak in quiet voices as we dig, the roar of the ocean drowning out our words. We speak as only lifelong friends can, carving out a moment of peace in these fragile times—

I am forever fortunate for the corsair's decision to build his home on this street, on this block where one day a rum scion would do the same, providing me with another sister.

When we've dug a nice-sized hole, I set the wooden box inside. My hand drifts to my stomach. Will I bring my child back here to dig it up with me? Perhaps I'll make a game of it—buried treasure indeed.

I cover the box with the cold earth, clutching the dirt in my hands until my fingers are caked with it, until it sneaks into the crevices under my fingernails. One day I'll bring our child here. I'll show our baby the letters we wrote, the ring its father slid on my finger, give it this part of our history, our love. The earth will guard my secrets, preserve this piece of Havana for me, my memories—

For when we return.

chapter thirty

Marisol

I search for your face in the men pouring into Havana. I dream of lying in your arms, of your lips against mine.

I miss you and I love you.

Where are you? When will you return?

You were right, you know. I understand that now. We weren't paying attention. We lived in our little bubble, and now the bubble has burst, and I do not recognize my country. Do not recognize my place in this world.

I read my grandmother's letters to Pablo—ones she gave to Guillermo before she thought Pablo was dead, after Fidel had taken Cuba, ones she sent my grandfather throughout their relationship. I started from the beginning of their romance, from that first letter she sent him, and now that I'm at the end, it's like she's sitting here beside me in bed, her words giving me the final push I need.

I wish I had done more. I wish I had fought.

I wake early the next day—my final day—the morning sun breaking through the clouds, the space beside me cold. After I came back from spreading my grandmother's ashes, after I read each of her letters, I found Luis. We fell asleep together on the tiny bed in my guest room at the Rodriguez house, our clothes still on, Luis's arm draped around my waist. But now he's gone.

I make my way through the house, trying not to break into a run, telling myself he's just gone for a walk, that nothing will stop us from leaving Havana today. With my grandfather's help I got access to a phone and called Lucia yesterday and begged her to help get us out, to get the plane, buy us tickets to Antigua, asked her to talk to our father about getting Luis into the United States. I didn't tell her the whole story, just the parts she needed for now. I'll tell her the rest on the back porch of the house in Coral Gables, mimosas in hand. A different life.

I find Luis on the balcony, staring out at the water. He doesn't turn when I open the door and walk outside, but he wraps his arm around me, bringing me against his side.

I exhale.

Neither one of us speaks.

The hand around my waist finds my hand, linking our fingers, his thumb running over my grandmother's ring.

I don't know what to say, don't know what he wants to hear.

If he stays, he will likely die. If he goes, I'm asking him to leave everything he's ever known, fought for, behind. Is Cristina right? Will he always feel like he abandoned Cuba? Will he resent me for the choice? Will he regret having left?

I don't know.

I think about the decisions I used to obsess over before I came here, the ones I likely will worry about in the years to come—am I too invested in my job? Am I not invested enough? Am I being challenged? Am I happy?

Those worries feel like luxuries now.

The decision in front of him is one of the most fundamental ones anyone can ever make, and he's forced to make it in the span of a day, forced to walk away from his family, his country, his life. But my grandfather made it clear; Luis only has a day or two before the government will realize what he's done, before they'll come looking for him.

We have to leave today.

"I'm sorry," I whisper.

Luis shakes his head.

"I'm angry, but not at you. I'm sorry if I've made you think that. I knew the cost to what I was doing. Knew the risk I was taking. This is my fault."

"Luis—"

"I love you," he whispers against my mouth.

The words sound like good-bye.

A tear trickles down my cheek.

"If you stay, what will it buy you? A few days? A week? What difference can you make in that time? Think of all the good you can do with more time. With more resources. Think of all the good you can do when your words aren't censored, when the government doesn't block your site, when you don't have to fear you'll be hit by a car when you cross the street simply because you don't think what they want you to think. You said I should write about my experiences here in Cuba. Help me. Think of all the good we could do together, think of the people we could help.

"What about your family? How long until they start coming after your grandmother? Your mother? Cristina? Because they can and will in order to stop you. My grandfather can only protect them so much, but if you continue agitating the regime, that will change."

He releases me. "You don't think I know that? That I haven't always weighed the cost of my actions against the threat to them? There's no winning here. Every path in front of me is problematic."

"You could leave Cuba."

"But I wouldn't be Cuban anymore, would I? I would be living with you in a mansion in Miami while my people are struggling. While my elderly grandmother works to provide for her family. What kind of man would I be?"

"You would be alive," someone says behind us.

We both turn at the sound of his mother's voice. She stands in the doorway, her expression tired, her gaze on her son.

"What about you? Abuela? Cristina? Who will take care of you when I'm gone?" Luis asks.

She crosses the distance between them, placing her palm against her son's cheek.

"We don't need you to take care of us. We've made it this far, and we will continue to do what we've always done. We grow where we are planted. This is our home, and we will die here. That's our choice. I could have tried to leave when you were younger, could have taken my chances with the raft and the sea.

"I didn't because I was scared to leave, scared to get caught and sent back, scared to die in the water. I watched people speak out and die for it, watched them disappear, and I told you to keep your head down, to go along with what they wanted, to accept your lot in life as a given.

"But now I know. Nothing changes no matter how much we work, how much we pray for change, and the pieces they give us aren't enough. I'm tired and I'm old. It's not my fight anymore. It's yours. Don't throw this opportunity away. Go. Go to the United States."

"Dad—"

She takes a deep breath. "Your father would agree with me. He believed you should live your life dedicated to a cause greater than yourself. I can think of no greater way to honor his memory than the life you are living. He would be so proud of you. Always."

A tear slips down Luis's cheek.

"Times are changing. Perhaps there's more you can do from outside Cuba than within." Her eyes swim with tears. "You will always be my son. I will always love you, and I'm sorry if I haven't said it enough. I'm proud of you. So proud. There are many ways you can serve, Luis. Sometimes the bravest thing you can do is decide to leave when it is no longer wise to stay."

"My students—"

"Will survive without you. We will all survive without you. And one day, things will change and we will see each other again."

Her words chip at the resolve, the fear, the doubts, until I see acceptance in his gaze, and at once, the man who has struck me as so confident, so self-assured from the first moment I stepped out of José Martí airport, now looks lost and unsure.

"I'll send money," Luis vows. "And I'll write."

"I know you will." She wraps her arms around her son for a moment before releasing him. "I need to go to the market. Don't forget to say good-bye to your grandmother." She glances in my direction, and I brace for whatever words she will throw my way. "I know what you did, the strings you pulled. Thank you."

I nod through the tears clouding my vision.

"Take care of each other," she says.

"We will," I promise.

She stands in the doorway for a moment, staring at Luis, and then she's gone.

I finish packing my bags while Luis says good-bye to Cristina. I put the letters my grandfather gave me on the Malecón in my carry-on along with the white rose and the letters my grandmother saved in the wooden box for when I explain the story to my family. I also carry the letter my grandfather has written to his son and asked me to deliver to my father. I leave the gifts I brought for Ana and her family as well as the leftover cash I brought with me, keeping just enough to cover our journey out of the country. Hopefully, it will help them.

Someone knocks on the door.

"Come in," I call out.

Luis opens the door. "Are you ready?"

"I am. How did it go with Cristina?"

"I said good-bye."

"Will she be okay?"

"I hope so. She has distant relatives in the Oriente. She may go stay with them; she hasn't decided yet. My grandmother and mother consider her family; I hope she'll stay here with them."

"Will you be okay?" I ask.

"I hope so." Luis holds out his hand to me. "My grandmother wants to see us off. My friend Oscar should be here soon to pick us up."

He takes my bags in one hand, holding on to me with his free one. A lone suitcase waits at the base of the stairs.

Pablo advised him not to take too much, that it would raise red flags if Luis looked like he was leaving for longer than a short trip—a romantic jaunt to Antigua with his American girlfriend. I hope they don't dig too deeply at the airport, that my grandfather was successful in shielding Luis for a day or two. It's a lot to hope for, but right now hope is all we have.

We make our way to Ana's sitting room, where she's seated on the worn silk couch, a smile on her face, her best china set out in front of us.

"It was my mother's," she answers when I comment on how beautiful the pieces are. "And her mother's before her. And her mother's before that. They came on a ship from Spain."

We sit on chairs opposite her while she pours us coffee, offering us a plate of snacks she's set out. There's an elegance to her motions, a ceremony to the whole process that speaks to a civility long since forgotten.

I sip my coffee while she and Luis make small talk about the dinner that evening, about the neighborhood, about anything and everything but the day ahead of us.

A knock sounds at the door, the noise ominous, intruding on the peace we've created in this little room.

It's either the police or Luis's friend come to take us to the airport.

Luis reaches out and takes my hand, squeezing reassuringly. My heart pounds as he excuses himself and greets whoever's on the other side, and when I finally hear the sound of his voice mixed with Oscar's, the tension subsides a bit.

Ana and I stare at each other across the sea of her family's china.

"You're doing the right thing. Both of you," she says.

"I hope so."

"You are. It was time for him to go, even if he wasn't ready to leave."

"We could—"

"—Get me out?"

I nod.

"It's fifty-eight years too late for that. Cuba is my home. I will die here, and I wouldn't have it any other way. Luis, though, is young. He deserves to have children, to be able to raise them in a world where they can have a bright future. Where they can dream. You'll bring them back one day and show them where we lived. You'll tell them our stories so they can know where they come from. So they can know their roots."

"Yes."

"I'm glad you found each other," she says. "Glad you returned. Elisa would be so proud of you. I pray she will watch over you and guide you on your journey ahead."

The sound of Oscar's and Luis's footsteps grows louder as they get closer, and we rise from our seats. Her arms wrap around me, holding me tight, her hands stroking my hair.

"Never forget where you come from. You come from a long line of survivors. Trust in that when things get hard. And in each other."

That trust feels tenuous when Luis and I have only known each other a week, but then again, what is certain in this world? Governments change, regimes fall, alliances shift—with so much that lies out of our hands, it seems like love is the easiest and only thing worth trusting.

Ana pulls away from me, smiling at Luis standing in the doorway.

"Come here." She motions to her grandson.

He walks toward her; he looks as though he's barely holding it all together.

She whispers something to him, and he nods, his arms around her. She pulls back, tears swimming in her eyes, her gaze beaming with love and pride.

We move to where Oscar waits in the entryway, Ana behind us, our bags already loaded in the trunk of Luis's convertible. We exchange kisses on the cheek, and then we're climbing into the car, Luis and I in the back seat, Oscar in the front, Ana watching over all of us, her presence both reassuring and a reminder of all he leaves behind.

Luis keeps my hand clutched in his as we turn back to glance at Ana standing in the doorway, at the only house he's ever known.

The big car rolls away from the driveway, kicking up gravel, drifting farther and farther away from the Rodriguez family, from Ana, until the house is little more than a speck behind us.

We turn and look forward, soaking in our last view of Havana. The city doesn't disappoint, and perhaps it's my imagination, but the sky seems more beautiful than before, the sounds of the street—

the people laughing, music spilling out of open windows—a melody all her own.

Oscar keeps up a steady stream of chatter as we drive through Miramar, his good-natured banter adding much-needed levity to a somber day. Cuba passes us by in flashes of color and an elegy of sounds from the street. I try to memorize the scenery, take a mental photograph I can carry with me until we return.

Does Luis do the same?

We reach the airport in what feels like a matter of moments.

I'm eager to leave, to return to the safety and security of my home in Miami, my family, the world I know. I'm loath to leave, to abandon the people who've become a part of my heart.

I'm scared they won't let him leave. I'm terrified they'll throw us both in jail.

Oscar and Luis exchange a half hug and slap on the back at the same airport where we first met. A look passes between them; how much has Luis shared with Oscar? Has he been involved in Luis's efforts all along? Is he one of the men whose names Luis guards? Does he realize what is really happening? Is Oscar also willing to risk his freedom to help us? Does he understand that this good-bye might be forever rather than for a few weeks?

He must, and once again, I am awed by the kindness and bravery of my countrymen.

"Good luck, man," Oscar says.

I exchange a quick good-bye with Oscar, doing everything I can to make it appear that everything is normal, that my insides aren't quaking with nerves and fear. Luis is stoic beside me, save for a twitch of his fingers against mine, a tensing in his hand as we walk through the airport.

The gun-toting soldiers standing around the airport are ominous specters now, and it takes everything inside me not to pay them more than a passing glance, to continue on with our business as though we have nothing to fear, as though we are ordinary travelers.

We check in to our flight and receive our boarding passes. I paste a smile on my face, exchanging words with the smiling woman behind the desk. My heartbeat thrums. Through the whole process I wait for her to say there's something wrong with our tickets, that our flight is delayed.

Instead, we go through the traveling process I've done countless times. After a few minutes of standing at the desk, we're waved on with a smile.

My legs begin to shake as we walk toward the customs area. We're just two more people in the departure hall, and yet it feels as though all eyes are trained on us, as if there is a spotlight shining down upon us.

Are these our last moments of freedom?

The story of exile has different origins. There are those, like my family, who were lucky enough to leave when it was possible to hop a flight to the United States, even if that avenue was fraught with government red tape and denials. Then there are those—the Peter Pan kids—whose parents were so desperate to get their children out of the country that they put them on a plane alone and sent them to the United States with the hope that one day they would be reunited, the dream of giving their children a better life than they would otherwise have in Cuba powerful enough to warrant such a sacrifice. There are those who came in the Mariel boatlift in 1980, when Castro let more than a hundred thousand Cubans leave for the United States. And then there are the rafters, the people whose ingenuity and courage drove them to brave the seas in makeshift rafts to forge the ninety-mile journey to freedom, facing death or— if they were captured before they reached U.S. shores—a life of imprisonment.

Cubans exist in a constant state of hope.

On the surface, *ojalá* translates to "hopefully" in English. But that's just on paper, merely the dictionary definition. The reality is that there are some words that defy translation; their meaning contains a whole host of things simmering beneath the surface.

There's beauty contained in the word, more than the flippancy of an idle hope. It speaks to the tenor of life, the low points and the high, the sheer unpredictability of it all. And at the heart of it, the word takes everything and puts it into the hands of a higher power, acknowledging the limits of those here on earth, and the hope, the sheer hope, the kind you hitch your life to, that your deepest wish, your deepest yearning will eventually be yours.

That same hope is in me now as we make our way through the airport. The hope that they won't stop us, that we won't spend the remainder of our days in a Cuban prison, that we'll make it to the other side.

The nerves running through Luis's body touch my limbs. There's a tremor in his hands, his jaw clenched, his gaze darting around the airport, looking at the uniformed soldiers, the guns in their hands, waiting to see if one of them will walk over to him and take him away, if he'll simply disappear like the others who have dared to speak out against the government. If I'll follow him.

I've never been more afraid than I am now or more apt to prayer.

I'm forever caught between two languages. I learned Spanish before anything else, grew up speaking both languages at home and at school. In my most vulnerable moments, the ones when I feel things most deeply, when I hope, when I fear, when I love, it's the Spanish that comes to me first.

The prayer runs through me now.

I go first, approaching the customs booth with a wary smile. I hand the official my passport and boarding pass along with the other half of the tourist card I received when I entered the country. We exchange a few pleasantries about my trip to Cuba, and out of the corner of my eye I watch as Luis walks up to one of the booths.

For the span of a few minutes white noise rushes through my ears, my entire body suspended as I wait. As I leave the customs booth and walk to the security checkpoint where my bag will be scanned and wait. Wait for Luis to join me.

I twist the ring on my finger, around and around again, while he talks to the immigration official, a smile on his face, one I now recognize as feigned. I strain to overhear their conversation, to read the words falling from the immigration official's mouth. And then it's all over—

Luis walks forward, past the customs booth, out the other side, toward me.

My knees sag.

Luis wraps his arm around my waist, tugging me forward, toward the security line where I place my bag on the belt, adrenaline pouring through my limbs.

His lips brush my temple.

"Almost there," he whispers in my ear, his hand stroking my back.

Minutes. Minutes pass as we go through security, as we take those final steps, sinking into our seats near the gate.

I imagine my family sitting here, waiting for a plane to take them to the United States, not knowing when—if—they would return. I understand a bit more the uncertainty they faced, the kind of pervasive uncertainty that invades your bones, that comes from not having a country to call your own, a land upon which you can lay your head.

A family of tourists sits next to us blissfully unaware of the tension emanating from Luis and me. I try desperately not to make eye contact, staring out the airport window, at the drab floor, up at the ceiling, but it is as though they will me to look at them, the sheer eagerness to speak to me pushing and shoving its way into my space.

Maybe they want to make a connection in this crowded airport of travelers venturing from a lost land, maybe they think Luis and I look like a nice couple, perhaps they don't see the open wound in both of us. Whatever it is, they can't seem to resist.

"Was this your first trip to Cuba?" the wife asks me.

I nod, suddenly exhausted by all of this—the fear, the sense of loss, the weight of hope.

"It's incredible, isn't it?" she asks, and I give another polite nod, ready to just get on the plane. "It's so nice to see it like this. In its natural state. Before the tourists come in and ruin it."

She says it as though we share a secret, as if we've stumbled upon a lost city.

Luis stiffens beside me, and I give her another clipped nod.

Disappointed, she leans back, turning her attention to her husband, to their children.

What is there to even say anymore?

The idea that this ruined beauty is Cuba's destiny is as depressing as the idea that its future is to be cruise ships and casinos. That the very things that stoked the fires of revolution will be reborn again—if they ever died at all. That there's something quaint and charming about the struggles I saw everywhere I looked. Everyone talks about Cuba being "open" and "free," but that means very different things to very different people. To some it is the hope for fast-food chains and retail giants; to others it is the freedom to live in a country they can call their own, to maintain some semblance of autonomy over their lives.

And now I know the anger that burns inside Luis, the inability to accept this as Cuba's natural condition. The hope for more.

Our flight begins boarding, saving us from more conversation.

We shuffle forward in the line, shoved between jubilant tourists, sunburned and chattering about the exotic adventure they had. We board the plane furtively, looking over our shoulders for a soldier's uniform. Luis tells me to take the aisle seat, and his hands grip the armrests, his knuckles white; I realize he's never flown on an airplane before.

How much is his life about to change?

The minutes in our seat become an eternity as we wait for the wheels to begin rolling down the runway, as we wait for the plane to soar into the sky.

It feels as though I've been traveling for a decade, and I no longer recognize myself. The plane rolls back from the gate, and my heartbeat steadies, my limbs relaxing, my breaths growing slower and deeper.

And then we're in the air, Cuba behind us, Miami in front of us, far off in the distance, an ocean away.

Home.

We land in Antigua, where my father's corporate jet is waiting for us. I've called in every family favor I can think of to get us to this point, and I offer a silent prayer of thanks to Lucia for coming through. I owe her big-time for this one, even as I know how much she likely enjoyed the adventure of helping to smuggle someone out of Cuba. This will turn into one of those stories that become lore, shared at Noche Buena dinners and at family brunches. My family has its flaws, but if a drop of Perez—or Ferrera—blood runs in your veins, then there is nothing they would not do for you.

We arrive in Miami hours later, and I go through the arrival motions in a daze. Luis is silent, taking in all of the sights and sounds. I feel a bit embarrassed about the private plane, the opulence of our surroundings, but that eventually dissipates in the face of what we've accomplished.

Our family's attorney is waiting for us along with the immigration attorney Lucia contacted for me. When my great-grandfather arrived in the United States in 1959, he made it his mission to rebuild his fortune, to insert himself and his daughters in Palm Beach society, to win the ear of politicians. Perhaps it was the image of his son's dead body lying on the dirt in front of his home that motivated him, or the need to protect his daughters and wife, the understanding that everything he built could be stolen from him in an instant with a change in government. Over the years, our family has given to Republican and Democratic candidates alike, and in this instance, I am grateful for the Cuban pragmatism.

My father has called in favors at the highest levels in the government to get Luis into the country on a visa. It's temporary and uncertain, but it's enough for now. Enough to keep him safe. Enough to buy us a little time before we can figure out what we will do next.

It would have been an easy feat not too long ago, but as with all things, Cuban-American relations are shifting, promises broken, agreements changing, our countries on the precipice of something new and uncertain. And still, in this we are lucky to be Cuban, where so many others face far greater hurdles to set foot on American soil.

Once we've dealt with the preliminary immigration matters, we're free to go. There's so much to be done in the coming weeks— getting Luis settled in, meetings with his attorney to find out the next steps, finding him a job, a place to live—will he want to stay with me? So many obstacles in front of us, and yet there's a natural rhythm to this; it is quintessentially Cuban to help another find a new life in the United States, just as those before me did for my family.

We get to my car in the parking garage and slide into the seats, and at once I begin to cry, the tears streaming down my face until I don't know what I'm crying for anymore—a mix of sadness and relief.

My grandmother. Luis's grandmother that we left behind. My grandfather that I didn't get a chance to know as well as I would have liked. The people who share my blood in Havana who I never got a chance to meet. The home I fear I'll never see again. The pain I fear Luis will carry with him from here on out.

He holds me, his face pressed against mine, his lips on my lips.

There is so much he will have to learn now—

We carry our home with us in our hearts, laden with hope. So much hope.

When Fidel dies, we'll return. You'll see.

chapter thirty-one

We spend the next three days holed up in my house in Coral Gables, our bodies tucked under the big duvet, lounging on the patio, as I dodge family calls. We're still adjusting to this change, growing used to our new life, mourning in our own way. And then I'm ready and it's time to go out in search of the last piece of the puzzle.

Throughout my childhood, there was always one person who would give me the unvarnished truth. She gave me the sex talk when I was curious about boys, filled in the blanks when I had questions about the Great Divorce and the rubber heiress.

My great-aunt Beatriz is the family secret-keeper.

She lives in an estate in Palm Beach rumored to have been given to her by a former lover. An heiress in her own right, she easily could have purchased the seven-thousand-square-foot mansion on her own, but I imagine she likes the romance of drifting through the rooms and feeling that connection to her younger years.

If the walls could talk.

I leave Luis settling into my house, getting acquainted with all of the changes in his new life, and make the drive to Palm Beach alone.

Beatriz answers the door in a cloud of Chanel, dressed in a floral shift I own in a different color—she looks better in it. Her face is that of a woman ten years younger. Her dark hair is pulled back in a dramatic bun, fat diamond studs on her earlobes.

She wore those same studs in the spread *Vanity Fair* did on her years ago. In certain circles, she is a legend.

Beatriz greets me with a kiss on each cheek before stepping back. "Come in, come in."

Her hands flutter in the breeze as she speaks, a canary diamond on her ring finger, another gift, another lover.

"Is Diana off today?" I ask.

Her longtime housekeeper is as much a member of the family as any of us. Now that my great-aunt is nearing eighty, she and Diana have become companions in their older years.

"She is. She went to visit her sister in Punta Gorda for the weekend."

I step over the threshold and follow her lead into the floral sitting room she's constantly redecorating. This time it's done in pinks and yellows, a new chandelier hanging from the ceiling. Palm Beach chic.

We sit on opposite couches, and she offers me a drink. Midway through the sentence she stops, her eyes gleaming.

"Something's different about you." Her smile deepens. "You met a man."

I grin. Beatriz is also remarkably perceptive. "I did."

She leans forward, the drinks temporarily forgotten. "Tell me *everything*."

"I met someone. He came back with me."

Her eyes widen. "Darling, you bring a questionable hat back with you, one you'll probably never wear but can't resist because you're on vacation. Maybe even a bottle of rum. But a man?" Her gaze narrows as she takes in my appearance. "You're in love."

She says the word cautiously, as though there's a world of danger contained there, as though it's a word that could topple governments, conquer kingdoms, lay siege to everything in its path. She says it as if she knows a thing or two about bargaining with love and isn't a satisfied customer.

"I am." A little laugh escapes my lips, the cocktail of nerves, excitement, and happiness too great to be contained.

Her smile widens. She stands, smoothing the shift with her pink-manicured fingers. "Well, that settles it, this calls for something festive. Champagne. You'll tell me about your man and your trip." Her expression turns somber. "Did you find the right spot for her?"

"I think I did."

"Where?" she asks.

"The Malecón."

She's silent for a moment, her eyes closing, opening again with the faintest shimmer of unshed tears.

"Elisa was happy there. She'll be happy there again."

I blink back tears of my own. "I hope so."

She walks over to the bar cart, a bottle of Bollinger chilling in a silver bucket. Most occasions call for champagne in Aunt Beatriz's world; no doubt she was prepared to toast my return, or the settlement of my grandmother's ashes, or whatever reason she invented to pop the cork.

"And your young man? What's his name?"

"Luis."

Her hand stills on the champagne bottle, a laugh escaping. "Of course it is. So you're in love with Ana Rodriguez's grandson?"

I nod.

"Your grandmother would have been thrilled. I bet Ana was."

"I think so. She treated me like I was part of the family from the beginning."

"Well, of course she would. You pretty much are considering how close she and Elisa were. I'm sure having you stay with her was like having a piece of Elisa back."

She releases the cork with a pop, pouring the gold liquid into two crystal flutes.

"What's he like?"

I smile. "Smart. Passionate. Dedicated. He was a history professor at the University of Havana."

"And what will he do now?"

"I don't know," I admit, Cristina's earlier words in Havana coming back to me now. "I hope he'll like it here. Hope he'll be happy. Hope he can stay here. We still have to figure everything out. He's passionate about Cuba, and there's a part of me that feels guilty for encouraging his decision to leave. At the same time, he didn't have much of a choice. The regime was no longer willing to turn a blind eye to his protests."

Her mouth tightens into a thin line. "They're known for that."

Beatriz carries the glasses over, handing one to me before raising hers in the air.

"A toast—to finding love in the unlikeliest of places." Her voice turns serious. "I know you, Marisol. I've seen you go through life, and I've watched you navigate all the things that have come your way. You wouldn't have taken this leap if it wasn't right, if you weren't sure. I know you're scared now, and you have doubts, but you'll both make it work. You'll build a life here."

Tears prick my eyes.

"Thank you."

I take a sip of the champagne, the familiar flavor coating my tongue.

"When will I meet him?" she asks.

"I'm bringing him to Lucia's birthday party."

My sister's turning thirty-three next week, and we're all gathering for a big bash at the farm in Wellington.

"Good. I can't wait." A twinkle enters her gaze. "I still have to come up with the right present for her."

Knowing Beatriz, it could be anything from a handbag to an exotic animal.

"Speaking of presents, what would you like for a wedding present?" she asks.

I laugh. "I didn't realize I was getting married."

"You will someday soon. A painting, perhaps." She drains her glass, and her expression turns serious. "Now tell me about Cuba. I see worry in your eyes, and not just because of your concern that things won't work out with your young man. You dredged up family secrets when you were down there, didn't you?"

"Yes."

"Then I think we need more champagne."

She refills our glasses far more than is fashionable, a tremor in her fingers as the liquid in the glass pitches and sways.

"I dream of Cuba," she confesses. "Of our last days as a family there. Constantly."

Of my three great-aunts, Beatriz has always been the least sentimental, less prone to deep emotion. She's the butterfly of the family, the only one who has ever resisted being pinned down.

"Would you ever go back?" I ask, a bit surprised by the depth of emotion in her voice, the pain in her eyes.

Beatriz sighs. "And see it how it is now? No. I've already had my heart broken multiple times—no need for Fidel to break it again. I lost everything trying to reclaim Cuba."

"When you left?"

"Then, too. I don't want to see it like it is now. I prefer the memories I keep in my heart, rather than the harsh reality of what it has become."

"Do you—"

"Want to be buried in Cuba?" she asks, finishing my thought.

"Yes."

She shrugs. "I don't know. I suppose I haven't thought of it. I have a date Wednesday with a very special man; I'm too busy to think about death. Besides, I suspect Elisa's reasons for wanting to return were a bit different from mine."

It's the entry I need.

"I found some things when I was in Cuba."

"I thought you might."

"Did you know?" I ask.

"About the baby? About the man?"

So she did.

"I suspected," she answers. "They told everyone your father came early, that she wasn't as far along as she was. Some people probably thought they slept together before they were married. I had a different perspective, though. I saw her with him in Havana one night."

"With Pablo?"

"Yes. She was the happiest I ever saw her. You can't hide love like that. I tried asking her about him, and she brushed it off, but I didn't take it personally. Those were different times. No one knew who to trust; we were all trying to do what we could to survive. I don't doubt that she wanted to protect us. To protect him."

"He's alive. Still lives in Cuba. I met him."

I've accomplished the impossible and managed to surprise Beatriz.

"Did he know who you are?"

"Yes."

I tell her about the rest of my trip, meeting Magda, the missing pieces she filled in for me.

"Are you going to tell your father? Your sisters?" Beatriz asks.

"Yes. He wants to meet them if they can travel to Cuba. I would want to know about him if I were them."

"I agree." She reaches out and squeezes my hand. "If you need me, let me know. I'm happy to help you break the news to them."

"Thank you."

"And how are you handling all of the changes?"

"I'm not sure. I'm glad I got to meet Pablo. Glad I learned the truth. I read their letters, and after talking to him, it seems like they really loved each other. I only wish I knew how she felt. I always thought she loved Grandpa Ferrera. But now I wonder."

"You're still young. And if you're lucky, your young man will be the only man you'll ever love in your life. I hope that for you. For some, there is only one true love. But not everyone is lucky enough to have that love work out for them. And for some, the love we cannot have is the most powerful one of all.

"Elisa was pregnant in a time when being a single mother wasn't an option. We were starting out in a new country, grieving the loss of our brother, our home, our friends, our way of life. When she met Juan Ferrera, she was young and scared. He was established in the United States, and his family did a lot to help us. He was a decade older than her, and he offered her the stability she craved, especially after the horrors of the revolution.

"I don't know that she loved him when they married, but I know she grew to love him, and he loved all of you so much. He was happy with her, with the family they built, and she felt the same way about him. Perhaps it wasn't the glitzy, sweeping romance, but they cared about each other. That can be enough."

"I feel like I didn't know her. Not the most important parts, at least."

"We can't always know the people we love as well as we think we do, Marisol. Our love is tangled up in our expectations, our perception of reality. And you never know what people really think. They often keep their deepest emotions locked away. She kept her secrets close, but considering what we lived through, who could blame her?"

Ana Rodriguez's earlier words come back to me now.

"When I was with Ana in Cuba and she gave me my grandmother's belongings, she mentioned that it was a common practice for families to bury items in their backyard to keep them safe for when they returned."

Beatriz nods. "The walls of their homes, too. It was our way of preserving hope, I suppose. And perhaps a sign of our arrogance as well. We never imagined the bastard would live as long as he did."

"She said that you had the one that was buried in your backyard. The one that contained the Perez family treasures."

Beatriz is silent for a beat. "I had it. For a moment. And then I lost it again."

"How?"

"How what?"

The doorbell rings.

"How did you get it back?" I ask. "Did someone smuggle it out of the country for you?"

She rises from the couch, glancing down at her watch, before staring back at me. "Sorry for the interruption. I have a massage scheduled for this afternoon."

Her lips curve into a blinding smile, one that offers more than a hint of insight into the trail of broken hearts behind her. She's the kind of woman who has likely been stunning her entire life and knows nothing else.

"His name is Gunnar, and he is a sight to behold."

My beautiful, glamorous, mysterious great-aunt.

"Why did you go back to Cuba?" I ask again.

Beatriz turns back and smiles at me, halfway to the entry. Her voice holds the same tone of insouciance I've heard her employ throughout my life.

"I went to assassinate Fidel Castro, of course."

. . .

I leave Beatriz's house and make the trek back to the house in Coral Gables, where Luis is waiting for me. I'm greeted by the sound of music playing—an Icelandic band I discovered on a trip to Reykjavik ages ago—and the scent of paella coming from the kitchen.

I set my purse down on the entryway table, flipping through the mail resting there—a few bills, a postcard from my sister Daniela, who's in Marbella with our mother, a fashion magazine.

Little by little I've put my stamp on the house, adding in my own oversize comfort pieces with my grandmother's predilection for the ornate and opulent, replacing Baroque antiques with framed photographs from my travels.

There's a photo of the Malecón at sunset hanging over my grandmother's favorite chair in the sitting room where she used to tell me tales of Cuba. I imagine the spirit of her there now, in the wind, in the waves crashing against the rocks, in the notes of the trumpet playing across the promenade, in the smiles of the couples in love, their fingers linked as they sneak off together, in the look in Pablo's eyes as we scattered her ashes over the sea.

When I first arrived in Cuba I felt like I'd come home, as though the part of me that had been traveling for so long had finally found a place to rest.

But now I know.

There is no home for us in a world where we can't speak our minds for fear of being thrown in prison, where daring to dream is a criminal act, where you aren't limited by your own ability and ambition, but instead by the whims of those who keep a tight rein on power.

I've known two versions of Cuba in my lifetime: the romanticized version of my grandmother's that was frozen in time, and the version I'm learning from Luis, one of harsh reality and relentless struggle. That's the Cuba that speaks to me now, the mantle I pick up, the cause to fight for.

We started working on a new article last night—a series of them, really—a chance to shine a light on life in modern Cuba; a call for change and an attempt to rally the international community.

Luis comes behind me, wrapping his arms around my waist, pressing his lips to my nape.

"How was your aunt?" he asks.

"Good."

I don't tell him about Beatriz's parting comment about Castro or the new questions running through my mind. That's a tale for another day, and besides, we Perez women must be allowed our secrets.

"I love you," he whispers.

"I love you, too."

We have dinner scheduled with my father next week. I plan on sharing the news about Pablo with him then. I'll tell my sisters after that.

I imagine they'll want to go to Cuba to meet our grandfather, will want to know this side of our family that we've lost for so long. Who knows what the future will hold? It's not safe for Luis to return now. But one day—

One day the regime will fall. It has to.

Until then, we'll do everything we can, for Ana, for Magda, Luis's mother, for Cristina, my grandfather, for everyone who deserves a chance to know freedom, imperfect though it may be. For everyone who deserves a chance to hope for a free and democratic Cuba. The Cuba my great-uncle died for, the Cuba Pablo fought for, the Cuba we were promised so long ago.

Luis pours us both a glass of wine as I tell him about my visit with Beatriz, as he fills me in on the details of his upcoming meeting with the immigration attorney we've hired. When he's finished, he raises his glass to me in a silent toast, and the words, the fidelity of them, filter out of me as naturally as breathing.

"Next year in Havana."

Elisa
1970

The days drift into weeks, and flow into months, and sail away into years, a decade, and still we remain.

Marriages are celebrated, babies born, lives lost and mourned, and still we remain.

Juan drives us down to Key West for the day. Otis Redding blares on the car radio speakers, and we all sing along, our voices slightly off-key.

The top is down on the cherry red convertible he bought me for my thirtieth birthday, the wind blowing my hair despite the colorful scarf that attempts to force it into submission. Our son, Miguel, loves going over the bridge, looking down at the water.

The ocean is a pretty shade of blue, the kind that will likely dazzle tourists from up north. If you haven't traveled farther south, you might believe it to be the most beautiful ocean in the world.

But if you have—

We stuff ourselves on Key Lime pie and stone crabs, washing down peeled shrimp with fruity drinks tempered by the sharp bite of alcohol. Miguel plays on the beach, his pants rolled up around his calves, the water lapping at his feet. He spots a group of children playing in the sand, their brightly colored pails swinging from their little hands. He walks over to them and joins in, his sturdy body ambling along, peals of laughter mixing with the sound of the waves.

Juan takes my hand, his fingers linking with mine.

"I love you," he says, his gaze on our son.

"I love you, too," I answer, the habit of the words comforting. And I do love him.

It's not blazing fire or mighty flame; it's steady, true, strong. There's peace in his love, and I've had enough war to last a lifetime. He's a fine man, a good husband, an excellent father, a bulwark against the madness of the world.

And then there's Miguel.

My son will grow up knowing freedom. The freedom to express his thoughts without fear of being jailed, the freedom to work to support himself, the freedom to dream that he can be anything he wants, do anything he wants.

Once he's tired of playing we pack up, strolling down the street. We point out the sights to him, stop and buy ice cream from a stand.

At the corner of Whitehead and South Street, there is a sign with a palm tree.

THE SOUTHERNMOST POINT OF SOUTHERNMOST CITY KEY WEST, FLA.

A woman stands in front of the sign in a floral dress, selling conch shells laid out on the ground.

Miguel is instantly captivated by the shells, and Juan smiles indulgently, taking his wallet out of his pocket. It'll make a good souvenir for our boy.

I watch as Juan shows Miguel how to hold the shell up to his ear so he can hear the sound of the ocean. Our son's face lights up at the novelty, the pride on Juan's face inescapable. He loves him as though he were his own flesh and blood.

I walk forward a bit, their conversation drifting away, the roar of the ocean and the sound of the wind blocking out all else. It's late in the day, the sun nearly setting, the sky a placid blue.

If I close my eyes, I can almost see it; if I look straight ahead, my gaze fixed on the point beyond the horizon, I imagine I do.

There's a girl in a white dress, strolling along the Malecón, a white silk rose clutched in her hand, her dark hair blowing in the breeze. And there's a boy. He's taller, older, his head slightly bent as he leans into her, as he strains to hear what she says over the sounds of the city, the honking of horns, the laughter of people passing them by. She wants to laugh, too, but the thudding in her chest robs her of the emotion, and instead she feels something portentous, like the moment before a storm rolls in over the water. It's in the air around them, carried on the wind—hope, anticipation, longing.

He will kiss her and everything will change.

They will march from the mountains to the sea and everything will change.

The girl is now in a pink dress, her figure altered by motherhood and time, the white rose left in a box, buried in a backyard in Havana, for when she returns.

She sees his eyes every day in another's. It is both her greatest pleasure and her deepest pain that all she has to do is look to her son to see the man she loved and lost.

But one day . . .

Her knowledge of God was formed in the pews of the Cathedral of Havana. Some of it has stuck; most of it ebbs and flows with age, with circumstance.

But there's an undercurrent of hope, whether brought on by religion or Cuban birth—

One day when she dies, she'll see him again. She knows this with a certainty that resides in her bones.

If there is a Heaven, surely it will be this—

Five miles of seawall. Havana behind her, an ocean before her. They'll walk hand in hand, their son between them, a trumpet playing in the background, the smell of jasmine on the air, coconut ice cream on her tongue.

But for now there's only the sea. And beyond it, ninety miles away, a country.

Home.

How long before we return?

A year? Two?

Ojalá.

NEXT YEAR
in Havana

CHANEL CLEETON

Discussion Questions

1. The novel alternates between Elisa Perez's life in Cuba in 1958 and 1959 and her granddaughter Marisol Ferrera's trip to Cuba in 2017. Which woman did you identify with more? What parallels can you see between their personalities and their lives? What differences?

2. The first chapter ends with Elisa wondering how long her family will be away from Cuba. The final chapter ends over a decade later with her posing the same question. How are the themes of hope and exile illustrated in the book? How does the weight of exile affect the Perez family?

3. When Marisol arrives in Cuba she struggles with identifying as Cuban because she grew up in the United States and because she has never set foot on Cuban soil. How much does a physical place define one's identity? How does Marisol's trip alter her views about being Cuban and change her perception of herself? How do Marisol and her family attempt to keep their heritage alive in exile? Are there stories and rituals handed down through the generations in your family?

4. Like her grandmother, Marisol falls in love with a man who has revolutionary political leanings. What similarities can you see between Pablo's and Luis's dreams for Cuba? What differences are there in their worldviews? How do they go about achieving their dreams for a better Cuba?

5. Sacrifice is a major theme that runs throughout the novel. How do the characters make sacrifices for one another, and what are some examples of them risking their safety and security for their loved ones? How do you think you would have acted in similar situations?

6. Family plays an important role in the novel, and each of the characters face their own struggles in their attempts to live up to their family's expectations. What are some examples of this? Did you identify with one character's point of view more? Are there certain expectations in your own family? Do you feel the need to live up to them? How have they shaped your life decisions?

7. Elisa's final wish is to have her ashes scattered over Cuban soil. Do you agree with her decision? Would you have wanted your ashes spread in Cuba or would you have preferred to be buried on American soil? Do you think Marisol picked the best place to spread Elisa's ashes? Where else would you have considered scattering them? Have you scattered the ashes of a loved one? What was the experience like?

8. What initially attracts Elisa to Pablo? Do you believe they would have been able to overcome the differences between them if

they weren't caught in the midst of the Cuban Revolution? Or was their love fueled by the urgency of the times?

9. Elisa chooses to save her letters from Pablo and her memories of their romance by burying them in a box in the backyard. If you had a box in which to bury your most precious possessions, what would you choose to keep safe?

10. What parallels do you see between life in modern Cuba and life in pre-revolutionary Cuba? What differences?

11. Pablo tells Elisa that everything is political. Do you agree with him?

12. Despite coming from very different backgrounds, Marisol and Luis share many similarities that bring them together as a couple. What are some examples of this? Why do you think they get along so well? Do you think they are a good influence on each other?

13. Pablo believes that the best way to change his country is from within. Others like Elisa's family choose to leave Cuba because they can no longer support the regime. Which approach do you identify with? What are the differences between the Cubans who remained in Cuba and those who live in exile? What are the similarities?

KEEP READING FOR AN EXCERPT FROM
CHANEL CLEETON'S NEXT NOVEL,
FEATURING BEATRIZ PEREZ . . .

WHEN WE LEFT CUBA

AVAILABLE WINTER 2019 FROM BERKLEY!

Beatriz

The thing about collecting marriage proposals is they're much like cultivating eccentricities. One is an absolute must for being admired in polite—or slightly less-than-polite—society. Two ensure you're a sought-after guest at parties. Three add a soupçon of mystery, four are a scandal, and five, *well*, five make you a legend.

I peer down at the man on bended knee in front of me—*what is his name?*—his body tipping precariously from an overabundance of champagne, and mentally catalogue his appeal. He's a second cousin to the venerable Preston clan, related by marriage to a former vice president, and cousin to a sitting U.S. senator. His tuxedo is understated elegance, his fortune modest, if not optimistic, for the largesse of a bequest from a deceased aunt or an unexpected inheritance landing on his doorstep. His chin is weak from one too many Prestons marrying Prestons, his last name likely to be followed by Roman numerals.

Andrew. Maybe Albert. Adam?

We've met a handful of times at parties like this in Palm Beach, ones I once would have ruled over in Havana but now must bow and scrape in order to gain admittance. I could do worse than a second cousin to American royalty; after all, beggars can't be choosers, and exiles even less so. The prudent thing would be to accept his proposal—my auspicious fifth—and to follow my sister Elisa into the sacrament of holy matrimony.

But where's the fun in that?

Whispers brush against my gown. I feel the weight of curious gazes on my back, some more malevolent than others, and the words clawing their way up my skirt, snatching the faux jewels from my neck and casting them to the ground.

Look at her.

Haughty. The whole family is. Someone should tell them this isn't Cuba.

Those hips. That dress.

Didn't they lose everything? Fidel Castro nationalized all those sugar fields her father used to own.

Has she no shame?

Perhaps it would be different if we were men, if we weren't threats to the marital prospects of their friends, nieces, or daughters. If we slid seamlessly into the social fabric they've created here.

But we aren't men, and our sex too often has a particular affinity for hitting where it hurts. With a look, we are dismissed, some indescribable quality identifying us as different, as separate from the society we've fled to. We're treated as cuckoos in a nest, as though our presence here will only serve to snatch up the limited marital resources and steal some of the spotlight that is apparently in meager supply in Palm Beach. The truth is, they can keep their prospective husbands; I've little use for men these days.

My smile widens, brightening, flashier than the fake jewels at my neck and just as sincere. I lift my chin an inch and scan the crowd, sweeping past Alexander on his knees, looking like a man who hasn't quite acquired his sea legs, past the Palm Beach guard shooting daggers my way. My gaze rests on my sisters Isabel and Elisa, standing in the corner, deep in conversation, flutes of champagne in hand. Elisa's husband hovers nearby in that protective way of his. She might no longer be a Perez in name, but the sight of them, the reminder to bow to nothing and no one . . .

I turn back to Alistair.

"Thank you, but I fear I must decline."

I keep my tone light, as though the whole thing is a giant jest, which I *hope* it is. People don't go falling in love and proposing in one fell swoop, do they? Surely that's . . . inconvenient. I've seen the havoc love has wrought on my sisters' lives, and I'm more than a little glad to have escaped a similar fate.

For a moment, poor Arthur looks stunned by my answer. Perhaps this wasn't a joke after all. Slowly, he recovers, and the same easy smile on his face that lingered moments before he fell to his knees returns with a vengeance, restoring his countenance to what is likely its natural state: perpetually pleased with himself and the world he inhabits. He grasps my outstretched hand, his palm clammy against mine, and pulls himself up with an unsteady sway. A soft grunt escapes his lips.

His eyes narrow a bit once we're level—nearly level, at least, given the extra inch my sister's borrowed heels provide. It truly is a tragic thing when God doesn't give you the height you deserve. I would like to be an Amazon, preternaturally tall, stalwart and fierce, towering over my foes, rather than a curvy slip of a woman bent by the winds of revolution.

The glint in Alec's eyes reminds me of a child whose favorite toy has been taken away and will make you pay for it later by throwing a spectacularly effective tantrum. I think I prefer the honesty of it compared to the smile.

"Let me guess, you left someone back in Cuba?" he asks, enough of a bite in his tone to nip at my skin.

Men so do enjoy pursuing that which they cannot have.

My diamond smile reappears. Honed at my mother's knee and so very useful in situations like these, the edges sharp and brittle, warning the recipient of the perils of coming too close.

I bite, too.

"Something like that," I reply in a casual drawl.

Now that one of their own is back on his feet, no longer prostrate in front of the interloper they've been forced to tolerate this social season, the crowd turns its attention from us with a sniff, a sigh, and a flurry of bespoke gowns. We possess just enough money and influence—it turns out sugar is nearly as lucrative in America as it is in Cuba—that they can't afford to cut us directly, but not nearly enough to prevent them from devouring us like a sleek pack of wolves scenting red meat. Fidel Castro has made beggars of all of us, and for that alone, I'd thrust a knife through his heart.

And suddenly, unexpectedly, the walls are too close together, the lights in the ballroom too bright, my bodice too tight, and my heart bleeds out over the elegant parquet floor. Acting as though everything is effortless is surprisingly exhausting, and pretending that their disdain is beyond my notice even more so.

It's been nearly a year since we left Cuba for what was supposed to be a few months away, until the world realized what Fidel Castro had done to our island—before Cubans came to their senses and understood he wasn't the savior they sought, but rather a charlatan hungry for power. Hardly better than President Batista, and with each day that passes, I fear far worse.

America has welcomed us into her loving embrace—almost.

I am surrounded by people who don't want me here, even if their contempt hides behind a polite smile and feigned sympathy. They look down their patrician noses at me because my family hasn't been in America since the country's founding or hadn't sailed on a boat from England, or some nonsense like that. They think their sons are too good to dance with me, their daughters too precious to speak to me. Thanks to my education, I speak English well enough, if not for the faintest accent, but that's not enough for them. My features are a hint too dark, my voice too foreign, my religion too Catholic, my last name too Cuban. I am not one of them, and they won't let me forget it.

And at the same time . . .

There is no quarter in Cuba right now for differing from Fidel in the slightest. They're killing Perezes in Havana, so we must make do with the life we borrow in Palm Beach.

It is a strange thing to lack a corner of the world to call your own, to feel as though you are reviled wherever you go. In Havana, we are ostracized for having too much. In Palm Beach, we are written off for not being enough, dismissed as being of little use by a society that defines itself by how high one has climbed until one has reached a rarified status and can prevent all others from occupying the same space.

In truth, we did the same in Havana, and look where it has landed us.

The past tugs at me each moment, the memory of what we left behind a constant ache. The present hurls me back to the airport lounge at Rancho Boyeros airport—now renamed by Castro to Jose Martí airport—waiting in between our old life and an uncertain future. It's easy to not feel like any of this counts, as though this year we've spent in Palm Beach is a placeholder, a dress rehearsal for a different life. What will we care for their contempt when we have returned home?

In a flash, an elderly woman who looks suspiciously like Anderson's mother approaches us, sparing me a cutting look no doubt designed to knock me down a peg or two—as though a pair of steely gray eyes compares to the face of a firing squad—before turning her attention to her son. In a cloud of Givenchy, he's swept away until I'm left standing alone, my fall from grace on full display.

If I had my way, we wouldn't attend these parties, save this one, wouldn't attempt to ingratiate ourselves to Palm Beach society; they and their stuffy opinions can hang, for all I care. Of course, it isn't about me and what I want. It's about my mother and sisters, and my father's need to extend his business empire through these social connections so no one ever has the power to destroy us again.

And of course, as always, it's about Alejandro.

I perform another visual sweep of the ballroom. There must be two hundred people here tonight, surrounded by walls adorned in gold leaf, entombed in their unwritten rules and code. We had them in Havana, too, and while some things translate, others don't. I've learned the basics, but there are subtle nuances I've yet to grasp.

I turn on my heel and head for one of the open balconies off the ballroom, the hem of my gown gathered in hand, careful to keep from tearing the delicate fabric. We have a system in place for re-wearing and repurposing gowns; there's an art to appearing far wealthier than you really are.

I slip through one of the open doors and step out onto the stone terrace, a breeze from the water blowing the skirt of my dress. There's the barest hint of a chill in the air, or at least as close to one as South Florida experiences, the sky is clear, the stars are shining down, and the moon is full. The sound of the ocean is a dull, distant roar. It's the noise of my childhood and my adulthood calling to me like a Siren's song. I close my eyes, a sting there, pretending for a moment that I'm standing on another balcony, in another country, in another time. What would happen if I left the party behind and headed for the water, removed the pinching shoes and curled my toes in the sand, let the ocean pool around my ankles?

I close my eyes, moisture gathering in the corners, a tear trickling down my cheek. Just one.

I never imagined it was possible to miss a place this much.

When I open my eyes again, I turn, rubbing my damp cheek with the back of my hand, my gaze on the corner of the balcony, the palms swaying in the distance—

A man stands off to the side of the house, one side of him shrouded in darkness, the rest illuminated by a shaft of moonlight. He's tall. Blond hair—nearly reddish, really. His arms are braced against the railing, his broad shoulders straining the back of his tailored tuxedo, as though he, too, knows a thing about cramped ballrooms and strangling obligations.

He's so still he could be a statue.

I didn't come here for company, and if I'm honest, I've more than had my fill of Americans. I take a step back, and then another, about to turn around, when he turns—

Oh.

Oh.

The thing about people telling you you're beautiful your whole life is that the more you hear it, the more meaningless it becomes. What does "beautiful" even mean, anyway? That your features are randomly arranged in a shape that someone, somewhere, arbitrarily decided is pleasing. "Beautiful" never quite matches up to the other things you could be—smart, interesting, brave. And yet . . .

He's beautiful. Blindingly so. Shockingly so.

For a moment that stretches on and on, I can't look away.

He appears as though he's been painted in broad strokes, his visage immortalized by exuberant sweeps and swirls of the artist's brush, a god come down to meddle in the affairs of mere mortals.

Irritatingly beautiful.

In that moment, I hate him just a little bit. He looks like the sort of man who has never had to wonder if he'll have a roof over his head, or if his father will die in a cage with eight other men, or face a firing squad, or had to flee the only life he has ever known. Surely he's never held his murdered twin in his arms, blood spilling over that pristine tuxedo. No, he looks like the sort of man who is told he is perfection from the moment he wakes in the morning to the moment his head hits the pillow at night.

He's noticed me, too.

Golden Boy leans against the balcony railing, his broad arms crossed in front of his chest. His gaze—piercing blue eyes—begins at the top of my head, where Isabel and I fussed with the style for an hour, cursing the absence of a maid to help us. From my dark hair, he traverses the length of my face, down to the décolletage exposed by the gown's low bodice, the gaudy fake jewels that suddenly make me feel unmistakably cheap, as though he can see that I am an impostor and he is the real deal, to my waist and my hips, lingering there.

A tingle slides down my spine, goose bumps pricking my skin.

I take another step back.

"Am I to call you cousin?"

I freeze, his voice holding me in place as surely as a hand coming to rest possessively on my waist, as though he is the sort of man used to bending others to his will with little to no effort at all.

I loathe such men.

His voice sounds like what I am now learning passes for money in this country: smooth, crisp, and devoid of any hint of foreignness— the wrong kind, at least. The kind of voice that is secure in the knowledge that every word will be savored.

I arch my brow. "Excuse me?"

He reaches between us and grabs my hand, his skin warm, his thumb rubbing over my bare ring finger. His touch is a shock to my system, waking me from the slumber of a party I tired of hours ago.

His mouth quirks in a smile as he looks up, his gaze connecting with mine, little lines crinkling around his eyes. How nice to see that even gods have flaws.

"Andrew's my cousin," he offers by way of explanation, his tone faintly amused.

I find that most rich people who are still, in fact, rich, manage to pull this off, as though a dollop more amusement would be atrociously gauche.

Andrew. The fifth marriage proposal has a name. And the man before me likely has a prestigious one—is he a Preston, or merely related to one, like Andrew?

"We were all waiting with breathless anticipation to see what you would say," he comments.

There's that faint amusement again, a weapon of sorts when honed appropriately. He possesses the same edge to him everyone here seems to have, except I get the sense that under all of that seriousness, he is laughing with me, not at me, which is a welcome change.

I grace him with a smile, the edges sanded down a bit. "Your cousin has an impeccable sense of timing and an obvious appreciation for drawing a crowd."

"Not to mention excellent taste," he counters smoothly—*too smoothly*—returning my smile with one of his own.

My breath hitches.

He was handsome before, but this is simply ridiculous.

He leans back against the stone railing once more, his long legs crossed at the ankle. My gaze drops to the soles of his shoes, to the scuffs there, seizing on that imperfection.

"True," I agree. I have little use for false modesty these days; if you're not going to fight for yourself, who will?

"No wonder you've whipped everyone into a frenzy," he replies, appreciation in his gaze.

I arch my brow once more, for a moment feeling as though I have indeed gone back in time to when I was a different person, my problems far simpler. To when I enjoyed flirting with men on balconies and in ballrooms and the like.

"Me?"

He chuckles, the sound low and seductive, like the first sip of rum curling in your belly.

"You know the effect you have." There's that admiration again. "I saw you in the ballroom."

How did I miss him? He's not the sort of man who blends in with the crowd.

"And what did you see?" I ask, emboldened by the fact that his gaze has yet to drift.

"You."

My heartbeat quickens.

He pushes off from the balcony railing, taking a step toward me, then another, and then another, until only a foot separates us, his golden, blond frame looming over me.

"Just you," he says, his voice barely loud enough to be heard over the sound of the ocean and the wind.

His eyes are the color of the deep parts of the water off the Malecón.

"I didn't see you."

My own voice sounds husky, like it belongs to someone else, someone who is *rattled* by this.

My gaze has yet to drift from him, too.

His eyes widen slightly, a dimple denting his cheek, another imperfection to hoard, even if it adds more character than flaw.

"You sure know how to make a guy feel special."

I curl my fingers into a ball to keep from giving into temptation, to keep from reaching out and laying my palm against his cheek.

"I'd venture a guess that you have plenty of people making you feel special all the time."

There's that smile again. "That I do," he acknowledges with a tip of his head.

I shift until we stand shoulder to shoulder, looking out at the moonlit sky. He gives me a sidelong look. "I imagine it's true, then?"

"What's true?"

"They say you ruled like a queen in Havana."

I have no time left for such frivolities. Over a year ago, I would have accepted the distinction as my due. Now—

"There are no queens in Havana. Only a tyrant who aims to be king."

"I take it you aren't a fan of the revolutionaries?" he asks, interest in his voice.

"It depends on the revolutionaries to whom you refer. Some have their uses. Fidel and his ilk are little more than vultures feasting on the carrion that has become Cuba." I walk forward, sidestepping him so the full skirt of my dress swishes against his elegant tuxedo pants. I feel him behind me, his breath on my nape, but I don't look back. "Batista needed to be eliminated. In that, they succeeded. Now, if only we could rid ourselves of the victors—"

I turn, facing him.

His gaze has sharpened from an indolent gleam to something far more interesting. "And replace them with what, exactly?" he asks, his tone silk sliding over my bare skin.

"A leader who cares about Cubans, about their future. Who is willing to remove the island from the Americans' yoke," I say, caring little for the fact that *he* is an American and acknowledging the line that has already been drawn in the sand between us. I am not one of them and have no desire to pretend to be. "A leader who will reduce sugar's influence," I add. "One who will bring us true democracy and freedom."

He's silent, his gaze appraising once again, and I'm not sure if it's the wind, my imagination, or his breath against my neck, but goose bumps rise over my skin again.

"You're a dangerous girl, Beatriz Perez."

My lips curve. So he asked someone for my name.

I tilt my head to the side, studying him, trying desperately to fight the faint prick of pleasure at the phrase "dangerous girl" and the fact that he knows my name.

"Dangerous for who?" I tease.

He doesn't answer, but then again, he doesn't have to.

Another smile. Another dent in his cheeks. "I'll bet you left a trail of broken hearts behind you."

I shrug, registering how his gaze is drawn to my bare shoulder.

"A proposal or two, perhaps."

"Rum scions and sugar barons, or wild-haired, bearded freedom fighters?"

I laugh. "Let's just say my tastes are varied." I turn so it's no longer just his profile that's visible to me. "I kissed Che Guevara once."

I can't tell who is more surprised by the announcement. I don't know why I said it, why I'm sharing a secret not even my family knows with a total stranger. To shock him, maybe; these Americans are so easy to scandalize. To warn him that I am not some simpering debutante, that I have done and seen things he cannot fathom. And also, perhaps, because there's some power in it—the lengths to which you will go to secure your father's release from Guevara's hellhole of a prison, La Cabaña. It makes a good story, even if I inwardly cringe at the young girl whose hubris made her think a kiss could save a life.

Whatever arrogance I had, Fidel whittled away.

"Did you enjoy it?" Golden Boy asks, his expression utterly

inscrutable, a clever and effective mask sliding into place. I can't tell if he's scandalized, or if he feels sorry for me; I far prefer their scorn to their pity.

"The kiss?"

He nods.

"I would have preferred to cut his throat."

To his credit, he doesn't flinch at my bloodthirsty response.

"Then why did you do it?"

I surprise myself—and perhaps him—by going with the truth rather than prevarication.

"Because I was tired of things happening to me, and I wanted to make things happen for myself. Because I was trying to save someone's life."

"And did you?"

The taste of defeat fills my mouth with ash.

"That time, I did."

The problem is that the wave of power brings another emotion with it, the memory of the life I couldn't save, of a car screeching to a stop in front of the enormous gates of our home and the door opening, my twin brother's still-warm, dead body tumbling to the ground, his blood staining the steps we once played on when we were children, his head cradled in my lap while I sobbed.

"Is it as bad as everyone says?" he asks, his tone gentled to something I can hardly bear.

"Worse."

"I can't imagine—"

"No, you can't." I take a deep breath, the cool night air filling my lungs, staving off the panic creeping toward me. "You have no idea how fortunate you are to be born in this time, in this place. Without freedom, you have nothing."

He doesn't take his gaze off me, the solemnity in his eyes speaking to the sort of man he is. The understanding there surprises me and gives the impression that, despite the differences in our nationalities and stations in life, we might be more similar than I originally thought.

"And what would you tell a man with only a few minutes of freedom left?" he asks.

"To run," I reply, my tone wry.

A ghost of a smile crosses his face, but it's obvious he isn't buying what I'm selling, and I like him a bit better for it, for seeing past the facade.

"To savor the last few minutes he has," I answer instead.

I know a thing or two about cages.

He nods as though he can read the truth in my answer.

Who is he?

Part of me wants to ask his name, but my pride holds me back a bit. And if I'm being completely honest, it isn't just my pride—it's my fear.

Such luxuries have no place in my life at the moment.

I blink, only to be greeted by an outstretched palm, waiting for mine to join it.

"Dance with me," he says, and even though the words are phrased as a command, the question contained there is what strikes me the most—that and the earnestness.

I swallow, my mouth suddenly dry, cocking my head to the side, studying him, pretending my heart isn't thundering in my chest, that my hand isn't itching to take his.

"Now, why does that feel more like a challenge than an invitation?"

The music is a faint hum in the background of the evening, the notes drifting out onto the balcony.

"Will you dance with me, Beatriz Perez, kisser of revolutionaries and thief of hearts?"

He's too smooth by half, and I like him far too much for it.

I shake my head, a smile playing at my lips. "I didn't say anything about stealing hearts."

He smiles again, that full wattage hitting me. "No, I did."

Do I really even stand a chance?

He steps forward, obliterating the space between us, his cologne filling my nostrils, my eyes level with the snowy white front of his shirt. His hand comes to rest on my waist, the heat from his palm warming me through the thin fabric of my dress. He takes my hand with his free one, our fingers entwined, our bodies closer than I normally dance with men I don't know.

What is happening to me?

My heart turns over in my chest as I follow his lead, as the music fills me. Unsurprisingly, he's a natural, confident, elegant dancer.

We don't speak, but then again, considering the conversation between our bodies—the rustle of fabric, the brushing of limbs, the fleeting touches that imprint themselves upon my skin—words seem superfluous and far less intimate.

The thing about collecting marriage proposals is that people assume you're a flirt. And perhaps I was, once, long ago, but now, it feels unnatural to play the coquette. I am somewhere between the girl I was and the woman I want to be.

The song ends and another begins with far too much speed, the dance equal parts stretching for eternity and ending with a blink. He releases me with a subtle heave of his shoulders, the cool air between us, my fingers missing the twine of his, the shock of his absence surprisingly sharp.

I tip my head up to look into his eyes, steeling myself against the onslaught of flirtation that is likely to come, the invitation to lunch or dinner, the compliments about my dancing, the heat in his gaze. I have no use for romantic entanglements at the moment, even though part of me thinks I would very much like to be temporarily entangled with this man.

He smiles. "Thank you for the dance."

A glimmer of something that might be regret flashes in those eyes—or perhaps it's my own imagination—before he inclines his head and turns back for the ballroom.

I watch him walk away, rooted to the spot, my heart hammering in my chest, secure in the knowledge that he will turn around and look back at me.

He doesn't.

I turn once he's disappeared back into the ballroom, into the world where he clearly belongs. I stare at the swaying palms, at the water, attempting to get my traitorous heart under control. Minutes pass before I'm ready to return to the ballroom, to the glittering chandeliers, the harsh glint of the other guests. The world where I will never belong.

I pass through the balcony doors to find Isabel standing off to the side, Elisa nowhere to be seen.

"She wasn't feeling well," Isabel says when I ask about our sister's whereabouts. "Juan took her home."

A waiter approaches us with a tray of champagne flutes in hand, more waiters around the ballroom doing the same thing. A murmur resounds through the ballroom, whispers tucked behind cupped hands, names on everyone's lips, the calm before a scandal breaks.

Curious as to the piece of gossip they're all eager to seize upon, I scan the crowd, looking for Golden Boy, looking for—

He stands next to the orchestra near the front of the ballroom with an older couple and a woman.

Oh.

Oh.

There's no point in dissecting her flaws, for I fear it would be a useless endeavor and do me no favors. It's clear as can be that her family *did* hail on a great big ship at this nation's founding, that she's stunning with her blond hair and delicate features, the perfect complement to his golden looks. Her gown is the height of fashion, her jewels certainly not paste, a pretty smile affixed to her face.

And who can blame her for smiling?

I join the rest of the ballroom in lifting my champagne flute and toasting the happy couple, as the bride's father announces his daughter's engagement to Nicholas Randolph Preston III. He is not just a Preston—he is *the* Preston. The sitting U.S. Senator rumored to have aspirations of reaching the White House one day.

Our gazes meet across the ballroom.

How could I not see this coming a mile away? In the end, life always comes down to timing. It's New Year's Eve, 1958, and your world is parties and shopping trips; it's New Year's Day, 1959, and it's soldiers, guns, and death. You meet a man on a balcony, and for a moment you forget yourself, only to be reminded once again how mercurial fate can be.

I drain the glass in one unladylike gulp.

And then I see *him*—the one I came for—and nothing else matters anymore.

A different sort of awareness hums through my veins as I spy a man in the corner, standing on the fringes of the party, Nicholas Randolph Preston III a ghost of a memory.

This man is short and stout, his hair balding at the top, his nose better suited to a larger face. He wears his tuxedo like it's strangling him rather than as though he was born to it. Through the research I've done, I know he's invited to these parties for one reason and one reason only: His wife is the darling of the charity circuit, her maiden name whispered with reverence throughout the ballroom. He clearly prefers the comfort of the shadows, every inch of him reinforcing the intelligence I've received. He's a man who isn't afraid to roll up his sleeves and dirty his hands, who enjoys moving world leaders around like they are pieces on a chessboard, wiping the whole lot of them out with a crushing and fatal blow.

He is the CIA's man on Latin America. They say he has been suspicious of Fidel from the beginning, even when others in the agency were not. In the growing exile circles in Miami and Palm Beach, people whisper that he has a plan to do something about Cuba, about the situation ravaging my country.

I didn't come here to dance with a prince on a moonlit balcony, and I lied before, when Nicholas Randolph Preston III— soon-to-be-married U.S. Senator—asked me about freedom. I would savor it for a moment.

And then I'd fight like hell to make sure it was never, ever taken away from me again.

As nice as moonlit dances with princes are, I came here with more important business at hand. I came to meet the man who is going to help me avenge my brother's death and kill Fidel Castro.

Photo by Chris Malpass

Originally from Florida, **Chanel Cleeton** grew up on stories of her family's exodus from Cuba following the events of the Cuban Revolution. Her passion for politics and history continued during her years spent studying in England, where she earned a bachelor's degree in international relations from Richmond, the American International University in London, and a master's degree in global politics from the London School of Economics and Political Science. Chanel also received her Juris Doctor from the University of South Carolina School of Law. She loves to travel and has lived in the Caribbean, in Europe, and in Asia. Learn more about her at chanelcleeton.com.

Ready to find
your next great read?

Let us help.

Visit prh.com/nextread

Penguin
Random
House